Vampir

Sparkle

Deathless Book 3

Chris Fox

This novel is fiction, except for the parts that aren't.

Chrisfoxwrites.com

ISBN-10: 1517796571
ISBN-13: 978-1517796570

For Trevor. You are and always will be my friend.
None of this would have been possible without you.

The Old Gods

There are quite a few gods mentioned in this book, more so than either of the previous two. I've created a lexicon to explain who each one is, and how they relate to each other. Hopefully this will make it a little less confusing. Those readers familiar with Egyptian lore should see a lot of familiar names.

Anubis- Also known as the Jackal. Husband of Anput, servant of Ra.

Anput- Husband of Anubis, daughter of Osiris.

Hades- Greek god of the underworld, companion to Vulcan.

Horus- Eldest son of Isis and Osiris.

Irakesh- Youngest son of Ra, and all around pain in the ass.

Isis- Also known as the Mother. Wife of Osiris, mother to Horus.

Nephthys- Wife of Set.

Osiris- Husband of Isis. Father of Anput.

Ra / Sekhmet- Mother of Irakesh, once a near-sister to Isis.

Set- Brother of Osiris. Father of Wepwawet.

Vulcan- Roman god of the forge, companion to Hades.

Wepwawet- Son of Set, servant of Ra.

Previously On Deathless

Whenever I pick up the 2nd or 3rd book in a series I'm always torn. Should I re-read the first books, or just dive right in to the latest? I usually want to do the latter, but I can't always remember what happened in the previous books. This page is for all those people like me who can't quite remember everything that went down in *No Such Thing As Werewolves* or *No Mere Zombie*. I've decided to recap it just like a TV show. For those who just finished *No Mere Zombie* feel free to skip to the prologue.

In an announcer voice 'Last time, on deathless..."

A giant black pyramid bores from the earth in Peru, and a team of soldiers have been dispatched to investigate. They encounter a werewolf dressed in Egyptian style clothing, which tears through their ranks before escaping. They bring in a team of scientists to help them investigate the pyramid, and quickly find the central chamber is full of very lethal radiation. They desperately seek a way into the pyramid's control room, while the escaped werewolf with the bad fashion sense (Ahiga) begins slaughtering innocents. Some of those innocents rise as werewolves, and a plague begins spreading across South America.

The desperate team of scientists recruits Blair Smith, a brilliant anthropologist working at a local junior college as a teacher. Blair finds a way into the inner chamber, where the team discovers a woman sleeping inside of a high tech sarcophagus the ancients called a rejuvenator. Unfortunately, the act of opening the door to the inner chamber injects Blair with an unknown virus and Blair dies (it's all very sad, really). Within hours he rises again as a werewolf and begins slaughtering his former companions.

Blair wakes up in a small Peruvian village not far from the pyramid, where he meets Liz, a beautiful young redhead from the United States. The pair are pursued by Commander Jordan, the leader of the forces controlled by the mysterious (terribly mysterious) Mohn Corp. Liz is killed and brought back by Blair as a werewolf, and we learn that female werewolves are much larger, and much scarier than males. The pair flees north, deciding that if they can get to California Liz's brother Trevor might be able to help them find some sort of cure.

Meanwhile Ahiga tries to catch up, because he realizes Blair has inadvertently stolen the key to the Ark (the pyramid). That key is required to wake the woman inside, who Ahiga refers to as the Mother. It turns out she's the progenitor of the entire werewolf species, and when Ahiga finally catches up to Blair he tells him that without her the world is doomed. He explains that the world is about to enter a new age. The sun will go through a Coronal Mass Ejection, which will wipe out nearly all technology. This CME will also activate a virus that will turn all the people who currently have it into zombies (oh crap).

Blair decides to be a dumbass and tells Ahiga to go screw himself. He and Liz continue on to California where they meet up with Trevor and begin investigating the werewolf virus. It turns out Trevor is a helio-seismologist who just so happens to be investigating a giant sunspot (what a coincidence, right?). He confirms that a CME could royally screw the entire planet, and agrees to help Blair and Liz get back to Peru to wake the Mother.

Before they leave, Commander Jordan and his comic-relief sidekick Yuri show up with a bunch of soldiers in power armor. They blow up Trevor's house and his '67 Mustang, but fail to catch Blair. The werewolves escape back to Peru where they gather some furry allies and invade the Ark. They battle Mohn Corp's ever growing army, and there are casualties on both sides. The werewolves win and wake the Mother, who slaughters poor Commander Jordan and every soldier under his command. It's very sad, because by this point we feel bad for poor Jordan.

In the epilogue, the asshole author (that's me) dropped a really, really messed up cliffhanger. One of the scientists had the virus that would cause her to turn into a zombie when the CME hits. Not only does she turn into a zombie, but Trevor gets bitten within the first 30 seconds of the zombie apocalypse. Poor readers were left wondering what would happen to Trevor.

No Mere Zombie

Did the asshole author answer the question right away? Nope, he made you wait until chapter 5 to find out what happened to Trevor.

The book opens in 11,000 BCE just before the Arks went into hibernation. Irakesh, the son of Ra (the Mother's greatest enemy), concocts a plan to sneak into the Mother's Ark. When it returned, he planned to steal the access key for the Ark of the Redwood, located near San Francisco.

Fast forward to the present. Jordan wakes up, his last memory the Mother ripping his arms off (ouch). He quickly realizes he's a werewolf, and has no choice but to join Blair, Liz, Cyntia, and Bridget in their fight against the endless sea of zombies washing over the world.

Led by Isis (the Mother), they attempt to save as many people as possible, setting up a refuge at a church in Cajamarca. Unfortunately, that plan goes to hell when Irakesh steals the access key and runs for it. Liz and Blair pursue, but have no choice but to turn back to protect the Mother's Ark when Irakesh sends an army of zombies to invade it.

We finally learn Trevor's fate. He's become a zombie, and can't remember who he is. Fortunately, Trevor quickly discovers he can grow smarter by consuming, you guessed it, brains. He begins to recover his memory, and is one of the zombies Irakesh seizes control of.

Irakesh realizes Trevor is smarter than most zombies, and begins grooming him as an apprentice. They head north, aiming for a Mohn installation in Panama that Irakesh learned about by snacking on an officer's brain. Cyntia, love sick for poor Trevor, leaves the others to go find him. She eventually catches up to Trevor and Irakesh, and is recruited by the deathless.

Cyntia begins feeding indiscriminately on zombies, people, and even other werewolves. Irakesh encourages this behavior, because he knows it will make her stronger. Of course it also makes her crazy, so maybe not the best long term plan.

Blair, Liz, Bridget, and Jordan pursue Irakesh knowing they must stop him and recover the access key before he can reach the Ark of the Redwood in San Francisco. Isis remains behind to repair the catastrophic damage done to her Ark during the final battle with Mohn in the previous book.

We get a new point of view character, Director Mark Phillips (that's THE Director). He's squirreled away at the Mohn research facility in Syracuse, New York, where Mohn Corp is experimenting on zombies and living in luxury. Unlike the rest of the world, all their technological toys survived the CME, including their nifty X-11 power armor.

It isn't all rosy for Mark, though. He's learned that the Old Man has some dark secrets. He's not what he appears to be, so Mark begins investigating. He dispatches Yuri to Panama to recover the nuke they'd intended to detonate in Peru, and to learn what happened to Commander Jordan.

Meanwhile Blair, Liz, Bridget, and Jordan are hot on Irakesh's trail. They arrive in the city of Medellin to find an encampment protected by werewolves. It turns out they know two of them, Doctor Roberts and Steve (aka Captain Douchey). They have a tense reunion, but it's broken up by an army of zombies sent by Irakesh to ruin their day.

Trevor, Irakesh, and Cyntia make it to the airport where Mohn has their secret facility. They find the airplane carrying Mohn's nuke, which Irakesh decides to steal. By now Trevor has developed the powers of a deathless, and has regained all his memories. Unfortunately, Irakesh is mentally dominating him. Worse, Cyntia is growing more powerful and more unstable by the day.

Blair and company finally catch Irakesh at the airport. There's a big battle with lots of pew pew pew, rawr, etc. Blair's side loses, Irakesh gets away, and Yuri arrives just in time to capture Jordan and Liz. They're brought back to Mohn corp in Syracuse.

Blair, Bridget, and Steve decide to pursue Irakesh, but not before Blair sleeps with Bridget (yes, his cheating ex. Poor Liz). They catch up with Irakesh in Larkspur, just before he finds the Ark of the Redwood. Blair once again gets his ass kicked, and this time the cost is higher. Bridget dies, and even though she cheated on him, we still feel bad because she redeemed herself at the end. Well most of us feel bad. Some fans wrote in to say the bitch got what she deserved. Heartless, people. Just heartless.

Meanwhile, Director Phillips continues his investigation of the Old Man. It turns out the Old Man is *really* old, nearly two hundred. He serves a deathless named Usir, a name we later learn is a synonym for Osiris.

The Director starts a brief civil war, freeing Liz and Jordan. He arms Liz with Object 1, a super-powerful magical sword. Of doom. Since that's a really long title, let's just call it what the Director does: Excalibur.

Yuri pilots Liz and Jordan to San Francisco, where they link up with Blair and Steve. They attack Irakesh on the Golden Gate bridge. During the fight Trevor (very predictably) breaks free from Irakesh and joins the good guys. But not before shooting Jordan in the face. Again. It happens like four times in the book.

Unfortunately, they aren't able to stop Irakesh. He detonates the nuke he stole, destroying a chunk of the Golden Gate bridge. He channels the energy from the explosion into the Ark of the Redwood, charging up the battery and giving him control of a fully powered Ark.

Meanwhile an enraged Blair attacks Cyntia, desperately seeking vengeance for Bridget. Cyntia's much stronger, and more powerful, so he comes out on the losing end. His body is shattered and broken, but before Cyntia can kill him Liz uses Excalibur to slay Cyntia and drain her essence.

The heroes are in pretty bad shape, especially Blair. He realizes their only hope is throwing everything they have left at Irakesh. Steve convinces him to give up the access key to the Mother's Ark, which powers up Steve.

Irakesh attacks, showing what a fully-powered Ark Lord can do. The heroes get their collective asses kicked, and it looks like this is going to be the last book since Irakesh has basically won.

Then Blair throws the hail Mary. He uses his shaping to alter Irakesh's helixes. Since Irakesh is a deathless, and the Mother designed the access keys to only work for werewolves, the key leaves him. It shoots into Blair, who is now a super-powered Ark Lord. He turns all the zombies on the bridge to ash, and kicks the crap out of Irakesh. The heroes teleport inside the Ark, where they imprison Steve and Irakesh.

Director Phillips calls Jordan using a satellite phone, warning him that the Mohn Corp is compromised. He lost his civil war, and the Old Man is handing Mohn over to a deathless named Osiris. They're heading to London, where Very Bad Things (tm) are happening.

Just to throw a little salt on the wound, the book ends with Steve telling Irakesh he can light walk (teleport) from the cell, so they can escape and head to the Ark of the Cradle, where Ra rules.

The cliffhanger for *No Mere Zombie* wasn't as bad as the one in *No Such Thing As Werewolves*, but we were still left with a lot of questions. You're about to get answers, because you're holding *Vampires Don't Sparkle*, the third book in the series.

I hope you enjoy it!

If you do, please consider leaving reviews for any or all books in the series. I'm an indie author, and reviews are vitally important to my success. You might also consider signing up for the mailing list to hear when **Deathless Book 4: The Great Pack** is available (or my other tie in series,

Hero Born). If you do, I'm happy to give you a free copy of *The First Ark*, the prequel that explains a bit more about who the Mother is and where the zombie virus comes from.

Okay, enough rambling! On to *Vampires Don't Sparkle*...

Prologue- Osiris Locked Out

11,000 BCE

Osiris surveyed the assembled druids as he strode down the path and into the stone circle. Eleven of the most powerful men and women in his domain, each tending to one of the tribes. They were unperturbed by the steady drizzle, a near constant that had developed over the last few decades. It was one more sign the world was changing.

The assembled figures encircled the raised dais as he stepped atop it, kneeling in unison as they'd done many times. The cowls of their hoods shrouded their faces in shadow, but he didn't need to see them to know who they were. He'd selected each during their childhood for their talent in shaping, and he knew them as intimately as he did his own limbs.

"The time has arrived at last," he began, a rare note of sadness running counterpoint to the rain. "I must leave you, to slumber away the gulf between ages."

"Master," Alaunus said, rising to his feet and throwing back his cowl. His long fiery hair was bound with a leather cord, not so very different from Osiris's own. "My visions have failed me. I see little of the coming days. I do not know the way. What is to become of us?"

The distress in his voice pained Osiris, but there was nothing he could do to forestall it. He owed them honesty, particularly Alaunus. The man had the sight more strongly than any servant Osiris had met in the last nine thousand years. "You will age and die. The power you draw from the sun is fading, and in a matter of hours it will vanish entirely."

No one spoke, save the rain. Osiris couldn't blame them. How would he react to such news? Even having known it for so long, it still shocked him to his core. He possessed a link to the First Ark. He would continue on, slumbering away during the dark time, until the sun's strength returned in the Age of Aquarius.

"Is there nothing to be done?" Britannia's clear voice rang out as she too rose to her feet. She raised delicate hands to remove her cowl, dark hair spilling down her shoulders as she met Osiris's gaze.

"The cycle turns," Osiris said, wishing it were otherwise. "But all is not lost. Many places of power remain. These Sources will contain energy for a dozen generations. Hundreds, if they are not tapped too heavily. Some part of your power will survive with them, if you husband it. So too will artifacts survive."

He illustrated the latter by sliding the tooled leather sheath from his shoulder and offering his sword, hilt first, to Britannia. Her mouth fell open as she stared at the golden hilt, and shocked whispers broke out from many cowls. The weapon was sunsteel, one of only a handful in the world. Its power was incalculable, and Osiris had wielded this one longer than these people's civilization had existed.

"My lord, I am not worthy of this. None of us are," Britannia protested, yet she took the hilt reverently. She slung the scabbard over her shoulder, tears in her eyes.

His gift made it all real to them. He was departing their world, and by leaving the weapon he was passing his stewardship to another. "The weapon's strength is incredible. It may well last your descendants until the next age. Teach them. Let it become a symbol, a remembrance of the great power their ancestors wielded, and that they will one day wield again."

"As you say, my Lord," Britannia replied, dropping to her knees and wrapping a protective hand over the golden hilt.

"There is much you must prepare, and precious little time to-," Osiris began, but broke off as unexpected power stirred within him.

It began as a low buzz, but quickly built to a crescendo of gathering energy. He lurched forward, barely aware of Alaunus as he rushed in to catch him. Power gathered within Osiris, much as it did whenever he shaped. Yet this wasn't his doing, wasn't his command. Whatever was happening was beyond his control, the strange power bubbling within him like a cauldron about to boil. Then silver light burst from his eyes and mouth, the fire of the universe searing his very consciousness as it departed.

This cannot be. His risen whispered, an odd mix of awe and shock.

Osiris shuddered as the access key left his body, bereft of the Ark's incredible power for the first time in many millennia. He lay against Alaunus's chest, shivering in the rain as he struggled to understand what had just befallen him. There was only one explanation. Someone had bound the First Ark using a Primary Access Key. It should be impossible, but the proof was undeniable.

"A terrible calamity has just befallen the world," he said, forcing himself to his feet. The assembled druids watched him in silence, their expressions horrified. "The First Ark has been stolen. I must reclaim it, or I too will perish along with all of you. The thief will take its power into the next age, and the other Ark Lords will be unprepared when next they awaken."

No one spoke. What could they say? Osiris didn't wait. He gathered himself, blurring north with all the speed and fury he could muster. The wind and rain whipped at his cloak as he bounded over hills and through valleys. He ran for long minutes, crossing the land he knew so well, faster than it had ever been crossed.

At long last he arrived at the Valley of Hidden Voices, the place he and his companions had discovered so many millennia ago. Back during the last ice age when the world had been frozen and harsh. He stared up at the massive black pyramid, the First Ark. Its sleek surface was untouched by the rain, untouched by time itself. It hadn't changed in any way since the first time he'd laid eyes on it, though the land itself was different now.

A low thrum of power resonated through the land around Osiris. The Ark itself vibrated, then the structure began to sink, descending into the earth with alarming finality. Osiris understood what he was seeing, but he could scarcely believe it. Whoever had stolen the Ark was putting it into stasis, preparing for an age bereft of power.

It was exactly what Osiris had been planning to do, but now he was trapped outside with no way to reach the safety of the rejuvenators. No sanctuary to weather the ravages of time.

There was only one god who could have orchestrated this, could have found some loophole that allowed him to break Osiris's bond with the Ark. Set. His treacherous brother had returned, and now controlled the most powerful of the great Arks.

Did he know of The Well? What if he opened it? He could doom them all, and even if he did not he would possess an advantage over every other Ark Lord. The rest would slumber away the gulf of time, but Set would be able to wake periodically, to use the vast reserve of power to sustain his life. The others would have to husband their reserves, gambling that it would carry them forward to a day when the sun would again sustain the Arks.

Not so Set. He would emerge more powerful than ever, and this time Osiris would not be there to oppose him. Could not be, for no matter how clever he was there was simply no way to survive for thirteen millennia without the aid of an Ark.

Chapter 1- Angel Island

Trevor reflexively reached for his cell phone to check Facebook. Then he remembered Facebook no longer existed. Neither did his iPhone, or any other electronic device. They'd all been destroyed in the wake of the sun's coronal mass ejection, or CME as it they'd come to call it. Had that only been eight weeks ago? How ironic that he should find that more strange than the fact that he was, for all intents and purposes, a walking corpse. His heart no longer beat. He didn't need to breathe. His skin felt cool to the touch.

Then there was the mouthful of razor sharp fangs. Not quite as obvious as the black claws where his fingernails had been, but much more unnerving whenever he smiled. It was impossible to miss the almost palpable aura of fear he left in his wake as he passed through the encampment. It was a different flavor than that caused by his companion, despite the fact that both were mythological predators. People trusted werewolves—more so than walking corpses, anyway.

He and Commander Jordan made their way past the last knot of refugees, finally reaching the top of Angel Island. The heavily forested little spur of land was just a few miles across, connected to Sausalito via a ferry that had stopped running when the CME had wiped out most of the electronics required to run it.

Now the only way to reach the island was using one of the more conventional sailboats that ringed it, a vast fleet of them gathered from all over the bay. They bobbed up and down on soft blue waves, sails blindingly white in the afternoon sun. Trevor glanced up at the fiery orb, untroubled by its brilliance as he would have been while still alive.

"We're running out of room," Jordan said, stepping up to join Trevor. The beefy man wore a black T-shirt and grey cargo pants, which somehow managed to look like a uniform despite the fact that he no longer worked for Mohn Corp. "Food isn't an issue yet, but space is."

He was right. The entire island was dotted with small clusters of multicolored tents, most liberated from the REI store in Corte Madera. They were up to almost three thousand people, which was more than the island was able to support. Sanitation was fast becoming a problem, as was supplying the place with fresh water.

"Maybe it's time to start clearing the rest of Marin," Trevor suggested. He turned to gesture at the blackened remains of the Golden Gate bridge. A full quarter had been destroyed in the nuclear blast that Irakesh, the ancient Egyptian god, had unleashed a few weeks ago. "Thanks to baldy, the southern border is clear. If we can block the Richmond bridge, all we have to worry about is any zombies that wander down from the north."

"How many can you control, do you think?" Jordan asked, peering at Trevor through unreadable sunglasses.

"I don't know yet," Trevor replied with a shrug. He faced north, staring up the harbor towards Larkspur. Bad memories there. That was where he'd helped Irakesh kill Bridget. He wasn't sure if Blair had forgiven him for that. He certainly hadn't forgiven himself. "I'd guess a few hundred. At the very least I can set up a beacon to draw them to me. You and the others should be able to kill them."

"That's going to take a long time," Jordan said, shaking his head. The wind played through his hair. The military buzz cut had given way to blonde curls, and it humanized him somehow. "There are hundreds of thousands of zombies that way, and more will come south every day. I'm not saying we shouldn't try, but we could be at this for years before we get rid of them all."

"How's the training going? It looks to me that you've got a couple dozen promising soldiers down there," Trevor asked, nodding at a cluster of tents near the visitor center. It was patrolled by about a dozen men and women, each wearing black. They were all armed, most with rifles.

"They're not ready to deal with combat on this scale. Besides, that's not why I'm training them," Jordan said, scratching at stubble threatening to become a beard. Trevor no longer had that problem. His hair had stopped growing when he died, leaving him with a permanent goatee. "We're going to need them to defend the refugees. A militia of sorts. If we want to clear the zombies we need to do it ourselves, at least until we find a safe place for the survivors to hole up."

"I thought that's what this place is," Trevor said, a bit confused. They'd worked hard to set up the island as a sanctuary.

"It's temporary at best. People can't live here, not long term. The bay has been overfished for too long, and there's no farmland. We need to reclaim Marin and Sonoma, set up military compounds where people can start rebuilding their lives," Jordan replied, folding his arms as he stared north. The wind ruffled his hair, cool enough that it would have made Trevor's teeth chatter had he still been alive.

"You're right," Trevor said, returning his attention to the refugees gathered near the docks. "We're going to have to do that sooner, rather than-."

He trailed off, eyes narrowing as he focused on the soft waves lapping against the shore. The sun was sinking below the hills to the west, but there was still more than enough light. Especially to his enhanced senses.

"What is it?" Jordan growled, taking a step closer to Trevor.

"There," Trevor replied, stabbing a finger in the direction of the water. Right off the shore. "Something moving under the water. Something big."

Big didn't begin to describe it. A pair of hairy shoulders broke the water not far from the dock. The creature's face was inhuman, with long incisors and too-large eyes. Those eyes flared green, twin to Trevor's own. This thing, whatever else it was, was clearly deathless. Smaller shapes broke the water all around it, these ones far more recognizable as once having been human. They moved too quickly and with too much purpose to be simple walkers, though. Their eyes glittered with intelligence as they sought targets.

"Get down there and see what you can do," Jordan said, giving Trevor a shove.

Trevor fought down the urge to clock the commander, but he did turn to face him. "And just what the hell will you be doing?"

"Contacting Blair," Jordan shot back, tone full of contempt. "We're going to need help on this one, or people will die. Now get the fuck down there and stall. I'll see if I can get Blair and Liz here to help."

He was right. Trevor gave a tight nod, then turned back to the dock. He summoned the reserve of power deep within him. It had been growing for days, fueled by the sun. That seemed to be one of the advantages deathless possessed over werewolves. He could gain strength daily, while they had to rely on the moon to fuel their abilities. It looked like he was about to need every bit of that strength.

Trevor blurred, leaping down the trail toward the dock. He flew over rocks, bounded off pines. Faces peered up at him from in between tents. They were scared, but also curious. He ignored them as he rapidly approached the dock. The screams had already begun there, mostly from fear, but more than one shriek of pain. Trevor slid down a twenty-foot cliff, rolling back to his feet when he hit the bottom. He was near the water, close enough to get a good view.

Careful, my host. You are dealing with true deathless now, not the nascent deathless you so often encounter. They may be every bit as powerful as you.

"Great," Trevor muttered, peering over a boulder as he sized up the attack. He'd known they'd eventually have to deal with greater threats than zombies, but he'd hoped they would take longer to show up.

His risen was right. The attackers were leaping through refugees much more quickly than a zombie could manage. They also attacked more intelligently, incapacitating without killing. He watched as a pale-skinned deathless in a black tank top and jeans shattered an Indian man's leg. The man collapsed, clutching his knee with agonized grunts. The deathless kept going, downing another target as he moved on.

They are gathering food. Once they have enough they'll return and feed at their leisure. His risen said, tone emotionless.

Trevor was revolted, but also painfully aware of the rumble in his stomach. He badly wanted to feed, something he'd resisted as often as possible. He'd confined his meals to zombies, and even then he'd made sure no one saw him feed. If they found him disturbing now, that would only make it worse.

A roar drew his attention, and Trevor's mouth fell open now that he was close enough to see the larger figure emerge from the water. It was easily fifteen feet tall, and now that he was close he could clearly see it had once been a gorilla. A silverback, unless he missed his guess. He hadn't realized other primates could contract the virus, but apparently they could. What's more, this one had been feeding often and well to have already grown so large.

Its meaty black fist closed around a middle-aged woman one of the other deathless had incapacitated. She gave a single shriek, which was cut off as the thing stuffed her entire torso into its maw. Trevor gagged at the horrible crunching sound, cringing as the woman's entire body disappeared into the gorilla's mouth.

It would be wise to wait for aid, my host. That one is beyond your ability.

"Maybe," Trevor said, leaping over the boulder and blurring toward the gorilla. "But we don't have time to wait."

He leapt into the air, landing on the back of the gorilla's neck. Its thick fur gave him a solid grip as he swung one arm around to slash at its neck. A gout of cold black blood spilled to the ground, and the creature gave another bellow as its arms came up to seize Trevor. It was fast, but not blurring. Maybe it hadn't learned that ability yet, if he were lucky. Trevor instinctively transformed to green mist as the boulder-sized hands passed through the space he'd occupied.

He concentrated, summoning a wave of green light. It washed over the gorilla, cooking the thing's skin and filling the air with the stench of burnt meat and hair. The creature slashed wildly through the air where Trevor's cloud of energy hovered, its hands passing harmlessly through. It looked like he could hurt it, though the wounds closed as fast as he made them. At least it was no longer attacking refugees.

"Why do you fight us?" came a low feminine voice from below and behind him. Trevor shifted to see an Asian woman in her mid-twenties. Well, she'd been in her mid-twenties before dying, anyway. Now she had the same black claws and hideous green eyes Trevor did. She licked her lips, exposing a mouthful of razored fangs. "You are one of us. You should be feeding, not defending these cattle. You have fantastic abilities. You could teach us much. Join us."

The other deathless had stopped their attack, and were returning to encircle him. Trevor drifted a bit higher, now out of reach of the still-enraged gorilla. What the hell could he do now? He couldn't fight them all, and his experience with Irakesh had taught him that controlling the will of a sentient deathless was extremely difficult. So that was out. He needed backup, and he needed it now.

Maybe he could keep them talking until the others arrived.

Chapter 2- Light Pulses

Blair floated several inches above the ground, legs locked underneath him in a full lotus he'd never have been flexible enough to manage before his transformation. He drank deeply of the Ark's power, allowing his consciousness to flow through the entire structure. It was fascinating. Heady. In many ways he *was* the Ark, and could use it to extend his senses. More than that, he could capitalize on its senses, and the Ark had thousands of them. He could feel the ocean, feel the Ark's connection to something deep in the earth.

It was this latter that he focused on, trying once more to tease out the nature of the connection. Something powerful ran hundreds of miles into the earth, a sort of conduit. It was dormant, but he sensed it was capable of carrying enormous amounts of energy. That energy could flow both ways, which had piqued his curiosity. Where did it send the energy it gathered? If it could also draw energy, how and what did it draw that energy from? Blair understood conceptually that there was a network of Arks across the world, but how or why they'd been created remained a mystery.

Blair. Jordan's voice thundered in his brain. He winced, losing his concentration. That severed his connection to the Ark, and he fell heavily to the stone. *We need you out here. There's an attack. Not just zombies this time. Deathless. At least a dozen.*

We're on our way. Just give me a minute to grab Liz. Blair replied.

He concentrated for a moment, using the Ark to locate Liz. She was down in the training ring, where she spent almost all of her time. The ring displayed locales just like a holodeck, though so far as he knew the things it created were real. In this case, it had created a maze of black stone. Liz was prowling through it, golden sword extended. She wasn't shadow-walking, which was probably some new form of training.

Liz. He thought at her. She rolled backwards, disappearing into darkness before he'd even completed the thought. That didn't sever the connection though. She could still hear him. *I'm going to light walk to Angel Island. There's an attack and Jordan needs us.*

"Acknowledged," she replied aloud, emerging from the shadows once more. The ring wavered around her, stone walls disappearing.

Blair willed the energy in the Ark to coalesce around each of them. It was more difficult than when he'd used it to transport them into the Ark after the battle with Irakesh, because he and Liz were in different locations. That was a good thing though. He'd been pushing his shaping, in the same way Liz pushed her combat abilities. They both had demons to battle, and each was atoning in their own way.

The world vibrated around him, then beautiful, clear light flooded the room. There was a moment of weightlessness, and then he was simply elsewhere. He stood near the summit of Angel Island, Liz next to him in human form. She wore skin-tight black yoga pants and a matching tank top. Her hair was done up in the customary pony tail, a look he very much liked.

They'd appeared in a ring of rocks that had been erected for just this purpose. Blair still wasn't sure what would happen if they materialized in the same space someone else was occupying, so it seemed safest to designate an area they'd light walk to.

"Sit rep," Liz barked, stepping from the ring of stones. The golden blade of her sword rested casually against one shoulder as she approached Jordan. He towered over her, but if she was intimidated she didn't show it.

"Nine hostiles. One heavy," Jordan said, turning to point to the dock. "Eight smaller ones that seem like full deathless. Like your brother, basically. The larger one might be like the giant we fought in the hangar back in Panama, I don't know yet. They've stopped attack for now. Looks like they're talking with Trevor."

Blair didn't like Jordan's tone, but he understood it. Jordan and Trevor didn't trust each other, and that was made worse when a force of hostile deathless stopped their attack to have a little chat with Trevor. What the hell were they talking about? He peered down at the dock, noting the cluster of deathless around the larger, hairy figure. Trevor hovered above them, using the green cloud of energy he'd learned from Irakesh.

At least two dozen figures writhed on the ground, injured refugees no one was going to help. The militia was massing on the far side of a hill, under Yuri's direction. Blair turned to face Jordan. "If Yuri assaults those deathless, the whole militia will probably be slaughtered. We need to get down there."

"We'll blur," Liz said, tone hard. "Blair, I'll ride your shadow. When we get there, take down the smaller ones first. That will minimize the number of hostiles that can attack our people. Blair, see if you can use the Ark to deal with the larger one."

She didn't wait for a response, instead shifting to wolf form even as she slid into his shadow. He had a brief impression of a massive auburn creature, then she'd vanished entirely.

"Get your game face on," Jordan rumbled, already shifting into a tall, blonde-furred male. Blair followed suit, ignoring the brief pain as bones snapped and re-arranged to make room for his larger wolf-form.

Jordan blurred toward the docks, hopping down hillsides and over trees. Blair matched his pace, kicking up a cloud of dust that spun lazily in the air around him as the world slowed. They bounded toward the dock, crossing the quarter mile in a dozen hops. It was difficult to measure time while blurring, but Blair guessed no more than five or six seconds passed.

The commander barreled into the first deathless, an Indian woman in the tattered remains of a Fitbit T-shirt. She started to spin, but Jordan was far faster. He clamped his hands around her head, twisting with a sudden jerk. An awful crack echoed over the water, but the commander wasn't done. He twisted further, the muscles in his arms bunching as he gave another jerk. The woman's head came off with a pop, spraying desiccated gore into the air as her body collapsed to the sandy shore.

The other deathless spun to face the Commander, none noticing Blair where he crouched a few dozen paces away. Blair waited, turning his attention toward the larger figure. It was a fucking gorilla, probably liberated from the San Francisco zoo. He focused on the putrid green eyes, summoning his energy as he prepared to shape. He doubted it had anything like the mental defenses Irakesh had used, which meant he could probably bend its will fairly easily.

He was dimly aware of Liz appearing behind another one of the deathless. Her blade pierced its chest, lifting the man into the air. He twitched and flailed as pulses of sickly green light flowed down the blade. Blair didn't know how much strength Liz gained when she drank someone's essence, but even having done it just a few times she was clearly stronger than she'd been when she first changed.

Focus, Ka-Dun. His beast rumbled. *Deal with the bestial deathless before it endangers your pack.*

So Blair did. He envisioned a dagger of pure mental energy, thrusting it into the gorilla's neck at the base of the skull. It slid past the creature's defenses with little effort, and just like that the world vanished. He appeared in the thing's mind, immediately noting the differences between it and a human. Instead of the vast complex of neural connections he was used to, there was a more primitive network of thoughts. They were more primal, more focused on feeding to the exclusion of all else. This thing was a peerless predator, well-equipped to feed and grow stronger in this insane new world.

Blair's consciousness swelled to fill the beast, and suddenly he could see through its eyes. He flexed its fingers experimentally, tasting the air with enormous nostrils as he observed the world around. Only a few moments had passed, and the combat flowed around the gorilla's feet. Trevor had returned to the fray, grappling with one of the larger deathless. Jordan battled two more, a pair of women that were comically short, but devilishly fast. These two knew how to blur, even if some of the others didn't.

Three of the remaining deathless were bounding up over the hill. At first Blair feared they were fleeing, but then he realized they were heading for the militia. The crack of gunfire sounded around them, and the deathless saw a threat they could deal with. Blair forced the gorilla to lumber after them, crushing the spine of a deathless as the beast split the gathering evening with a thunderous roar.

The remaining deathless spun to face the gorilla, clearly confused. They scattered as it charged them, nimbly dodging as the beast launched a few clumsy swipes. The creature was large and powerful, but ungainly. He couldn't catch the deathless, but it might be able to keep them occupied.

Ka-Dun, be wary. Something stirs within the Ark.

That was all the warning Blair had. He was dimly aware of something stirring within the Ark's deepest systems, and then enormous power flowed through the entire structure. The bay was lit like noon, as a trio of clear white pulses blasted into the sky. The energy draw made him dizzy, and Blair lost hold over the gorilla's mind as he caught himself against a stunted tree. He felt weaker than he had in months, and a dozen alarms competed for his attention as systems failed all over the Ark. What the hell had just happened?

He tried to focus, tried to make sense of the conflicting demands the structure placed on his consciousness. Blair was barely aware of the approaching roar. He could feel the ground shaking as heavy footfalls sent up puffs of dust. His vision focused in time to see the gorilla, its putrid gaze focused hatefully on him as it approached.

"Oh crap," Blair said, staggering behind a larger tree. He wanted to blur, to leap away with the agility his form normally granted. But he couldn't. His body was sluggish, his mind thick as molasses. It pissed him off. Why the hell couldn't he ever get a straightforward fight? He was supposed to have the Ark on his side, not have it hamstring him at a critical moment. It wasn't fucking fair.

He cringed as a giant, hairy fist snapped the tree into splinters and continued into his gut. Ribs shattered as he was launched skyward, tumbling end over end into the dirt a good fifty feet away.

"Oww," Blair said, struggling to regain his footing. The gorilla was already charging again.

Chapter 3- Hesitation

Liz stumbled forward, staggered by the blow from behind. Claws ruptured her kidney, hot pokers jabbing into her again and again. She gritted her teeth, rolling onto her back to see her attacker.

The man standing above her had been an athlete in life, maybe a boxer or football player, judging by the broad shoulders. He had long, stringy, black hair, with a thick beard to match.

"Not so tough, are you, little puppy?" he growled, eyes flaring toxic green as his grin widened.

Liz considered a witty response, but settled on kicking a spray of gravel into his face. He winced, knocking the stones away. That bought her a moment, which she used to swing her sword in a low, tight arc. It hummed through the air, meeting brief resistance as it sliced through both his legs just below the knees.

She rolled to her feet, planting the blade in his chest, and willed the weapon to drink his essence, bracing herself for the cold shock as the pulses of light flowed up the weapon and into her. Each one was like a shot of espresso, bringing strength and clarity, along with a small portion of the host's memories.

The latter were troubling, but she shrugged them off. She needed to focus on the combat. Being a female werewolf meant she was the only combatant on the field without the ability to blur. She was strong and she was stealthy, but she was also the slowest one here.

"Liz!" Jordan roared from somewhere off to her right. "The militia's in trouble. They need immediate support."

She glanced in the direction he was pointing, up the hill to a cluster of rocks just off the path. About a dozen men and women had taken shelter there, and were firing their weapons into a trio of deathless.

Those deathless appeared unfazed by the assault, and all the militia had accomplished was drawing attention to themselves. She watched in horror as a deathless bounded into their ranks, disemboweling a woman with a wicked slash. It snatched up her rifle, and brought the stock down on the man next to her. His skull cracked in a spray of blood, and he collapsed onto the ground next to his companion.

Liz was about to charge, but the ground began to shake. She darted a glance to her right, noting the massive undead gorilla charging at Blair. She'd expected him to have already dealt with it, but he wasn't even looking in the creature's direction

He was focused on the Ark, and a moment later she understood why. The entire surface glowed white hot, then a burst of light shot from the tip into the sky. Another followed, then a third. Liz had no idea what they were, but she was more concerned about their affect on Blair.

He collapsed into the dirt, trying to pull himself to his feet as the gorilla approached. The creature shattered the tree he was sheltering behind, sending him flying through the air. Blair's silver fur was matted with dust and blood, and he didn't rise. She knew the blow hadn't been enough to kill him, but he was clearly in serious trouble.

"Liz," Jordan roared again. She darted another glance his way. He was squaring off against two more deathless, who were driving him steadily backwards toward the water. "The militia. Now! People are dying."

She looked their way again. The trio of deathless assaulting them had done hideous damage. Over half the militia was down, and the rest were fleeing. Liz steeled herself, committing to the decision. She slipped into the shadows, charging the closest deathless.

It was completely unprepared as she launched a two handed swipe at its neck. Her blade sheared through bone and flesh, severing its head in a spray of gore. The creature's headless body tumbled to the ground, but Liz was already cloaked in shadow once more.

The second deathless had noticed the fate of its companion, and was spinning slowly in an attempt to find her. It apparently hadn't learned to command the shadows, or it would already be hiding. That was good, because as long as it was looking for her it wasn't killing militia.

Liz bounded after the third deathless, who was chasing down a teen with an old carbine. The deathless blurred, darting forward and ramming a fist through the girl's back. The carbine tumbled to the ground in a clatter, and the deathless gave a cackle any Disney villain would have envied.

Liz saw red, baring her fangs as she leapt into the air. She came down on the deathless's back, crushing its spine and grinding in into the concrete. She drove her sword through its throat, pinning it to the ground as she leaned in close.

"I hope the last thing you feel is the same terror you inflicted on that poor kid," she growled. Then she twisted the blade, and drank the deathless's essence.

She rose to look for her final opponent, but it had fled back into the water. It disappeared from sight, wisely fleeing from her wrath. Liz turned to face Jordan, but either he'd dispatched his foes, or they too had fled. He'd already moved to assist Blair, who'd regained his footing and was dodging clumsy strikes from the gorilla.

Liz cloaked herself in shadow, sprinting up the hill in Blair's direction. By the time she arrived, Jordan had already entered the fight. He darted in close, disemboweling the gorilla with wickedly sharp claws, then dancing backwards when it tried to retaliate. The blow didn't faze the creature, but it did keep its attention.

She used the moment to launch herself into the air, timing her strike with all the precision she'd earned through dozens of hours of practice in the ring. Her blade came down on the gorilla's skull, splitting it cleanly in half and continuing down the spine. The blow continued all the way through the beast's body, which collapsed into two separate piles. The right half twitched once, then lay still.

"Blair, are you all right?" she asked, moving to his side. He looked dazed, his gaze glassy and unfocused even in wolf form.

"I think so," he said, cradling his head with one furry hand. "Something's happening with the Ark. Systems are failing all over. We need to get inside and find out what the hell is happening."

"What the hell were you thinking?" Jordan snapped, grabbing her shoulder. He spun her to face him, and she let him. She was far stronger in wolf-form, but she didn't resist. "You're a battlefield commander. You can't afford to hesitate, Liz. Out here you aren't Blair's girlfriend. You aren't a woman, or a friend. You're a leader. People died back there, people you could have saved. You came up with the plan. Next time, you need to goddamn follow it."

"I know," she said, gritting her teeth. She wanted to yell at him, to say that Blair had needed her. But Jordan was right. Blair had been fine, and her hesitation had cost lives.

Chapter 4- Escape

Steve sat up abruptly, cocking his head. Something thrummed through the Ark, deep and powerful. None of the driblets of information he'd pilfered from the Mother's sleeping mind suggested a cause, but he sensed it was unusual. What was Blair up to?

He rose from the bronzed bench, peering through the crackling blue energy net between him and freedom. Nothing stirred, not even the air. His companion hadn't moved; the white garbed deathless sat motionless on the bench on the far side of the cell.

His dark skin suggested Nubian ancestry, something that tugged at the anthropologist in Steve. Perhaps his kind had been the ancestors of the Africans who had given rise to ancient Egypt, and its rival, the mighty Nubia. Of course those descendants lacked the putrid green eyes and razored fangs that revealed just what kind of predator Irakesh was.

"If we go," Steve said, breaking the silence for the first time in nearly two days, "we go now."

"Now?" Irakesh answered, uncoiling languidly. He rose from the bench, folding his arms as he peered at Steve. His expression was unreadable, probably a survival trait in the world he'd grown up in. "For thirteen days I have railed at you to keep your promise. We could light walk from this cell at any time, yet you've whined about caution and the right time. What has finally caused your cowardice to ebb?"

Steve took a long, slow breath, schooling his features to conceal the surge of rage. Those had come often since his change, a legacy of the beast within him. "I can see why you lost, Irakesh. Why a half trained Ka-Dun that I manipulated easily was able to best you."

Irakesh staggered backwards as if struck. He caught himself on the wall, mouth working as if seeking the right insult to hurl. Then he straightened, jaw clicking shut. "I will not allow you to bait me again. They caught you just as easily, if you remember."

"Yes," Steve smiled, knowing he was about to win another verbal sparring match. "But I came away from the encounter with an access key. I achieved my goal of becoming an Ark Lord. Did you?"

Irakesh blurred, crossing the cell in the space between heartbeats. Steve could have matched his blur, but chose to conserve his energy. Let the deathless grandstand. A fist connected with his jaw, sending a jolt of pain through his face as he was hurled back into the wall.

Kill him, Ka-Dun. Why suffer such an affront from this wretch? You could tear him apart. He has nowhere to flee. His beast roared, its outrage clear.

Steve didn't answer directly. He didn't need to. The beast could hear his thoughts, and it knew why he didn't fight back, why he affected the posture of a beaten dog as he rose to his feet. It knew why he hadn't killed Irakesh, though he could have taken the deathless unaware days ago.

"Do not push me, Ka-Dun," Irakesh growled, chest heaving as if from exertion. Odd, that. Deathless no longer breathed, so the gesture was nothing more than a vestigial response from Irakesh's days among the living. "You have dangled the carrot of freedom for too long. I'll have it now, or this mockery of a partnership is at an end."

"Very well," Steve allowed, wiping blood from his lip. "I've waited until now, because we need Blair to be distracted. I can light walk to the central chamber, but from there we have to reach a light bridge in order to travel to the Ark of the Cradle. If we are not careful, he will intercept us before we can escape. If I reveal that I can light walk, Blair will close that route and we'll be truly trapped."

"So what is it that makes you think he is now distracted?" Irakesh asked. His expression was dubious, but curiosity lurked there.

"A few moments ago a tremendous surge of power rushed through the Ark," Steve explained, turning to face the lattice of energy bordering the cell. He took a step back from it, just in case. If he were too close, it might interfere with light walking. "I don't know the source of that energy, but either it's something Blair doesn't expect, or he's busy with something massive and delicate. That kind of shaping will take focus."

"Ahhh," Irakesh allowed, giving a shark-toothed smile. "Either way, he will be distracted. Clever, Ka-Dun Steve. Perhaps I have underestimated you."

"Perhaps," Steve said, extending a hand and grasping Irakesh tightly on the shoulder. "Come, let us be away from this prison."

Chapter 5- Imprisoned

Mark came to by degrees, gradually returning to consciousness. The room was bright, but he couldn't close his eyes for some reason. Couldn't blink. In fact, he had no motor control at all. His body lay limply on something cold and metallic, and he was staring upwards at a chrome ceiling. It was cold, but whatever muscle relaxant he'd been dosed with prevented him from shivering.

A door to his right hissed open and a figure entered. He saw the movement, but couldn't make out anything specific. It was frustrating, but he willed himself to stillness. If they wanted him dead, he already would be. If they wanted to interrogate him, they wouldn't have used a muscle relaxer, because that would dull any pain they'd inflict. So they must be here to talk.

"Good morning, Mark," came a familiar voice, pleasant and cultured. Leif Mohn, the Old Man himself. The victor of the brief civil war Mark had instigated at the Syracuse facility. He had no idea where he was, but he knew it wasn't Syracuse. He knew that installation, and this room wasn't a part of it. "I trust you're feeling more like yourself. It will probably take some time for the grogginess to fade. You've been in a medically induced coma for three and a half weeks."

"Why?" Mark tried to ask, but it came out as little more than a croak. He swallowed. Damn, but his throat was raw.

"Here, drink some of this," Mohn insisted, moving into Mark's field of view. He pressed a straw gently into Mark's mouth. Mark sucked greedily, not caring about the water's metallic taste. "Not too much now. Just a little at first."

Mark cleared his throat, then tried speaking again. "Why am I alive?"

"Because you are Mohn Corp's most senior surviving director. The rank and file all but worship you, and in this new world that makes you a very, very valuable commodity," Mohn explained. He dragged a plastic chair close to Mark's bed, sitting with exaggerated care. He folded his trench coat over his knees, the grey fabric beaded with drops of rain. So a wet climate, wherever they were. "We're facing threats most men can't bring themselves to accept as real. Without strong leadership, the men will break, and mankind's last shield will shatter. I cannot allow that to happen."

"You can't possibly believe I'll help you and whatever monster you work for," Mark replied, trying to turn his head to face the old man. A strap held his forehead in place, but at least he could move his eyes now. "I rebelled for a reason. I've seen what these things can do. We need to fight them, not give them the fucking keys to the kingdom."

"I can understand why you'd believe that," Mohn said, leaning back in his chair. He removed an ornately carved wooden pipe from the pocket of his trench coat, and a leather pouch from another. "When he first took me as a servant I believed much the same. I rebelled repeatedly. In my limited understanding, I thought he was some sort of demon, that he was trying to bring about an apocalypse."

"But at some point you sold your soul instead?" Mark replied. A thousand tiny pinpricks were making their way up his limbs as feeling began to return.

"In a manner of speaking," Mohn admitted. That surprised Mark. "It took three decades. During that time, I had the briefest taste of immortality, saw the world in a way few men do. I came to realize my master was guiding the fate of our species. Doing so requires many short term sacrifices, it means individuals matter not at all. It has to be that way, if we expect to survive in this new age."

"Can you even hear yourself?" Mark snapped. "You sound like a Bond villain, justifying his poorly conceived plot." He immediately regretted the loss of control, not because Mohn didn't deserve it, but because right now his wits were his only tool. "What is it your 'master' wants?"

"One of the many titles he wears is the Guardian of the West, the protector of mankind," Mohn explained, adding a pinch of tobacco to his pipe. "It's a responsibility he takes seriously, one he's borne for a very long time. When the first pyramids were built in Egypt, he was there guiding them. Imhotep, they called him. When the Mayans built their civilization three millennia later he was there, guiding them. Cambodia. Stonehenge— my master was there shaping humanity, preparing us for *this* day.

"Mohn Corp is one small piece of his plan, a way to harness technology his contemporaries know nothing about," the old man continued, finally lighting the pipe. He took an experimental puff. The stuff was pungent, but not unpleasant. "A war is about to begin, Mark. A war between gods who drew breath when the most complicated human tool was a stone hand-axe. When we lived in caves and could only dream of writing. The winner of that war will decide the fate of our species. You assume my master is a monster, an evil to be stopped. Mark, he is the best hope we have. You know of Irakesh. There are far worse evils gathering strength even now. My master is the only one strong enough to oppose them."

"I get that you believe that," Mark said, blinking rapidly. The smoke burned his eyes. "I don't. I'm not going to sell my soul, Leif. I'm better than that. I'm loyal to humanity. I sent Jordan to deal with Irakesh. He's the best of the best. He'll deal with you and your master too, eventually."

"Will he now?" Leif asked, rising from the chair. "Osiris will be here soon, and I promise after you meet him you'll feel quite differently about things. Not only will you serve the Master, but you'll count yourself privileged to do it."

The old man turned and slipped from the room, leaving that cloying smoke in his wake. For the first time he could remember, Mark was terrified. These ancients possessed abilities they barely understood. One thing had been quite clear: they could control minds.

Chapter 6- Oh Shit

"Oh shit," Blair said, rising unsteadily to his feet. He blinked away spots, the afterimage caused by the glow the Ark had emitted. The massive structure had returned to a flat black, and was little more than a looming shadow now that full night had fallen.

"What is it?" Liz asked, turning to face him. Her tone was hard. It had been since the fight, not that he could blame her. A lot of people had died.

"Steve and Irakesh," Blair said. He tucked his hands in the pocket of his windbreaker to ward off the chill. "What if the system malfunctions shorted out their cell?"

"They'd still be trapped inside, right?" Trevor asked from his place in the shadows beneath a nearby pine. Blair started. He'd almost forgotten Trevor was there.

"Maybe," he said, directing his answer to the twin pools of green shining in the darkness. "I still don't know everything the Ark can do, but at the very least it does have a light bridge. They might be able to use it to light walk out, though I'm not sure where they could go."

"Then you're right. We need to get inside," Liz said. She sounded so tired, her usual determination faded to a dull monotone. "Trevor, will you go grab Jordan? The three of you can investigate. I'll stay to oversee the island until you get back."

"On it," Trevor said, trotting off into the darkness. Blair could hear Jordan bellowing orders down near the dock, so not far.

"It wasn't your fault, you know," Blair said, quietly. He approached Liz, giving her shoulder a squeeze.

She wrapped an arm around his waist and leaned her head against his shoulder. It was as intimate as she'd been with him in a while, especially in the last few weeks. They'd never really returned to the close bond they'd developed when they'd been on the run from Mohn.

"The attack wasn't my fault," she said, disengaging and meeting his gaze. "The moment of hesitation when I couldn't decide whether to stop the deathless or help you was. I screwed up, and I cannot allow that to happen. Jordan's right. Emotion can get us killed."

Blair wanted to trot out a counterargument, or at least say something to make her feel better. What would that be, though? He'd made a lot of mistakes in the last several months, most of them caused by giving in to one emotion or another. They had to be above that.

Liz settled her arms around his waist again, soft curves pressing against him. It felt good, and he decided to enjoy the moment. They might not get another any time soon, at least if their track record for crises continued unabated.

"I'm glad I met you, Liz," he whispered. She didn't reply, but she did squeeze him a bit tighter.

Footsteps crunched on the gravel, approaching quickly. Liz released him immediately, her back straightening as she became the warrior once more.

"Let's move," Jordan said, striding up boldly. "Trevor filled me in."

"Great," Liz said, turning to face him. "Handle the situation, then get back here as quickly as you can. I'll handle the defense for now, and see if we can recruit a few more people to replace our losses. Is Yuri still in command?"

"He is," Jordan said, giving a tight nod. "I've ordered him to organize the remaining militia into smaller squads for more coverage. You're right, though, we need more people. Starting recruitment is a good idea."

"You're wasting time," Liz said, her tone frosty. Her eyes were fastened on Jordan. "If there's a chance Steve has escaped we need to stop him. This time we listen to you. If he's left that cell, he dies. No more imprisonment. He's too much of a risk walking around."

Jordan nodded. His expression was...approving.

"I'm going to initiate the light walk," Blair interrupted, drawing everyone's attention.

It was harder than usual, perhaps because the Ark had less to give. Warning klaxons were still echoing in his mind, and he was aware of several hundred systems that were still offline. Whatever the Ark had done had taxed it to the edge of its abilities, even with the enormous infusion of power Irakesh had given it when he detonated the bomb.

Blair used some of his own energy, closing his eyes and willing them to appear within the central chamber. There was a moment of resistance, then they were surrounded by clear white light. When it faded they stood in the central chamber.

Chapter 7- Pursuit

The lights in the central chamber flickered, occasionally flaring brighter, yet never reaching their full illumination. The place reeked of ozone, though Jordan wasn't sure what had caused it.

"What the hell happened to this place?" Trevor whispered, spinning slowly in place.

"Doesn't matter," Jordan said, fixing Blair with his gaze. "Can you detect whether the cells are still occupied?"

"I don't know," Blair said, rounding to face him. He looked concerned. And angry. "I felt something, a surge of some kind."

"Like the pulses?" Trevor asked. Jordan noted the deathless had one hand around the .357 belted at his side. He might not like Trevor, but he respected his combat prowess.

"Sort of," Blair said. He spun slowly, one hand raised as if testing the air somehow. "Not quite, though. It was weaker, and it reminded me of something. It was just like whenever I light walk…"

Blair trailed off, and his eyes widened. "Oh crap."

There was a brief flash of light, then Jordan was elsewhere. He took in his surroundings once again, this time even more cautiously since he hadn't been expecting the second light walk. They stood in an arched hallway with bronzed walls. Every few feet, a small room with no door broke the flow of the hall. The one they stood in front of had a crackling lattice of energy.

"They're gone," Trevor said, pointing at the cell even as Jordan realized the same thing. There was no sign of Irakesh or Steve.

"Irakesh is a master of illusion," Jordan said, thinking out loud. "Is there any chance he's using that to fool our senses?"

"So we'd open the cell and let them out," Blair said, cocking his head as he approached the crackling blue energy. "I don't think that's it. I'd be able to sense Steve at least. He can't hide the presence of an access key, and I don't feel anything inside. They aren't here anymore."

"You said you felt light waking?" Trevor said. His words hung in the air as they all considered the implications.

"How far could he go using that?" Jordan asked. It bothered him that he didn't understand the tactical limitations of such an immense power.

"Not far," Blair said, shaking his head. "I think he's still in the Ark somewhere. He might have made it as far as Angel Island, but I doubt it."

"Where would he go inside the Ark?" Trevor asked.

"There are only a few tactical choices," Jordan said, voice deepening as he shifted. His clothing disappeared, replaced by thick blonde fur. He barely felt the pain. "He could be trying to wake the sleepers in those rejuvenators, or he could be trying to escape. Do you think he has some sort of power that would let him get through the bay?"

"Possibly," Blair allowed. He shifted as well, bones cracking as a muzzle sprang from his face. In the space of two seconds, he gained two feet in height, and his body was covered in thick silver fur. "There's another option, though. He could be trying to use the light bridge."

"Light bridge?" Trevor asked. The deathless withdrew his pistol, cradling it in both hands.

"No time to explain. I'm going to light walk us down to the light bridge. We'll start there, and if we can't find them we'll widen the search," Blair said.

Then they were bathed in light again, and Jordan was elsewhere. Damn, but he was getting tired of this light walking shit.

Chapter 8- The Nexus

Blair blinked twice, knees sagging as he gazed around him in wonder. He wasn't sure where the sudden weakness had come from; perhaps it was the enormous distance they'd apparently traveled. Wherever they were, it certainly wasn't anywhere near San Francisco.

You have entered the Nexus, Ka-Dun. The Beast rumbled softly. *Even The Mother does not understand it fully. Its age is incalculable.*

That surprised him. Gaps in Isis's knowledge were rare, though she'd already admitted they did exist. Whatever this place was, it predated even her. He studied the architecture carefully, immediately picking out common patterns. The fluted columns could have been found in 4th Dynasty Egypt, the scarabs and sphinxes the same style he'd grown up loving.

The resemblance to ancient Egypt ended there. The walls were a familiar black stone, dotted with diamond-shaped crystals every ten feet. Those were a perfect mirror of the ones found in the Ark of the Redwood, reinforcing what he already knew. The Builders had created this place as well.

Bridget would have loved it. Thinking of her was painful, but also freeing. They'd reconciled at the end, and in her final moments he'd learned just how much that had meant to her. She'd died content, and her sacrifice had not been in vain. He could finally lay her memory to rest, and move on to better things. Red-headed things.

That brought his attention back to his surroundings. Irakesh had been directly responsible for Bridget's death, even if it was Cyntia who'd done the killing. He and Liz had dealt with the crazed abomination, but Cyntia's death did little to quiet his thirst for vengeance. Irakesh and Steve were going to die, even if it meant giving up vital knowledge.

"This way," Blair said, stepping down from the platform. It was a raised golden disk about a dozen feet across, surrounded by a triangle of black stone that sloped gently to the floor.

Trevor disappeared into the shadows, while Jordan prowled ahead. His pistol was comically small in his huge furry fists, but Blair seriously doubted anyone would be foolish enough to laugh at the commander.

They followed the corridor between the fluted columns, each diamond-shaped crystal flickering to life as they passed. They shed a wan illumination, just a pale shadow of the brilliance Blair had witnessed in both the other Arks he'd seen.

"What's wrong with the lights? This place is even worse off than the Mother's Ark," he whispered softly. It was for Trevor's benefit. He was a master of the harder sciences, and far more at home with computers than Blair. If anyone understood what was happening here, it would be him.

"This place has to run on power of some sort. I imagine it's running out," came a disembodied whisper to his right.

Jordan made a sudden shushing motion, then glided into a chamber at the far end of the corridor. Blair followed, stopping in the doorway to gawk. The chamber was a large domed room, the ceiling thrusting some seventy-five feet into the air. It was perfectly clear glass, and it held what appeared to be an ocean at bay, the kind that was so deep light no longer penetrated.

"We're at the bottom of the sea," he muttered, taking a step into the room.

A flicker of light at the room's center drew his attention. Several gemstones along the floor had flickered to life—a ruby, an emerald, and a pair of diamonds. They pulsed once, then a holographic form appeared above them.

"What the fuck is that?" Jordan rumbled, aiming his weapon at the hologram's head. Blair assumed the gesture was reflexive, as Jordan's posture was too relaxed for real combat.

"I think we're looking at one of the Builders," Blair said, taking several steps forward until he stood before the hologram.

It was roughly six feet tall, with mottled green skin the color of summer-cut grass. It had large black eyes, like a shark's. Its arms were a bit too long, its limbs a bit too thin. Each hand had four fingers.

"Holy. Shit," Trevor said, joining Blair near the hologram. "That thing is right out of the X-Files. Are you telling me the pyramids really *were* built by aliens?"

"That assertion is incorrect," the figure hummed, its voice digitized but still recognizable English. "The structures you refer to as pyramids were constructed by humans during the early Holocene. They were created by a culture you refer to as the ancient Egyptians, during the fourth dynasty. The first was constructed by pharaoh Khufu. The second was…"

"He meant the Arks," Blair interrupted. Part of him wanted to listen, wanted to ask how this thing knew so much about human history. It had been dead-on about Khufu's pyramid. What else did it know? If only they weren't so pressed for time. Steve and Irakesh were getting away even now.

"Ahh, the Arks were not constructed by aliens either," the figure corrected. It flickered, fading a bit. A moment later it returned to full illumination. "They were constructed by the Builders, an early hominid that predated your species by six point four million years."

Blair's jaw sagged open. "So these Builders, they were born on earth then? How many years from the current date did they build the Arks?"

He'd asked the question to see when this thing considered humanity to have begun. That could mean Homo Sapiens, which was roughly 200,000 years old. Or it could mean Homo Erectus, or an even earlier ancestor. If that were true, it would make the Builders over 10,000,000 years old.

"Six point six million years," the being answered, cocking its head. "Your genus first appeared roughly 200,000 years ago, while your species is nearly three million years old."

"That's great," Jordan interrupted, finally joining them near the hologram.

"Has anyone else passed this way recently? We're looking for two humans."

"Ah, the Ka-Dun and the deathless," the figure said, nodding. It focused its gaze on Jordan. "They departed this room three minutes and sixteen seconds before your arrival."

Blair stifled the urge to ask how this thing knew what a Ka-Dun was. "Where were they going?"

"To the light bridge in the southeastern section of the Nexus," it explained, shifting those flat black eyes back to Blair. "I believe they are seeking the Ark of the Cradle."

"Let's move," Jordan snarled. He stalked forward several paces, then turned a sheepish look to Blair. "Do you know which way the southeastern corridor is? I can't get my bearings down here, and something is playing havoc with my compass."

"That way," Blair said, starting towards one of the doorways leading to the room. He counted seven of them, now that he'd torn his gaze from the hologram. Each doorway had a slightly different Ark glyph above it.

"Ka-Dun Blair," the figure called as they started for the doorway. Blair turned, shocked that it knew his name. "Be aware that the Nexus has reached critical power reserves. If a conduit to a powered Ark is not restored within the next three hours, power will fail entirely, and this entire complex will be crushed by the ocean above."

"Lovely," Trevor said, already moving for the doorway. He looked back at Blair even as he glided forward. "Can we trust this thing?"

"I don't know," Blair shrugged, glancing at the hologram. It seemed benign, but appearances could be deceiving. "Either way we have to stop Steve and Irakesh. Let's see if we can catch them before they reach the light bridge."

The race was on.

Chapter 9- Osiris

An unremarkable servant in plain white clothes led Mark into the sitting room, the kind of library with all mahogany furniture and the thick smell of tobacco. A fire roared in one corner. It was the only source of light, as the windows were covered by heavy curtains. A figure sat in the corner opposite the fire. His features were thick with shadow, but his hands revealed a great deal. Too-pale skin with long fingers. Each nail had been expertly manicured, and his forearms revealed the heavily muscled frame of an athlete.

The door closed behind Mark. A floorboard creaked as the guard shifted outside. Then the figure rose, stepping into the light of the fire. His perfectly styled hair was dark. Not quite black, but something close to that. It bore the faintest hint of red, if that wasn't a trick of the light. He wore a dark blue suit with a thread count as high as any Mark had ever seen. Armani, unless he missed his guess. This man could have swam with any of the sharks who ran the super-corporations springing up around the world. Until you reached his eyes. They glowed with a faint inner light, the horrifying green that conjured thoughts of Chernobyl. Those eyes made it abundantly clear this man wasn't even remotely human.

"Ahh, the legendary Director himself," the man said, his voice reinforcing the polished appearance, his accent not anything Mark was familiar with. "I'd offer you a hand, but I doubt you'd take it. Please, have a seat. It's time we talked."

The man, or whatever he was, sat back down in his chair. Everything but his horrifying eyes and charming smile were swallowed in shadow. He nodded at a plush armchair neighboring his. Mark hesitated for an instant, considering. If he sat, that would open a very small door. Agreeing to one task led to accepting another, then another, until it became natural to accede to the next one. That was a dangerous road, especially when the one guiding him down it was a creature reputed to control minds.

If he remained standing, he might make it through a short audience, but even now his legs had begun to tremble. He'd been unconscious for days, maybe even weeks, and if he pushed it, his body would fail. Fainting during the middle of the meeting would throw him far more off balance than agreeing to a simple request.

Mark sat. He leaned into the chair in spite of himself, letting out a more audible sigh of relief than he'd have liked. Then he waited as the silence stretched. This was the next test. Most people could not abide an uncomfortable silence. They'd say almost anything to fill it, often revealing things they'd never intended. Mark had used the tactic to great effect many times, and he wasn't going to fall for it here.

"What must you think of me?" the man began, leaning forward in his chair to catch the firelight. He reached up with one thumb and pushed at his upper lip until it exposed his teeth. His canines were elongated in a way Bela Lugosi had made famous nearly a century before. "I have fangs. Unnatural eyes. Your brain senses I am a predator, and every instinct screams to flee. Even now your limbic system is flooding your system with adrenaline. Given your weakened state, that will carry quite a price in seven or eight minutes."

He paused, giving Mark a chance to speak. Mark remained silent.

"Worse, you know I am affiliated somehow with the virus which wiped out over ninety percent of your species, a crime greater than any committed in your recorded history. So far as you know, I have, in a way, killed more people than all other causes combined," the man continued, leaning back in his chair so only his eyes were visible. The effect was eerie, and no doubt quite intentional. "If there was ever an embodiment of the word evil, surely it must be me. You long to destroy me, yet even now there is another emotion slithering through your mind: fear. Fear that I can compel you to serve me. Fear that I have an unnatural means of control."

He paused, placing his pipe between too-white teeth. Then he waited, no doubt studying Mark's reaction. It was the smart tactic. Time was on this thing's side, not Mark's. The clock was ticking, and he had to find a way to gain some tactical leverage. "You know who I am," Mark said, finally. "Why don't you grant me the same courtesy?"

"A fair request," the man said, giving a half chuckle. He leaned forward again, eyes gleaming. "You'd know me under many names. I was Ah Puch among the Maya. Brahma among the Hindu. Usir is my current name, a mispronunciation of an ancient one. One you'll recognize, I'm sure. Among the Egyptians I was called Osiris."

Mark swallowed, blinking rapidly several times as he sought to process what he'd just heard. Part of him knew the physical tells would be used against him, but that just didn't matter. This thing had been multiple gods throughout history. The revelation was nearly unthinkable. This being had likely guided the human race since the Pleistocene, and possessed the accumulated knowledge of that entire span of time.

"You'd like to ask about my motivations, I'm sure. What benefit could there possibly be in wiping out humanity? Why kill so very many people?" Osiris asked, giving an exaggerated shrug. He wore the type of smile that suggested he was enjoying this. "The situation is far more complex than that, I assure you, Director."

"If you're just going to compel me, why bother with the recruitment speech?" Mark asked. It was uncharacteristically blunt, but he was losing ground and had few options. He reached up to loosen his tie before realizing he still wore his hospital gown. Another tactic to keep him off balance.

"Oh, I'm not going to compel you, Director," Osiris replied. He leaned forward again, his gaze deadly earnest. "I am so positive you will see things my way that I am simply going to give you all the facts. Once you know the extent of the situation, you can choose to stay and help, or I can have you flown to any destination in the world. Simply name it. Is that a fair enough arrangement, do you think?"

Mark hesitated for a long moment. "Go on."

Chapter 10- Ark of the Cradle

Trevor kicked off a wall, using the momentum to fling himself around a corner. He rolled past a column, the strange black stone pitted and scarred. Maybe that was natural erosion, but it looked more like this place had seen battle at some point, probably recently from the bits of stone on the floor.

Lights flickered on as he passed, lending credence to the story the strange hologram had related. That alarmed the hell out of him, for a damn good reason. It was clear this place was at the bottom of the ocean, and just as clear it was ancient. Whatever power reserve kept it running was on the verge of running out, and if they were still here when it expired there would be no escape. They'd either starve, or the ocean would crush that big glass dome and everything inside, including them.

"We're getting close," came Jordan's guttural voice, as an eight-foot-tall streak of blonde passed Trevor.

The commander's furry form came to a halt outside a doorway that mirrored the one they'd come through when entering, though the glyph set above it was a little different. His enormous black nose sniffed, ears twitching as he listened. Trevor took the opportunity to drop back into the shadows, prowling to the edge of the doorway as well. Blair appeared a moment later, dropping into a crouch beside Jordan. They needn't have bothered; their quarry was already aware of them.

Two figures stood on the center of a raised golden disk, just like the one they'd arrived on. Irakesh wore a condescending smile, green eyes flashing as he folded his arms. His ivory garments caught the light, making his dark skin almost black in the dim room. The figure next to him was much more recognizable, perhaps because Steve was bathed in a silver aura. It was the same aura Trevor sometimes saw around Blair, presumably when he used the power granted by the Ark's access key. It made sense, since Steve had stolen just such a key.

The disk began to hum, a sound just beyond the edge of hearing. It was unmistakable, and Trevor knew what came next.

"We have to stop them now," Jordan roared, blurring into the room. His pistol was already in his hands, and it coughed several rounds in Steve's direction.

The time between deafening gunshots lengthened as Trevor began a blur of his own. There was a sort of doppler effect as his entire body accelerated. He leapt through the doorway, circling wide to the left as he watched events unfold. Irakesh had also begun a blur, carefully positioning himself between Steve and the rounds Jordan had fired. The bullets corkscrewed through the air, moving unerringly towards Steve's face and chest. Each left a visible wake in the air, crawling towards their target as if in no particular hurry.

Irakesh plucked them from the air one by one, then flung each one back at Jordan, but Jordan easily evaded them. He dropped his pistol, leaping into the air above Steve. It was a smart tactical move for several reasons. Steve was the one initiating the light walk, so if they could stop him then they could also stop Irakesh. If they failed, their opponents would escape. It also forced Irakesh to stay engaged in the fight. If they went after him he could simply vanish—or, worse, create an illusion to distract them.

Trevor briefly considered drawing his own pistol, but decided against it. Firing it would give away his location, and he wanted to maintain the element of surprise. He glanced behind him, seeing Blair enter the room. Blair had a hand extended towards Steve, but whatever shaping he was doing was invisible. Trevor shifted his attention back to Jordan, who was descending towards Steve's still human form. Then a bolt of green energy shot from Irakesh's hand, catching Jordan in the chest and knocking him away from Steve.

Now, my host, his risen crooned. He didn't need the encouragement; he was already in motion.

Trevor intensified his blur, planting a foot against Irakesh's face and launching himself at Steve. The move caught the deathless off guard, and he knocked Irakesh to the edge of the platform as he sailed into Steve. Trevor's flying tackle knocked Steve prone on the disk. Unfortunately, it didn't seem to have broken his concentration. The deep thrumming intensified, and the room was bathed in familiar white light. A moment later they were elsewhere.

Trevor gave it a once over, knowing he only had moments before combat resumed. The room, wherever they were, was dimly lit by the familiar diamond-shaped lights he'd grown used to back in the Ark of the Redwood. Fluted columns lined a pathway leading from the room, just like they had in the Nexus. The disk they'd landed on also mirrored the Nexus, which meant they were in another Ark. The Ark of the Cradle, if the hologram had been telling the truth. Trevor gathered that meant somewhere in Africa, where Irakesh's mother ruled. Lovely.

"Fuck," Jordan roared, flipping to his feet and blurring towards Irakesh. His meaty werewolf fist sailed harmlessly through the illusion of Irakesh's face.

"Dammit," Trevor muttered, leaping off Steve and back into the shadows. They'd failed to stop Steve from initiating the light walk, and it looked like Blair had been left behind in the Nexus. That meant the fight was two on two, more or less even. Except that Irakesh was older and more powerful than he and Jordan put together.

Another bolt of toxic green energy lanced from the darkness at the edge of the room, briefly illuminating it. The bolt sailed into Jordan, picking him up again and hurling him into the wall with a sickening crunch.

Trevor unleashed an eldritch bolt of his own, catching Steve in the face. The bolt knocked Steve from the platform, sending him slamming into the black stone wall where he collapsed. Right at Jordan's feet.

Jordan leapt on Steve, tearing and biting as the two males snapped at each other. Jordan had the twin advantages of size and experience, so Trevor turned back to combat.

"Clever, my apprentice," Irakesh's voice whispered from the shadows. Trevor darted right, then left. He rolled behind a pillar. His evasive moments were probably unnecessary, but the last thing he needed was Irakesh getting the drop on him. The deathless had far better control of his powers, and centuries more experience. Trevor doubted he could take Irakesh on his own, but hopefully he could delay him long enough for Jordan to deal with Steve. "What will you do now, Trevor? We've arrived at the cradle, and without Blair you can't escape. Even if you beat us, you'll still have my mother and her attendants to deal with. Surrender, and she may show mercy."

"Fuck you," Trevor said, turning his attention back to Steve and Jordan.

Steve was on the bottom, clearly getting the worst of the exchange. Jordan hadn't come away unscathed though. His fur was matted with blood, and one of his eyes scrunched shut in obvious pain. The two were apparently more evenly matched than Trevor had expected. He could do something about that, though. Trevor blurred forward, planting a hand against Steve's shoulder. He reached into his reserves, flooding Steve's body with the same awful radiation he'd just used at range. The move caught Steve off guard, and he began flopping about like a fish.

Jordan instantly seized the opportunity, ripping out Steve's throat with his fangs. Then Jordan leapt to his feet, planting one furry foot against Steve's chest as he seized Steve's right arm with both hands. Jordan ripped with all his strength, tearing off Steve's arm in a shower of hot, coppery blood. Trevor found himself licking his lips where some of the blood had splattered. A tide of hunger rose within him, but he forced it down as he dropped back into the shadows. Just in time. A bolt of green fire shot past him, catching Jordan in the shoulder. It knocked the Commander back from Steve, though Steve didn't seem in any shape to capitalize on it.

Steve scrambled away from Jordan, finally pulling himself to his feet at the base of one of the columns lining the room. He clutched his severed stump with his remaining hand, but Trevor knew it would only be a minute or two before the limb regrew. They had the advantage, but only for a few moments. He had to find a way to capitalize on it, but what the hell could he do?

Be wary, my host. A new danger approaches.

Trevor rolled into a crouch next to a column, studying the darkness. There was no sign of Irakesh, and both Jordan and Steve were recovering in different corners of the room. He sensed nothing, so what had caused his risen to speak?

The head of a massive scythe erupted from Jordan's chest. The haft shone gold, very much like the sunsteel sword Liz wielded. The two-foot-long curved blade at the end was also gold, but had an enormous ruby set into the center. It gleamed cruelly for a moment, then it wrenched loose from Jordan's chest. Jordan's furry form collapsed to the ground, eyes glazed. He was totally unresponsive, possibly unconscious. What the hell had done that?

Trevor kept perfectly still, waiting to see if the attacker revealed himself again. If he did, his likely target would be Steve, as he was the only visible person in the room. So Trevor watched him, waiting to see what would happen. A few moments later, the same golden scythe burst from Steve's throat. He reached up to free himself; the axe jerked. The motion slammed Steve's body into the column next to him with so much force all three remaining limbs shattered. His broken body tumbled to the ground, unmoving.

It was a damn good thing Trevor neither breathed nor had a heartbeat. Either would have given him away. He stood there next to the pillar, waiting. Long moments passed, then a rolling wave of green energy burst from the center of the room. It came from the strangest figure Trevor had ever seen, much like a werewolf but with the head of a jackal. It wore golden armor, but he didn't have time to see more before the energy burned his eyes from his face.

He fell to the ground screaming, praying for the pain to end.

Chapter 11- Stabilizing the Nexus

Blair stared dumbly at the light bridge as the white light faded. All four figures had been whisked to wherever the bridge had taken them. If his theories about the glyph over the door matched the hologram's claims, then that meant all four had just light walked to Africa. They were now in the stronghold of the enemy, locked in a fight for their lives.

Take caution, Ka-Dun, his beast rumbled. *You seek to protect your pack, but if you follow blindly you may share their fate. That would deliver not one, but two access keys into the hands of your enemies.*

The beast wasn't wrong, but Blair still took a step towards the light bridge. Either he acted decisively and followed, or he accepted the fact that Trevor and Jordan were lost. They'd need an Ark Lord to guide them back to the Nexus, and there was no way they could coerce Steve to do that.

"I have to go after them," he decided, hurrying towards the light bridge.

"That is inadvisable," buzzed a cheery voice. Blair spun to find the hologram hovering not far from the doorway. Oddly, there were no gems projecting the light that formed the strange green figure. Somehow it had manifested on its own.

"Inadvisable why?" he asked, stepping onto the light bridge.

"Inadvisable, because as previously mentioned the Nexus is doomed unless you forge a conduit to the Ark of the Redwood," the alien said—Blair couldn't think of it as anything else, since it very much resembled the little green men that had so bedeviled Fox Mulder. "If you leave, the ocean will destroy this place. This act will isolate all seven great Arks. They will no longer have a shared connection, and light walking between them will be impossible."

"Yeah, I'm not sure I'm willing to buy what you're selling," Blair replied, taking several cautious steps toward the hologram. "It seems awfully convenient that this place is suddenly in trouble, right at this precise moment. Why now? Hasn't it stood for millions of years?" The anthropologist in him was intensely curious. He'd always dreamed of discovering a lost culture, but an entirely lost species that had, in many ways, exceeded their own? That was beyond incredible. Yet he wasn't willing to let his enthusiasm override his caution. This thing had its own agenda.

"Indeed," the hologram said, giving a jerky little nod. Its tone remained unfailingly cheerful. "The Nexus was created after the fifth Ark, four point eight million years ago. It has stood the entire time, though its location has moved several times since its creation."

"So why is it suddenly in trouble now?"

"The problem began nine millennia ago when the conduit to the First Ark was severed," It explained, cocking its head to the side. "Until that time the Nexus was always sustained by a steady flow of energy, which kept it safe during the intervals when the sun produced less energy. Once the conduit was severed, the Nexus began losing power, and this process has continued until the present day. This process has greatly accelerated over the last few years, because several groups have used the light bridge to enter and leave. Doing so costs enormous power, and has taxed the Nexus to its final limits."

Blair closed his eyes, considering. "So this place ran off its own battery, and the First Ark recharged that battery. Since that connection is severed you need a new one. Basically I have to jump start the Nexus using the Ark of the Redwood. Is that about right?"

"Precisely," It said. Blair opened his eyes, staring down at the cheerful little alien. "Your arrival is quiet fortunate. So far as I know the Ark of the Redwood is the only one with reserves large enough to sustain the Nexus."

"How much power will that take from the Ark?" Blair asked.

"Approximately 63% of the Ark's current power capacity will be required to sustain the Nexus. This percentage will drop as other Arks come on line and establish their own conduits," It explained, blinking once.

"You said the connection to the First Ark was severed. Who severed it?" Blair asked, changing gears. He wasn't sure whether to cooperate with this thing yet, but at the very least he could learn as much as possible. Assuming it was telling the truth.

"I do not know," the hologram said, somehow managing to look troubled. "At first I suspected the progeny of the Builders, but they are unable to access the Arks or the Nexus."

"That doesn't make sense," Blair said, running his fingers through his hair as he considered the hologram's words. "If the Builders created this place, why wouldn't they or their progeny be able to use it?"

"They lost access through my own intervention," the hologram said, giving what sounded like a sigh. "I helped shape the helixes of the progenitors of what you know as the Deathless, as well as those of your own sub-species. Your Ka, the entity you address as the Beast, is a shard of my existence. A copy, if you will. That is the reason for the name, as I am called Ka."

Blair was silent for a long moment, the revelation shocking. Ka was the Egyptian word for spirit, and he already knew that ancient Egypt possessed many markers that had to hail from an earlier civilization. It all made sense. Ka had been created by whoever or whatever the Builders were. Isis, the Mother, had somehow met Ka. Possibly right after the brief memory she'd shared with him. He'd witnessed her discovery of the First Ark, and it was quite possible that she'd met Ka inside.

He didn't let that derail him, though. As momentous as this new information was, he still needed to know who had intentionally cut this place off, and why. "So you helped Isis create the deathless. Why did that block the Builders and their progeny from using the Arks?"

"Isis used the Primary Access Key to modify each of the Arks as they were discovered," Ka explained. "She created secondary access keys like the one you possess. Prior to the creation of these keys anyone could use an Ark. Once the keys were created they became the only method to control the Arks. Since the keys are bonded to your DNA only a hominid with the mutagen Isis and I engineered can control an Ark. This prohibits the Builders or the progeny from seizing control."

Blair had about fifty million questions. Why would Ka help humans take control of the Arks? Why did it seem to be working against its creators? He stifled that line of logic, focusing on the current problem. "So if the Builders didn't sever the conduit, then who did? And why?"

"The identity of the saboteur is unknown," Ka said, heaving a very human sigh. "As for motive, there can be only one. They sought the destruction of the Nexus."

"You've been here monitoring things the entire time?" he asked.

"I have only been in the Nexus for a very brief interval," Ka said, cocking its head. "I returned mere hours ago, as soon as I sensed the flow of power from your Ark. Before that I'd been shunted to the Ark on the continent south of yours, colloquially called the Mother's Ark."

"Did you meet the Mother?" Blair asked, shooting to his feet.

"Assuredly," Ka said, nodding rapidly.

"And?" Blair asked.

"And what?" Ka asked, blinking rapidly. Another head cock.

"And what did the two of you discuss? When was this? Is she all right?" Blair asked, all in a rush. This thing was maddening to deal with, like a computer program. It took exacting precision to talk to, and he'd never had the patience to do that. Not with computers anyway. What he wouldn't give to have Trevor back here, even for five minutes.

"We discussed little, unfortunately. Her Ark was also out of power, and I could not sustain myself there. I was shunted into backup systems until I was able to manifest here," Ka explained. "Our brief conversation occurred approximately seventeen days ago. At that time she appeared in perfect health."

"Okay," Blair said, beginning to pace. He studied the hieroglyphs lining the walls. Part of him wanted to begin recording them, but he knew there were more important things to deal with. "Let's focus on creating this conduit, then. Is there any way for me to automate the flow of energy from my Ark, so this place doesn't collapse? How can I do that if I can't return there?"

"Yes, such a feat is possible. I can guide you through the proper sequence, though you will need to grant me access to the systems in the Ark of the Redwood," Ka explained.

Blair hesitated. This thing seemed benevolent, but could it be trusted?

"Before you decide, you should know that you are no longer alone in the Nexus."

Chapter 12- Set

Set swept into the central chamber, backhanding a demon that got too close. The blow shattered its horned face, sending the ebony creature sprawling to the floor near one of the lesser obelisks. Other demons took note, pouncing on their doomed companion the moment they were certain Set wouldn't visit the same fate upon them. He smiled grimly behind his dark armor, pleased at the palpable aura of fear his servants exuded.

His steps slowed as he approached the black throne at the base of the central obelisk, which pulsed with its own inner light. He'd not yet allowed the Ark to surface, so power was drawn exclusively from the Well, deep within the earth. Unlike the other great Arks, his had an endless supply of power, keeping it well-fueled during the long ages when the other Ark Lords slumbered. That had allowed him to grow in both power and knowledge, and when he confronted his enemies they'd find he'd greatly eclipsed their limited abilities.

Particularly in light of the powers bestowed upon him by his new masters. That term galled him, chafing like a collar. It was difficult acknowledging another as master, but the fact that these beings had created the Arks made swallowing such a bitter pill easier. They had immense strength, and if he wished to one day rule this world he would need to learn everything they had to teach.

"What troubles you, my husband?" Nephthys hissed from the shadows.

He glanced in her direction, noting the glittering red eyes in the darkness. Even she was wary of approaching him, though she stood higher than all others. "The Nexus should have fallen by now, crushed by the ocean."

"It has not?" Nephthys said, stepping into the faint light exuded by the central obelisk. Her features were hidden behind a truly horrifying helm, one he himself had designed. It closely mirrored his own, and he longed for the day when his irritating brother quailed at the sight of them. Osiris would recognize the power in the corrupted metal, and know despair.

"It has not," he snapped, turning from her to face the central obelisk. Her penchant for stating the obvious wore on him. "Someone or something must have forged another conduit, which I find most troubling."

"Osiris?" she asked, voice quavering at the name—rightly so. His brother's name often sent Set into a rage, and who could blame him? He'd suffered countless injustices at the hands of his brother.

"Possibly," Set replied, sitting upon the black throne at the base of the obelisk. "Yet I do not think so. A conduit would require an Ark, and I robbed my brother of his. Either he has found an ally, or there is a new player on the board. Either way my spies will soon know the truth of it."

Set waved a hand, dismissing his wife. She crept back into the shadows, which writhed with the forms of many other servants. All were careful not to approach the light. The room was silent, save for the crunching and slurping that came from the corpse of the demon he'd slain.

Chapter 13- Intruder

"Can you show me a map of the Nexus?" Blair asked, wolfish ears twitching as he sought some sound of the intruder Ka had mentioned.

"Of course, Ka-Dun," Ka answered, gesturing with a translucent four-fingered hand. A second hologram sprung to life, hovering in the air not far from the construct. It showed a top-down view of the Nexus, which was much, much larger than Blair would have assumed.

The few corridors he'd explored were just the topmost section. They radiated out from the room where he stood, seven spokes connecting to light bridges that linked the entire Ark network. Below that level were a number of thin passages that connected to outlying structures.

Most of those outlying structures were pyramids, and there were perhaps a dozen of various sizes. If he used this room for scale, at least a few were the size of the great Arks, large enough to contain an entire city. The Nexus could house a million people. Maybe more. Just what the hell had the Builders been like?

A red dot appeared near one of the light bridges. It was advancing up the hallway, coming for this room. Blair sank into a combat crouch, prowling to the edge of the room. He lurked near the door, trying to remain as silent as possible. The red dot was coming closer, but wouldn't reach him for another minute or more.

"Ka, when the intruder reaches this room, I want you to engage them in conversation," Blair rumbled, as close to a whisper as he could manage in wolf form.

"Assuredly, Ka-Dun," Ka said, as cheerfully as it had said everything else.

The next forty or fifty seconds took years to elapse. Blair watched the dot grow closer, and when it was close enough he focused his attention on the corridor where the figure would emerge. He heard nothing. Whatever it was made no noise.

"Greetings, Ka-Ken," Ka said, causing Blair to jump even though he'd been waiting for it.

The instant a silver figure emerged from the corridor, Blair leapt, blurring as fast as he ever had. Time slowed, Ka's too-wide mouth moving so slowly it might have been frozen. Blair extended both sets of claws, opening his jaws as he came down at the figure's throat. He had time to register that it was a female werewolf, and that she looked familiar.

Then she blurred, faster than he could perceive. A fist tightened around his throat, and he was jerked like a rag doll. The figure dragged his face close to her own, and he read death in her eyes. He dropped his blur and went limp, quite proud he'd managed to avoid wetting himself this time.

"Hello, Ka-Dun," Isis said in a low growl. "I'm pleased to see that-"

Something golden flashed. It blurred, not nearly as fast as the Mother had, but still a blur. The figure barreled into him, and Blair felt teeth sink into his crotch. He gave a panicked yelp, struggling in the Mother's grasp as something chewed on a part of his body he'd very much *not* like chewed on.

"Yukon, *no*," the Mother growled.

Yukon stopped immediately, releasing Blair's crotch and backing away. He gave Blair a single growl, then turned those big brown eyes on Isis. He started wagging his tail, suddenly a harmless golden retriever—a golden the size of a North American wolf. Jesus. He was twice the size he'd been when Blair had seen him last.

Isis relaxed her grip, and Blair tumbled to the floor. He caught himself awkwardly, scrambling back to his feet and backing away a step or two. After gaining control of the Ark of the Redwood he'd felt incredibly powerful, yet beside Isis he was still just a whelp.

"I'm, uh, sorry about that," Blair explained sheepishly, giving her a shrug and a grin. "I didn't know who to expect."

"I was in on the ruse," Ka interrupted, cocking its head. "I thought it might be interesting to see how the Ka-Dun fared against you. Not well, it seems."

"Be silent, Ka," Isis snarled, giving Ka a baleful stare. "You've done quite enough damage. Don't think I trust you in the slightest, and I'll see that my progeny is aware of your deceitful nature as well. Do not speak unless one of us queries you directly for information."

Ka opened its mouth to speak, then closed it. The hologram gave a brief nod, lapsing into silence.

Isis turned back to Blair. "I must know all that has transpired since last we met. Mindshare with me."

"Of course," Blair said, though with quite a bit of trepidation. It wasn't just that he was embarrassed by some of what had transpired. There were memories he'd rather not visit.

Isis stretched out a furry hand, resting it on his forehead. There was a dizzying rush of vertigo, then he floated in darkness. Before him stretched a sea of glittering jewels, each playing a memory just like a different channel on TV. A moment later Isis appeared within his mind, this time in human form.

Her otherworldly beauty struck him like a physical blow. She was a petite four ten with long silver hair and glittering green eyes. Her creamy face was a perfect oval, the kind men everywhere would stop what they were doing to stare at. Yet the instant Blair saw her eyes any attraction died. That gaze had been hardened in a crucible twenty-five millennia deep. Isis was, in every way that mattered, no longer human.

Open your mind, Ka-Dun. she thought, drifting towards him. Her eyes closed, and she came closer until her forehead pressed against his. There was a flash of heat, a rush of emotion. She was in his mind, replaying memories faster than thought.

He saw the pursuit of Irakesh, the battle in Panama when he'd first realized Trevor was deathless. Being intimate with Bridget, and later her death in Larkspur. He saw the final battle with Irakesh, the detonation of the nuclear bomb. The energy being sucked into the Ark, and the lingering devastation in its wake.

Blair felt a flush of embarrassment as the image of giving the key to Steve flitted through his mind, but it was replaced by pride when he accepted the key he managed to steal from Irakesh. His memories moved on, showing Isis the weeks after taking possession of the Ark. Their efforts to gather the survivors on Angel Island, supply runs into the city, and hasty training of a militia. Finally he showed her Steve and Irakesh escaping, the brief pursuit, and then meeting her here.

Isis finally pulled away, drifting backwards into the blackness as her gaze held his. It was unreadable. Then the blackness disappeared and they were in the Nexus again. Isis was a werewolf once more, her ferocity terrifying even to Blair.

"Much has transpired, not all of it bad," she allowed, crossing her arms. "You did well, given your lack of training. I am less than pleased you relinquished the key to this treacherous Ka-Dun you call Steve, especially given that he delved my sleeping mind. Yet you managed to capture the key to the Ark of the Redwood, and Irakesh's mad plan has ensured that it has the energy to give you an edge in the coming decades."

"So, uh, what do we do now?" Blair asked.

"We prepare the conduit Ka has mentioned so the Nexus will not collapse," Isis said. She barred her fangs, a low growl escaping. One Yukon mimicked. "Then we invade the Ark of the Cradle, and bring justice to the whelp Steve."

Chapter 14- Sucker

Mark's gut clenched the moment he sat down. Osiris was already seated at the narrow mahogany table, filigreed porcelain china atop a scarlet place mat in front of him. He cradled a glass of red wine—probably a Cab, from the smell and color. A similar glass had already been poured for Mark, alongside identical china.

"Hello, Mark," the monster said, swirling his glass as he glanced at the wall-sized television hanging against the far wall. The screen was paused, showing a fanged teen sparkling in the sun. Mark recognized the movie, of course, though he couldn't remember the name of the actor. Someone all the teen girls loved, no doubt. Osiris turned back to him. "The wine really is quite spectacular. That's one of the things I most love about this new world. Our beer was palatable, but our wine was barely worthy of the name."

"What do you want?" Mark asked, slipping the napkin onto his lap out of habit.

"A dinner companion. At my age, conversation is one of the greatest treasures left. It's so rare to hear a different perspective, and few men are as openly hostile as you," Osiris said, exposing a pair of too sharp fangs as he smiled. "You know what I am, or have some idea at least. This age has some odd ideas about my kind. I don't sparkle, but the term *vampire* was first coined to describe my progeny. While that may terrify you, the fact doesn't govern your actions."

"I'll play along then. What's for dinner?" Mark asked, his heart thudding in his chest.

"Filet mignon," Osiris said, gesturing at a white garbed servant in the corner. The man wheeled a tray over, flicking a latch with a hiss of air. The mouthwatering scent of beef filled the room. "Over the last several millennia

I endured many hardships, so one of my rewards is dining well."

The servant, a middle aged Indian man nearly as wide was he was tall, began setting plates before them. There were mashed potatoes that smelled of garlic, some of the most succulent steaks Mark had ever seen, and heavenly-smelling brussels sprouts.

Osiris picked up a small silver remote and aimed it at the television. The image of the sparkly vampire disappeared, replaced by a top-down feed over Stonehenge. Mark recognized it immediately as belonging to one of Mohn's satellites.

"Why is satellite five aimed at Stonehenge?" Mark asked. His stomach rumbled as the servant added a filet to his plate.

"I'm sure you've guessed. Why don't you share your theory?" Osiris asked, picking up his utensils. He sliced a generous morsel of beef, and popped it into his mouth. His eyes never left Mark as he began to chew. The whole thing was cultured. Refined.

"You're clearly waiting for something. Judging by the amount of attention you're paying to this location, and by the fact that no other Ark has appeared in Europe, I'd guess you expect one to appear here." Mark tasted the mashed potatoes, blinking in surprise. They were beyond amazing. They might have been the best thing he'd ever tasted.

"Astute, as expected," Osiris said, pausing for a mouthful of wine. "I'm not waiting for just any Ark. The one that will appear here is called The First Ark, because we believe it was the first ever created."

Mark picked up his wine glass, taking the tiniest sip. He watched Osiris thoughtfully, but said nothing.

"Satellite five is watching for the Ark, because when it returns the war will begin." Osiris set his wine glass down. "Every weapon Mohn Corp has at its disposal will be launched at the force that emerges. It is a confrontation we are doomed to lose, and when we lose, the demonic horde will begin scouring the world of all sentient life. I can delay it by hurling the dead at it, but that is nothing but a stalling tactic."

Mark considered the statement very carefully. It didn't sound like a lie. "So who is this bogeyman you expect to emerge? And why fight if you expect to lose?"

"He is my brother, an ancient just as old as I am. You'd know him as Set," Osiris explained, cutting his steak into bite-sized morsels as he continued his explanation. "As for why I fight? Because if I do not, then this world is doomed. You think me a monster, but you've never seen my brother. You have no idea what he is capable of. He will devour all life from this world, leaving us naked before an even greater threat."

"A greater threat," Mark said, shaking his head. He heaved a sigh, setting his fork down. "You have to know you're going to have to present some sort of evidence if you expect me to buy any of this. Right now it sounds like the plot to a Michael Bay movie. That means the plot sucks, in case you're not familiar with Michael Bay."

Osiris laughed, a deep belly laugh that boomed through the room. He set his wine glass down without drinking. "Yes, I definitely like you, Mark. You have spirit, which will be needed in this age. You want proof, and I will offer it. Let us start with a few questions, shall we? Have you ever wondered who built the Arks? They are impossibly old, far older than Homo Sapiens, older even than Homo Erectus or Home Ergaster. If my theories are correct, the Arks were likely built during the time of Australopithecus. Possibly even before that."

Mark picked up his wine glass and drank deeply. Osiris's statement rocked him to the core, because it gave voice to quiet doubts that had plagued him since Peru. Someone or something had created the Arks before the dawn of humanity, and that terrified him. Who had they been? Where had they gone?

"You've often wondered about Project Solaris, I'm told," Osiris continued, a wry smile slipping into place. He took a moment to spear another piece of beef, popping it into his mouth and chewing before he continued. "I created Solaris, and it was at my direction that the Old Man kept you in the dark. I wanted you ignorant, both because I needed you focused on the Arks, and because you were not yet ready to know the truth."

"So what is Project Solaris, then?" Mark's appetite fled, despite the tempting aroma of steak.

"The Builders, as we call them, have returned. They've been experimenting on humanity, and Project Solaris is the means by which we are fighting back," Osiris said, savoring a mouthful of mashed potatoes. "Simply exquisite. Have you tried them?"

Mark ignored the question. "So let's say I'm willing to accept that these Builders are a threat. How does this Set figure into things? Why are we wasting men and material fighting here, if you claim these Builders are the true enemy?"

"The Builders may not return for decades, Mark," Osiris said, shaking his head as he stared at the wall-sized view of Stonehenge. "Set is here now. We need the world united, but Set will never allow that."

Mark clutched at his stomach as a cramp sent a spike of pain through his innards. He gritted his teeth until it subsided. A side effect of morphine withdrawal? Maybe. Or maybe not. "Okay, so you need to stop Set. You said we lack the power to do that, so why squander what we do have in an attempt you know will fail?"

"I don't plan to," Osiris said, steepling his fingers and resting his chin atop them. "I am gathering allies, something I'll need your assistance with."

"Who?" Mark began, but the question was choked off by another cramp. He gritted his teeth again, groaning against the pain.

This time it didn't subside. He fell from the table, writhing on the floor as the creeping pain spread throughout his body. It engulfed his senses, and when the whiteness faded he found himself staring up at Osiris. The monster was smiling down at him, mere inches away.

"Relax, Mark," he whispered, eyes flaring green. "There will only be a few more moments of pain. When you awaken to your second life, I will make everything clear to you."

Oh, God. The bastard had put something in the wine. Mark flashed back to the Syracuse facility, to staring through a skylight down at an operating table with one of the zombies strapped to it. That was where they'd first isolated Virus A2493, which he'd just been infected with.

Chapter 15-Audience

Trevor awoke with a groan, hauling himself to his feet as he blinked away the grogginess. Where the hell was he? He scanned the room, a tiny eight-by-six cell that looked entirely too familiar. The bronzed walls were identical to the room where they'd imprisoned Steve and Irakesh, though this time he was on the wrong side of the crackling blue bars.

He could see into the cell across from him. It was occupied by a very disgruntled-looking Commander Jordan. The man had returned to human form, and sat on the bench that ran along the cell's back wall. Well-muscled arms were folded across his chest and he stared balefully in Trevor's direction. That pissed Trevor off for no good reason, but he stifled the anger.

You were attacked by a powerful deathless, my host. One fabled among our kind. The mighty Anubis.

Trevor considered that, turning away from the Commander and stalking to his bench. He sat down, swinging his legs up as he rested his back against the wall. He wasn't very well versed in Egyptian lore, though he'd picked up a few things from Blair. The Mother's Egyptian name was Isis, and they'd recently learned about Osiris taking control of Mohn Corp. Those were names he knew, as was Anubis. Unfortunately, most of his knowledge came from Stargate, and he had no idea how accurate any of it was.

Heavy footsteps sounded in the distance, coming towards his cell with a deliberate cadence. Trevor rose from his bench, peering through the bars to see who might be approaching. The creature carried the same weapon that had been used to disembowel Steve and Jordan, a six-foot staff with a wide fan blade at either end. The figure who carried it didn't look like he needed the weapon to kill, though. It stood a good eight feet tall, with either black skin or very short black fur. At first he thought it was a werewolf, but there were subtle differences. The muzzle was too long and a bit too thin. The eyes were a little too narrow. The teeth more numerous, and a bit smaller.

The creature, whatever it was, wore the strangest armor he'd ever seen. Golden sandals were strapped to its feet, the straps winding their way up to the knees. A pair of thick golden bracers covered the creature's wrists, each bracer containing an oval sapphire. A similar torque covered its neck, with a larger sapphire set there. The headdress it wore was familiar to every school kid in the world. It could have belonged to King Tut.

The figure stopped in front of Trevor's cell, sharp green eyes sizing him up. It barred its fangs, finally speaking. "Your name, pup—give it to me."

Trevor was silent for a moment, several thoughts competing for his attention. The color of this thing's eyes were the same as his own, and so far as he knew those only belonged to the deathless. It also spoke English, despite the fact that it clearly came from the ancient world.

"My name is Trevor. Trevor Gregg," he finally said.

"I am Anubis," the creature growled, pressing one of the sapphires on its wrist. The bars disappeared. "You will accompany me. If you attempt to flee, or show mighty Ra even a hint of disrespect, I will dismember you and scatter your entrails across the great desert."

"That sounds unpleasant," Trevor said, stepping into the hall. "I'll cooperate."

A wise choice, my host. Anubis is ancient and powerful. If you can befriend him, he can teach you much.

Trevor remained silent, falling into step as Anubis made his way back up the hallway. That too was familiar, a perfect mirror of the Ark of the Redwood. It was reassuring, since it meant he wasn't totally lost. He glanced into Jordan's cell as he passed. Unsurprisingly the Commander glared at him, though he didn't utter a word.

Anubis led him through many corridors, eventually taking a series of stairs up to the central chamber. It was almost identical to its counterpart in Blair's Ark, save that the decor was different. This one had clearly given rise to the Egyptian culture, with golden pillars dotted with a sea of hieroglyphs. A small flight of steps had been erected at the base of the largest obelisk, and they led up to the most ornate throne he'd ever seen. The chair appeared to be cut from one solid block of black marble, and was covered in golden hieroglyphs that glowed with their own inner light.

Yet it was the woman sitting on that throne that caught his attention. She was gorgeous. More than gorgeous. She was breathtaking, if he'd had breath to take. She had long hair of the deepest scarlet, a more elegant version of his own. Her skin was perfect alabaster, and her eyes were the sharpest emeralds he'd ever seen. She wore simple white garb nearly identical to the Mother's, and a golden spear was propped against the side of the throne next to her.

It took several moments for Trevor to notice she wasn't alone. Two figures stood at the base of the stairs, both familiar. Irakesh and Steve. Irakesh wore a triumphant smile, while Steve simply watched Trevor with that calculating gaze. A fresh shiver of fear rippled through him. He was well and truly in the house of his enemies.

"I bring Trevor of the house Gregg, mighty Ra," Anubis rumbled, his staff sweeping forward in a blur. The move caught Trevor behind the knees, knocking him into a kneeling position. Anubis sank to one knee next to Trevor, lowering his voice as he hissed. "Avert your gaze, you fool."

Trevor did exactly that, forcing his gaze to the black stone floor as he awaited Ra's answer. He wasn't sure what he'd expected. According to his limited Egyptology, Ra had been a man. He knew she was a sun god, but that was about it.

"Rise, mighty Anubis. Bring the pup forward, that I might examine him," came a musical voice. Trevor couldn't place the accent, but it was very similar to Irakesh. The closest he could come would be to call it English.

A hand seized Trevor by the shoulder, hauling him to his feet and shoving him forward. He stumbled, recovering after a step, and marched forward, careful to keep his gaze averted as he made his way to the base of the steps. Anubis's heavy feet clinked on the marble behind him, and he could feel the thing's presence as they approached the throne.

"Look upon me, Trevor of house Gregg," Ra commanded. Trevor felt his gaze rise before he was even conscious of it. She was even more beautiful up close, though that beauty had the same stark austerity of the desert where he'd lived outside San Diego. "Why have you come to the Ark of the Cradle? What do you seek here?"

"I came to kill that bastard," Trevor said, nodding at Steve. He knew Irakesh was related to Ra, but she'd probably know if he was lying. So he told the truth. "If we were able to kill Irakesh too, that would have been even better."

Ra steepled her fingers, expression unreadable. She studied him for long moments before finally speaking. "The Ka-Dun I can understand. He is the mortal enemy of our kind, after all. But why seek the death of my son? He is one of your kind."

"I couldn't care less about our 'kind'," Trevor spat, glaring at Irakesh. "Your son is a slimy coward who killed some of my friends. He forced me to do some pretty fucked-up things, and he enjoyed doing it. I bet he was the type of kid that pulled wings off of flies for fun." Trevor shifted his gaze back to Ra. "Steve isn't quite as bad, but he's more intelligent and a lot more dangerous. Killing him isn't personal. It's just smart."

Ra began to laugh, soft peals that echoed through the room. She stopped after several moments, glancing down at Irakesh. "How would you answer his words, my son?"

"If he wishes to kill me, let him come," Irakesh spat, all sign of his earlier smile gone. His eyes narrowed, black eyebrows knitting together as he glared at Trevor. "He's nothing but a half-trained kitten, easily dispatched. Give me leave and I will devour his corpse."

"Come and get it, baldy," Trevor shot back. Not smart maybe, but he was willing to try his luck.

"Silence," Ra thundered. She rose from her throne, descending the stairs with a grace that drew the eye of every man in the room. She stopped before Trevor, a tall woman with the muscles of a lifelong athlete. She cupped his chin, tilting it one way, then the other. "You are well made, Trevor. And resourceful, if my wretch of a son is truthful in his accounts of his time at the Ark of the Redwood. I may let you live, if you please me."

"He will betray us, most holy," Anubis snapped, taking a step closer. Trevor could feel him looming, though he couldn't turn to face the jackal-headed god with his chin still cupped in Ra's hand.

"You speak out of turn, Anubis," Ra snapped, her eyes flaring green.

Metal rang on stone as Anubis sank to his knees. "My apologies, mighty Ra. I seek only to protect. This pup is from this new world. He keeps company with your enemies, Isis and her newly created pantheon."

"Perhaps, but he does so from ignorance," Ra said, releasing Trevor's chin. She returned her attention to him, gaze touching his. If his heart still beat, Trevor was sure it would have been thundering in his chest. "You have heard all sorts of lies from Isis and her get. No doubt my son made matters worse, made you think our kind are nothing but malicious gods. Capricious and petty. Let me assure you, that is not the case. You are an immortal now, Trevor Gregg. As the decades blur by you will begin to see time as we do. You think us callous, but we are merely pragmatic. Decisions that seem harsh may in fact save the world millennia from now."

"So, what then?" Trevor asked, forcing the words out. "You expect me to join you? Just like that? A quick recruitment speech and I betray my friends. Again. Lady, you can shove that speech right up your ass. You may as well kill me now, because I will never work for you."

Trevor felt the rush of wind as something moved behind him. He had enough time to turn his head, but even blurring he wasn't fast enough. Anubis's fan-bladed axe arced towards his skull, and he was powerless to stop his death.

The weapon froze.

Ra had blurred faster than he could see, her right hand pinching the blade between two fingers. The weapon had stopped a hair's breadth from Trevor's face.

"If I must chastise you a third time, you will feel my wrath, Anubis," Ra said, her voice arctic. "This pup is mine to do with as I will, not yours. I know you do not trust him. I know his disrespect burns your honor. But you *will* hold your temper. Is my will clear?"

"Forgive me, most holy," Anubis said, dropping to one knee. Ra released the axe, and the weapon clattered to the floor. She turned back to Trevor, gaze cold now. "You have a choice, Trevor Gregg. You can swear to abide by my rule and learn our ways, or I can incinerate you where you stand. I know you have no wish to betray your friends, and I would not ask you to do so, not unless there is no other choice but to fight them. This leaves you in a difficult position, I realize. You risk having to fight your allies, but consider the alternative. If you die here you will never be able to aid them again. If you live, then who knows what the centuries will bring? What say you?"

It wasn't a hard choice.

"I agree," he snarled, unable to hide the anger. Here he was being forced into the servitude of another, yet again. Probably forced to kill his friends. Again. Yet it was better than immediate death. As long as he was alive he had a chance to correct matters.

"Your words are insincere, and I know you will attempt to betray me," Ra said, mounting the steps and sitting in her throne once more. "When that day comes I will destroy you, but until then I will treat you as any other vassal. You will learn to be one of us, one of the royal court of Ra. Before I dismiss you to begin your tutelage I have one final matter to discuss. This other Ka-Dun, the one you call Jordan. Tell me of him."

"Jordan used to be an enemy," Trevor began, unsure what to reveal.

Telling her the truth couldn't hurt. She'd have learned all the facts from Steve anyway. "He's competent, one of the best soldiers of our generation. He's even stronger now that he's become a Ka-Dun. He serves the Mother, and he's loyal to her and her pack. You'll never turn him, if that's what you're asking."

"Interesting," Ra said, giving a half-smile that chilled Trevor more than her earlier fury. She looked to Anubis. "Escort Trevor to Anput. Have him prepared for the banquet. As an equal, Anubis. Not a thrall."

Trevor glanced at Anubis, catching the hatred in the jackal's eyes.

Chapter 16- The Gift

Isis swept down from the light bridge into the Ark of the Redwood. It was the first time she'd been here in thirteen millennia, yet it was hardly the joyous homecoming she'd wished for. Instead, she was awash in fury. Not at her surroundings, but at the circumstances. Nothing in this new age had gone as she'd planned. From Ahiga's death, to Irakesh's theft of the key, to this sudden news that the conduit from the First Ark to the Nexus had been severed.

Only one person could have severed it: the Ark Lord who'd ruled The First Ark for millennia. Her estranged husband, the man she'd created the virus for. Osiris, the first deathless. Isis pushed the thought away, focusing on the task at hand.

She shifted back to human form, turning to the Ka-Dun Blair as he too stepped off the raised disk. "Letting Ka enter the systems here could have dire consequences, but I do not see any other choice. Your beast can guide you through the process."

"Are you leaving?" Blair asked, blinking owlishly. He looked so harmless in his human form, a blessing whether he knew it or not. Other gods would underestimate him in the millennia to come.

"No, but I have business to attend to. Use Ka to build a conduit from the central chamber to the Nexus, and do it quickly before the ocean claims it. Once you are finished, come find me on Angel Island," she instructed, already exiting the chamber.

Yukon trotted at her heels, patient in a way no wolf would have managed. He followed her through many passages, until they finally reached the central chamber. To the untrained eye it was identical to her own Ark, each obelisk in exactly the same position. Yet to her eye the two couldn't have been more different.

She ran her hand along the black stone wall, remembering the carving of every glyph. Her hands had sculpted the magnificent statues flanking the doorway to the rejuvenation chamber. One was her, of course. All her work bore such a statue, a signature of sorts. The other was unique, however, a tribute to her daughter Jes'Ka.

It showed a fierce Ka-Ken armed with a golden spear. Her eyes blazed with fury, and her gums had been pulled back over a mouthful of impressive fangs. It was an expression Isis remembered well, once she'd both dreaded and loved. Dreaded, because it often accompanied a tirade from her strong-willed daughter. Loved, because it meant Jes'Ka had the same untamable spirit as her father, Osiris.

The Mother swept past the statue and into the room beyond; she paused there, studying the two occupied rejuvenators. One held Lucas, the dark-skinned male a long time servant of her daughter. The other held Jes'Ka herself; proud, and stubborn, and beautiful. Her golden locks blanketed the bed around her, alabaster skin shining in the white light of the chamber. She looked at peace, though that would change when she woke.

A rare moment of indecision washed through the Mother. Isis so badly wanted to wake her daughter, yet she knew it would be a mistake. She was about to embark on a dangerous quest to investigate the first Ark. For good or ill, Osiris lay at the end of that path, and if he'd truly manipulated history as she suspected he had, then he might very well have become her greatest foe.

If it came to battle between them she wasn't sure which side her daughter would choose. It was hardly fair to put Jes'Ka in that position, and more than that it was dangerous. If Jes'Ka supported her father the two of them would be more than a match for Isis. More than a match for Sekmet, if she could even convince her near-sister to join forces. Together they'd be all but unstoppable.

Isis turned from the rejuvenator and strode back into the central chamber. She could not afford to dally in such personal matters. She had work to be about. She closed her eyes, feeling the Ark around her. It was immediately clear why Steve had been able to escape. Blair had initiated none of the proper security measures. Any Ark Lord could utilize this place. She'd have to teach him to defend it, but there wasn't time for that now.

She reached into the Ark's well, pulling in enough power to initiate a light walk. Then she was elsewhere, standing on a dock she'd plucked from Blair's memories. It lay on Angel Island, the place where the Ka-Ken Liz was gathering her growing flock. That was to the good. Liz had impressed her, doubly so after combing Blair's memories.

The Ka-Ken was strong. Intelligent. More than that, she was bold enough to make hard choices, and that would make her an incredible leader. If she were given the time to learn.

In the distance lay the ruins of a truly impressive bridge, painted gold by the waning sunlight. Beyond it lay a dense city, every bit as grand as anything from her world. She'd glimpsed skyscrapers in memories, and seen a few in Cajamarca. None like this. San Francisco was an impressive city. A city of the dead, unfortunately. Figures moved in the distance, most shambling between buildings. Enough to clog even the wide streets.

Isis turned her attention back to her immediate surroundings. She scanned the dock, where a jumble of men were unloading metal boxes from a battered-looking boat. They ignored her, which made her smile. To them she was a girl just out of adolescence. Liz was smarter than that though. The Ka-Ken obviously sensed something, whirling to face Isis.

"Hello, Ka-Ken," Isis said, giving a warm smile. She opened her arms, taking a step forward to embrace Liz. "Your struggles have been difficult, and there are more to come. But I am proud of all you have accomplished."

Liz all but engulfed Isis in a hug. "I can't believe you're here. Thank God."

"Would that we had time to reminisce, but the situation is dire. We must depart this place within the hour," Isis said, stifling a sigh. In a way, every

Ka-Ken was her daughter, and she longed to comfort Liz. Yet doing so would be no favor. Liz needed to learn to stand on her own.

"Leave?" Liz replied, taking a step back. She brushed a lock of hair from her face, staring in confusion. "We can't leave. These people just weathered an attack by deathless. We drove them off and killed most of them, but a few escaped. They'll be back, sooner or later."

Isis folded her arms, turning toward the setting sun. She was silent for a long moment, considering. "The crisis we face is more important than any single settlement, yet I'd not abandon even a single bastion. Yukon, to me."

The dog had been sniffing about several refugees, tail wagging as he made new friends. One of them was a girl about twelve, on the cusp of adolescence. She had long, dark hair, and a dirty face. Well, dirty until Yukon began licking it furiously.

At her command he reluctantly abandoned his new friend, trotting over to Isis. She lay a hand on the side of his face, smiling grimly down at him. "This place is in great danger. The not-deads come in ever greater numbers, and without protection these people are doomed."

No. Yukon's thought was loud and angry. *We will protect them. We will slay the not-deads.*

"I must leave to face a graver threat, my friend. Will you stay and protect these people?" she asked. Isis was conscious of Liz's tense form next to her. The Ka-Ken couldn't hear Yukon's responses, of course.

Yes, but I am not strong. I cannot do it alone.

"Nor will you need to, my friend. I want you to reform the Great Pack. Find other dogs, find coyotes, and foxes. Gather them to you. There is strength in numbers, and in time they will awaken as you have," she explained, her smile growing warmer. "Will you do this?"

I will do this thing. Yukon said, mind firm with resolve.

"Isis," Liz began, more timidly than Isis would have liked, "will a pack of dogs be enough to protect these people?"

"No," Isis said, extending a hand. The Primary Access Key flowed into it, a pool of gold that gradually elongated into a familiar staff with a winged scarab at one end. She turned to face the refugees, the sapphire in the scarab's thorax flaring blue as it sent out a spiderweb of wispy blue tendrils. "We need champions as well."

"What are you doing?" Liz asked, her gaze following the tendrils.

One found the girl Yukon had been licking, and it flared brightly, leaving a glowing blue mark on the girl's forehead. Four others found their mark within the crowd, but that was all. So few.

"Those with the mark have the greatest chance of returning from the dead," Isis said, gravely. She faced Liz. "It is not certain, but their helixes bear the greatest likelihood of bonding with the virus."

"You're going to kill them," Liz said, clearly aghast. "Isis, she's a child. You can't."

"I'm not going to kill them," Isis said, gaze catching the Ka-Ken. She took a step toward the larger woman. "You are. This is your domain, your pack. If you wish these people to survive your absence, you must provide them with champions. It is a difficult task, I know. Yet what chance do they have if you are too weak to do what must be done?"

Liz's face fell. Tears welled up as she looked at the child. Several moments passed as indecision warred across her features. In the end the battle was won, and Liz's face hardened with resolve.

Chapter 17- Anput

Trevor eyed Anubis warily as the jackal-headed god escorted him through a myriad of passageways. They probably corresponded to their counterparts in Blair's Ark, but Trevor had never been in this area so he couldn't identify the high-ceilinged hallways. They were black stone with golden hieroglyphs, which seemed to cover every available surface. Similar glyphs were present in Blair's Ark, but fewer and in a different style.

Anubis climbed a steep stairway, pausing at the top for Trevor to join him. He summed up Trevor with that awful canine gaze. "You are unworthy of existence, pup. Yet I am loyal to Ra, she who gave us all life. She commands me to give you into the care of my wife. Know this, however: If you speak ill of or to my wife, if you look upon her with lust, or if you offer her any offense, then I will destroy you. Not even memory of your name will survive."

Be careful, my host. Show no resistance, his risen counseled. Unnecessarily. Trevor knew better than to pick a fight with something much stronger and much older than he was.

"Listen, Anubis. It's Anubis, right? I came here for one reason, and one reason only. To kill Steve," Trevor explained, meeting the jackal's gaze evenly. "I didn't plan on any of this, but since I've been adopted into your little pantheon I plan to mind my manners. I won't offer your wife any offense, and if I offer you any please give me a chance to apologize before you ram that axe through my chest. Remember, I'm ignorant of your ways."

"I promise nothing," Anubis snarled, though he seemed mollified.

The jackal stalked up the next corridor, eventually pausing outside the entryway to a large chamber. The chamber was roughly twice the size of the one Trevor had occupied back in Blair's Ark, and, unlike his, had been heavily modified. Ornate rugs covered the floors, and statues of various Egyptian deities dotted the chamber. A massive four poster bed dominated one corner, and the far side of the room even contained a pool-sized bath.

A figure emerged from that bath, naked and dripping as she stepped onto the stone and picked up a towel. She made no move to use it, instead sizing up Trevor like a puzzle she was trying to solve. The woman was beautiful, no doubt about that. She had long, dark-skinned legs, and patient wide eyes. A river of black hair cascaded down her back, twisted into fine braids, each with a golden bead at the end.

Trevor was about to look away, largely due to Anubis's warning, when he noticed something hanging brightly in the air above her. It was a multicolored sigil of some kind, a stylized likeness of Anubis. He wasn't sure precisely what it signified. Marriage maybe? Trevor dropped his gaze to the stone, waiting for either Anubis or the woman to speak. He noted that the woman looked completely human, no toxic green gaze, no razored teeth. That was an interesting tidbit to file away.

"My wife," Anubis rumbled, clicking his away across the floor until he towered over the woman. "Ra commands me to present you with this pup. He is a new god, from this strange age. She commands that you educate him in our ways. Know this, however, I have sworn to—"

"Leave off, husband," the woman said, placing a hand on Anubis's forearm. His jaws snapped shut, though his gaze still smoldered. "I can tell already that you have no love for the pup, and you and I will discuss the reasons later. In private. For now, please allow me to discharge the obligation Ra has given me. The pup will learn nothing with you looming over him, ready to mete out violence. Leave us."

Anubis gave a curt nod, whirling and stalking past Trevor. He passed far closer than was strictly necessary, furry muscles gliding past Trevor's face as if a reminder of how close to death he came.

"How are you called, newling?" the woman asked, toweling the water from her naked body.

"My name is Trevor. Trevor Gregg," he amended, still trying to avert his gaze. The basic human needs for sex were supposed to be gone, but he experienced a very human lust. He hadn't felt that way with Ra, despite the fact that the fiery-haired goddess was much more beautiful than Anput.

"I am called Anput, wife of Anubis and daughter of Osiris," she said, giving him a wide smile. Her teeth were perfectly white, and, as he'd noted earlier, perfectly straight. Illusion, perhaps? If that was the case he should have been able to detect her shaping.

No illusion, my host. She is cousin to the deathless, but a wholly separate creature. She cannot be trusted. Your desire for her is unnatural, one of the abilities her kind possesses.

"So, you're supposed to teach me how to fit in here?" Trevor asked, mainly to fill the silence that lingered in the wake of her statement.

"Just so," Anput said, giving a soft nod. She reached for a sheer black shift and pulled it on, then moved to a high-backed wooden chair near a window.

Trevor moved to join her, sinking into a second chair. They sat at the edge of a balcony, which overlooked the Giza plateau. The view was breathtaking, showing Cairo in all its glory. The city was huge, possibly bigger than Los Angeles. Yet it was also empty. He could see no movement there, not a single corpse or even a bird.

"I have been tasked with teaching you to survive here, no easy feat given that you are an outsider," Anput said, crossing one shapely leg over the other as she studied him. "To do that I must understand more of what you are. How did you come to be here?"

"By accident. I was pursing a Ka-Dun who stole an access key," Trevor explained. He wasn't sure how much he should reveal to Anput, but right now he didn't have many choices. She was the only thing approaching an ally he was likely to find here. "Your husband ambushed my companions and I at the light bridge. After he kicked our collective asses, I woke up in a cell. I was presented to Ra, and then escorted here."

"Interesting," Anput said, resting her chin on the palm of her hand. She leaned her elbow on the arm of the chair, still studying him. "Anubis said you are of this age. Obviously you've had some training. Who sired you?"

"If by sired you mean trained, then I guess that would be Irakesh. Though I have no loyalty to that bald bastard," Trevor snapped, instantly regretting the loss of control.

Anput cocked her head back and began a musical laugh. Her eyes twinkled when she stopped, and he noticed for the first time that she wore dark eyeshadow. It was so skillfully applied it could have been part of her skin.

"You are refreshingly honest, Trevor Gregg," Anput said, her expression suddenly unreadable. "If you wish to survive in the court of the mighty Ra, that must change, and change quickly. Here, honestly is a liability. It reveals your true intentions, and such predictability will allow your enemies to engineer your death."

"You're implying some people aren't my enemies," Trevor shot back. He knew he was out of his depth. Politics weren't his strong suit. Hell, social situations in general weren't his strong suit. Before all this had begun, the happiest nights of his life had been spent observing the night sky at Palomar in San Diego. He was completely alone, save for the data and perhaps one or two grad students interested in that data.

"So you have a glimmer of intelligence then," Anput replied, giving a coy smile. With anyone else Trevor might have assumed she was flirting. "Everyone here will seek to use you for one end or another, but that is not the same as being an enemy. Take me, for example. I've been given the task of making you presentable to the court. If I fail in this, I will lose status with Ra, and thus with the court. It is in my best interest to ensure that you are well groomed, that you have the tools needed to flourish here."

"And in so doing you earn my gratitude. I'll owe you a favor, right?" Trevor asked, narrowing his eyes. He already detested this game, though he thought he'd learned the first rule.

"Precisely," Anput replied, giving him a warmer smile. "There is much to discuss, but before we begin you'll need to quiet your mind. To do that we must first unburden it. I will permit you three questions. Choose wisely."

Trevor felt like he'd just rubbed a lamp. Fortunately, long years of Dungeons & Dragons had prepared him for just such an occasion. The mistake people often made with questions like this was trying to learn too much. Aim lower, and you were more likely to get what you wished for.

"How can I make an ally of Anubis?" Trevor asked, giving Anput a wry smile.

Anput merely blinked for long moments, then burst into musical laughter once more. "You are a bold one, aren't you? Anubis is not easily swayed, not even by me. If you wish to earn his patronage, you must prove yourself in battle. He respects strength, and little else. It will also benefit you if you adopt our cause, and prove your loyalty to Ra. Does that answer suffice?"

"It does," Trevor nodded, considering her words. He needed a way to prove himself, but there was no immediate solution. One would present itself eventually, however. "For my second question, how can I convince Ra that I am useful enough to outweigh any threat I pose?"

Anput reached across the space between them, resting a cool hand on his leg. She stared up into his eyes, her own half-closed and sensuous. "I begin to believe you may survive here, Trevor Gregg. You may even thrive, if your third question is as inventive as the first two."

Chapter 18- Conduit

Blair settled into a half-lotus at the foot of the central obelisk. Ka floated next to him, a ghostly green hologram. Its translucent form appeared stronger here in the Ark of the Redwood than it had in the Nexus. He still found its alien appearance strange, as he did its command of the English language. "What do I need to do?"

"It is simple, Ka-Dun," Ka said, cocking its head. "Merely think of the Nexus, and envision its heart. Generate a flow of energy from the heart of this Ark to the Nexus, and the conduit will be complete."

Blair did as asked, though he found the process strange. So much of shaping was about visualization, which made sense from a scientific standpoint. The brain generated electrical impulses based on thought, and shaping tapped into those impulses. He envisioned a river of light flowing from the massive heart of power at the base of his Ark, the river snaking through the ocean until it reached the Nexus. A moment later an enormous shudder passed through the Ark. The lights dimmed for a split second, then returned at full strength.

"It is done," Ka said, giving a tight nod. It blinked with those too large eyes, pools of unreadable black. "This conduit will be enough to sustain the nexus until other Arks are strong enough to add their own flows."

"Ka, can you tell me about those pulses earlier? The ones that shot into the sky? They shorted out hundreds of systems. I've never seen anything like it," Blair asked, hoping the creature would both possess the knowledge and be willing to share it. The Mother had warned him to be cautious around Ka, but thus far the intelligence had been nothing but helpful.

"Accessing logs," Ka said, its eyes going unfocused. They focused again after a moment. "I see the event you reference, Ka-Dun. The pulses were a communication generated by all Arks on the network with sufficient strength to create them. Each fired a trio of pulses designed to alert the Builders to the current climate of this world."

"Current climate?" came a voice from behind Blair. He scrambled to his feet, abandoning the lotus.

Isis strode toward him, with Liz in tow. The diminutive goddess crossed her arms, glaring at Ka through narrowed eyes. So much distrust there.

Liz followed Isis into the chamber, looking dazed and more than a little ill. Blair caught her gaze, but she gave a slight shake of her head and looked away. Her eyes were red and puffy. What the hell had happened back on the island?

"Yes, Ka-Ken. The climate of this world is warmer than it has been in over three million years. The age you refer to as the Pleistocene has ended, and the Holocene has begun. These conditions are perfect to support the Builders, who prefer a much warmer climate than humanity can tolerate," Ka explained, cocking its head to the other direction. "The pulse the Ka-Dun referenced was a means of alerting the Builders to this new climate, so they can begin re-colonization of this planet."

"So this warning was generated automatically?" Blair asked.

"Unfortunately, no," Ka said, giving a very human sigh. "The energy required to fire such a pulse is more than any Ark is capable of mustering at this time, with the exception of this one. This required an external power source to fuel the bursts in those Arks unable to produce them. Only an Ark Lord could have done this."

"The Well," Isis growled, taking a step closer to Ka's translucent form. "You're saying someone tapped into the Well to generate this pulse."

"Just so, Ka-Ken," Ka nodded vigorously. "Someone was able to tap into the vast reservoir of power offered by the Well. This allowed them to send a message, one that will reach the Builders in approximately four years, seven months."

"And the Builders will return when they hear this message?" Blair asked, moving to stand next to Isis. "How long will it take them to return to earth?"

"Unknown," Ka said, pursing its green lips. "When they departed this world, the Builders did so as pure energy, broadcast to their new home as light. This process was much like the pulse you just witnessed. During the intervening eons their technology has changed. They now use craft for transport, or at least their progeny do."

"Progeny?" Blair asked, blinking.

"Yes. The Ka-Ken knows of their existence," Ka said, nodding at Isis.

"I know a little," Isis admitted, looking at Blair. "Ka claims they've been here for millennia. Ka, what do you know of these progeny?"

"The progeny have been orbiting this world for many centuries, possibly longer," Ka explained, giving another cock of its head. "I do not know how long, precisely, as they did not transmit any signals until they were ready to begin exploration."

"Exploration?" Blair asked, raising an eyebrow. He did not like the sound of that. The idea that the pyramids really *had* been built by aliens pissed him off more than a little.

"Yes, I believe they were sent as scouts by the Builders. Their mission was to measure the appropriate climatological data, and ensure that the planet was ready for their masters' return," Ka explained. "This process involved seizing control of the Arks, but my involvement in helping the Ka-Ken create the first mutagen has prevented this. All Arks are now occupied, so the progeny were unable to seize control."

"Apparently that's changed," Liz said, finally joining the conversation. She still looked a little nauseous. "How did they send a message? And what is this Well you spoke of?" Liz addressed the last question to Isis.

"The Well is a source of enormous power," the Mother replied, folding her arms. "The center of our planet is a molten ball, and the Well connects to the power contained there. It supplements the energy of the sun, but it is located in the heart of the underworld, and therefore is nearly impossible to reach."

"The underworld?" Blair said, blinking. "You can't be serious. THE underworld, as in the one referred to by the ancient Egyptians and the Greeks?"

"I am quite serious, I assure you," Isis said, eyeing him frostily. "The underworld is described in your myths, though the true place bears little resemblance to your fanciful tales. It is located under our world, hence the name underworld. To our knowledge there are only two ways to gain entry, and the progeny of the Builders would have had to use one or the other. The first is beneath The First Ark, in what you know as England. The second is Olympus, the stronghold of a rival group of gods. You'd know them as the Greek pantheon, led by Zeus and his brothers."

Blair rested a hand against the central obelisk, steadying himself. It made sense, in a way. If the Egyptian pantheon was based on real people, why not the Greeks and Romans? Yet the sudden revelation still made him dizzy. He turned to face Isis. "So you believe these progeny are either in control of the First Ark, or have somehow used Mount Olympus to reach the underworld? That's how they sent their message?"

"Possibly," Isis replied, frowning. "We have little to go on, other than the fact that a message was sent. That message would have required access to an Ark, or to the Nexus directly. I do not think such access could have been granted from Olympus, as it is not directly connected to the Ark network. However, it could still have been used as a method of entry. If someone got in that way they could have travelled through the underworld until they reached the Well under The First Ark."

"This hypothesis is correct," Ka said. "Someone, or something, would have had to gain entry to the Underworld. Once there, they overrode the Ark Network's security and forced it to send the message to the Builders. This is alarming, as the progeny of the Builders do not possess this ability. They would have needed the aid of a Homo Sapien to accomplish this. All Arks are genetically locked to your species, a side effect of the creation of the access keys."

94

"So how do we use this information?" Liz asked, pragmatic as always. She tucked a lock of copper hair behind her ear.

"We must learn more," Isis said, clearly irked by the situation. "If we can reach Olympus before Ra, we might be able to speak to Hades, or whoever controls the place now. If someone used that gateway to enter the underworld Hades will know of it."

"How do we get there?" Blair asked.

"We use the light bridge," the Mother said, her mouth tightening into a determined expression.

"I thought the light bridge only connected to other Arks," Blair said, thinking out loud. "If we use the light bridge, wouldn't that mean we either need to come out in the Ark of the Cradle, or the First Ark?"

"That's exactly what it means," Isis agreed. "We will light walk to the Ark of the Cradle."

"Won't that mean a fight with Irakesh's mother?" Liz asked, paling.

"It might, but we have to risk that. I will attempt to parlay with Sekhmet. Once she understands the threat she may be willing to work with us," Isis explained. "She'll want to learn the answers to the same questions we ourselves are asking."

"So you just want to walk into her stronghold? Won't she have a pantheon of gods?" Blair said. "I know you're strong, but wouldn't she be able to overwhelm us?"

"Her servants are powerful, but none so old or powerful as me," the Mother said. The Mother extended a hand and gold flowed up her arm. It coalesced into a golden staff with a winged scarab at the tip. The fist-sized sapphire in the thorax caught the light from the rejuvenation chamber on the far side of the room. "She has no idea I possess a Primary Access Key. This will even the odds enough that she'll deal in good faith."

"You're certain she doesn't know you have it?" Blair asked, raising a dubious eyebrow.

"Absolutely. There are only two, as I said. One is possessed by Osiris in the First Ark. The other was stolen from her by Sobek, who fled to the continent you call Australia. That means I have one, and she does not. With this I can wrest control of her Ark from her, and she'll know that. I'm hoping she'll be willing to parlay rather than risk battle," the Mother reasoned.

Blair had a hard time finding fault with her logic, but he was still nervous. Invading the Ark of the Cradle sounded like suicide to him.

Chapter 19- I know Kung Fu

Trevor's quarters were all golden metal and black stone, just like the ones back in Blair's Ark. That much was similar, but there were definite differences.

A sea of hieroglyphs covered nearly every surface, and wooden furniture dotted the room. The nightstand next to the strange foam bed might have been mahogany, though he didn't know a lot about wood. The statue on top of it was clearly Anubis, though. That probably meant something significant, but he had no idea what.

Trevor flopped down on the bed, allowing the contours to form to his body. He didn't feel exhaustion in the same way he had when he'd been alive, but sleep was still welcome. It allowed him respite from his new existence, allowed him to lose himself in dreams of being alive.

His younger self would likely have been thrilled by the turn of events. After all, he was blessed with all sorts of crazy superpowers. But this was different than some Saturday night roleplaying game. He didn't get to wake up on Sunday and return to normal life. He was dead. Immortal, sure. But still dead.

"Get up," a heavy voice rumbled from the doorway.

Trevor blurred from the bed, dropping into a combat crouch. He reached instinctively for the pistol usually belted at his side. When he realized it was gone, he moved for the combat knife normally tucked into his boot. That was gone too, of course.

"What do you want, Anubis?" he asked, eyes narrowing. He knew the jackal could kick his ass, but if the thing wanted a fight he'd at least go down swinging.

The jackal didn't answer, instead advancing into the room. He cradled that strange double-fan-bladed axe loosely in one hand, while the other rested on the hilt of a sword belted at his side.

This sword was more like a traditional scimitar, narrow at the hilt and wider as it approached the tip. It had a slight curve to it, and the weapon was probably heavier than a na-kopesh.

Anubis paused, unbuckling the leather belt that held the scabbarded sword. He tossed the weapon at Trevor with enough force to knock down a mortal. Trevor caught the weapon awkwardly, blurring slightly to do it.

"What's this?" he asked, holding the scabbard at the midway point.

"Suspicious, are you?" Anubis asked, taking several heavy steps closer until he loomed over Trevor. "Perhaps there is something approaching sense in that head of yours, though I still remain doubtful on that count. That, young pup, is a sword. You have seen a sword before, have you not?"

"Of course I've seen a sword," Trevor snapped, glaring up at Anubis. "Why the hell are you giving it to me?"

"Because you are useless in a fight," Anubis rumbled, giving a very toothy smile. "Ra has asked me to remedy that. I have been given the monumental task of honing you into a soldier, though doing so may take more centuries than I have remaining to me."

Trevor's first instinct was to attack, to show Anubis he was wrong. Unfortunately, indulging that instinct would only prove the jackal right. He'd lose. Again.

"All right," Trevor said, buckling the scabbard around his waist. "Teach me, then."

"I have already begun, you mewling, pathetic wretch," Anubis roared, looming closer with bared fangs. He waited for a long moment as Trevor simply stared up at him, waiting. "Good, you can contain your anger. Perhaps there is a tiny sliver of a chance I can make something from you. Follow me."

Trevor did so, unsurprised that he recognized the path Anubis led him down. They wound through many corridors, arriving at a familiar room, one Trevor had used often in Blair's Ark.

It was a spacious chamber, with an enormous ring in the center. The ring was set about two inches above the rest of the floor, black stone with a gold trim just like in the Ark of the Redwood. Trevor had used it many times for training bouts against his sister. Liz had almost always kicked his ass, though he'd definitely improved through the experience.

"Who's that?" Trevor asked, nodding at a pale-faced deathless that knelt next to the edge of the ring. It was a man of perhaps sixty, or had been before he died and risen as a deathless. Now, alert grey eyes sized up Trevor from a rotting face as he approached.

"I am Abdul Azked Akbar," the man said, his voice hollow and raspy. He rose slowly to his feet, and Trevor noticed a scimitar belted at his waist.

"Is this guy going to teach me the basics?" Trevor asked, turning to Anubis. The jackal watched him impassively.

"In a way," Anubis growled, blurring across the chamber so quickly Trevor couldn't track the movement. The jackal reappeared next to Abdul, his fan-bladed weapon scything through the man's spine with alarming ease. The man's broken body collapsed to the stone, his eyes now dull and lifeless. "Abdul was barely more than a nascent deathless, but he retains something you are in grave need of. Knowledge. He spent a lifetime learning the sword, though I gather such knowledge was deemed of little use in this age."

"You want me to eat him," Trevor said. It wasn't a question, because he already knew the answer. He'd feasted on zombies before, but never one that could speak. It smacked of cannibalism. "And if I refuse?"

"Refuse?" Anubis asked, kicking Abdul's body to the ground outside the ring, near Trevor's feet. "Why would you do such a thing? If you wish to survive, you require this knowledge. We don't have years for you to learn to wield a blade. You must gain that knowledge swiftly, and this is the only way for that to occur."

Anubis speaks wisely, my host. If you do not accept this gift he will think you weak. He will be right.

Trevor hesitated, staring down at the corpse at his feet. Somehow this was crossing a line he knew he couldn't uncross, though he couldn't find any logical fault with feeding on a corpse specifically to gain memories. He'd done that, back in Panama, when he'd devoured a man's mind to learn how to pilot an aircraft.

He knelt swiftly, embracing the decision. Abdul's body was nothing more than matter now, and feasting on it was no different than a normal human eating a steak.

Trevor began to feed. It was quick, grisly work. Before long, a torrent of memories flooded his mind. A young man on the streets of Cairo, born in a time when survival meant quick work with a knife. That man had been adopted by a beduin, the last of a breed that still valued the sword. Decades passed, and with them Abdul's mastery increased. He trained dozens of students, some idly, others going on to become masters in their own right.

The knowledge of sword forms seeped into Trevor, first into his mind, and then into his body as muscle memory. Fascinating, but terrible. Part of Trevor cried out at the crime of it, but mostly he was grateful for the knowledge he gained. Only through strength could he ever hope to escape Ra's court.

"I am a blade master," Trevor said, rising to his feet. He whipped his weapon from its scabbard, twirling it expertly as he tested the weight. It wasn't identical to the scimitar that Abdul had known so well, but it was close enough that he was confident he could fight with the weapon.

"Show me," Anubis said, stepping into the ring. He beckoned for Trevor to follow as the ring flared white. The steady rhythmic pulse he'd grown used to was gone, perhaps because neither he nor Anubis had a heartbeat for it to sync with.

Trevor entered the ring, which instantly shifted. There was a moment of vertigo, then everything changed. A deep, otherworldly cavern sprang into existence around them. Stalactites and stalagmites broke the room at uneven intervals, and the floor was slick with condensation. It was damnably hot, and a faint red glow came from the corridor leading into the distance. It played across the jackal's golden armor, glinting off the fan-bladed axe. The rest of the jackal was lost in darkness though, his midnight fur blacker than whatever Trevor was allowing himself to become.

"Where is this?" Trevor asked, circling a stalagmite as he assumed a combat stance. It felt so natural, something he'd been doing his entire life.

"The underworld," the jackal rumbled, also dropping into a combat stance. He began twirling his axe in slow arcs as he circled the same stalagmite.

Trevor blurred, rushing the jackal. He came in low, aiming an upward slash at the jackal's belly. There was a surge of elation as his blade closed in, apparently faster than Anubis could track. The instant the blade touched fur, the jackal exploded into green mist. Trevor's weapon sailed harmlessly through the cloud, and he stumbled forward. It only took a fraction of a second to recover, but that might as well have been an eternity. Fire exploded in his back as the fan-bladed axe burst through his chest. Trevor toppled to the ground, dropping his weapon with a clatter.

Chapter 20- Vampire

Awaken, master.

Mark tumbled from the bed, rolling to his feet with an arm extended protectively. He took several deep breaths as he attempted to calm his thundering heart. Or rather, he tried to. Only he wasn't breathing. His heart wasn't beating, not that he could feel anyway.

It is part of the change, master. You are greater than you were. Beyond the ravages of time, or the need to draw breath.

"Fuck," was all Mark could manage. He straightened, drawing on decades of discipline to still the tempest of rage and loss. What the hell had Osiris done to him?

He has imparted the greatest of gifts, master.

"Do not speak, unless I direct a question at you. Do you understand?"

As you wish, master.

He remembered stories from Jordan about the beast in his head, and this thing sounded a great deal similar. That terrified him, because he knew it could hear his innermost thoughts. Yet he couldn't change it, so that left only one option. He'd use it. Treating it like a virtual assistant was a good start.

"Osiris slipped me the virus, or some version of it. Is that correct?" Mark asked. He squared his shoulders as he studied his surroundings. The room was small, containing a narrow metal bed with a stained mattress, and a single nightstand and lamp. It smelled like grease and dust.

That is correct, master.

"I've retained my memories. Why aren't I like one of the zombies we saw just after the CME?" Mark asked, moving to a thick metal door with a slot set at eye level. He threw back the slot, peering as best he could into the hall. It was dimly lit, and empty.

You are no paltry deathless, my host. The oily tone was layered with disgust. *You have become a Draugr, what you would know as a vampire. We are more noble, more graceful. Deathless are brutes. We are artisans.*

"I see," Mark said. There was still no movement in the hallway, not that he could see anyway. He reached down to the cool handle, turning it gently. Much to his shock it opened. "These vampires. How are they, we rather, different than the deathless?"

All he knew of deathless came from Jordan's reports of Irakesh, and from the brief studies they'd conducted on zombies back in Syracuse. That was precious little, other than the fact that they possessed fantastic abilities and were very, very difficult to kill.

Vampires are always sentient, always retain the greater part of the master's consciousness. We require less direct sustenance, and prefer blood over flesh. Blood contains the helixes of the host, giving us what we require without the need to kill. As I said, artisans.

"Great," Mark muttered, stepping into the dimly-lit hall. There was a single lightbulb at the far end, which flickered dully. The walls were whitewashed concrete, and hadn't been tended to in at least a few years. The place was also damp, as if they were underground. "So you're saying I drink blood instead of eating people? That's loads better, thanks."

In time you will understand the benefits, master. Our strength will be needed in the coming days. We feed upon the unblooded, but use that strength to protect.

Mark moved up the hallway, rounding the corner. He passed two more doors and one flickering light before the hall ended at another door. He stopped in front of it, listening. To his amazement he could hear everything beyond. Heartbeats. Breathing. The clacking of keys, and the low hum of computers.

He took a deep breath, then opened the door. The room was a low-tech version of the ops center back in Syracuse. Perhaps a dozen techs worked at hastily erected stations, each tapped into data feeds he recognized. Most were the satellites Mohn had launched prior to the CME, but several techs were doing simple data analysis.

A familiar one looked up as he entered, her jaw dropping. She shot to her feet, snapping to attention. "Director on the floor."

The techs rose as one, delivering a hasty salute. His attention was reserved for the first woman who'd risen, though.

"At ease," he said, threading through the workstations until he reached Benson. "You're looking well. I was worried you'd be brought up on charges for your role in my little coup back in Syracuse."

"No, sir," Benson said, giving him a wide smile. It made her almond-shaped eyes crinkle in a way he found damnably attractive. Should he be able to do that now that he was dead? "I was detained briefly, then brought to London to meet with the Old Man. He explained that I'd be reassigned, and you'd still be my CO. He didn't give me a lot of choice, but I'd have agreed to pretty much anything once I heard you'd still be in charge."

"Your loyalty is appreciated," he said, giving her the warmest smile he could muster. She blanched, face draining of color. "What is it?"

"Your, uh, teeth sir," Benson stammered, blinking rapidly. "They're, uh sharp. The canines."

"Lovely," Mark said, feeling his teeth with his tongue. Sure enough, his canines were elongated. Whatever monster Osiris was, he'd become the same. "I can't change it, so I'll have to adapt to it. Give me a sitrep."

"We're observing points of interest, sir," Benson said, clearly relieved to slip back into routine. She glanced at her computer, exposing a delicate neck. A vein thudded there, in time with her heartbeat. "Stonehenge was given a priority of ten, with Cairo at nine. Cambodia, San Francisco, and Peru are all listed as eights."

Mark processed that. Mohn Corp was focused solely on London.

"Flags?" Mark asked, focusing on Benson's heartbeat instead of her neck. It was slow. Steady. She wasn't alarmed by his condition. Part of him found that flattering, but the analytical mind knew it had to be deeper than that. If she wasn't alarmed, then seeing monsters like him had become normal. She'd been working heavily with Osiris, in all likelihood.

"We haven't seen anything of note in London," Benson said, gesturing at her screen as she pulled up several feeds. "Cairo has been the most interesting. Whoever or whatever is in control there has gathered an army, a large one."

The satellite feed showed a massive cloud of dust. Benson zoomed in, and he could see row upon row of figures. Dead figures. Someone clearly possessed the ability to control tens of thousands of zombies. Who? And what were they planning on using them for?

"Noted," Mark replied, filing the events away. He'd dissect them later. "How about the other targets?"

"Peru has been quiet, for the most part," Benson said, sweeping dark bangs out of her face. "It looks like whoever is in charge there is rebuilding Cajamarca. There's a lot of traffic going back and forth, but beyond clearing the city of undead they haven't made any notable advances."

"Interesting. San Francisco?" Mark would have held his breath, if he had any.

Benson pulled up the feed. She was quiet for a moment as the camera focused. "We're not entirely sure what happened—but, sir, look at that blast crater. It's consistent with a nuclear detonation, but the devastation stops after just a few hundred yards. It's too small to be one of our assets."

She was right. The first quarter of the Golden Gate bridge had been melted to slag, but the latter section hadn't been touched. The entire area around the San Francisco side was a charred hole, but that hole was far smaller than the hole the 500-megaton nuclear asset Irakesh had stolen should have created. A lot smaller.

"Theories?" Mark asked, holding off on speculation until he'd gathered all available data.

"None, sir," Benson said, giving a very uncharacteristic shrug. "The energy had to go somewhere, but it isn't clear where."

"Show me the Ark," he said, pointing at the object at the corner of the screen.

Benson zoomed in, revealing a massive pyramid twin to the one in Peru. It stabbed out of San Francisco bay, not more than a mile from Angel Island. The bulk of the structure was covered by water, and there was no visible means of entrance. If it resembled its counterpart in Peru, the entrance would be under five hundred feet of frigid water.

"What's that?" he asked, pointing at Angel Island.

"That's the new settlement Commander Jordan has created," Benson explained, zooming in on the island. She continued to zoom, past the clusters of tents and the small army of boats tethered to the dock. She didn't stop until she reached a small cluster of men.

The men were drilling, and the drill was a familiar one. As familiar as the man leading those drills. "My god. Yuri survived."

"Indeed he did," came a polished voice from behind. Mark whirled to find Osiris just a few inches away. He could hear the creak of every shoe, yet this man's approach had been completely undetected. It underscored just how new his abilities were, and how little he knew about them. "I've worked with Yuri in the past. I'm not surprised he found his way through the CME."

"Have we attempted to establish contact?" Mark asked, choosing not to react to Osiris's arrival.

"We don't have the means," Benson said, shrugging helplessly. "If they have a surviving sat phone they haven't used it, so as far as we know they're off grid. We'd have to physically send a bird to make contact, and we don't have more than a handful left."

"Those birds are needed here, for the time being," Osiris said, turning to Mark. "Will you take a walk with me, Director Phillips? I'd like to discuss your new condition, and your role here going forward."

Chapter 21- Collared

Jordan came to with a start. He hadn't meant to fall asleep, but he wasn't sure how long he'd been down here. It was difficult staying alert when you couldn't mark the passage of time, especially when there was no apparent end to your confinement. That was no excuse, though. He couldn't let himself get weak. Now, more than ever, he needed his strength.

There is truth in that, Ka-Dun. Yet you cannot blame yourself for our current circumstances.

"Who the fuck else is there to blame?" Jordan replied, rising from the bench and approaching the crackling blue bars to his cell. He knew roughly where he was in the Ark, and he also knew how to reach the light bridge where he'd entered.

That knowledge was useless, though. Steve had been able to escape a cell like this one, but he'd been an Ark Lord and had used his ability to light walk. Jordan had no such ability, and that meant for the time being he had no method of escape.

Heavy footsteps clinked their way on the marble in the distance. They were growing closer. Jordan tensed, moving to the far side of the cell so he had the best view of the hallway where the steps had originated. Long moments later, a familiar jackal-headed figure stepped into view. It carried the same golden staff, each end capped with a fan-blade like some wicked doubled-bladed scythe.

Jordan could immediately see the usefulness of the weapon, which capitalized on the wielder's speed. You were always in a position to launch a blow at your foe, and the force of that blow couldn't be countered with a conventional parry. If you hit your target, your target died.

The jackal stopped outside of his cell, tapping a blue sapphire set into one golden gauntlet. The crackling bars of energy abruptly ceased. He said nothing to Jordan, instead gesturing at the hallway. The meaning was clear. Walk. Now.

So Jordan walked. There was no point in resistance. Not yet, anyway. This thing had already mopped the floor with him, and if he got into another confrontation it would have the same end. He needed to bide his time until he understood exactly what this thing was. It had to have a weakness, and if Jordan had enough time he'd find it.

The jackal shoved him roughly from behind, and Jordan stumbled forward. He regained his footing quickly, resisting the urge to round on his tormentor and attack. That was no doubt exactly what the jackal was goading him into. Jordan kept walking.

Eventually they reached the central chamber. Jordan slowed his pace slightly, a play for a bit more time to study his enemies. Irakesh stood on the lowest step of a short stairway leading up to a massive throne. Below him stood Steve on one side, and Trevor on the other. Right now Jordan wasn't sure whom he disliked more.

A few steps above Irakesh stood a woman with long dark hair. To her left, another attendant to the throne, a wolf, but something was off about the creature. Definitely male, but he stood a good nine feet tall, on par with most females. As Jordan approached the throne, he caught a whiff of something rotting.

That is no Ka-Dun. It is a dead wolf, shaped into being by the twisted deathless. Wepwawet, he is called. A vicious, cruel god.

Then his attention shifted to the figure presiding over the court. A warrior goddess occupied the throne. Dark red hair spilled down well-muscled shoulders. Piercing green eyes studied him, exactly the way he was studying her. This woman was the veteran of a thousand wars, a soldier born and bred. She was gorgeous, long-limbed and pale skinned, but then so was his ex-wife.

As she smiled he caught sight of the same razored teeth Irakesh and

Trevor bore. Her eyes smoldered with green flame, reminding him she was every bit his enemy. A spear very similar to the dead wolf's was propped against her throne, within easy reach.

"Mighty Ra, I have brought the prisoner as you commanded," the jackal rumbled. A huge hand settled over Jordan's shoulder, forcing him to his knees. The jackal fell to one knee beside him, dropping his voice to a low rumble. "Avert your gaze, or I will take your eyes, whelp."

Jordan stared Ra right in the face, daring her to take some sort of action. The jackal's gauntleted hand swept up in a backhand, but Jordan was ready this time. He blurred, catching the gauntlet in both hands. He summoned his telekinesis, using it to help lift the jackal. Then Jordan flung the creature directly at Steve and Irakesh, stripping the strange fan-bladed axe from its grip as the creature sailed past.

Jordan settled into a combat stance as he scanned the room, searching for a means of escape before they recaptured him.

The jackal was still in midair when the figure on the throne twitched. That was the only way Jordan could describe it. Her position shifted as if she'd blurred, yet it happened so quickly he couldn't track it. He blinked twice, staring down at his hands as he realized his stolen weapon was gone.

He looked up to see the jackal crash into Steve, knocking the man to the ground under his tremendous weight. Irakesh managed to dodge out of the way, though his feet never left the step he'd been standing on. Jordan glanced up at the throne again, jaw dropping as he saw that Ra now held the axe he'd stolen from the jackal.

"I'll devour your heart," the jackal roared, leaping to his feet and blurring in Jordan's direction. Even though Jordan blurred, he couldn't avoid the attack.

A gauntleted fist hit his jaw like a freight train, shattering bone as he was flung back twenty or more feet. He skidded along the marble floor, trying to roll to his feet. The jackal gave no quarter, and Jordan felt more than one bone break as blows rained down on him.

"Enough," Ra's voice cracked. The blows didn't slacken. "Anubis, your disobedience is becoming a dangerous habit."

That stopped the blows. He was aware of Anubis moving away; that was apparently the jackal's name. The creature fell to one knee, facing the throne. "Forgive me, mighty Ra. I lost my temper. This whelp has embarrassed me in front of the court. Please, let me take his heart."

"Be silent, and contemplate your disobedience lest I take *your* heart," Ra snapped. The jackal merely nodded, remaining in his kneeling position.

Jordan took the opportunity to rise to his feet, snapping his forearm back into place. Two ribs cracked into position, and he couldn't stifle the groan of pain.

"Approach the throne, Ka-Dun," Ra commanded, eyes smoldering. Jordan considered his options, then decided he had no choice. He walked painfully to the base of the stairs, stopping next to Steve and Irakesh. Trevor was lurking there as well, avoiding Jordan's gaze. "I must decide what to do with you. Tell me, Ka-Dun, whom do you serve?"

That was a harder question to answer than Jordan would have thought. Who *did* he serve? Not Isis. He respected her, but he didn't share her goals. She was too callous, too focused on things that wouldn't occur for millennia. Blair then? No, Blair was more of an ally.

"I serve the Ka-Ken, Liz," he said, squaring his shoulders. "She leads my pack."

"I am unfamiliar with this Ka-Ken," Ra said, rising from her throne. She swept past the wolf-thing, past Steve and Irakesh, until she stood before Jordan. She was his height, a rarity among women. "If this Liz could issue you an order, what would it be? What would she wish you to accomplish in my court?"

"To kill that fucker," Jordan rumbled, nodding at Steve.

"Ahhh," Ra said, raising a delicate eyebrow. "So this Liz serves Isis. Unsurprising."

She turned from Jordan, focusing her gaze on Steve. "What of you, Ka-Dun? Whom is it you serve?"

"I serve you, mighty Ra," Steve replied, sinking to one knee, as the jackal had. He kept his eyes downcast, and his tone was as deferential as Jordan had ever heard. "It was I who saved Irakesh and brought him here. I offer myself to your service, and I offer the key that I bear. The key belonging to Isis and her Ark on the jungle continent."

Jordan struggled against the urge to shatter Steve's face, barely containing his fury. The betrayal had been expected, but to give the key to the Mother's Ark to a woman who'd given birth to a monster like Irakesh? That was beyond stupidity.

"I see," Ra said, folding her arms as she stared down at Steve. "You are not the first to profess such loyalty, and I am not inclined to trust you. Why should I, after you betrayed your former master? You would do the same to me, like as not."

Steve looked up at her, fear etched in his features. "Mighty Ra, I have told the truth. I seek only to serve. To live and die in your service. Please, I know much of this age. I am a trained scholar, well-versed in our history. I can teach you a great deal. Even show it to you, if you'll permit me to mindshare."

"Allow you to touch my mind?" Ra said, disbelieving. She threw her head back and laughed. Jordan was aware of Irakesh flinching behind his mother, and it wasn't hard to guess why. The mockery in that laughter cut deeply. Eventually it stilled, and Ra turned to Irakesh. "Step forward my son."

Irakesh did so, descending a step to stand next to his mother. He made no attempt to disguise his fear, not that Jordan could blame him in this instance.

"Place this around the Ka-Dun's neck," she commanded, extending her hand. Gold pooled there, forming a perfectly round ring just large enough to fit around a man's neck. Glowing glyphs like those lining the walls covered the surface.

Irakesh took it, fear melting as he took a step toward Steve. He snapped the object around Steve's neck with an audible click, and there was a brief flash of golden light. Then the collar sealed, now apparently one unbroken piece of metal.

"He is your responsibility, Irakesh. If you train him well you will be allowed to keep him. If not...." She shrugged.

"How do I control him, Mother?" Irakesh asked, the hunger in his gaze plain.

"With this," she said, offering a bracelet to match the collar. Irakesh all but snatched it from her hand, slapping it around his wrist. It snapped into place and a look of ecstasy came over him.

"Lie down, dog," Irakesh commanded, gesturing at Steve with his hand. The bracelet glowed golden for a brief instant, then Steve collapsed to the floor. Irakesh's grin nearly swallowed his face.

"Step forward, Trevor Gregg," Ra commanded, turning to face Trevor. Jordan's eyes narrowed, and he shifted to a combat stance. "Place this around your Ka-Dun's neck."

She extended a similar collar, which Trevor took reluctantly. He met Jordan's gaze, and Jordan saw something odd there. Was that pity? Trevor eventually took a step forward and gently slid the collar around Jordan's neck. Jordan briefly considered batting Trevor's arm aside, but what would that accomplish? Better to keep his dignity.

"And the method of control," Ra said, offering Trevor a bracelet to match Irakesh's. Trevor placed it around his wrist, a look of distaste flitting across his features.

"How do I use it?" Trevor asked, still looking at Jordan.

"Simply will pain through the bracelet," Ra explained, gesturing at Jordan. "The Ka-Dun will feel it for as long as you will it so. What's more, any shaping the Ka-Dun attempts will be cancelled, unless you allow it. This includes shifting. He is nothing but a mortal unless you allow him to be more."

Jordan gritted his teeth and glared at Trevor.

Chapter 22- Spy

Mark looked up from the narrow desk, surprised by the soft rapping at his door. He'd just left Osiris, and besides, the knock seemed too timid. Yet he didn't hear a heartbeat on the other side. Interesting. He rose to his feet, pulling open the heavy steel door.

A woman in all-black nylon stood on the other side. It covered her from head to toe, even her face. She was short, maybe five foot three. Mark took a step back, concerned she might be some sort of assassin. Yet she produced no weapon, and hadn't made any threatening gestures.

"We can't talk here," the woman whispered, with a faint Irish accent. "Head down a level. Go to the storage closet at the south end of the hall."

Then she was gone. She didn't step into the shadows, as Mark had seen with other supernaturals. She simply vanished, and somehow he knew it wasn't an illusion. He sensed that she was gone entirely. Some new power? Perhaps the voice in his head knew.

It is, master. Vampires possess the ability to instantly traverse space. The ability can only be used to cross short distances, but may save your life.

Short-range teleportation, then. That was beyond amazing, especially if he could master it.

Mark started up the hallway toward the door leading to the stairwell. He'd already decided to meet the strange woman, though he had no idea what her motives might be. Curiosity, cats, and all that.

The door to the stairway was a single solid piece of steel, its pitted surface painted a deep brown. The place screamed bomb shelter, and he wondered briefly why and when it had been built. World War Two? Mark opened the door, which creaked far too loudly in protest.

No one seemed to have noticed, so he started down the narrow concrete stairs. The hallway was dimly lit by a single bulb, but his new senses made incredible use of the illumination. He could pick out the gradations of the concrete, the grease on the walls where thousands of careless hands had brushed.

He hurried down one flight, stopping outside the next door. He took a deep breath, or rather mimed taking one. His body was no longer aerobic, and apparently it functioned without the aid of oxygen. Despite that, the muscle memory was powerful, and he could feel the air as he sucked it in.

The door opened more easily on this floor, with only a slight creak. Mark stepped into the hallway, which was virtually indistinguishable from the one above. It too was lit by a single dim bulb, with a series of steel doors lining both sides.

He hurried up the hallway, moving far more quietly than he'd have been able to manage in life. That was a curiosity. His loafers were the same, yet he didn't hear a single scuff, despite taking no special effort to prevent them.

This too is one of your abilities, master. You possess the ability to smother sound, much the same way a Ka-Ken does when shadow walking.

Mark filed that away for further study later. He needed to learn more about his abilities, and he needed to learn it as soon as possible.

The door at the far end of the hall was different than the others, this one cut from heavy oak instead of steel. Mark tried the handle, which turned easily. The door slid open silently, revealing a darkened closet filled with brooms, mops, and various cleaning supplies.

He stepped inside, glancing up the hallway to ensure he wasn't being followed. Nothing. Mark closed the door, plunging the room into darkness. A pair of sharp green eyes flared to life at the far end of the closet.

They gave off just enough light to illuminate the stranger's face. She was a young woman in her mid twenties. Blonde curls dusted her shoulders, and her cheeks dimpled as she gave him a warm smile. It couldn't have been more at odds with the hellish eyes.

"I've come down here on good faith, but you've reached the limits of my cooperation," Mark said, just above a whisper. He straightened his tie, then folded his arms as he waited for a response.

"Thank you, Director Phillips," she said, giving a gracious nod. It exposed a long, slender neck, which led down to a generous expanse of cleavage. Mark appreciated a beautiful woman as much as the next man, but he was shocked by the depth of the lust that simple glance provoked. "I know you have many questions, and I will answer what I can once I've explained why I called you here. You are a pawn, Mark. May I call you Mark?"

Mark nodded brusquely. He was already tired of this game.

"Osiris hasn't sired progeny in over a century," the woman said, licking her lips. That too, was sensual. "The fact that he would now is troubling, and my associates are quite concerned."

"Associates?" Mark asked, eyes narrowing. "I don't even know your name. Who are you? Who do you work for?"

"You can call me Elle," the woman said, the Irish strong in her words. "As for who I work for, you'll find out if you choose to meet them. We're a faction of what you know as vampires."

"You're clearly working at cross-purposes with Osiris, or you wouldn't be doing all this cloak-and-dagger crap," Mark interrupted, trying to speed things along. He could be missed at any time, and he didn't want to have to explain his absence. "I thought he was the first vampire, which means he created all of you. So what's with the familial spat?"

"It's far more than a simple argument," Elle said, giving a heavy sigh. "Osiris is insane, Mark. He was left outside the Great Ark during the span between ages. He spent thirteen millennia scavenging enough energy to survive, and he did whatever it took to ensure that. It changed him. He's not the same benevolent father we knew, and I fear what he intends for the world. You've already seen what happened, the zombies everywhere. You realize he's responsible for that, right?"

"Is he?" Mark shot back. He'd had time to think on it, and the move didn't seem to be Osiris's style. If there was anything he'd learned about the ancient god, it was that Osiris was ever the showman. Killing the entire world deprived him of an audience. "And even if he is, why should I trust you? What makes you any different?"

"My people were left behind to care for the world," Elle said, cocking her head as she studied him with those intense green eyes. "None of us are ancient, because we died off or slumbered as the power diminished. Yet some of us sired progeny, and passed down the legacy."

"Okay, so let's say you're on the level. What exactly do you want from me?" Mark asked.

"We need to know what Osiris's plans are. For whatever reason, he seems to trust you. If you value the few survivors and want to help humanity survive the next decade, then you'll help us," she said, gaze earnest. Mark sensed no deception, but didn't discount the possibility that she could be using an ability to manipulate him. "Listen, Mark. I know you don't trust me. You have no reason to. All I ask is that you agree to meet with my associates. Speak to them, and see if they can convince you. If not, then we go our separate ways."

Mark was silent for a long moment. He didn't trust her, but then he didn't trust Osiris either. What was the right side? Was either one better than the other, or were they two shades of the same darkness?

"All right," he agreed, giving a tight nod. "I'll meet with them, as long as we can do it safely. But I'm going to want something from you."

Maybe he leered at her, or maybe she was just used to men looking at her in a certain way. She glanced down at her chest, then back up with a wicked smile.

"Not that," Mark snapped. "You're going to teach me that teleporting trick. Do that, and I'll meet with your masters. Deal?"

Chapter 23- Banquet

Trevor finished dressing and surveyed himself in the full length mirror set into the wall of his new chambers. He thought he looked ridiculous in the shiny white vest and harem pants. His chest, though well-muscled and hardened by combat, felt exposed...naked. Anput had insisted he dress the part if he wanted to fit in. All the court wore the garments, with the exception of Anubis. Trevor felt like frigging Aladdin. Now if only he had Robin Williams around to grant wishes.

Footsteps sounded behind him, and Trevor turned to see Anput enter the chamber. She wore a flowing white blouse cut from the same fabric as his vest, though hers was trimmed in gold. Her makeup was as skillfully applied as last time, and she wielded a smile with the same degree of skill.

"Are you ready for your first banquet, Trevor Gregg?" she asked, taking a step into his room. He noticed for the first time that she wore nothing on her feet. He'd expected some sort of expensive slippers, like she'd insisted he wear. Instead she walked barefoot, making no sound as she moved.

"No, but I doubt anything else you can teach me in the next few minutes will prepare me," he said, stifling a sigh. He glanced down at the golden bracelet around his right wrist. It seemed an unnecessarily cruel invention, one even worse than the slave collars he'd read about in the Wheel of Time. If Jordan hadn't hated him before, then he certainly would now.

"A fair answer. Follow me, and I'll escort you. Do as I do, and avoid speaking unless spoken to," Anput said, offering him her arm. Trevor took it, allowing her to lead him from the chamber. "These affairs are all about position. Others will attempt to spar verbally, those who win gaining favor with Ra."

"You called it a banquet," Trevor said, unsure how to broach the subject.

He took several more steps up the corridor before continuing. "What exactly are we eating?"

"Ahh, I forget how little you know," Anput said, shooting him a sly smile. "We will consume the hearts and minds of exotic thralls. This will gift us with potent memories, and we will share what we learn as we dine. It provides an easy method of conversation. Doubly so, since every memory is new in this strange age. Almost everything we learn is vastly different from our own time."

Trevor felt a moment of revulsion, but he stifled it. It was unlikely that the victims supplying their meal would be consumed alive. More likely they were already dead, zombies harvested for this grisly meal.

You must set aside this squeamishness, my host. Power comes from feeding. Even were that not so you are no longer human. You are deathless, and must consume the flesh of others to survive.

He was still gnawing on the problem when they entered a spacious chamber. They threaded through row after row of dark wooden tables, probably a legacy of when Ra's court had been far more numerous. Each was covered with an array of animal pictographs, though many were faded from simple age. He was amazed they still held the weight of Ra and her court.

Anput leaned closer, whispering low enough that only he could hear. "The man seated to Ra's left is Horus, son of Isis and Osiris. You already know Anubis, and you met Wepwawet briefly."

Wepwawet, the wolf-headed creature that so closely resembled a werewolf, now wore golden garments. There was no sign of weaponry on his person, though Trevor had no doubt he could produce one if needed.

Anubis sat between Wepwawet and Ra. The jackal-headed god glared grimly at Trevor, though his earlier ire seemed muted. Perhaps because of Anput. Trevor glanced furtively at Ra, who lounged in her chair just as she had the throne earlier. She'd donned a sheer gown cut from a silky material Trevor had never seen.

The figure on her other side, the one Anput had called *Horus*, was strange. He was a shorter man with black skin and a shaven head. He was also the only god Trevor had seen to wear glasses, something he hadn't even known had existed during the previous age. Horus straightened in his chair, peering through the gold-rimmed lenses as they approached.

"Irakesh has already seated himself across from his mother. He does this to steal prestige," Anput said, guiding Trevor toward the table.

Trevor considered for a long moment, then took the seat to Irakesh's left. That put him directly across from Horus. Anput gave a tight nod of approval as if he'd done something intelligent, then settled into the empty seat to his left.

"Welcome, Trevor Gregg," Ra said, in that musical voice. He was once again struck by her beauty, though he did his best to suppress that. "I trust that Anput's instruction in our ways is adequate?"

"It is, mighty Ra," Trevor said, ducking his head in what he hoped she'd take for a seated bow. "I have much to learn, and I hope I don't embarrass her too badly. If I do so, it's my fault. Not hers."

Ra raised a delicate eyebrow, and conversation ceased as everyone focused their attention on him.

"You are an interesting creature, Trevor Gregg," Ra said, straightening in her seat. She clapped her hands once, and a set of doors at the far end of the chamber swung open. Several zombies garbed in simple black robes pushed trays into the room. They began setting covered platters in front of each person.

"It is unheard of for someone to preemptively show weakness," Anput whispered as a platter was set before her.

The servants removed the platters' covers, revealing porcelain bowls containing brains, hearts, and stomachs. Trevor wanted to be nauseated, but a tide of hunger immediately filled him. He forced himself to watch the others, particularly Ra.

She deftly picked apart each organ, savoring tiny morsels for long moments before she'd take another. He looked to Anput, who appeared to be the only person at the table with utensils. She used a knife and a two pronged fork to cut thin slices of flesh.

It was only when he saw her open her mouth to eat one that Trevor finally understood why. Anput had two sharp incisors, the kind of fangs you'd expect to see on a vampire. The rest were as flat as any normal human's.

*She **is** a vampire, my host. A child of Osiris. They are quite different than the strange legends I glimpse in your mind.*

Interesting. Trevor turned his attention to his own food, forcing himself to rip off small bites. Each brought a small rush of memory, which revealed that his host had once been a tour guide. The man knew all sorts of things about Sakkara, the Pyramids, and the Sphinx. He'd spent countless days exploring them as a child.

"Do you find the meal satisfactory, Trevor?" Ra asked, in that strangely musical voice.

He looked up at her, forcing himself to focus past the rush of memory and emotion from a large morsel of the man's prefrontal cortex. "More than satisfactory. This is the first food I've had in nearly two weeks."

"You did not eat when you were with Isis's pack?" Ra asked, raising a curious eyebrow.

"I didn't want to alarm the humans we were protecting. They already distrusted me enough," Trevor said, shrugging as he popped a hunk of heart into his mouth.

"This is why we rule the humans, and not they, us," Ra said, raising a delicate eyebrow in what Trevor took for gentle admonishment. "They live to serve, while we guide the world they live in."

Trevor wasn't sure how to respond to that, so he shifted the topic of conversation. "I notice Anput is different from the rest of you. My risen calls her a vampire. My people have myths, but I don't understand how or why that's different than the deathless."

"A shrewd question," Ra said, nodding at Anput. "Tell him, daughter of Osiris."

Anput used her napkin to dab blood from the corner of her mouth, then set down her utensils before speaking. "In the beginning there were only the deathless, fathered by Osiris and my foul uncle Set. They were powerful, but my father felt they lacked control. He hated what he'd become, hated how his former tribesmen viewed him.

"So it was that Isis led Osiris to the repository at the base of the Ark of the Cradle. The Ark in which we now stand," Anput explained. The tale was clearly one she'd learned, rather than experienced. "She helped him shape the virus that had changed him, to remake himself into something more human. Something that could blend more easily among his human followers. Osiris became the first vampire, and after his change he was indistinguishable from a normal man.

"My kind are blessed with the same gifts as a deathless, but we prefer to feed on blood rather than flesh," Anput explained, wearing the same posture Trevor had seen on grad students defending their thesis. "This is why I use utensils, while the rest of you dine with your more…natural attributes."

"That is the heart of the tale, but Anput leaves out much," Ra interjected, dabbing her own mouth with her napkin. "Osiris and his desire to be more human became a source of weakness for our people. Many chose to follow, diluting their bloodline with his newly modified virus. It caused a schism among our people, one that eventually erupted into war. At the end of this war I stood triumphant, and Osiris was banished to the frozen north to administer to his few followers."

"Are deathless and vampires all that different?" Trevor asked.

"Different enough," Ra shot back, something violent smoldering in her eyes. "It is not so much the change in physical appearance, but rather what it represented. Osiris sought the love of his people, but they'll never love us. To them we are monsters. He sought to cloak that fact, to curry favor with the sheep. I realized we'd never have their love, so instead I take their fear. I show them my true face, so all know precisely who and what they pray to."

Something incredibly bright played outside the balcony window, slicing the night like the atomic bomb that had so recently detonated in San Francisco. Trevor rolled from his chair, diving under the table. A smattering of laughter echoed around the room, and Trevor's cheeks heated in a very un-deathless like fashion. He rose to his feet the room full of mocking smiles.

"What the hell was that?" he asked, glancing back at the balcony. The brightness was gone, like a flash of lightning. Something still crackled in the air though, an afterimage he could almost see.

"The pup's ignorance is limitless," Anubis rumbled, broad muzzle splitting into a grin. "Calm yourself, boy. It was merely a sun flash."

"You have no idea, believe me," Irakesh muttered, mostly under his breath. He eyed Trevor sidelong, and something beyond hatred lived there.

"Sun flash?" Trevor asked, sinking back into his seat.

"Sun flashes herald a sunstorm," Anput explained, resting a hand delicately on his shoulder. She withdrew it a moment later. "Sun storms strike without warning, cooking the unprotected."

"Unprotected mortals," Ra interjected, leaning forward in her chair. She caught Trevor's gaze, eyes flaring green. "Humans can be destroyed if caught in a sunstorm. We, however, can draw on their strength. Imagine drinking in the sun's light for a week or more, but in an instant."

"What mighty Ra suggests is dangerous," Horus said, his voice a high, lilting tone that contrasted with everyone else at the table. "Those who drink from sunstorms risk burning themselves up. The power is near limitless."

Trevor leaned back in his chair, shifting his gaze from person to person. He finally let it settle on Ra. "The event that finally triggered this new age was a coronal mass ejection. I was studying that event before it occurred, and I watched as it crackled across the sky. What you're describing can only be more CMEs, each more violent than the one I saw."

Ra raised an eyebrow, eyeing him curiously. "You studied sunstorms?"

"You might say that, yes. Before I became deathless I was a scientist," Trevor explained. He turned to Anput, since he was more likely to get a straight answer there. "Am I right? Are the sunstorms more CMEs?"

Anput didn't answer him, at least not directly. She turned to Ra, giving a deferential nod of her head. "Mighty Ra, may I have permission to take the pup up to the observatory?"

"You have an observatory?" Trevor asked, struggling to suppress his sudden excitement. The observatory at SDSU had been his second home and he'd clocked endless hours there, each spent studying the sun or other astronomical phenomena.

"You may accompany us," Ra said, dropping her napkin as she rose to her feet. She waved to one of the dead servants, who began to clear the dishes. "Come, pup. I would hear more of the science in this new age. Perhaps you have learned things even we did not know."

Chapter 24- Sun Study

Ra swayed from the hall, shapely legs drawing Trevor's eyes as he followed. Anput rose to join them, but the rest of the figures remained seated. Trevor caught Irakesh's gaze on the way out, and if anything the hatred had deepened.

His jealousy is palpable. You have gained much prestige, while he broods silently. Left behind like a child.

That was definitely ironic. He'd gained prestige by diving under a table like a superstitious yokel. Trevor turned his attention back to Ra, following her from the chamber and up a dizzying array of halls. They climbed stairwell after stairwell, gradually making their way to the apex of the pyramid. The hike would have winded him had he still breathed. Instead, he felt nothing as he climbed.

"Ahh, we arrive at last," Ra said, cresting a final stairwell. She hurried up the black stone, entering a chamber that made Trevor gawk.

Each of the walls was sloped, and they met in a single point at the top of the room. The floor was the same black marble, the walls solid gold. Unlike the rest of the Ark there were no hieroglyphs of any kind; the place was bare of any decoration.

"This is an observatory?" he asked. The walls were opaque, which seemed to preclude any such observation.

"Indeed," Ra said, sweeping her arms out in an encompassing gesture. The walls faded to transparency, and they were suddenly standing in space. "Watch, and I will show you."

Trevor spun in a slow circle, marveling at what he was seeing. There was the moon, larger than it could have been anywhere on earth. The sun hung in the distance, impossibly bright, since there was no atmosphere to mute its brilliance. It was as if the Ark had linked to a satellite, and he was observing a holographic representation of whatever that satellite saw. Maybe it had. Maybe the Black Knight satellites were more than just a conspiracy theory.

"This is incredible," he whispered, truly awed in a way none of the rest of the Ark had been able to provoke. This place made the Kepler program look archaic. Hubble was nothing but an infantile experiment, clear proof of just how far modern science had lagged behind whoever had built this place.

"You've not seen even a fraction of the capabilities the observatory possesses," Anput said, giving him a warm smile.

Ra gestured and a holographic sphere appeared in the center of the room; she stretched out delicate fingers, touching various points on the sphere's surface. The room answered, zooming their perspective until they were much closer to the sun.

Normally its brilliance would have been blinding, but their transformed eyes made it easier to see. He could make out massive flares all over the sun's surface, far more numerous than anything in recorded history. At least four looked like they would result in coronal mass ejections sometime in the next several weeks.

"Jesus," he muttered, taking a step closer to the sun. "Four at once. We've never even conceived of that kind of solar violence. It's a wonder the world is surviving at all. How does that not overwhelm our magnetosphere?"

"Your words are strange, but I have tasted of several scientists," Ra said, joining him near the edge closest to the sun. "What you refer to as the magnetosphere, we referred to as the shroud. It protects this world from the fury of the sun, but it is limited and easily depleted. The violence you see now is a tiny precursor to what this world will experience over the next dozen centuries."

"How will we survive?" Trevor asked. He knew far more than most about helio-seismology. There was no way the world could make it through that kind of prolonged exposure. "All life will be wiped out. Not even plants will survive."

"That would be the case, were it not for the Arks," Ra said, resting a hand on his shoulder. He turned to see her standing closer than she had before. He was acutely aware of her scent, clean and intoxicating. "The network is controlled by the Nexus, which you passed to reach us here in the Cradle. Each Ark drains a portion of the solar storms, using that energy to cleanse the shroud. In short, life exists on our world because the Arks regulate our atmosphere."

Trevor wasn't sure how to respond. The implications sent his entire world spinning. If the solar storms were cyclic, then only the creation of these Arks had kept the cycle of life moving. This explained the previous mass extinctions. The dinosaurs hadn't been wiped out by a meteor. They'd likely been killed by the sun.

"How does humanity survive?" Trevor asked. "There's no way they could live on the surface, not if things get as bad as what you're describing."

"You are an astute one," Ra said, beaming a brilliant smile. For once the razored teeth didn't bother him. "Humanity flees to the underworld. They take shelter in the bowels of the earth, waiting out the worst of the solar storms. Those storms will not be upon us for decades, but if humanity is not guided to safety by then, they will be annihilated."

Ra turned to face Anput, folding her arms across her chest. "Have you learned anything further about the burst of light?"

"No, mighty Ra," Anput said, dropping her head in apparent shame. "We have no idea what caused it. Something seized control of the Ark's systems, and not even Horus understands how or why. He does not believe Ka was involved, as the creature would have left some sign of its passage."

"You're talking about three pulses of blinding white light that fired up into the sky?" Trevor asked, with a sinking feeling.

"Just so," Ra said, shifting her attention to him. "You know of them?"

"A little," he admitted, combing his fingers through his goatee. "We experienced the same thing at the Ark of the Redwood. An entity we met in the Nexus, while pursuing Steve and Irakesh, claims the pulses were sent either by the Builders, or possibly something it referred to as their progeny. Can you show me the direction the pulses were fired in?"

"Of course," Ra said, closing her eyes for a moment. The perspective changed, showing a trio of pulses blasting into space from Northern Africa. It followed them into space, drawing a line in the direction they were fired.

"That path looks familiar," Trevor said, biting his lip. "I could be completely wrong, but they're aimed in the rough direction of a habitable planet my people recently discovered. We call it Kepler 425B."

Trevor would have continued, but metal cracked on stone as something large approached up the stairway they'd taken to reach the room.

"Mighty Ra," Wepwawet's towering form growled as he ducked into the room. "We are invaded. Isis has breached the light bridge with a small pack. Horus has gone to delay her."

Chapter 25- Horus

"Are you ready?" Blair asked, stepping onto the light bridge.

"Ready," Liz said, stepping up to join him. Her gaze was hard. Resolved. She'd come a long way from the timid doctor back in Peru.

"Before we depart I must offer one last warning," Isis said, stepping onto the disk. "When we arrive, whoever Ra has left in control will sense us immediately. It is my hope she will be willing to parlay, but we must assume they will respond with all the force they can muster. I will handle the greatest part of those enemies, giving you the time to reach the central chamber. From there you must light walk to Olympus."

"Yeah, I'm still a little unclear about that," Blair said, shaking his head. "What happens when we arrive? You're known to these Olympian gods, but they aren't going to respect us."

"True, but you are resourceful," Isis said, her features tightening. "I trust you to learn what we must know: whether the way to the underworld is open. If so, you must convince them to allow us passage. If not, you must find out why. Remember they will see you as standing higher than they. We are the true gods, they are merely sorcerers. They lack the virus, and are far weaker. Even an old god will think twice about attacking you."

"Why don't you go with us? If we're going to light walk I can grab you on the way out," Blair offered. He didn't like the idea of separating from Isis. They were dealing with incredibly ancient gods, and while he and Liz fought well as a team he doubted their ability to overcome gods who'd spent millennia learning to fight.

"Would that I could," Isis said, giving a sigh. She turned to Liz. "Keep him safe. I will join you when I can, but until then I must slow Ra's march, first to Olympus and then to The First Ark, should it come to that."

"How will you do that?" Liz asked, folding her arms underneath her breasts. "You're strong, but you're only one against many."

"True," Isis said, giving an encouraging smile. "But I will not be alone when I face Ra and her forces. I will turn one of her most potent weapons against her, a creature that devours entire armies. The Sand Kraken will not be enough to stop her, but it will force her to deal with it, or risk losing her army."

"And you can just control this thing?" Liz asked, more than a little dubiously.

"Of course," Isis said, blinking once. "I tamed it to begin with."

"You've made some really frightening things, Isis," Blair said, heaving a sigh. "I don't like anything about this plan, but I guess we don't have a lot of choice. If we're going to do this, then let's do this."

"Begin," Isis commanded. Blair met Liz's gaze. She gave a tight nod, squaring her shoulders.

He concentrated, willing the Nexus to activate the light bridge. There was a moment's hesitation, then brilliant light exploded around them. A moment later they stood on an identical bridge, though the room itself was different. The hieroglyphs here were much more numerous, and clearly created by a different hand.

Blair gawked openly at them. Egyptology had always been a passion, but his training in anthropology had carried him across the world. He'd worked with Mayan, Cambodian, Indian, and Welsh writing. He knew their stylistic differences, which was why he was so positive he was looking at the precursor to both the Sumerian and Egyptian languages. This room held proof that not only were the two cultures linked, but they had a common parent culture.

"Blair, focus," Isis's voice cracked. She'd already moved from the light bridge, shifting as she did. In the blink of an eye she was ten feet of silver-furred muscle. "Liz, I'm going to teach you a new ability. You can use the shadows to cloak those around you for short period of time. That should keep you safe until we know how we'll be received."

"I'd say it's too late for that, Mother," came a wry voice from the doorway. Shadow rippled, revealing a man of average height with a pair of golden spectacles. Well-muscled with bronzed skin and a hawk-like nose, he somehow managed to look like a scholar.

"Horus," Isis said, stretching out a hand towards the newcomer. Her voice was thick with emotion, and Blair saw tears in her eyes. "You survived the gulf of time. I was sick with worry."

"Worried that Ra would leave me to wither and perish?" Horus asked, taking a step into the room. He extended both hands, and his golden bracelets melted and flowed into his hands. A moment later he held twin weapons like large pickaxes, but with three blades each. They resembled the enormous talons of some bird.

"I don't claim to know her mind," Isis said, assuming a defensive stance. A look of infinite sadness passed over her face. She turned her head slightly toward Liz, but kept her eyes on Horus. "Draw Blair to your chest, then summon the shadows. Your beast will show you how. Be aware that the ability is taxing, so use it only as long as you must to reach the central chamber. I will tend to my son, with violence if necessary."

Horus blurred toward Liz, burying one of those massive talons in her gut. He flung her into the wall with bone shattering force, blood splattering his face. Blair saw red, shifting unconsciously even as he took his first step toward the strange deity.

"No," Isis snapped in Blair's direction. "Tend to Liz. Get her to the central chamber. This fight is beyond you."

Blair restrained himself, blurring to Liz's side. She'd already begun to heal, but he helped her to her feet anyway.

"He hits like a Mack truck," she grunted, spitting out a little blood.

"Get in my shadow, you can heal on the way," Blair said, watching Horus. The god stared cruelly at Isis, as the pair circled each other.

Liz flowed into inky tendrils of smoke, her body disappearing as she slid into his shadow. It no longer bothered him as it once had. If anything, it was reassuring. If they ran afoul of another god, maybe Liz could surprise him.

Blair blurred, as fast and hard as he could. He whipped past Horus, ducking under the casual swipe the god launched with one of his talons. Blair rolled out of the room, bounding off a wall as he blurred up the corridor. He knew the layout of this place intimately, having spent time in the Ark first in Peru, then later in San Francisco.

Blair continued up corridors, blurring past several slow-moving figures. From their garb he took them for servants, slow and nearly mindless deathless he didn't bother to dispatch. It was possible they could report to their masters, but he was hoping by the time they did he'd have activated the light bridge and carried Liz to safety.

Or potential safety anyway. He still had no idea what to expect at Olympus. The idea that it wasn't a mountain was exceedingly strange, and he found himself wondering again just what the place that had spawned so much legend was like.

Focus, Ka-Dun. You must tend to your surroundings, or you risk being ambushed by your enemies. The learning of secrets is laudable, but we've other prey this night.

Blair sighed, redoubling his pace as he leapt up a stairway in a single bound. The beast was right, but it still annoyed him to no end.

At long last Blair blurred up a familiar hallway, slowing as he approached the doorway. Faint light shone from within, and his breath caught as he started down the ramp into the central chamber. The place was markedly different from either of the other Arks he'd encountered. For starters, the walls glistened with golden hieroglyphs, but it went far beyond that.

Thick, plush carpet of the deepest scarlet led in a narrow path down the ramp to the base of a small set of stairs. The stairs led up to a throne that had its back set against the central obelisk, itself towering over both the throne and the rest of the room.

"You must be the Ka-Dun Irakesh warned us to expect," came a warm feminine voice. A figure melted from the shadows, coalescing into a pretty woman with dark hair bound in hundreds of tiny braids. She gave him a too-white smile, split by a pair of fangs. "Have you come to seize control of the Ark then, little wolf? A bold move, Ka-Dun."

She seemed friendly enough, but he knew she was likely lulling him into complacency. He'd have to deal with her if he expected to use the light bridge. That would take concentration for at least several seconds, and he doubted she'd allow him that time.

"You know who I am," Blair rumbled, circling the room to keep distance between them as he approached the central obelisk. "Do you have a name?"

"I am called Anput. As I understand it some legends of me survive, though they mistakenly think me some meek little servant of my husband," she said, taking several unhurried steps in Blair's direction. The movement kept her close to the obelisk.

"Your husband?" Blair blinked, recognizing her name. "You're married to Anubis?"

"I see you're familiar with the imaginative tales of our exploits," Anput said, giving a soft, feminine laugh.

"Maybe more so than anyone else in this age," Blair said, taking another cautious step toward the central obelisk. "I'm an anthropologist. I study the past, particularly legends of your age."

"Marvelous," Anput said, sauntering closer still. She had an athletic build, and from the graceful way she moved Blair was certain she was a fighter. "I'll be sure to visit your cell. We can talk often of these legends as we await Ra's return."

"Yeah I don't think that's going to work out," Blair rumbled, only a few steps from the stairs leading up to the throne.

"And what makes you think you can stop me from imprisoning you, little wolf?" Anput asked, delivering a truly alarming smile that made clear just who was the predator here.

"Because I didn't come alone," Blair grinned, ready for Liz to make her move.

"Neither did she," rumbled a voice from behind Blair.

Her turned to see the stuff of nightmares. The black-furred Jackal must be Anubis. The grey-furred wolf could be none other than Wepwawet, the stench of decay making Blair gag. Yet it was the woman behind them who turned his bowels to water.

A fiery-haired woman with toxic green eyes stalked past the others, her gaze seizing Blair like a wayward mother scooping up a toddler.

Chapter 26- Secret Meeting

Mark closed the door to his tiny room, listening for several tense moments to ensure no one was lurking outside. He'd spent the last two hours in the makeshift ops center Osiris had constructed here, ostensibly so he could learn the ropes enough to be placed in command.

Osiris seemed to place a great deal of trust in him, and had given him leave to hand-pick his command staff from anyone in Syracuse. It was all a little too neat, and he sensed there was more at play here.

Mark straightened his tie, then concentrated as Elle had instructed him. He'd practiced using the ability to move across the room, but he'd yet to try something as audacious as teleporting the three hundred yards to the surface.

He could end up in the middle of a wall, or back in ops. Elle claimed the risk was low, but any risk was more than he liked.

A wellspring of energy flowed up inside him, bubbling to the surface and begging to be harnessed. Mark guided that energy as he'd done previously, visualizing his destination. He picked a small stand of oaks just beyond the fence ringing the compound.

There was a sharp pop, then he was elsewhere. He blinked several times, eyes rapidly adjusting to the reduction in light. It was a cloudy night with no moon, which meant the area was dark as pitch. The complex had no external lighting, which he'd have ordered if they hadn't already been doing it. No sense letting enemies know anything of note existed here.

Mark surveyed the nondescript warehouse, with cracked paint and dirty windows. The place looked like it hadn't been used in years. Perfect camouflage.

He turned on his heel, trotting into the darkness. Mark's newfound powers ensured that he made no noise, and he found himself enjoying his rapid dash through the shadows. He had to be clocking at least twenty miles an hour, and it didn't tax him in the slightest.

"You came," a voice came from his right, and he nearly yanked the pistol from his jacket before he realized it was Elle. She materialized from the shadows near him, playful smile visible despite the limited light. "Follow me. It's not far. They're waiting."

Mark fell into an easy trot behind her, loping through the wet grass as they climbed a gentle slope. Elle leapt over a chain link fence, moving silently onto a residential street. Mark followed, carefully noting their path in case he needed to flee back the way they came.

Long minutes later, they arrived in front of a two story brick house with boarded-up windows. Elle rapped twice at the door, which opened immediately to reveal a scowling man with thick black eyebrows. He ushered them inside wordlessly, scowl deepening as he took in Mark.

"Rest are downstairs. Bring the whelp, and be quiet about it," he rumbled, closing the door and turning to peer through the peephole.

Mark's doubts grew louder. If their sentry was trying to keep watch through a peephole maybe these people weren't as impressive as Elle had made them out to be.

"Come on," Elle said quietly, tugging at his trench coat. She led him to a narrow white door, which revealed steep stairs that descended into darkness. She started down, so he followed.

They arrived in a spacious basement that was clearly the reason this house had been chosen. It had been cleared, and now held a half-dozen hastily erected card tables with mismatched computers. Several were in use, though the people using them were now staring fixedly at Mark.

"So you managed to lure the progeny out of Osiris's lair," a gravelly voice rumbled from the back of the room. A man with thinning grey hair rose from one of the tables, clutching at a simple black cane. "Welcome, Director Phillips. We are pleased to make your acquaintance."

"You know my name," Mark said, licking his lips. "How about you share yours?"

"Very well," the man said, delivering a cold smile as he clicked across the concrete to stand next to mark. He offered his free hand, which shook with age. "You may call me Acula. Doctor Acula."

"You have got to be kidding me," Mark said, raising an eyebrow.

"I told you it was terrible," Elle muttered, mostly under her breath.

The man let his hand fall, giving an apologetic smile. "I thought that if I must use an alias, I might as well chose an amusing one. We can't be too careful, until we're sure where your loyalties lie."

"They aren't with Osiris, if that's what you're thinking," Mark said, folding his arms. He surveyed the room with a critical eye. "Not with you, either, if this is the best you have to offer. I don't know what your plans are, but I can tell you they're going to fail. Osiris is a professional. You lot are amateurs."

"A sadly accurate assessment, I'm afraid," Acula said, frowning. He gestured at Elle with the hand Mark had refused. "Elle is one of our best— promising, but young. We lack resources, and are faced with an impossible task. We have to stop Osiris, before he destroys the world."

"I'd say you're a little late for that," Mark shot back, considering whether to start back up the stairs. He decided not to. Yet. "What's your real name, and who are you people?"

"Grandfather, tell him," Elle said, tone sharp. "He's going to leave if you don't offer him a reason not to."

"All right," the man said, adopting a shrewd look. "My name is Alaunus. Like you I was sired by Osiris, though my rebirth came a very, very long time ago. I served the man unquestioningly for centuries, until the world changed. When the sun robbed us of our powers, Osiris became a different man. Like the rest of us, he was forced to scavenge for power in order to survive, draining other gods, and artifacts of their precious strength.

"Somewhere along the way madness began to grow," Alaunus continued, sadness sliding over his features. Mark wasn't sure whether it was feigned or not. "Perhaps it was jealously of his brother, or perhaps he's simply lived too long. Regardless, Osiris concocted a plan to wipe out all life on this planet."

"So you and the Brady Bunch here decided you were going to stop him?" Mark snorted. "Where do I fit into this grand plan?"

"Osiris hasn't sired progeny since the last age," Elle said, resting a hand on Mark's. "You're his right hand. If you could feed us information, then maybe we can stop whatever he has planned."

Mark was silent for a long moment. Something didn't add up. If Osiris had to scavenge power in order to survive, what had this Alaunus needed to do? "I'll think about it. Give me a few days."

Alaunus and Elle shared a very alarming look, and Mark sensed movement behind him.

"Now that you know of our existence we can't let you leave," Alaunus said, straightening. All hint of the weak old man vanished. "I'm sure you understand."

Chapter 27- Parlay

Isis stalked the shadows, prowling the edge of the room as she sought some sign of Horus. It was a delicate game she played. If she didn't offer some sign of herself, then her son would likely assume she'd fled. If that happened, he'd head straight for the central chamber, very likely stopping Blair and Liz from light walking to Olympus. So she had to give him a sign.

"I am still proud of you, my son," Isis said, moving slowly through the shadows. "You have accomplished much, both in the last age and already in this one. Getting Sekhmet to carry you forward to the present is no mean feat, and it suggests she relies on your counsel. It gladdens me that you are a check on her rash behavior."

"Your opinion means little, Mother," Horus snapped. The voice came from the far side of the room. "You abandoned us. Abandoned me. You should be the voice checking Ra's violent nature. You should be guiding her and Father to a wiser course. Yet instead you fled to another continent and set up your own empire. You deserted us, and everything fell apart. Hypocrite."

It stung more than she'd expected, perhaps because she knew he was right. Isis could have stayed, could have argued longer and more loudly against the actions of Sekhmet, then later Osiris. Yet she hadn't. She'd taken the easy route, giving up here and starting over.

"I apologize, Horus. You are not wrong," she admitted, taking a cautious step from the shadows. Isis lowered her defenses, waiting. "If you wish to kill me I will not stop you. Come, vent your fury."

It was a calculated risk. She didn't truly believe her own son would kill her, but the truth was she barely knew the god he'd grown into. There was every chance Horus would end her life now. Yet Horus was her own offspring. She could not kill him, could not even harm him.

Long moments passed. Horus neither showed himself nor spoke. "Horus? My son, say something. I cannot bear this silence."

Nothing. Isis felt a moment of deep terror. Horus had tricked her. Even now he made for the central chamber, that had to be it. Isis blurred, leaping off walls and around corners as she desperately sought to reach the central chamber before her son.

Faster and faster she moved, at last skidding into the shadows just outside the doorway to the central chamber. Blair had reached it, but he wasn't alone. He knelt at the base of the stairs leading up to the First Throne, the one Isis had commissioned so many millennia ago to celebrate her near-sister's rule.

The woman had changed little, her face proud as she stared imperiously down at the Ka-Dun. Rendering judgement, as always. Her court was scattered about the room, some of more concern than others. Anput would flee. Anubis would fight, as would Wepwawet. Horus was no doubt lurking in the shadows as well. She couldn't fight them all.

"Sekhmet," Isis boomed, striding into the chamber. She shifted back, flowing into human form by the third step. Her pace didn't slacken, and she ignored the others as she passed them. Her attention was reserved for her near-sister. "I call for parlay. What say you?"

Sekhmet, or Ra as she styled herself, looked up in shock. Her eyes widened, and her mouth worked silently as she stared down at Isis. Isis merely waited, folding her arms across her breasts as she waited for Sekhmet to regain her composure.

"You send your pack to invade my Ark, not once, but twice. Then you have the temerity to ask for parlay?" Sekhmet said, leaning forward on her throne. She speared Isis with her gaze, and Isis knew a moment of terror. She quickly suppressed it. "Why shouldn't I slay you and your impudent pack? I already posses the key to your Ark, as you are no doubt aware."

"I have asked for parlay out of remembrance of the friendship we once shared. I honor the woman you *used* to be," Isis said, resisting the urge to shift. She extended her right hand, summoning the Primary Access Key. It flowed into her hand, strength welling up within her as it manifested. "I will say this but once. Accept parlay, or I will show you bloodshed the likes of which not even you have seen. You are a peerless warrior, Sekhmet. Yet you know I am the world's foremost shaper. Do you really wish to see what I can do? Your key to my Ark is meaningless. I can use the Primary Access Key to take yours from you right here and now."

Gasps rustled through the room like a hot breeze. The tension thickened as Sekhmet's court prepared themselves for battle. Younger members, like Irakesh, wore their confidence like armor. The older and wiser, like Anubis, grimly prepared for death. They'd heard legends of the weapon she held.

"Very well," Sekhmet finally said. She rose to her feet, descending the steps gracefully. "I grant your parlay, in remembrance of the woman *you* used to be." Sekhmet stopped before her, resting one hand on each of Isis's shoulders. She leaned forward, kissing one cheek, then the other.

Isis tensed, but there was no subterfuge here. That pleased her, as it showed that some part of her friend remained inside the cold, undead shell.

"The rest of you, leave us," Sekhmet said, waving a hand dismissively.

"What of the Ka-Dun?" Anubis rumbled, taking a threatening step toward Blair.

A golden sword materialized from the shadows, its blade pressed against the Jackal's neck. Liz leaned in close, growling loudly enough for the room to hear. "How about we leave him be, 'kay?"

Sekhmet laughed, turning back to Isis. "Your latest daughter has spirit. I like her. Anubis, Isis and her pack are now under the aegis of parlay. They have full guest right. Trevor, step forward."

Isis turned toward a figure she hadn't noticed, perhaps because he'd been cloaked in shadow. The flame-haired youth walked guiltily into the light, refusing to meet his sister's gaze.

"Yes, mighty Ra?" he asked.

"Escort the Ka-Ken and her Ka-Dun to your quarters. They may rest there until the parlay is concluded," she ordered, turning back to Isis once more. "Now near-sister, let us speak."

Chapter 28- Get in the First Shot

Liz eyed Trevor sidelong as he led them through the Ark, letting the silence linger until they entered the room that must belong to him. It was well-decorated, though it didn't match her brother at all. Of course neither did the strange flowing white clothing he wore, or the sword that now rode at his hip.

"You've changed a lot. It's only been a few days. What the fuck happened?" she asked, quietly in case there were other ears about.

"Uh," he said, more than a little sheepishly. "I've done what I had to in order to blend in."

"Mighty Ra?" Blair asked, his tone more than a little accusatory.

"Listen, I didn't have a lot of choice. It was either join the enemy camp and do what I can, or spend my time in a cell," Trevor snapped, eyes flaring green. "That's assuming they didn't just kill me outright, which was a very real possibility."

"Where is Jordan?" Liz asked, keeping her tone carefully neutral. Trevor had a defensive streak, and if they both ganged up on him they'd get nowhere.

Trevor avoided her gaze, pausing so long she nearly asked him the question again. He didn't look up when he finally spoke. "They put a collar on him, and gave me the bracelet that controls it. It's awful. He's…basically a slave. They let him roam free, but he can't shape, or change. He answers to me, I guess."

Liz, he's gone native. Or is going native. Blair's voice echoed in her head. *I'm not sure we can trust him anymore.*

"Did you speak up in his defense?" Liz asked, stalking to a chair and dropping into it. She tried to keep her tone level, but knew some accusation had crept in.

"No," Trevor said, hanging his head. He paused again, finally looking up at her. He was in anguish. "I can't, Liz. My position here is tenuous at best. Ra is learning to trust me, and she listens to my advice. I'm in a position to do some good. If I tried to free Jordan it wouldn't accomplish anything. They won't let him get away, and it would just weaken my position here."

"Trevor, you're a friend," Blair said, sitting in the chair next to Liz. He folded his hands in his lap. "I'm not passing judgement, but you have to see how this looks. They're assimilating you. You look different. You're acting different. The choices you're making aren't in the best interest of our pack, and you know that. If they were, you'd be asking us about escape right now. You're not. You're ready to do whatever Ra asks."

Trevor recoiled as if struck, but didn't reply. He looked helplessly at Liz, but all she could was avoid his gaze.

"Guys, I *am* different," he finally said, sitting on the edge of his bed. "I know we don't like to talk about it, but I'm deathless. I'm not a champion. Like it or not, these are my people. Maybe that means we're on opposite sides of a war, but we are different species. If we're lucky, Isis and Ra will hammer out some sort of agreement. If not, I'll do everything in my power to help you escape. But I'm staying. I can do some good here. I'm learning so much, growing stronger every day."

Liz felt a tear slide free, and wiped it brutally away. She rose restlessly, pacing the spacious chamber. "Do what you think is right, of course."

Blair looked askance at her, but she shook her head. She didn't want him delving Trevor's mind, coercing him in any way. If Trevor wanted to stay, well, he'd made his choice.

"You," Isis snapped, sweeping into the chamber. The comment was directed at Trevor, who rose nervously to his feet. "Out. Find somewhere else to be. Maybe Sekhmet will have space in her bed. Wherever you go, make sure it is out of earshot. If I detect you anywhere near this room I will end your miserable existence."

"I get it. I'll give you guys some space," he said, giving Liz a nod as he departed. His sandals clacked on the stone, growing distant after a few moments.

"You're back already?" Blair asked, rising to his feet and peering down the hallway after Trevor. He returned a moment later.

"The parlay was short. Sekhmet permitted a mindshare, providing I allowed certain safeguards. We communicated much in a short time," Isis said, looking more than a little distracted. If she'd been a cat her tail would have been twitching.

"So what happened?" Liz asked, listening to see if Trevor had remained. She seriously doubted it, as he hated eavesdropping. But who knew how much he'd changed?

"I explained to Sekhmet what I knew of the Nexus. She was as alarmed as I that the conduit had been severed," Isis explained, mouth going sour. "That was the end of our agreement. She, too, believes Osiris may be responsible. She wishes to marshall her armies and march immediately for Olympus, to recruit the gods there to wage war. I counseled caution. We do not know for certain Osiris is behind this, and even if he is we know nothing about his motives."

Isis shattered a porcelain vase with her fist, eyes flaring silver. "She called me a besotted fool. She thinks me unable to act, because of my feelings for Osiris. That led to a quarrel, and it did not end well. She suggested we continue in the morning, but I know her well enough to know that will accomplish nothing."

"Isis," Blair asked cautiously. "Why do you call her Sekhmet when everyone else addresses her as Ra?"

"It is a long tale, but I'll give it to you in brief," she said, obviously still agitated. "Sekhmet was part of my tribe, along with Osiris. We came to the Cradle many millennia ago, in pursuit of Set. When we arrived we found that a vast empire already existed here. They were called the Nubians, and they were led by a powerful god who called himself Ra. We didn't know exactly how old Ra was, but he was thousands of years older than us. He was immensely powerful, but through many struggles we eventually defeated him.

"Sekhmet adopted his mantle, changing her name and taking the Ark of the Cradle for herself. She set up her empire on the ashes of his, even continuing the same religion," Isis explained, features contorted in disgust. "I was horrified, and that began the rift between us, though we did not split for many more centuries. I will not address her by Ra's title, because she has no claim to it."

"I see," Blair said, quietly. "Thank you for explaining."

"You're planning on fleeing, aren't you?" Liz said, stopping her pacing and settling her attention on Isis's tiny form.

"I am," the goddess said, giving a quick nod. "We will follow through with the original plan. The two of you will light walk to Olympus, where you will contact Hades and learn where he and his brothers stand in all this. I will distract Sekhmet by seizing control of the Sand Kraken."

"Okay. I still don't like the plan, but we'll do as you ask," Liz said. She took a deep breath. "What about Jordan? He's here, and apparently Ra has enslaved him. Can we rescue him?"

"We cannot risk it," Isis said, shaking her head. "If we attempt it then Sekhmet will know what we intend. We must move swiftly. The Ka-Dun will have to fend for himself, at least for the time being."

Chapter 29- Saved

Mark took a single step backward, surveying the vampires encircling him. There were seven, all older, and more experienced than he was. He couldn't fight them, but he *could* run. Mark drew on the well of energy inside him, pulling up enough strength to teleport to the street outside. It built more swiftly than it had the last time he'd tried it, perhaps because of his desperation. Then the power shattered, evaporating like mist in the dawn.

"Did you really think it would be that simple?" Alaunus said, gripping the middle of his cane in one hand. He used the other to pull a long, slender blade. "We'd never have shown you the ability if we feared you using it to escape."

"How did you stop me?" Mark asked, mostly to play for time.

"You're little more than an infant," Alaunus sneered. He whipped the blade experimentally through the air. "It's a pity you couldn't be persuaded to join us."

"Grandfather, maybe we could give him another chance," Elle said, biting her lip. "Asking him to trust us immediately is difficult. He may just need time to see what we're about."

"It's too late for that," Alaunus said, shaking his head. His eyes narrowed. "We will not win his loyalty under duress, and if we keep him here to train him, then he'll never be able to go back. Osiris will know he's compromised, which would make him useless."

Mark considered arguing his case, but knew it was useless. So he attacked, launching a rabbit punch at the old man's gut. Alaunus flowed out of the way, backhanding Mark with the hand that held the cane. The blow sent Mark rolling into one of the tables, spilling the computer to the ground in a shower of sparks. He expected the others to fall on him, but none moved to do so. Apparently they were allowing Alaunus to execute him.

"At least I'll have the satisfaction of knowing your cause is doomed," Mark said, rising to his feet. He wiped blood from his mouth with the corner of his hand. "Your organization is pathetic, and I'm sure it's only a matter of time before Osiris wipes you out."

"That might be more difficult than you think," Alaunus replied, a predatory grin splitting his wrinkled face.

"I doubt it," came a rich tenor from the shadowed corner near the basement stairs. Dress shoes clicked on the concrete as Osiris stepped into the light, a silvery rapier clutched loosely in one hand. His eyes glowed with emerald power, and his mouth was tight with anger. "Director Phillips is right, Alaunus. Your organization is pathetic."

"How did you find us?" Alaunus asked, backpedaling toward the opposite wall as he glanced around the room in panic.

"Why do you think I finally sired progeny after waiting centuries?" Osiris said, taking another step into the room. His stance was fluid, something between a dancer and a soldier. "I created Mark so my enemies would see the opportunity, and attempt to turn him to their cause. I knew your group existed, though I confess I had no idea who was leading it. How did you survive, Alaunus? What did it cost you?"

"You used me," Mark snapped, stalking over to Osiris. "Why didn't you warn me?"

"Think it through, Director," Osiris replied, his gaze never leaving Alaunus. "I had no way of ensuring your loyalty. For all I knew you could have chosen to join Alaunus, and I'd have had to wipe you out too. I'm pleased it didn't come to that, but keeping you ignorant both allowed me to test you, and to guarantee you'd give this lot a convincing performance."

"Grandfather, what does he mean about you surviving?" Elle asked, gaze shifting between Osiris and Alaunus. Mark stifled his anger, taking a step closer to Osiris.

"Yes, grandfather, why don't you tell her who you really are? How you survived into this age?" Osiris said, slowly circling the tables to a more open section of the basement. Mark followed, keeping Osiris between himself and the others.

"A necessary fiction, Elle," Alaunus said, glancing at her briefly. "I am much older than I pretended. I walked the earth during the last ice age, when Ark Lords like Osiris ruled us. I was one of the first progeny—"

Osiris blurred, his sword carving a line of light in the air as he separated a woman's head from her body. He glided through their ranks, carving like a butcher. The vampires scattered, some wearing a look of concentration. Alaunus was one of them. He eyes narrowed, and he gritted his teeth as Osiris carved through his compatriots. There was a sharp swelling of shadow around him, and then he was gone.

"Blast it," Osiris snarled, dispatching another vampire. Only Elle remained now. He turned his attention on her, then to Mark. "Can she be trusted?"

"I don't know," Mark said, eyeing Elle critically. "I think so, but I can't guarantee it."

"What do you have to say for yourself, girl?" Osiris demanded.

Elle merely stood there, eyes wide as she surveyed the room full of bodies. "He abandoned us. I can't believe he just left."

"Elle," Mark snapped. That finally drew her attention. She looked at him, then paled when she turned her gaze on Osiris.

"If I let you live, what will you do?" Osiris said, taking a threatening step forward.

"I'll flee," she said in a small voice. "I won't oppose you again. How can I? You've wiped us out, and Grandfather deserted us."

"Good," Osiris said, giving a quiet nod. "Know this: I am not the monster he painted me to be. Leave here in safety, and try to find a place where you can weather the coming storm. I'd make it far from England, the further the better."

Elle gave a grateful smile, then swirled into the shadows as Alaunus had done.

Mark was silent for a long moment before leaving. "Why did you let her live?"

"Because I truly believe she's innocent in this. Alaunus manipulated this entire nest, convincing them I was the true threat," Osiris said, flicking the blood from his sword. He withdrew a white handkerchief from the breast pocket of his suit, wiping down the blade.

"You let Alaunus go, didn't you?" Mark asked. If Alaunus could block him from teleporting, then it stood to reason Osiris could have done the same.

"I did," Osiris said, eyeing Mark thoughtfully.

"Why?"

"Because he will report back to his true master, Set," Osiris explained, resting the tip of his sword against the concrete. "He will tell Set he overpowered my shield, which may lead Set to believe me weaker than I am. Set will also assume that I believe I've purged my organization of spies. I haven't, but it is best he not know that."

"So what happens now?" Mark asked.

"We ready ourselves for war."

Chapter 30- Light Walk

Liz gasped as the shadows flowed around Blair, pulling him closer. They were colder than she'd expected, numbing her skin as they washed over her fur.

"Well done, Ka-Ken," Isis whispered from a neighboring shadow. "As I said, it will be taxing, but you can bring your Ka-Dun to the central obelisk undetected. From there you can light walk to Olympus."

"Won't the Ark be locked?" Blair asked, his voice curiously disembodied.

"I will unlock the Ark's defenses. Sekhmet will sense that immediately, and send minions to deal with me. She may even face me herself," Isis explained. Her voice was moving closer to the door. Liz trailed after. "Use that distraction to escape. Light walking will only take a moment. By the time she feels you it will be too late. But be swift, or risk losing the shadows before you arrive."

"We're going," Liz-wolf rumbled. She quickened her pace, sprinting up the corridor. Carrying Blair was taxing, and more than just physically. It drained her energy, the reservoir she'd been building over the last several weeks. So many nights basking under the moon, and all of it would soon be gone if she wasn't swift enough.

They crossed a familiar maze of corridors, passing silently by undead servants until they reached the central chamber. The room was dim, only the faint glow of the obelisks providing illumination. The throne was empty, its vast black expanse still somehow threatening. There was no movement in the room, not even the stirring of air. It appeared the place was deserted.

"Okay, do your stuff," Liz whispered, releasing Blair. He slid from the shadows, stumbling forward until he caught himself.

"On it," he said, weaving like a drunken sailor as he made his way up the steps toward the central obelisk. He stood on the throne, reaching above it to touch the obelisk.

"You seek to depart already? Was our hospitality not to your liking?" a feminine voice said. A moment later Anput emerged from the shadows at the base of the throne, her wicked smile revealing a pair of fangs as she swayed her way up the stairs toward Blair.

Liz disliked her immediately. She'd known other women like her, the kind that drew every male eye in the room. They knew it, too. Used it to get whatever they wanted. She felt a low growl growing in her chest, but stifled it. Anput didn't know she was here. Yet.

"And you're here to stop me?" Blair said, turning to face her. His hackles rose, and he bared his teeth. Liz would never have a better chance.

She darted forward, ramming her claws through the small of Anput's back, while savaging the tiny woman's neck with her fangs. Cold, brackish blood showered the marble, but a moment later the god melted into tendrils of dark smoke. She flowed into the shadows and was gone. Liz did the same, nostrils twitching as she hunted for a scent.

Careful, Ka-Ken. This is no mere deathless. You face one of Osiris's get. They are more cunning, more subtle than those you have faced.

"Keep her off me," Blair said, turning back to the obelisk. He planted a hand against it, closing his eyes in concentration. Liz didn't know how long he needed, but she knew Anput would strike before he completed whatever he was about.

"Wait," came a melodic voice. Tendrils of smoke began flowing together, until a figure stood next to Blair. She wasn't more than a few feet away, but hadn't made a threatening gesture yet.

Liz didn't wait. She charged, bursting from the shadows in a whirl of fangs and claws. Anput vanished, her voice suddenly behind Liz. "Please. You're accessing the light bridge. To do that you need an access key. The only way your key would be recognized is if someone had first disabled the Ark's defenses. That can only be done with a Primary Access Key."

Blair didn't stop, and Liz could feel energy gathering around him.

"I can help you deal with the gods of Olympus," Anput burst out.

Blair paused, opening his eyes and staring at Anput. "What makes you think we're going there?"

"Neither Isis nor Ra would be foolish enough to march on the First Ark without first knowing the fate of Olympus," Anput said, relaxing. "It makes sense that she'd send an emissary."

"What can you tell us of Olympus?" Liz asked, neither confirming nor denying Anput's assumption.

"During our age, Olympus was one of the few strongholds to maintain independence from Ra," Anput explained. She peered at the shadows near Liz, as if searching. "Zeus was their leader, but it is Hades that Ra will seek. He was given charge of the underworld, which meant he was the only member of their pantheon with direct access to the Well. He will know why the conduit has been severed. He may even be the one who severed it."

It matches the little Isis has told us. Blair's thoughts echoed in Liz's head again.

"I realize you have little trust for me, but please listen," Anput said, straightening. She raised her hands, palms facing them. "I have nothing to gain in battling you. At best, I kill or subdue you. What then? I gain little prestige from defending Ra's Ark. If I let you go, then I gain favor with Isis. That will very much please my father."

"Your father?" Liz rumbled. She knew she was cloaked in the shadows, but she moved after speaking any way. It couldn't hurt.

"Osiris," Blair interjected, taking a step closer to Anput. "The husband of Isis. It sounds like you have a complicated family history. You want to score points with Isis? Let us be about our work. We use the light bridge, and then we're out of your hair."

"Done," Anput said, giving a tight nod that set the beads in her hair to clacking.

"Just remember, if you attack Blair while he is shaping I'll scatter your damned entrails all over the Ark," Liz rumbled. She summoned Excalibur, settling the flat of the blade against Anput's throat.

"Where did you get that weapon?" Anput said, gasping in obvious recognition.

"Does it matter?" Liz said, pressing the blade a little tighter against the woman's throat. "I have it. Let that be enough."

"Yes it matters," Anput hissed, eyes narrowing. "That is my father's blade, bonded to him since time immemorial. He'll come for it, I assure you. Take care, little pup, my father is not as forgiving as I am."

Chapter 31- First Born

Isis blurred through the Ark, passing through a seemingly endless array of dark stone corridors. She knew the place intimately, and arrived at the repository within seconds. The giant aquamarine dominating the valley below drew a pained breath from deep within her chest. The first virus had been concocted in a room just like this, so many millennia ago.

"I knew you'd come, Mother." Horus's voice came from behind her, smug and angry all at the same time.

She turned to face him. Emotion overcame Isis as she stared at her eldest son. It had been countless millennia since last she'd embraced him, but she still remembered his first tottering step. Still remembered how proud and amazed she'd been at the miracle of his birth. She and Osiris had labored for decades to change his physiology enough to have children, and Horus had been the fruit of that labor.

"We do not have to be at odds, Horus. Step aside. Allow my pack and I to leave," she rumbled, assuming a defensive stance.

Horus merely watched her for long moments. His shaved skull still looked odd, as she remembered the thick mane of dark red hair he'd worn in his youth. His bronzed skin was the same, as were the tri-talons he wielded. She still remembered his discovery of the weapons, in the dark corners of Nubia.

"By invading the Cradle, you have placed us at odds," Horus snarled, eyes narrowing. He took a threatening step forward. "You agreed to leave these lands forever, to stay on the jungle continent to the south. We'd have left you to it, if you abided by the oath you swore to uphold."

"Things have changed, my son," she said, softly. Isis took a step backwards, trying to appeal to his reason again. "The Well has been disconnected from the Nexus. We do not know who controls the First Ark, but whoever it is threatens us all. It may not be your father, whatever Sekhmet has told you. Even were that not the case, you must surely have felt the surge of light that was broadcast from this place. Someone sent a signal to the Builders, and we need to learn the cause."

Horus cocked his head, considering. Then his gaze hardened once more. "If these things are true, you should have parlayed with Ra, yet instead you are sneaking away. You came for your own reasons, as always. I do not know what your true goal is, but I have sworn to defend this place, and I will do it. Return to your quarters, or I will do as I must."

"Oh, Horus," she sighed, shifting into wolf form. She loomed over him, though she wasn't foolish enough to believe her height provided much advantage to one with his peerless speed. "Please do not force a confrontation. I do not wish to hurt you."

"Hurt me?" Horus laughed. "You think because you can assume this bestial form you frighten me? I battled Set when you and Father were powerless to stop him. I was accorded the mightiest warrior of the final age, as you well know. You are powerful, Mother, but don't think your sorcerous tricks will avail you here. This will be a test of combat, and you know you will lose such a contest."

"I am not the same woman you knew, Horus," Isis said, the first pangs of anger stirring in her gut. She extended her left hand and commanded the staff to reveal itself. Gold flowed down her forearm, pooling as it extended into the Primary Access Key. "I have spent millennia fighting, since you last knew me. I am a stronger warrior than you, or your father. As you are about to learn."

Horus leapt skyward, transforming as he did so. Isis blurred, taking a single step backward toward the bronze railing as she readied her defenses. Her son was fast, perhaps the fastest being alive. But he was also predictable. He'd grown too used to surprising his enemies.

Feathers leapt from his skin, and there was a flash of gold as the tri-talons melded with skin. When the transformation was complete a massive falcon dived at her, six golden talons flexing as they sought flesh. She allowed them to find purchase on her shoulder—perhaps *allowed* was a generous term. She wasn't fast enough to stop it, even blurring as she never had.

The talons dug into her flesh, as Isis shot out her free hand. She seized Horus by his feathered throat, slamming his body into the black marble walkway with as much force as she could muster. Bones broke in an explosion of feathers and blood. Isis did not relent. The fight had just begun, and her only chance was overwhelming force.

She swung the Primary Access Key down in a tight arc, the weapon humming through the air as it descended towards the falcon's head. It struck stone as the bird hopped away, shifting back into a man on the third hop. Horus spun, circling her as his eyes narrowed.

"You've grown stronger, it's true," he said, wiping blood from the corner of his mouth. His wounds were already healing. "Yet I am faster. Do not think the access key will save you. I will strip that lofty weapon from your corpse, Mother."

Isis blinked in surprise. It was in that moment she finally understood the stakes. If she hoped to survive, she'd have to kill her first born. So be it. She concentrated, summoning power from the Ark through her staff. Horus blurred, launching an aerial attack. He came down with both tri-talons extended, and she knew there was no way she could dodge. So she didn't.

Again, Isis allowed the weapons to find her flesh. They tore into her shoulders, biting deeply as they sought her heart. She ignored the pain, ignored the greater pain of what she was about to do. Isis summoned still more energy, pulling in as much as she could drink from the Ark. Then she released it in a blinding pulse of blue light. It exploded out from every pore, boiling away everything it touched. Flesh, stone, bronze—it all ceased to exist as the wave passed over it.

Horus gave a single scream, so like the falcon he'd come to resemble.

Then the light finished its work, and he ceased to exist. Isis fell to her knees, sobbing bitterly.

Your pain is unendurable, Ka-Ken. Yet we have work to be about. We must wake the worm.

Chapter 32- To War

Jordan slipped on his sunglasses as he emerged into the wall of heat. He'd spent a long time in the gulf, so Cairo's oppressive sun wasn't anything new. He still hated it though, and it shocked him that this was supposed to be the cradle of humanity. It was a damnably hot place to have set up the first city. Hot and dusty. His lips were dry and cracked, his skin continuously burning in the blistering sun.

"Come on, the army is departing soon," Trevor said, starting towards a line of immense beasts clustered about fifty yards outside the Ark.

The leathery-skinned creatures looked a great deal like mammoths, but instead of shaggy fur they had something closer to the thick hide of an elephant. They were far, far too large to be that, though. They towered over him; their tusks were easily a dozen feet of dense ivory. Each had a huge brown wicker basket on its back, outfitted with palm fronds for shade. Each basket was large enough to hold maybe eight people, and a rope ladder dangled from the base.

Jordan started after Trevor, eyeing the sword now belted at the man's side. It should have looked out of place, but it rode there like an extension of Trevor's body. That wasn't the only change, either. Trevor had abandoned his jeans and t-shirt, and now wore the strange flowing white garments favored by most of the gods in Ra's pantheon. In short, the fucker had gone native.

Jordan had tried experimenting with the collar the night before, but any attempt to remove it resulted in an electric shock that left him twitching on the ground. He could move of his own accord, but the farther he got from Trevor the more pressure built up in his skull. Anything beyond a few hundred yards, and he developed a splitting migraine. Of course, that might actually be worth it to avoid the stench of elephant dung mixed with rotting flesh.

Trevor shimmied up the rope, pausing about halfway up. Jordan turned to see what had drawn Trevor's attention, squinting at the glare even through his sunglasses. "Holy. Fuck."

Thousands upon thousands of corpses stood in neat, even rows. They covered the entire plain, from the Ark all the way to the muddy waters of the Nile. If they were anything like a modern army, he'd guess a dozen regiments or more.

He turned back to the elephant, when a plopping sound came from his right. The beast had just deposited a pile of shit roughly the size of a Subaru near Jordan. Lovely. He held his breath, climbing the rope after Trevor. They'd nearly reached the basket when Trevor stopped and turned again. Jordan followed his gaze, and suddenly understood why Trevor had paused. A dozen massive zombies towered over their smaller brethren. They were misshapen and ugly, not quite human-shaped any longer. Their mouths were too large, their eyes too far apart. Their skin was a hodge podge of colors, as if they'd been made from hundreds of different people all glued together.

"What the fuck are those?" Jordan muttered, mostly to himself.

He was surprised when Trevor paused, leaning down the ladder to face him. His eyes were the same muted green as Irakesh's, his teeth just as horrendous as ever. "They're called Anakim. You encountered one, though it was a lot smaller. Remember the giant zombie in Panama? Irakesh made it to slow you down. Ra's been growing these things for a lot longer. Let's hope Blair and Liz don't end up having to fight them."

Jordan didn't answer, following as Trevor disappeared into the basket. It was interesting that Trevor was still thinking about Blair and Liz. That surprised him, at least a little. It didn't change how he felt, though. Right now Trevor might be trying to stay normal, to be loyal to his friends. But Jordan had seen Stockholm syndrome. He'd watched troops gradually assimilate into foreign armies. It was a tactic Mohn had employed often. It might take time, but Trevor's loyalty *would* shift to Ra.

Not that it mattered, really. Even if Trevor was completely loyal to their pack, it was unlikely he'd be able to do anything to help himself, much less Jordan. They were watched constantly, especially by the Jackal. On top of that, Irakesh clearly nursed a singular hatred for Trevor, which meant he and Steve were watching them at all times as well.

Take heart, Ka-Dun. Time flows on a scale you have yet to comprehend. Even if it takes years, you will have your freedom. The collar mutes your abilities, but it does not stop them entirely. You can shape, and the more you strain at your bonds the stronger you will grow.

That drew a grim smile from Jordan. He'd simply treat this like working out. The time would come for him to make his move, and when it did he'd be ready. It wouldn't take years, either. He'd be free before he knew it.

Chapter 33- Hades

"Holy. Shit," Blair said, jaw dropping open as he gaped up at the sky. A torrent of competing thoughts rushed through his mind, because what he was seeing explained so much of the history of the western world.

"What the hell is that?" Liz asked, shading her eyes as she stepped up next to Blair along the trail. Each step sent up little puffs of dust, and Blair waved them away absently.

"That has to be Olympus," he replied, studied the shimmering city high above. It flickered and danced in the sky, maybe a mile above the stunted hills around them. The fluted columns and heavy marble architecture would have been at home in Rome, though this was clearly beyond anything the ancient Romans had created. Clouds boiled all around the base, shot through with veins of pink, gold, and red. It reminded him of a sunrise, though this particularly sunrise was created by the floating city.

He'd guess there were two or three dozen structures, ranging from temples to a colosseum. There were even houses—well, mansions, actually. If he were a god, this was definitely where he'd want to live. "How the hell is it hovering there?"

"You're the shaper; you tell me. It's like the frigging cloud city from *Empire Strikes Back*. What was it called? Bespin," Liz replied, fishing her sunglasses from her pack and sliding them over her eyes. She added a green baseball cap a moment later, tucking her hair through the back in a simple pony tail. "Why does it keep shimmering like that? It's like a mirage."

"I don't know," Blair said, shaking his head slowly. He could feel something each time the city shimmered. It would disappear for a split second, and he would feel an absence. When it returned he could feel it, like the sunrise on his face. "A better question is: how are we going to get up there? I'm guessing that's what Isis meant when she said Olympus."

"I thought it was *Mount* Olympus. Where's the mountain?" Liz asked.

"It is," Blair said, starting up the trail. At the very least they could get to higher ground and get a look around them. A number of monuments had been unearthed and, given what he could see, Blair had a suspicion he knew exactly where they were. "The Greeks claimed their gods lived on Mount Olympus. It's not even the highest mountain in Greece, but it is a real place. My guess is they created it in remembrance of this place. Their ancestors probably worshiped here."

They made their way to the top of the hill, and by that time the sun had plastered their clothing to them in a thick layer of sweat. It was definitely over a hundred degrees. It might have been a hundred and ten.

"What's that city?" Liz asked, pointing at a series of ruined buildings below them. None stood more than two stories, but the complex was massive. Far larger than man should have been able to construct before agriculture.

"That's Gobekli Tepe," Blair said, scrambling down the trail as he made his way toward the ruins. He slid down some gravel, catching himself as he made it to even ground. "These are, so far as we know, the oldest human ruins in the world. They're from about nine thousand BCE, well before man had learned to farm or build permanent settlements. The anthropological community teaches that we were nothing more than hunter-gatherer tribes back then. It was the tail end of the Pleistocene, the last ice age."

"Weren't we cave men back then? Like the Cro-Magnon?" Liz asked, tucking her hat low to block the sun as she scanned the structures.

"That's what universities teach, but this place proves that theory wrong," Blair replied, starting towards a pillar just a few dozen yards ahead. "See these animals? There's a fox, a cow, that's probably a raven. There are a couple I don't recognize that are likely extinct. This kind of iconography shouldn't have been possible, but clearly it was."

"So what do you think happened?" Liz asked, leaning close to examine the pillar.

"Well, so far as we know, this complex was used for about two thousand years, then in about seven thousand BCE it was deliberately buried. We don't know by who, and we haven't the faintest idea why," Blair explained, walking slowly around the pillar. "It's a good thing, though. Otherwise this place would never have survived."

"The fact that it sits right beneath a floating city certainly seems suggestive," Liz said, peering back up at the shimmering city. "I'm not an anthropologist, but it doesn't seem like the dates line up, though. From what we understand the Arks submerged around eleven thousand BCE right?"

"I can see where you're going with this, and you're right," Blair said, peering up at the city himself. "If the dating is accurate, this place was built two millennia after the Arks disappeared. If that's the case, maybe they could still see that city. That would definitely explain why they went through so much effort to build it here. Can you imagine what that place would have looked like to primitive cultures?"

Be wary Ka-Dun, we are no longer alone, the beast rumbled.

Blair spun, looking for whatever had alarmed it. A figure stepped from behind one of the buildings, a man with long white hair in dark blue robes. He wore golden slippers completely unsuited to the hot gravel, and leaned heavily on a gnarled wooden stick a little taller than he was. If he'd been wearing a hat he would have given Ian McClellan a run for the part of Gandalf in the *Lord of the Rings*.

"You are the first to come here since the sky turned," the man called in a quavering voice. He started down the path towards Blair, tottering like he might fall at any moment. "Judging by your companion's hasty departure, I'm guessing you're either of Isis's bestial get, or perhaps that of Osiris. Am I correct?"

Blair realized for the first time that Liz had disappeared. Good on her. She'd probably gotten into position to attack, which very well might save their lives. There was *no way* this was just some kindly old man. No god they'd run into was benevolent, not even Isis.

"We're champions of Isis," Blair said, shading his eyes as he moved to meet the man. He concentrated for a moment, feeling for the na-kopesh he'd taken from Irakesh when they'd beaten him. The weapon was there, melded with his body and waiting to be called. Blair didn't really have much idea how to use it, but the sword still gave him comfort. "I'm Ka-Dun Blair. Who are you?"

"I am known by many names," the man said, giving a gap-toothed smile. Every part of him looked harmless, except for the steely grey eyes. "You would know me as Hades, I think."

Blair blinked a few times, considering the legends he'd heard. Supposedly Hades was bound to the underworld, though clearly that couldn't be the case if he was standing before them. "Isis sent us to negotiate with you. We're, uh, emissaries I guess."

"I see," Hades said. He gestured weakly at a neighboring building that might once have been a temple. "Perhaps we could get out of this hot sun? I enjoy it no more than you do."

That was an interesting tidbit. Deathless drew strength from the sun, and they didn't sweat. Hades had a clear sheen across his brow, and seemed to be genuinely suffering in the heat.

"Of course," Blair said, following the elderly man inside the temple. It was a single story adobe building. One corner of the roof had caved in, and whatever drawings had once adorned the walls were long stripped by time.

Hades stopped in a corner, sitting atop a large rock that had fallen from the roof. He propped his staff beside him, then wiped the sweat from his brow before finally turning his attention back to Blair. "So, you claim Isis sent you. Why did she not come herself?"

How much do you think I should tell him? Blair thought at Liz. It wasn't difficult pinpointing her location, just a few feet to his right in the shadow cast by the crumbling wall.

Well, the Mother did tell us to strike a deal. I guess we should be honest about why we're here and what we're after.

"An interesting trick, that," Hades said, raising a thick snowy eyebrow. "You can communicate with the Ka-Ken despite not being able to see her. That's something I haven't seen before."

"Isis sent us to find out what's happening with the Well," Blair said, ignoring the god's comment about his ping ability. "The conduit to the Nexus has been severed, and it is in danger of collapse."

"Interesting," Hades said, folding his arms across his robes and leaning back against the wall. He coughed once, wiping the back of his hand across his mouth before continuing. "And just what does she think I can do about it?"

"According to Isis, you're one of only two gods with direct access to the Well," Blair said. He looked about for a place to sit, but didn't spot a comfortable perch. Damn, but it was hot. "From what I gather, there's a portal here leading to a place she calls the underworld."

"Do you know what the underworld is, Ka-Dun?" Hades asked, clearly amused.

"I have our legends to go by, but they're clearly based on mythology. If there is any truth to them, the underworld is where souls go when bodies die. The Egyptians believed Osiris was the caretaker of the underworld. The Greeks believed you were."

"Both are right, after a fashion," Hades said, rolling one shoulder as he massaged his forearm. "The underworld is the world under ours, hence the name. Spirits don't go there. So far as we know there is no such thing as a spirit. I suspect the legends arose from the armies of the dead that both Osiris and I accumulated over the millennia. Before he went mad, that is."

"Osiris went mad?" Blair asked, blinking.

"Indeed," Hades continued with a nod. "He was once the best of the gods, not just the first, but the most just and most powerful. After the Arks went into hibernation he changed. In a few centuries he grew callous, far more concerned with his own survival than that of his people or of the gods who would one day return. He began a campaign to seize the underworld.

"I resisted at first. I am not without power, after all. Yet I was doomed from the first. Osiris had direct access to the well, you see. He could use the First Ark to create endless soldiers. Demons of exquisite power. I was left with my paltry forge, manned by one of my few surviving companions. You'd know him as Vulcan, I think," Hades explained. He paused, watching Blair. "Or perhaps Hephaestus?"

"I'm familiar with both names. Vulcan is the Roman god of the forge," Blair offered. He was less familiar with Roman lore, but he'd studied it for a semester once upon a time. "So you have a forge of some kind, and you were battling Osiris?"

"Indeed," Hades continued, immersed in the tale again. "Osiris encroached further and further upon the underworld. From the frozen north to the distant east, he launched a campaign of conquest. My army of the dead was shattered, as were those of every other surviving ruler. In the end my connection to the Well was severed, and I was left to my own devices. This occurred roughly four thousand years ago, and I have been losing strength ever since. That is what has brought me to the wretched state you see before you. Now that the true energy we thrive upon has returned, I am growing in strength, but it will be months before I am hale and able to fight again."

"So Osiris conquered the underworld, and you were stranded up here?" Blair asked, trying to digest the information. The idea that early human mythology was rooted in fact still floored him, and he wasn't sure how close it lay to the truth.

"He is a treacherous snake, and while I do not know what he intends for this new world, it is clear we will not enjoy it," Hades said, offering a sigh. "Without the conduit to the Well, I cannot fully return Olympus to this dimension. Those of my brothers who took shelter there are trapped, if they survived at all once the conduit was severed."

That gave Blair pause as he considered the ramifications. If Osiris were truly trying to conquer it made sense. Lock away the Greek gods and cut their power supply. Then your only competition would be the returning Ark Lords.

Thunder rolled across the sky behind them, ominous and distant. Blair glanced through the hole in the roof, but the sky remained an unbroken blue.

Chapter 34- Training

Mark felt strange wearing the nylon body suit. It wasn't at all like the tailored suits he preferred; it was too tight and far less professional. Seeing Osiris wearing a similar one was just as jarring. One of the few things they had in common, other than both being vampires, was their taste in clothing. Osiris had a wardrobe most billionaires would envy.

"I've had basic combat training," Mark said, shifting his stance as he prepared to launch another grapple. He glided forward, but Osiris flowed around the attack like a cat that didn't want to be petted.

"Indeed, but that training was for and against mortals," Osiris said, tapping Mark on the chest with a finger. "You need to learn to think differently, to anticipate abilities other supernaturals will employ. Try again."

Mark did. He rushed forward, ducking lower and aiming a kick at Osiris's knee. Osiris exploded into mist, solidifying the instant Mark's blow had passed harmlessly through. He lunged, tapping Mark on the chest again. "Deathless, champions, and vampires all have their respective abilities. Some overlap, some do not. You need to learn each, and learn how to counter them. Again."

Mark gritted his teeth, but obligingly launched another attack. This time he sent a right hook at Osiris's jaw. Osiris vanished, but Mark had expected it. He summoned his energy, willing himself to vanish. Mark reappeared behind Osiris, triumphantly kicking at the back of his knee. His foot passed through…nothing. It was an illusion.

Osiris reappeared, tapping him on the back this time. "You are still thinking linearly, but that was much better. Let's take a break."

"Are you sure?" Mark said, rolling his shoulder. The motion was instinctive. An old injury that bothered him in life. "I'm happy to keep going."

"Training is as much visualization as it is muscle memory," Osiris explained, walking to the edge of the training mat. "The best way to learn is to study one concept, then master it. Spend time thinking about what we've discussed, then we'll try again tomorrow."

"That's fair," Mark said, moving to join Osiris. He tugged off his gloves. "I just wish I was progressing faster."

"So do I," Osiris sighed. "But we can't simulate centuries of training, not in a few days anyway."

"The data we accumulated suggested that your kind, our kind I guess, has the ability to ingest memories," Mark offered. There had to be a reason Osiris hadn't suggested it, but Mark was too curious not to bring it up.

"That's a dark path, Mark," Osiris said, frowning. "You can ingest the memories of others, but it muddies your personality. Changes you in small ways. I avoid it at all costs, and haven't done it in centuries. Trust me, it's a line you don't want to cross."

That took Mark aback. He removed his knee pads, dropping them on the table next to his gloves. Osiris had done the same, and was tugging off his shirt. To Mark's surprise his chest was littered with scars, dozens of them.

"Earlier you mentioned going to war. I know you're waiting for Set to make a move, but I don't get why. Wouldn't a preemptive strike make more sense?" Mark asked. He tugged off his own shirt, then shucked off the tight nylon pants. Once he'd added them to the pile, he pulled on his dress shirt.

"It would, if it were possible," Osiris said, shaking his head. He expertly tied his tie, a black silk affair that had probably cost as much as most people's cars. "The Ark is all but impregnable, so we can't make a move until Set comes out. He won't do that until he thinks we're vulnerable."

"Ahh," Mark said. "That's why you let Alaunus go."

"Precisely," Osiris nodded. "Set will smell blood in the water, and soon he'll come for us."

Chatper 35- Olympus

"We must seek shelter," Hades said, rising to his feet as he peered out at the sky.

"Shelter from what?" Liz asked. She finally emerged from the shadows, still in human form. This god looked harmless enough, but they'd yet to meet someone from the old world who wasn't both incredibly powerful and cunning beyond measure.

You learn swiftly, Ka-Ken. This one is the kin of Zeus. It was they who overthrew the titans and laid dominion to these lands. Mortal sorcerers with unlimited ambition.

"From the coming sunstorm. It will be upon us soon, and this one will be bad. It could last days," Hades explained. He'd begun limping into the shadows, and for the first time Liz realized something was cleverly hidden there. A stairwell leading down.

"Blair?" she asked, turning to face him. He looked just as puzzled as she felt. If anyone would know about these sunstorms it would be Trevor, though of course he wasn't here.

"Ra is coming here, if Isis is correct," Blair said, directing the comment to Hades. "If we're trapped for days, she'll be on us when we try to leave. Assuming she doesn't just follow us."

"Ahh, I should have known," Hades replied, giving a low chuckle. He stopped on the top step, turning to face them. "You've few choices then. Does Isis seek to stop Osiris in his mad quest for power?"

"I believe she does," Liz said. She was certain it was true. From what she understood, Osiris had been Isis's husband once, but that was millennia ago. Now it seemed like they were enemies, and if they weren't before, they would be when Isis learned what he'd been doing in the underworld. "If he severed the conduit, then he's the reason the Nexus is failing. She'll want to stop him for that reason, at the very least."

"Very well," Hades said, giving a sober nod. "Follow me. I will grant you access to a slipsail. It can carry you swiftly away from here, though in return I must ask a great favor. If you do not dally, you may beat the storm's arrival, thus evading capture. I would advise that, as Ra is not known to be merciful to prisoners."

"What about you?" Blair asked, starting down the stairwell after Hades. "She's coming here. She'll be asking a lot of the same questions we are. Aren't you worried?"

"About Ra?" Hades asked, scoffing. "Bah, she'll leave me be. The woman is power-mad, but she's no fool. She'll see the threat posed by Osiris, and will want to stop him at all costs. She might even be willing to make peace with Isis to do it."

They headed deeper and deeper, Hades growing visibly tired as their journey continued. The only sound was the dripping of water, so odd below the desert. That, and their muffled footfalls scuffing the stone.

"We are nearly there," he said at last, pausing to rest on his staff. "In the next chamber we will find the slipsail dock. Have you ever used a slipsail?"

"No," Liz replied, circling Hades to get a look in the chamber beyond. Something silver glittered within.

"I haven't either," Blair admitted, joining her at the entryway to a huge room. It was empty, save for a single ship. That ship was a sleek silver vessel, not more than fifty feet long. The surface was smooth metal, without a single rivet or bolt. It looked like one solid piece of metal, with nothing resembling a sail.

"You're just going to give us this?" Liz asked, trying to keep the mistrust from her voice.

"Your surprise is proper," Hades said, hobbling into the room. "This is one of the last slipsails in the world. By giving it to you, I am giving aid to Ra's enemies, which could mean my death."

"Then why do it?" Blair asked, folding his arms as he peered suspiciously at Hades. Liz couldn't blame him. The whole 'old man bearing gifts' trope was pretty played out.

"You saw the city above, yes? Mighty Olympus?" Hades asked, pausing for a wet cough.

"It's pretty tough to miss," Liz said, drily.

"I currently lack the strength to pilot a slipsail. Only an Ark Lord or a being of incredible strength can do so," Hades explained, giving them another gap-toothed smile.

"I see where this is going," Blair interjected. "We carry you to the city, you let us keep a ship you can't use."

"Precisely. Besides, what happens in the coming days is more important than any bauble, even one so kingly as a slipsail," Hades said, giving an exaggerated sigh. He approached the vessel, running gnarled fingers along the metal. "If Osiris is not stopped, the world is doomed. His army of demons will swarm the world, and all the gods of my age will be extinguished. Osiris will plant new gods in their place, dark gods bent on conquest. They will reshape this world into a hellish place, one I do not think you or anyone else wishes to see. You may be able to stop that, if I aid you."

Liz met Blair's gaze. He raised an eyebrow. It all seemed a little too easy, but they couldn't just say no. This could solve their immediate problems.

"How do we pilot it?" Blair asked. His eyes widened when his fingers brushed the silver metal. Liz sensed more than saw a crackling energy pass between him and the ship. "Never mind."

"Ah, I see you begin to grasp the true worth of a slipsail," Hades said, giving a chuckle as he clapped Blair on the back. He turned to Liz, sharing a warm smile as he explained. "Powerful shapers can bond with such a vessel. In many ways, they *become* the vessel. It is powered by sun or moon, and will carry you faster than the fastest bird can fly. I'm told you have the like, or had the like before the sun devastated your technology. It is much like one of your airplanes, though far more nimble."

Thunder rumbled in the distance, or something like it anyway. There was something off about it, like a gigantic sheet of fabric being ripped. It echoed and reverberated around them, and Liz raised her hands to her ears. "If it will carry us away from whatever that is, then I'm game. How do we board it?"

Before she'd finished speaking, the silvered surface rippled, pulling Blair inside. Liz stretched out a tentative hand, laying it against the ship. A warm ripple passed over her hand, and the next thing she knew she was being sucked inside. She suppressed the hostile gut reaction.

Inside was a comfortable chamber that looked a little like the inside of the Arks, save that the stone was white marble instead of black. It lined the walls, forming an inner shell the silvery metal must be bonded to. The decor was spartan, enough for a single person, or maybe a couple to live comfortably.

The bed dominating the far side was smaller than the one in her chamber, but obviously cut from the same strange black foam. The sight of it reminded Liz how tired she was, but she refused to even think about that.

Blair stood next to a strange obsidian pillar, with a diamond-shaped console at the top. It resembled the obelisks in an Ark's central control room, though the glowing gems set into the console had a more advanced feel. Blair had already pressed his hands into two indentations that seemed made for that purpose. His gaze was far away.

Hades wizened form slid through the same spot she'd entered, and he leaned heavily on the nightstand next to the bed.

"Blair?" she asked, staring about her in wonder.

"Sorry," Blair said, blinking as his gaze focused. He turned to face her, wiping sweat from his forehead with the back of his hand. "This thing is amazing. Hades, you're as good as your word. I can guide us up the shaft above us, and we'll emerge above ground not far from where we entered."

"Excellent," Hades said, clapping Blair on the shoulder. "Guide us to Olympus. Keep your distance, at least at first. We'll need to sync with the temporal field in order to gain access."

"Temporal field?" Liz asked, more than a little alarmed. "That sounds dangerous."

"It's a trivial thing for an Ark Lord," Hades said, giving a shrug and an apologetic smile. "Your Ka-Dun should be able to manage the feat. The field is unstable, but predictably so."

"Maybe, but what is it, exactly?" Blair asked. His eyes were unfocused. There was a soft rumble, then the ship began to move.

"The gods of Olympus knew we were weaker than your kind," Hades admitted, though he looked like he'd swallowed something sour. "In order to survive the vast gulf of time, we needed to cheat. We decided the best way to do that was to slow time. For those trapped in Olympus, millennia would pass as years."

"Wow," Liz said, blinking. "I've heard some pretty impressive things from Isis, but that sounds like a massive undertaking."

"It was by far Zeus's most ambitious plan, but he had the full support of the pantheon," Hades said, eyes growing watery. He paused before continuing. "Sustaining a field that powerful requires immense energy, the kind of energy only the Well could provide. I was asked to stay outside so I might protect the conduit, ensuring the survival of my brethren."

"Oh, God," Liz said, catching herself as the ship lurched with sudden acceleration. "Osiris severed the conduit, and you want to return to see if your people survived."

Hades nodded, seemingly unable to find words.

"We're clear of the tunnel," Blair said, voice distant. The front end of the ship flickered, then dissolved. She could see the sky around them, though she couldn't feel the wind.

Liz looked up, shocked by how quickly they were approaching the city in the sky. Olympus grew larger, and as it did her heart sank. The buildings were pitted and scarred, with more than one column toppled to the ground.

There was no sign of movement, not so much as a bird. Olympus was a tomb.

Chapter 36- Into the Storm

Blair guided the ship higher, keeping the prow aimed at the floating city as he circled Olympus. He could feel the wind along the hull, the hot breath of the approaching storm. It was getting closer, though he guessed they still had an hour or two before it arrived.

"Head for that platform," Hades's voice sounded muffled and distant. "Go in slowly. You'll feel waves of energy washing over the ship. You need to match the slipsail's modulation perfectly. Your beast can guide you."

He is correct, Ka-Dun. Allow me, and I will guide us.

Blair relaxed his control, allowing the beast to surge through his mind. He studied what it did, feeling the strange pulses of energy from Olympus. They crackled blue as the slipsail entered, buffeting the ship far more than the wind.

He began to panic as the waves grew rougher, but the beast took action before Blair had to. The slipsail emitted a series of counter waves, a split second before the temporal field. Each wave grew closer to the pulse, until they were in perfect sync.

"Well done, Ka-Dun. Well done," Hades said. Blair felt a hand on his shoulder, though it was far more muted than the senses coming from the slipsail. "Guide us to that dock, the white stone platform. We can set down there."

Blair did as asked, feeling a strain as he forced the slipsail the last few feet through the field. There was a sudden lurch, then they were free. He gazed in wonder around him, though gaze might not have been quite the right word. He *sensed* Olympus from the slipsail's perspective.

The city was perhaps a mile across, stretched across gentle, rolling hills. There were dozens of buildings, all shaped from the same white marble they'd glimpsed from below. Wide gardens stretched between them, or what had once been gardens. They were withered and brown, the skeletal branches of stunted olive trees dotting patches of barren soil.

Some of the buildings looked like they'd been through a war. Scorch marks dotted their sides, and a few were now rubble. Most of those that were not still had damage, ranging from a single singed hole to entire missing walls.

"What happened here?" Blair asked, guiding the slipsail into a landing. It hovered a foot or two above the platform, bobbing gently up and down. He released the vessel, returning to his own senses.

"War," Hades said, sadly. He wept openly, and Blair wanted to look away. "I can imagine what happened. For the first years all was well, but once the conduit was cut the flow of time grew much closer to that below. Years became decades, and my brethren's strength failed them. They likely drained their batteries and artifacts dry, siphoning strength to stay alive.

"When that failed them," Hades said, voice cracking. He paused, mouth working for several moments before could continue. "They turned on the last source of available strength: each other. The weakest probably died first, but in the end time claimed them all. The city is a graveyard. Osiris murdered my people."

"What will you do now?" Liz asked, resting a hand on Hades arm.

"I'll stay, and try to rebuild," Hades said, clearing his throat. He wiped the tears away with the arm of his cloak, then turned to Blair. "My people are dead, but their sacrifice doesn't have to be in vain. Convince Isis to ally with Ra. Tell her of Osiris's evil. Do not let old loyalties trick her, or the world will pay a furious price. You have no idea the depths of Osiris's depravity."

Blair gave a sharp nod, moving to put an arm around Liz. "We'll do our best. If you'll debark we'll be on our way. It looked like that storm was about to start."

Hades gave Blair a guilty look. "I'm sorry, Ka-Dun. The temporal field is much weaker, but still potent. Hours have passed outside olympus, perhaps days. The storm may have already passed, or it could still be raging."

"It doesn't matter," Blair said, struggling to contain his anger. "We can't change it. All we can do is get out of here. Let's go, Liz."

Hades gave another apologetic nod, then started for the ship's hull. Blair ignored the old man as he rippled through the slipsail's wall. He focused on the console, willing the ship to depart Olympus and head back into the storm.

Chapter 37- Master

Hades waved at the departing slipsail, wiping at the tears on his cheeks. He watched as the vessel passed through the temporal veil, back into the boiling orange clouds on the far side. He hid his smile until it had disappeared.

The first seeds had been planted, but a wise farmer scattered many, knowing not all would bear fruit. Schemes were much the same, and even if the Ka-Ken and her Ka-Dun convinced Isis to attack Osiris there was still work to be about.

Hades cackled to himself as he made for the ruins of the central amphitheater. He knew his brother well, and if Zeus had met his end it would have been there. Eventually Hades would need to return to treat with Ra, but first he needed to recover the crown. It would be drained of energy, but that hardly mattered. He would expose it to the Well, and eventually it would brim with the power he needed to stand on equal footing with the Ark Lords.

He cast aside the staff he'd been using. It was an effective prop, but he wouldn't need it again until he returned to the surface to meet Ra. Gone too were his quavering steps, replaced with sure and powerful strides. Hades had been careful to retain his bedraggled appearance, knowing it would cause others to underestimate him. He could have bent light to achieve the same appearance, but there was too much chance that such shaping would be detected.

Better not to cloak his true form, lest a powerful shaper pierce his illusion. He could labor as an old man for a few years more until his schemes were mature and his power unquestioned. Then he'd return to youth and vitality, when it wouldn't matter what any thought of him.

He trotted along the charred road, weaving around the worst of the pitted surface. It took only moments to reach the archway leading into the amphitheater, though he knew much more time was passing outside. There was nothing to be done about that, save being as quick as he could here.

The archway was shaded, and it took his eyes a moment to adjust. He stepped over someone's ribcage, probably one of the last to assail Zeus. Aphrodite, maybe. Or Poseidon. Hades couldn't help but grin as he emerged into the amphitheater itself, rows of stone seats overlooking a simple stage.

A single white marble chair dominated that stage, and his pulse quickened when he saw the flash of gold atop the skeleton's brow. "Oh brother, you poor fool. You waited here until the last, withering away until there was nothing left."

Hades trotted down the walkway, leaping atop the stage. He paused before the throne, grinning widely as he stared down at the slack-jawed skeleton. Zeus had been the mightiest. The most handsome. The most charismatic. He'd easily commanded their brethren, none of whom respected Hades. They'd feared him of course, but that was different.

Now they were all dead, and only Hades remained. He plucked the crown from the skull and dropped it over his own brow. It settled there, instantly resizing to fit him. He felt the stirring of power within it, though it wasn't enough to accomplish much.

It would be enough. Hades took a deep breath, focusing on the energy he'd been gathering for the last several weeks. It would tax him to his limits, but he had little choice if he wished to escape the tomb Olympus had become.

Hades concentrated, willing his strength to fill the crown. He tapped into one of its many abilities, envisioning his destination. There was a crack of thunder, then he stood in a wide cavern.

"I've done it," he cried, thrusting a fist into the air. The Ka-Dun had enabled him to recover one of the mightiest artifacts from the previous age, all without alerting anyone that he'd done so. Not even his master would know.

He turned his attention to his surroundings. Most of the ground was covered by a bubbling cauldron of thick, viscous, black sludge. That sludge was equal parts oil and water, and it held a portion of the Well's trapped energy. It was here that most of his more powerful workings took place, for without access to Olympus or an Ark it was the only means of achieving his mightiest shaping. Hades knelt next to the water, peering carefully at the far end of the cavern before beginning his work. The corridor on that side led to Vulcan's forge, and thus far his compatriot was still ignorant of Hades's true loyalties. The time was coming when he could end that deception, but for now it was still useful.

A particularly vile bubble burst near Hades's feet, splashing his dark boots with the noxious liquid. He could feel the horror and loathing in the boots, which brought a smile to his face. He'd shaped them from a man who'd once offered him insult.

He knelt next to the sludge, thrusting his right hand beneath the dark surface. Deep within him the last reserves of stored energy surged, linking with that contained in this tiny pool of the vast Well. Hades created a swirling vortex around his hand, which rippled outward as it greedily drew in more power. It flared an unnatural green, easily the size of a man now.

At last he released the energy, now that it was strong enough to be self-sustaining. Hades guided it, forcing the vortex to establish a link with a far away part of the Well. This distant part was in the far north, beneath the First Ark. It resonated as someone on that far end joined with the energy. Hades could feel that person, knew their resonance as well as his own.

"I have news, my master," he intoned, sinking to his knees in genuine supplication. The day might come when he could overthrow the mighty Set, but Hades doubted it. Not that it concerned him overmuch. He'd spent millennia in servitude to his brother Zeus, quietly gathering strength while Zeus dealt with the mind-numbingly dull minutiae of ruling. It was much the same now. Hades paid Set nominal tribute, and in exchange was left alone to rule his own kingdom.

"Speak, vassal," the voice rumbled back, thick and powerful. More powerful than when last Hades had heard it, which stirred a bit of fear. How had Set grown so much stronger so quickly?

"I have spoken with the emissaries of your sister by marriage. Isis now believes the conquest of the underworld is the work of her husband. She is yet ignorant of your survival," Hades explained, bowing his head.

"Excellent. You have done well, vassal. What else have you to tell?" Set asked, voice tinged with dark pleasure.

"Ra approaches Olympus even now. I shall sow further seeds of discontent. She will believe that Osiris is the true evil, and that Isis seeks to be in league with her husband. War will come, weakening those who might oppose you," Hades explained, smiling in spite of himself. Oh, how he loved sowing discord. So much more effective than direct combat.

"This is to the good, my vassal," the voice said, still more pleased. "I would have you plant one further seed. Tell Ra the forces that drove you from the underworld have fallen back. You fear they are massing for an assault, and if she hastens to the First Ark she may find it undefended."

Hades immediately grasped the plan. Make her think Osiris controlled the First Ark, that he was taking his army to assault someone, thus leaving his stronghold undefended. "It shall be as you say, master."

"When Isis and Ra are disposed of, you will have the first of many rewards," Set said, voice thrumming with power. "Tell me, mighty Hades, what would you wish of me?"

"The Ark of the Cradle will have need of a new lord, my master," Hades said, cautiously. Only those with a Ka had ever served as Ark Lord. He was only a lowly shaper, a sorcerer who'd grown strong through artifice and ingenuity.

"Interesting," Set replied, then was silent for a long moment. "And what of Olympus? When first you came to my service you desired to reign there.

Is this no longer so?"

"By cutting off the conduit to that place I have murdered my brethren. I would rule over a dead city, my master," Hades offered, again cautiously.

"True," Set said, silent for a long moment. "I will grant you the Ark of the Cradle, the moment Ra is dead. You will have her key, and you will rule the vast desert continent."

Hades rejoiced inwardly. Better to reign in hell, than to serve in heaven.

Chapter 38- Big Ass Worm

"So that's a sunstorm," Trevor muttered, leaning out of the Howdah's flap to peer at the northern horizon. It was a wall of billowing orange clouds, like a dust storm that stretched from the ground to the tip of the sky. It blotted out everything in that direction, as if the very air had ignited.

"Forgive me for speaking, mighty deathless, but will Ka-Dun Jordan and I survive the sun's fury?" Steve's ingratiating voice came from behind him. Trevor turned around immediately, eyes narrowing.

Steve had his head bowed deferentially to Irakesh. Trevor had assumed Irakesh was too cunning to fall for Steve's crap, but it appeared he was wrong. Irakesh ate up the dutiful servant routine, acting as if it was only right for someone of his station.

"You will survive it, as will the mammoths. Ra will erect a bubble of force over our camp," the deathless replied, settling more comfortably atop his small mountain of pillows. He swirled the contents of a golden goblet, staring disdainfully at Trevor. "Trevor is a yokel, with no knowledge of such things. Let him gawk, but you needn't fear the sun's coming fury. It will be unpleasant, but it will pass over us quickly."

"You'd better hope so," Jordan muttered from his place on the wall opposite Irakesh. He tugged absently at the golden collar, and Trevor gave a wince of sympathy. He hated what had been done to the man, and he hated his unwitting role in it even more. "If we're going to buy it you can be damn sure we're taking you with us."

"My queen," a voice bellowed, so loud that Trevor was forced to clap his hands over his ears. He recognized the jackal immediately. "Wepwawet has found prey. In the skies above. A slipsail has emerged from Olympus, and is fleeing north."

A trumpet blew and the mammoth stopped. Trevor briefly debated asking Irakesh what was going on, but his former master was unlikely to give him a truthful answer. Instead he nodded at Jordan. "Let's go see what this is about."

Trevor leapt through the flap, landing in a crouch nearly forty feet below. The stench of the mammoth was thick, making Trevor gag. It overpowered even the rotting army of undead that trailed in their wake. Jordan's muscled form landed next to Trevor a moment later, his landing sending up a puff of dust. He was still in human form, and other than the golden collar looked exactly like the same man who'd blown up Trevor's house back in San Diego. The camo pants and skintight black t-shirt were sweat-stained and dirty now, but they still belonged on the man more than any other uniform.

"Looks like that's what's causing the commotion," Jordan said, donning his sunglasses as he nodded at the horizon.

Trevor turned to face that way, spotting the trouble immediately. The storm batted a silver ship all over the place, knocking it around like a plastic bag in a tornado. A bronze skiff had risen from the area near Ra's howdah. It made its way cautiously into the air, much less affected by the growing storm. Wepwawet's white-grey form hunched low over the skiff, which was slowly gaining on the silver vessel.

The caravan had halted, a small cluster of figures gathering at the head. Trevor recognized Anubis, who towered over the others. Ra was unmistakable as well, her scarlet hair a spot of bright color in a sea of white clothing. Trevor began trotting in that direction, Jordan falling into step beside him. He hadn't insisted Jordan follow his orders, or done anything to make his situation worse. Yet the man's already sizable animosity was clearly growing. Trevor doubted that would ever change, nor was he sure he wanted it to. Even now part of him wanted to kill Jordan.

Then do so, you'll never have a better time to strike. It might deprive you of a tool, but it will also prove your strength to the other deathless.

"Hang back a little," Trevor told Jordan, slowing as he reached the knot of figures surrounding Ra. Anubis eyed him balefully, but none of the rest seemed to notice his appearance.

"It seems clear Hades dispatched the slipsail," Ra was saying, her attention focused on the vessel landing in the distance. "The question is why? He clearly saw our approach, but I cannot think he would abandon Olympus. If he desired to, he'd have fled to the underworld. So why dispatch so precious a tool into the maw of a sunstorm?"

None of the figures surrounding her answered, but Trevor found himself speaking. "Because he wants us to pursue them."

Ra turned to face him, glittering green eyes sizing him up for long moments before she spoke. "And what makes you think you have the slightest inkling of the motivation of a god you've never met?"

"I don't have to know him to guess at his motives. If you're right and he knew we were coming why else would he have sent the ship? If he wanted to hide someone, couldn't he have them flee into the underworld? We'd never even know they existed. Sending them out in a ship he knows for sure we'll see seems pretty stupid," Trevor argued.

"Obviously. Yet, sadly, you are the only one among my retinue to see it. You are one to watch, Trevor Gregg," Ra said, giving a tight nod. "Anubis, make ready for battle in case this is some kind of trap. The rest of you...."

The ground bucked wildly, knocking Trevor to the dust. Jordan fell as well, though the rest of the gods somehow kept their balance. A deep rumbling sounded somewhere deep beneath them.

Trevor shifted into a cloud of energy, drifting a few feet off the ground in a cloud of crackling green motes. It was the best defense he could muster without knowing more. He peered around them. Ra's army was in chaos, zombies flailing to regain their footing with little success, as the ground continued to quake. Only the mighty anakim kept their footing.

"No. No, no, no," Ra wailed, spinning in place as if searching for something. A moment later, Trevor knew exactly what she'd been searching for, and why she seemed so disturbed by it.

An enormous grey creature burst from the ground in the distance. Up and up it went, a titanic worm hundreds of feet thick, dwarfing anything found on Arikas. A tiny figure clung to the worm's back, which gave it scale. Trevor couldn't make out much, save a shock of silver fur. Uh oh.

"She wouldn't dare," Ra whispered, as her minions scattered. The worm's body plunged into the sky, then began to fall. Its passage kicked up a whirlwind of dust and gravel, and had Trevor not been transmuted to energy he would have been blown backwards by the gale that knocked deathless and zombie alike to the ground. Jordan had erected a telekinetic dome around himself, much like he'd used to ward off the nuclear blast back in San Francisco. "Anubis, fall back and protect the army."

"But my queen, if we kill the Sand Kraken..." Anubis protested.

Ra whirled on him, expression thunderous. "Do you think I do not realize the cost? If we do not kill the Kraken it will lay waste to my army. When it is finished, Isis will free the beast, and we'll lose both the Ark's chief guardian and my fledgling army. That's no doubt exactly what Isis seeks here. It cannot be coincidence that it attacks us here, at this precise moment."

"What of the ship?" Anubis asked, nodding toward the silver vessel. It had made progress into the storm, but Wepwawet's skiff was still gaining on it.

A tremendous boom crashed over them as the worm's body finally struck the earth. Hundreds of deathless were crushed beneath its mass, including two of the giant Anakim. The colossal white body began rolling and thrashing, crushing dozens more under its thick hide.

"We have no time. The Kraken must die," Ra snarled.

Now is a time to gain much prestige, my host. If you aid in the killing of this beast, then you will secure your position here.

Damn it. Trevor knew the voice was right, but helping Ra carried a heavy price.

Chapter 39- Dog Fight

Blair struggled to adjust to the massive volume of data rolling through his mind. He'd suddenly gained a dozen senses instead of five. He could feel the ship's velocity and energy levels, and could perceive all directions at once. His breathing grew ragged as the ship passed through the temporal field and back into the storm on the other side

Seek your calm, Ka-Dun. This is not unlike every other skill you have mastered. In time it will be as natural as breathing.

Maybe the beast was right; he still wanted to panic. Enormous winds buffeted the ship, knocking it about like a kite. It was all he could do to keep it anything close to level, and he wanted to throw up from the vertigo.

He focused primarily on his vision, looking around the ship for points of interest. He found more than he'd like, all bad from his perspective. He willed the entire ship to become transparent.

"Liz, below us," he roared, scanning the horizon to the southwest. "Do you see them?"

Liz rested a hand on his back, the touch dimmed by his other senses. "Yeah, I see them. Looks like Ra is about to catch up with us. I see a bunch of elephants, and what I'm guessing are giant zombies like the one we fought back in that hangar in Panama."

"Shit," Blair said, commanding the ship to zip skyward. "Doesn't look like we have a lot of options. If Hades is right we need to find Isis, but I have no idea where she is. We need to find a way to deal with the storm."

"Maybe we can fly over it?" Liz asked, grabbing onto the control console as the ship picked up speed.

"I'll try, but we're already over a mile up, and I can't see the top of it," Blair said. He felt a buzzing in his ear, and focused on it. It was some sort of alert. "Shit. We're about to have company. There's another ship approaching. It's smaller, like a flying chariot. Is that—? It looks like there's a werewolf on it."

"Isis?" Liz asked. Blair could hear the hope in her voice.

"We're not that lucky. The thing looks male, but it's too large to be...." Blair realized what he was seeing. The sickly grey fur didn't belong to a werewolf. This was something else. Unless he missed his guess, it was some sort of deathless that had been shaped into a wolf.

"How long before it gets here?" Liz asked, resting a foot on the lowest rung of the ladder.

"I don't know," Blair said, commanding the ship to sail faster. He aimed it north, deeper into the storm. He wasn't sure that was a good idea, but he still had time to break off if he had to. Another buzzing in his ear. "Shit. Liz, those giant zombies? They're throwing rocks at us."

Blair forced the ship to dodge right, narrowly avoiding a chunk of stone the size of a compact car. It sailed past with a hum, arcing back down to the ground almost a mile below. How strong did those things have to be to hurl something that big, with that kind of speed and accuracy?

"Can you dodge them?" Liz asked.

Blair didn't answer for a moment, saving his concentration for flying. He dodged three more, increasing the ship's speed as they sailed toward the storm. "Yeah, but it's slowing me down. The skiff is getting closer. It will be on us in a moment."

"I'll deal with him," Liz rumbled. Auburn fur faded into the shadows as she disappeared out of sight.

Blair hoped it wouldn't come to that, but they weren't escaping unless he did something drastic. He gauged the distance to the storm. Maybe thirty or forty more seconds to reach those angry orange clouds.

You dance with death, Ka-Dun. Remember the words of the treacherous Hades. Such storms are not often survived, especially when flying.

"So what's your plan?" Blair growled, urging the ship to still greater speed. The skiff was approaching from below. He guessed it was no more than a few hundred yards away.

I have none, Ka-Dun. I wish only to advise you of the danger.

A bolt of eldritch fire, green and baleful, shot from the prow of the skiff. It struck the back of the slipsail, the energy playing across the silver metal like lightning. Pain rippled through Blair, and he clenched his teeth as he forced himself to focus on flying. The ship had slowed during his momentary lapse, and the skiff had taken the opportunity to narrow the gap.

It fired another green burst, but this time Blair dodged to the left. The bolt sailed harmlessly by—but another, then another, shot by. Blair did a barrel roll, drawing on instinctual knowledge provided by the beast as he narrowly avoided the staccato of fire.

It was only then that he realized what the skiff was doing. Each shot was timed to forced an evasion, and each evasion brought the skiff that much closer.

Liz, he thought. *We're about to be boarded. I have to focus on flying. See what you can do to keep this thing off me.*

Chapter 40- Boarded

Liz extended her right hand, summoning her sunsteel sword as she scanned the horizon behind them. A moment later the skiff burst into view, a jaguar pouncing. It closed rapidly, nearly touching the deck as a single figure leapt toward them.

Blair had left the the ship's surface transparent, so Liz was easily able to position herself to intercept. Their attacker was the strange, dead wolf-thing from Ra's court. Wepwajebus or whatever. His golden spear was cradled like a lance, stabbing into the hull as he landed.

Ripples of golden energy spread from it, and Blair gave a cry of pain. Then the dead wolf passed through the skin of the ship just as they had when they entered. His stench came with him: rotting meat, and less pleasant things.

Liz glided forward, bunching her muscles as she poured all of her strength into the thrust. She kept the blade parallel with her foe's spine, bracing herself as the weapon pierced bone and flesh. She swept upward in a tight arc, slicing his spine cleanly in two from the small of the back all the way to the base of his skull. She whirled, reversing her strike as she decapitated her opponent in one smooth motion. The blade passed through his neck with almost no resistance, and the headless body toppled to the deck.

"Impressive, especially for one so young," rumbled a voice from behind her. She spun, bringing her sword up defensively. There stood Wepwawet, apparently unharmed. He raised a paw-like hand in a placating gesture. "Peace. Command your Ka-Dun to land the slipsail and there need be no violence. Resist, however, and I will not hesitate to slay both of you."

"You know we can't do that," she growled, assuming a combat stance as she slipped into the shadows next to the console. "Ra will kill us as soon as we land."

"You know her that well, then?" the dead wolf asked, giving an expression of surprise. "Two of your pack invaded the Ark. Yet both live. One was made a prisoner, the other a vassal of Ra. Both you and your Ka-Dun will be treated fairly, if you surrender. I will not ask again."

Liz hesitated, glancing behind her at the storm. They were getting closer, but it would be another minute or two before they got there. If the dead wolf could use the illusions of a deathless, as he'd just demonstrated, then he almost certainly had their ability to blur. He could kill Blair before she could stop him. Even if she could get away, where would she go? She couldn't fly the ship, and even if she could she doubted Wepwawet would allow that.

"Trevor is alive?" she asked, playing for time.

"Alive is an interesting word to apply to a deathless, but he is no more dead than he was when he arrived," Wepwawet said, shrugging. He started walking toward the ladder leading into the hold. "The Ka-Dun Jordan lives as well. He has been given to Trevor, and if Jordan pleases Ra she may eventually grant his freedom. Now convince your Ka-Dun to set the slipsail down, before I must engage in violence."

"All right," Liz said. She dropped her voice to a tight whisper she knew his enhanced senses would still pick up. "Do as he says, Blair. I don't think we can fight this thing and have any chance of living."

In answer the ship began to descend smoothly. Liz tensed as the dead wolf shifted his weight, but relaxed when he rested his spear against the wall. He folded his arms, approaching slowly. "You have chosen wisely, Ka-Dun. I will see that you are both treated fairly when Ra boards this vessel."

Chapter 41- Demons

"What am I looking at?" Mark asked, staring at the feed dominating the main screen. It was tiny compared to the one in Syracuse, just a simple sixty-five-inch television that had been safely stored in an underground warehouse when the CME hit. He'd had it installed just the day before.

He ignored the hunger gnawing at his insides, capitalizing on an iron will he'd cultivated over decades. He wasn't going to kill one of his subordinates; he needed them. If he did have to feed, he'd speak to Osiris about options. In the meantime, he had an operation to run.

"Sir, it looks like another CME," Benson said, stepping up to the television to join him. "Preliminary research suggests it's larger than the one that wiped out power. We should be safe down here, but anyone in the Middle East or Northern Africa is about to be hit with another wave. If our data is accurate, a third CME will erupt within a week. We don't have telemetry yet, but we're guessing it will hit somewhere below the equator."

"Wonderful," Mark said, trying not to focus on the vein throbbing in Benson's neck. "Do you have an update on the army leaving the Cairo Ark?"

"Yes sir," Benson said, reaching down to tap her tablet. The feed on the TV shifted, now showing a cloud of dust. She zoomed in, showing towering undead figures. Mammoths lumbered along next to them, all heading in roughly the same direction.

"Why have they stopped?" he asked, noticing that the figures were no longer moving.

"We're not sure, though it could have to do with the solar storm," Benson theorized, panning out a bit to show the massive storm moving in their direction. "That much radiation could cook even those walking corpses.

Maybe the army is battening down and waiting for it to pass."

"Maybe," Mark replied, tapping his own tablet. He panned the camera around, stopping when he saw something erupting from the earth. For just a split second he thought it was another Ark, but the color and size were all wrong. Whatever this was, it seemed to be alive. A truly gargantuan creature with thick grey hide. Like a worm that had been growing for thousands of years.

The creature began thrashing out, crushing hundreds of undead as it tore through the army that had departed from the Cairo Ark. "Get Osiris up here. He's going to want to see this."

Chapter 42- Reunited

Blair had rarely felt this helpless, even in all the fucked-up situations they'd had to deal with recently.

"You have my respect, Ka-Ken," Wepwawet rumbled. He addressed the patch of darkness next to the bed where Blair sat, roughly where Liz hid herself in the shadows. "You could flee, and we couldn't stop you," Wepwawet continued addressing Liz. "Yet you choose to remain, to protect your Ka-Dun as best you are able. I will petition Ra to give you both into my care, much as the Ka-Dun Jordan was entrusted to the deathless Trevor."

"Exactly what does that entail?" Blair asked, rising from the bed. Part of him longed to fight, but he knew he was outmatched. There was no way they could take on someone as old as Wepwawet. Hell, they'd barely been able to take out Irakesh with their entire pack, and from what Blair understood Irakesh was considered a child in Ra's court.

"You will become my vassals, living or dying at my pleasure," Wepwawet rumbled, taking a step closer. The strange orange light from the storm played over his grey fur, giving him a hellish look. "I am a harsh master, but fair. Not so lenient as Trevor has been with this Jordan, but neither will I treat you cruelly as Irakesh does the whelp Steve." Wepwawet spat at the last.

"Yep, looks like you've definitely met Steve," Liz said, finally reappearing from the shadows. She was still in wolf form, but didn't have her sword out. Ready to defend if needed, but clearly not interested in picking a fight. Blair followed her lead.

"It doesn't look like we have a lot of choice, but I'll warn you: If you try to make us betray Isis, you'll be sorely disappointed. I'd rather die first," Blair rumbled, trying to look fierce. He had a feeling he more resembled a yapping puppy.

"You have some fire, then," Wepwawet rumbled, giving a toothy grin. "You remind me much of myself at your age. I was in a similar position, captured during the battle wherein my father was driven from the cradle."

"Your father?" Liz asked, raising an auburn eyebrow.

"Set," Blair supplied, folding his arms as he considered. "Brother of Osiris, also the enemy of Isis, Osiris, and Sekhmet."

"You are well versed in our lore," Wepwawet rumbled, clearly surprised. "Are you a lore-keeper of this age?"

"You might say that," Blair said. There was no easy translation for anthropologist. "So what happens now?"

A fist erupted from Wepwawet's belly. Before the wolfish god could react, a huge silver maw latched onto the back of his neck. A hail of teeth and claws rent his face and spine.

Liz moved protectively in front of Blair with her sunsteel drawn, ready should the fight require their involvement.

The foes moved so fast, Blair blurred in order to track the fight, and still it was more than he could take in. It ended as suddenly as it had begun.

Isis stood over Wepwawet's broken body, her muzzle coated in his blood.

"Isis," Blair said, wanting to cheer.

"Ka-Dun Blair," Isis barked, eyes firmly fixed on her prey. "Take us into the storm. Quickly. Sekhmet approaches even now, and it will not take her long to deal with the distraction I've wrought."

"What have you done?" Wepwawet rasped through a ruined throat. He seemed to be healing, but slowly. There was a lot of damage, after all.

"Be silent, nephew," Isis snarled, leaning closer. "I've half a mind to end you right now, but in honor of the esteem your uncle holds for you I will not. For now. Do not make me regret my leniency."

"If you are leaving, I ask that you return me to Ra," Wepwawet pleaded.

"Liz, push him through the slipsail's skin. Be gentle, if possible," Isis said, turning back to Blair. "As for you, time is not on our side. We must be away, and quickly."

Blair merged his senses with the ship, quickly assessing their surroundings. Absolute chaos had erupted outside. A titanic worm slammed down into the earth, crushing a large swathe of Ra's army. The impact caused the ship to shake, and Blair urgently commanded it to rise.

That didn't improve things. If anything it made the shaking worse, as they were buffeted by winds from the storm. "Hold onto something."

Then all Blair could do was fight. The winds reached gale force. Stronger, if that was possible. He did his best to guide the ship into them, but it was like a leaf being tossed about by a hurricane. He had almost no control, and the only success he had was gaining a little altitude. Good thing, too. They passed perilously close to the ground more than once, and he had a feeling that kind of impact would destroy the ship as easily as it would a regular plane.

Chapter 43- To the Rescue

Trevor blurred, dodging around boulders and leaping over walking corpses as he evaded the worm's titanic blows. Three times it had slammed its body into the earth, and three times it had crushed a large swath of Ra's army. A couple more hits like that, and Ra wouldn't *have* an army.

"Jordan," Trevor roared, rolling past a rock and coming to his feet not far from the blonde werewolf. The golden collar caught the strange light of the storm that was nearly upon them, making it easy to find him. Even if that were not the case, Trevor could feel Jordan through the bracelet. "You're with me."

Jordan gave a tight nod, blurring a dusty path towards Trevor. Trevor turned and started towards the storm, where the strange silver ship had landed. It shuddered for a moment, then lifted off again. The ship had reached maybe a hundred feet up when a body came tumbling out of the side. Wepwawet's body.

It impacted with a puff of dust, unmoving after the fall. Trevor blinked as the bronze skiff detached from the silver ship, zooming down to rest next to Wepwawet like a dog running to its master.

"What's your plan?" Jordan roared over the wind, following Trevor as he made his way into the fringes of the sunstorm. The heat increased, and energy crackled all around him, though it wasn't painful. He hoped that didn't change. If what he'd heard of these sunstorms was accurate, they could be lethal. The way the wind already tugged insistently suggested it was going to get far worse.

"There," Trevor said, nodding at a shape looming in the dust kicked up by the keening wind. Trevor blurred towards it, stopping next to the skiff

Wepwawet had used earlier. "I'm pretty sure I can fly it if I have to."

"You know who was on that ship, right? We could escape right now. There's no way they could chase us," Jordan roared back. "Let's get the fuck out of here while we can."

"Jordan, give me a hand with Wepwawet," Trevor ordered.

Jordan remained where he was, slowly drawing a holstered pistol. He aimed it at Trevor's face. "You're not going to go, are you? You're going to stay with Ra."

"We can deal with that in a minute," Trevor said, throwing Wepwawet's body over his shoulder. He heaved himself to his feet, though it wasn't easy. "Wep is in bad shape."

"Not as bad as you're going to be in," Jordan said. The pistol boomed, and Trevor's face exploded in agony. He tumbled backwards as several more shots found his gut. He tried to fight back, but Jordan seized his arm and broke it. A kneecap shattered.

The bracelet, my host. Use the bracelet.

Trevor felt a hot surge roll through him, and this time it wasn't caused by the storm. Jordan had been placed in his care and, while he hadn't wanted the responsibility, he'd done his best to protect the werewolf. Now Jordan was turning on him. It was just too much, after everything else the man had done to him. The '65 Mustang still loomed in the back of his mind—three years of work wasted when Jordan had blown it up.

"Fuck you," Trevor said, using the bracelet for the first time. He forced all the anger, all the resentment, into the gold band. Jordan's back arched as if he were being electrocuted. He collapsed to his knees, then dropped face first into the dirt. Trevor staggered to his feet, favoring his injured leg. It was healing, but it and about a dozen other wounds screamed for his attention. "Now pick Wep the fuck up and carry him onto the god damned skiff. I'm about done with your insubordinate bullshit. You understand what a chain of command is; I know you do. You might not like it, but right now you fucking work for me." Trevor was screaming by the end, completely overwhelmed by the rage. He didn't care. "Get the fuck up."

Jordan staggered to his feet, hatred in his eyes. He scooped up Wepwawet and carried him to the skiff, dropping the wolf-headed god none too gently aboard.

"You're in control right now, you fucking traitor," Jordan rumbled, glaring at him sullenly over the rail of the skiff. He watched as Trevor leapt aboard. "Sooner or later that's going to change, and when it does I'll be the one to put you down. Remember that."

"Yeah, because you've had so much luck before," Trevor snarled back. "You only survived the bridge back in San Francisco because I let you. Before that, I kicked your ass in Panama. You want to try again? Give it your best fucking shot."

Jordan lapsed into silence, and Trevor moved to what he took for a steering wheel on the center of the skiff. He placed his hands on it, wondering what the hell to do next.

Open your mind, my host. Allow the slipsail to bond with you. Your will join with it, and you can use it as an extension of your body.

So Trevor opened his mind. To his surprise, he found he could feel the skiff. Some quick experimentation allowed him to levitate a few feet off the ground. He stayed low, knowing that going any higher was an invitation to destruction. The storm was on them now, and the winds even more fierce. Something like thunder cracked above, making it brighter than day for just a moment. Then the light faded back into a muted dusk, the boiling orange clouds completely obscuring what had been noonday sun just a few moments before. Thankfully the clouds didn't seem to be pure flame at the edge of the storm, though if the baking heat was any indication, the center of the storm was pure death.

Trevor zoomed the skiff towards the ruins dotting the area underneath Olympus. Gobekli Tepe, the place was called. That had been where Ra was making for, so that was where she was likely to go next. Assuming she survived her battle with the worm. He brought the skiff to a halt near one of the more intact buildings, then spun to face the worm.

I know what you contemplate, my host. It is foolish in the utmost. Ra does not need your help.

"Fuck you," Trevor muttered under his breath. He turned to Jordan, raising his voice to a shout. "Take Wep into that building and wait there. If I'm not back shortly it means I'm dead, which ought to make your day."

Jordan didn't reply, instead scooping up Wepwawet and carrying the unconscious deity off the skiff. What the hell had kicked his ass so thoroughly that he was still out of it? Trevor could only think of one god capable of that and, given that he'd been adopted into Ra's court, that meant Isis was now an enemy. He sure hoped he didn't run afoul of her anytime soon.

Trevor commanded the skiff to rise, then zoomed towards the worm in a spray of dust. He'd finally figured out what Ra was trying to do. Her attacks were designed to annoy, not kill. They'd agitated the worm into following her, and she'd led it away from the battle. Now it was chasing her, but even as fast as she was, he wasn't certain she could evade it forever. It simply moved too fast, and didn't seem to tire.

If we must do this, my host, then I will aid you. The skiff possesses weaponry. It can focus your energy into a more potent blast, one that might get the beast's attention.

Trevor considered that as the skiff shot closer to the worm. There was something very close to a cannon strapped to the underside of the skiff, and he could somehow feel the weapon. If he fed his energy into the skiff and commanded it to fire, the weapon would apparently amplify the blast.

"All right, let's see what this thing can do," he muttered, though the words were torn away by the wind. Trevor shot skyward, battling the wind as he raced for the worm's head. Most of the attacks Ra had leveled had been aimed at the softer flesh inside the worm's mouth. He decided to do the same.

Trevor increased speed, circling up and away from the worm. Then he dove, curving earthward in a tight arc as he approached the thing's mouth. It was beyond colossal up close, the largest thing he'd ever seen. This creature could probably devour entire skyscrapers whole, and had the breath to match. The stench was awful.

He fed some of his energy into the craft, firing a quick trio of blasts into the creature's open maw. A bellow, even louder than the wind or the cracks of thunder above, split the air. Trevor resisted the urge to clap his hands over his ears, instead twisting the craft in midair as the creature's mouth snapped shut where Trevor had just been.

It hurled its body at him, but he dodged to the left and poured on more speed. Jesus, the thing was just so damned massive. He urged the craft to maximum speed, biting his lip as the shadow grew larger over him. An instant before it struck, he juked left, narrowly avoiding the beast. Unfortunately, there was no way to escape the wake.

The creature sent a roiling wave of debris in his direction, rocks and dust and bodies all bouncing off the skiff. Something heavy struck him in the back, and he was knocked from the craft in a split second of absolute terror. There would be no way to escape the worm without the skiff.

Then a hand seized the scruff of his neck. He was back on the skiff, slammed down against the railing. Trevor clung to it instinctively, gazing up at his savior. Ra's scarlet mane fluttered in the wind, dancing around her like a forest of tiny snakes. She seized the skiff's control wheel, urging it up and away from the worm.

"Clever," she shouted over the wind, pivoting the craft until it was in front of the worm. "You've enraged the worm enough that we can lead it away from the others. Once it's far enough away we'll take to the skies, assuming we survive the storm. Then we can circle back."

"Won't the worm just come back?" Trevor yelled.

"No," Ra said, shaking her head as they raced away from the worm, away from Gobekli Tepe. "It is incredibly powerful, but not very intelligent. Once there is no obvious threat, it will return to its hunting grounds, back at the Ark of the Cradle. A good thing, too. The Kraken is the most potent of the Ark's defenses. Isis plays the game well. She knew I couldn't let it die, but also that I couldn't allow it to crush my army. So she delays me, and I can do nothing save follow the course she has led me down."

Trevor didn't reply to that. Maybe he'd done the right thing after all. He'd proven his usefulness to Ra, but hadn't interrupted Isis's plan. Blair and Liz had probably made it to safety, though he had no idea where they'd go now. That was probably for the best. If he didn't know their destination, he couldn't betray them.

Chapter 44- Power Armor

Jordan clenched his fist, growling as Trevor sped away. He watched as the skiff gained altitude, totally unsurprised when it began firing at the worm. The worm that had been crushing Ra's army, but that was now chasing Trevor. The fucker had just saved their enemy from total destruction.

"Gahhh," he bellowed, shattering a nearby rock with his fist. He felt so damned powerless, not just because the collar prevented him from shifting. It was also because he couldn't stop Trevor, whose loyalties were quite obviously shifting to Ra. That would make him an enemy again, one that even Jordan had to admit was damned formidable.

"What troubles you, Ka-Dun?" a voice came from behind him.

Jordan spun, reaching for the gun belted at his side. Except his gun was gone, knocked away during the fight with Trevor. He was unarmed, for the first time since he'd become a werewolf. An old man with long, stringy white hair and a sun-weathered face stood before him—hardly a threat, though, at least not an obvious one.

"Who the fuck are you?" Jordan shot back, slipping into a combat stance.

"I could provide a litany of names, but I suspect you are a man of little patience. Please, call me Hades," the old man said, giving a friendly nod. He leaned heavily on a simple wooden staff. "How are you called?"

"Name's Jordan," he growled back.

Be wary, Ka-Dun. This one is old, and very powerful. A sorcerer who styles himself a god.

"Well, Ka-Dun Jordan, I can see you have a problem. One I may be able to assist with," the old man said, delivering a warm smile. It was somehow predatory.

"What problem might that be?" Jordan asked, narrowing his eyes behind his sunglasses. Thankfully they were wrap-around, which was the only reason the violent winds hadn't tugged them away. A particularly violent gust knocked him a step closer to the old man.

"You're wearing a collar of shi-dun. That means you are locked in human form, and are the plaything of the collar's owner," Hades said, shaking his head sadly. "If you pick up your companion and carry him below, then I will free you from the collar's limitations."

Jordan looked back at Ra's army. The worm was distant now, still chasing Trevor's skiff. That meant Ra and her troops would be here soon.

"All right, lead the way," Jordan said, leaning down to scoop up Wepwawet's unconscious form. The wolf-headed god gave a groan of pain, the first sign he'd exhibited that he might be returning to consciousness.

Hades turned without a word, walking quickly into a neighboring building. He moved like a much younger man, the pretense of age falling away as he quickly gained ground. Jordan struggled to keep up. He hadn't rested well in days, and it had been over a week since he'd seen the moon. That made his burden heavier than it should have been.

They made their way deep into the earth, passing down stairways carved into rock caverns. It reminded him of a trip he'd taken to the Oregon Caves a few years back, the wet stone illuminated by a very modern flashlight Hades had withdrawn from his bedraggled robes.

"How far is it?" Jordan grunted after a particularly treacherous stairwell. It was growing hotter, and he'd begun to sweat.

"Not far," Hades said, threading through stalactites as he crossed a wide chamber. He emerged into a room unlike any they'd passed thus far. This one had clearly been worked by human hands, far more than had been used to create the simple stairs they'd used to get down here.

The walls were smooth and flat, seamless granite extending hundreds of yards into the distance. Below was a hellish vista, huge iron cauldrons full of molten metal. The air stank of sulfur, and Jordan's eyes stung from the heat. Dozens of uniformly black figures moved about the room. Some worked at anvils that could have come from medieval Europe, while others worked on the type of machinery he'd have expected to see at a Mohn facility.

It was an odd mix, and it raised some troubling questions. Modern machining was delicate work, and required massive factories to produce. The robotic assemblies and conveyor belts here must have been manufactured elsewhere. That meant they'd been created before the CME. How long had this place been in operation?

"This way, this way," Hades said, beckoning Jordan to follow him into the factory. "Welcome to The Forge. It has been used for thousands of years to construct countless wonders. Even now it labors to create even greater works."

Jordan followed, his arms burning from the strain of carrying Wepwawet's heavy body. They threaded through the Forge, surrounded by a sea of pounding hammers and flying sparks on one side, modern robotic assemblies turning out recognizable pieces of power armor on the other. Eventually they reached the far side, where Hades finally paused. He stopped at a raised dais, where a single figure was working.

"Holy. Shit," Jordan said, depositing Wepwawet's body at the base of the stairs so he could get a closer look. "That's a modified X-11. Where the hell did you get Mohn power armor?"

There were some differences, but the man-sized suit of armor was unmistakable. It was the same type he'd worn in San Diego, and later in Peru. Both times he'd fought werewolves, and both times he'd lost. That didn't mean the suit wasn't powerful, though. It turned a normal soldier into a formidable killing machine, and the idea that someone was still manufacturing them was troubling. Especially when that someone was a god with unknown motives.

"I see you've some familiarity with my work," a man next to the armor said, rising to his feet. He was bare to the waist, his bald head slick with sweat and soot. He turned to Jordan and gave a respectful nod. "I am called Vulcan, the smith. Who might you be, little Ka-Dun?"

"Jordan," he replied, turning his attention back to the armor. "You built the original X-11?"

"No, I'd love to claim credit, but that goes to a man from this age. What I have done is dramatically improve upon his work," Vulcan said, crossing tree-trunk arms as he beamed a smile at his work. He patted the black metal arm. "I've made the metal stronger and lighter, and I've also insulated the internals. Sunstorms won't affect it, nor will bursts of electricity."

"That definitely sounds useful," Jordan admitted. The traditional X-11s were worthless after the CME, unless Mohn had some mothballed somewhere. Even if they did, those suits could only be used until a sunstorm showed up. If they were exposed, their internals would be cooked almost instantly. "What else have you done to make it different?"

"For starters, the metal can be charged with the same energy you absorb from the moon, or the deathless draw from the sun," Vulcan explained. He removed his thick black apron, dropping the leather to the ground. "The metal is malleable when charged, which means it can shift with you. My new V-11 will turn someone like you into a one man army. Even other champions or deathless would fear you. If you went up against someone like Anubis, I'd lay even odds a young whelp like you could take him."

Jordan studied the armor, daring to dream a little. It would dramatically enhance his combat abilities, allowing him to make a difference against Ra. It would make him far more than a match for Trevor, too. In short, it was too good to be true.

"I feel like you're setting me up to buy something," Jordan said, folding his arms as he stared Vulcan down. "The armor seems amazing, but I have nothing to pay you with. How about we end the pitch, and you tell me what it's going to take to get this collar off? That is what Hades here promised he could do."

Hades and Vulcan shared an unreadable look. Something significant passed there, but Jordan had no idea what it was. He wasn't all that good at the double-dealing social arena the Director had thrived in. He was a soldier, not a politician.

"It's very simple," Hades said, turning back to Jordan. "The collar cannot be removed, save by the person wearing the bracelet. However, its influence can be neutralized. Vulcan?"

"He's right," the shorter god replied, giving a tight nod as he slapped the armor with his palm. "If you wear the V-11 armor, the armor will siphon power from the collar. This process will prevent the collar from restricting your abilities, while simultaneously ensuring that the armor functions for an extended duration. In short, if you wear the armor you'll be free from the collar. You can shift and shape as normal, so long as you wear it."

"So I'm exchanging one prison for another then," Jordan said, maybe with a little more hostility than he'd intended. "Let's say I agree to this. What do you get out of it?"

Vulcan cleared his throat and looked away. Hades, on the other hand, gave a too-friendly smile and wrapped an arm around Jordan's shoulder. "Not more than three hours ago I met with a Ka-Dun named Blair. I believe he was a part of your pack. Blair and I share a goal. Are you familiar with the name Osiris?"

Jordan knocked Hades's arm from his shoulder and took a step back. He eyed the god balefully. "Yeah, I've heard the name. Is that where you got all this tech?"

"Hardly," Vulcan broke in. His glowered at Jordan. "We're not lapdogs to that tyrant. We've been stealing his tech for two decades, and he's none the wiser."

"What Vulcan means," Hades said, his gaze clearly warning Vulcan to keep quiet, "is that we're no friends of Osiris. He's conquered the entirety of the underworld. In doing so he's isolated our brethren in the city of

Olympus. You probably didn't see it in the sky above, as it was obscured by the storm. It is locked elsewhere, until we can restore our conduit to the Well deep within the earth. Osiris prevents that, which makes him our enemy. You are no doubt familiar with the phrase the enemy of my enemy is my friend?"

"Yeah, I've heard it," Jordan said. He didn't like this, not one bit. "Osiris is an enemy, so far as we can tell. So maybe we have that in common. Walk me through your plan. I take the armor, then what?"

"You take the armor, which makes you faster and stronger. It also frees you from the collar, so you can leave this place," Hades explained, putting on another magnanimous smile. "You head north to the land known as France, where you will overtake your pack. You add your now tremendous strength to theirs, and aid them in stopping Osiris. Once Osiris is stopped, Vulcan reforges our conduit to the Well, and we free our sleeping brethren."

"Sounds simple enough," Jordan said, though he knew it would be anything but. He nodded at Wepwawet's unconscious form. "What about our wolf-headed friend here?"

"Ra will be here shortly, as soon as she's dealt with the distraction left by Isis. When she arrives, I will give him into her custody. You needn't worry. Wepwawet will be fine," Hades said, his tone all assurances. "Have we a deal?"

Jordan was torn. There was more to this than Hades had explained, but he'd be damned if he could see the catch.

"All right, I accept," he said, offering his hand to Hades.

Chapter 45- Baiting the Trap

Hades stared after Jordan, grinning widely. That had gone better than he could have dreamed. Another seed planted.

"I do not condone this, Hades. If not for the sake of our brethren, I would oppose you," Vulcan said, frowning darkly as he hauled Wepwawet to his feet. "Giving that Ka-Dun a set of my armor is one thing. He is young, and his need is dire. He might be willing to pay the price the armor will ultimately demand, but this? We are forcing a god to don it without choice."

"I understand your reservations," Hades said, as placatingly as he could muster. He breathed deeply, enjoying the hot stench of coal and metal. "Yet we do what we must. If we do not force Wepwawet to don the armor, then we have no way of knowing Ra's movements. Doing so will be critical. If she is in league with Osiris we must know it, and if she is not then we can at least learn the answer this way."

"It is wrong, Hades. As is much you have asked me to do," Vulcan said, snarling. Yet he pushed Wepwawet's unconscious form into the dock where the second set of armor lay. He propped the body up, and began the sequence that caused the robotic arms to mount the armor.

"I don't disagree," Hades said, giving what he hoped was a genuine sigh. Would that he didn't need Vulcan's cooperation, but he was not yet ready to betray his companion. He had use for him still. "It is wrong. Yet so is what Osiris has done to our brethren. Do you wish to see Zeus again? Poseidon? If we do not overcome Osiris and restore the conduit, our family is lost forever."

"They may be lost already. How could they have survived so long without the energy of the conduit? They'd have been forced to turn on each other," Vulcan said, his voice quavering.

The robotic arms in the stall began to whir and buzz as they affixed armor to Wepwawet's body. Hades couldn't help but smile. Once the process was complete, Wepwawet would have no means of removing the armor. He'd be trapped, as surely as the unwitting Ka-Dun had been.

"Haaaaades," came a roar, louder than thunder. It suppressed even the din of the Forge, an impressive feat. The voice was both feminine and terrifyingly familiar. "Show yourself, you treacherous little weasel."

"Complete the process. I will stall her," Hades snapped, whirling and heading towards the voice. He threaded his way back through the Forge, careful to avoid the numerous automatons carrying out Vulcan's work.

He was playing a very dangerous game. Ra had the power to kill him, and even if by some miracle he overcame her, Anubis wouldn't be far from her side. He had to convince her both that he was no threat and that his actions had been in her best interest. Damn Set and his pride. Had he not required Hades to plant a spy with both Isis and Ra, then he wouldn't be in this position.

"Ahhh, mighty Ra," Hades said, giving a low bow as Ra swept into the mouth of the Forge. She wore the same ivory and gold regalia he'd seen over a dozen millennia before. Her stark beauty hadn't changed a whit, nor had the lethal way she twirled her spear. "I have been expecting you. I have much news to share, and I can even offer a potent new weapon."

"Where is Wepwawet? And what of the Ka-Dun Jordan?" she demanded, stalking forward until she stood mere inches from Hades. Hades was not a short man, yet Ra stared him in the eye, her lean body coiled, ready to strike.

Hades licked his lips, eyes flicking to the figures with her. He'd expected Anubis, but there was no sign of the jackal-headed god. That surprised him. Ra usually brought her enforcer everywhere. In the jackal's place stood a pair of deathless, one with red hair and freckles. The other Hades dimly remembered. Ra had a son, if he recalled. What was his name? Irakesh, yes that was it.

Behind Irakesh stood a Ka-Dun, one also ensnared by a collar of shi-dun. He waited in clear deference to Irakesh, a proper servant in every way. Interesting.

"Apologies, mighty Ra. Follow me and you'll have your answers," Hades said, threading back through the Forge. Ra and her entourage followed. Irakesh appeared bored, but both the shifty-eyed Ka-Dun and the fiery-haired deathless surveyed the room with curiosity. Intelligence lurked in both gazes, though only the deathless had the bearing of a true warrior.

Hades stopped at the platform where Vulcan waited, turning to face Ra. He clasped his hands, bowing low. "Vulcan has given Wepwawet a potent new tool. He wears armor crafted from the finest technology this age has to offer. It will greatly increase his strength."

"Wepwawet," Ra barked, stalking up the dais and stopping before the wolf-headed god. His body was completely enshrouded by the armor and he didn't answer.

"It will be a few moments before the armor wakes him," Vulcan said, stepping up to join Ra.

If he feared her, he didn't have the good sense to show it. That was alarming. Always Ra and her kind had stood above them, and they had never let Hades forget that his pantheon had once been lowly mortals. They lacked the raw power of Ra and her ilk, and relied on their weaker shaping.

"What is wrong with him?" Ra snarled, turning to Vulcan. She appeared a hair's breadth from violence.

"He was attacked by Isis, mighty Ra," Hades said, drawing Ra's eye. "I do not know what prompted the fight, but the Ka-Dun Jordan was clear on this point. The fight rendered him unconscious, but the armor will help him recover from his injuries."

"What of Jordan?" Ra snapped, eyes flaring green. "I'll crack his spine myself if he's betrayed me."

"I released him, mighty Ra," Hades said, raising a palm in supplication.

"Please, hear me out. I did so for a grave purpose. I have dispatched the Ka-Dun to find Isis, for she must know the same news I am about to share with you."

"Speak, worm," Ra growled, eyes narrowing. Hades knew he was one word from death.

"Your anger is righteous, but when you understand my reasoning you will forgive me, I think," Hades said, dropping to his knees. Ra wasn't stupid, but she was also vulnerable to flattery. "Osiris has done much while you slept. The world is in danger, and our only hope lies in an alliance between you and Isis."

Ra relaxed half a hair, cocking her head to the side. "Explain. Quickly."

"After the Arks entered hibernation, Osiris awoke. He used the power of the Well to craft a potent army, one very similar to those once used by his brother Set. Demons of the most hideous variety," Hades explained. Now that the hook was set he'd use a piece of the truth, one she could verify. "His army stormed across the underworld, cutting off all conduits to the Well. All save his own. We were left powerless, growing old while he grew strong. Many gods perished, while Osiris did the unthinkable: he emerged to enslave and shape the nascent cultures of man. You can see his touch everywhere."

"This could explain much," Ra said, pursing her lips. "I have seen his fingerprints across the globe. The culture known as Egypt clearly aped our own, as did several others on other continents. Tell me, if your tale is true, how did you survive? Without a link to the conduit, you'd never have had the energy to cross the gulf of time to this new age."

"It is a shameful tale," Hades replied, hanging his head. His long grey hair screened his smile, or so he hoped. He adopted an agonized tone, one that part of him really felt. "Vulcan and I had no choice but to reverse the flow of energy from the conduit we forged with Olympus."

"That's monstrous," Ra snapped, eyes going wide. She rounded, stalking back and forth like a caged cat as if weighing his fate. Even her followers looked concerned, particularly the fiery-haired deathless. "You siphoned their energy to keep yourselves alive. You understand this means all your brethren are likely dead?"

"We do, mighty Ra," Hades said, real tears falling. He regretted what he'd been forced to do, though he'd do it again in an instant if needed. "My brother Zeus likely died cursing my name, yet what choice did we have? We are lowly sorcerers, unable to oppose someone with the strength of the deathless. We fought, but Osiris brushed us aside like gnats. Had we not reversed the conduit, my brethren would have died anyway. Vulcan and I would be dead as well, and you and Isis would have no knowledge of the treachery of Osiris."

Ra folded her arms, staring hard at Hades. A sudden clicking and whirring drew her attention, and Hades followed her gaze. Wepwawet's now armored form staggered from the stall. Vulcan caught him before he could fall, using those powerful arms to hold up the god's enormous weight.

"Wh-what happened?" Wepwawet asked, his voice strangely mechanized by the armor's voice synthesizer. His faceplate angled down as he raised an armored arm for inspection. "What have you done to me? And where am I?"

"Peace, Wepwawet," Ra commanded, turning back to Hades. "You have done what you must. I still think you are a treacherous snake, but I will take this gift in the spirit it is offered. I will even overlook you aiding my enemy. Sending a messenger to Isis may be to my benefit."

"Peace?" Wepwawet roared. "I will show you peace."

His armored fist smashed Ra in the chest, launching her backwards into the stall where he'd donned the armor. She rolled to her feet with cat-like quickness, but Wepwawet was already making for Hades.

"You!" he screamed, a trio of black blades erupting from the fist of his gauntlet. He rammed them at Hades, his arm blurring too quickly for Hades to have any prayer of evading.

Yet somehow Ra was there, interposed between Wepwawet and Hades.

Her sunsteel spear had blocked the blow, and she whirled it low, knocking Wepwawet onto his back with a terrible clatter.

"Contain yourself, Wepwawet, or I will take your life here and now," she yelled, sliding into a defensive stance. Her companions looked ready to join the fray, but as of yet had done nothing.

"The armor is terrible," Wepwawet snapped, climbing slowly to his feet. "I can feel it pressing at the edges of my mind."

It sounded like an apology, and it seemed to have the desired effect. Ra relaxed a hair. "If you raise arms against me again, your life is forfeit. Head back to the surface. Now."

Wepwawet stalked off, smashing an automaton with a balled fist as he passed by. Ra watched his passing until he was out of sight.

"Thank you, mighty Ra," Hades said, bowing low. He held his deferential pose for long moments.

"Now, what other weapons have you created for our use?" Ra said. "It seems we are to go to war with Osiris, and I'd not fight it unprepared,"

The seed was planted. Set would be pleased.

Chapter 46- Run

Jordan ducked as a boulder the size of a bus crashed down behind him with a deafening boom he could feel even in his armor. The wind screamed, whipping trees, rocks, and the occasional body around with equal ferocity. He'd never seen anything like it; the entire horizon was painted in violent orange, blotting out most of his immediate surroundings. Visibility was a paltry hundred feet, and even the armor's vast array of sensors picked up little.

Despite the life-threatening peril he felt like a god-damned god. Jordan gathered his legs underneath him, the mechanical whirring of the armor audible even over the wind. Then he leapt skyward, over the crest of the hill and onto a boulder on the far side. What had that been? A hundred and seventy five feet in one bound? His already incredible strength was vastly augmented by the armor, but it was more than that. He had limitless energy, as well. Jordan laughed exultantly.

I do not trust this strange mechanical device, Ka-Dun. The beast rumbled. *We'd be better served with our own abilities.*

"Maybe I'd ditch it, if I was able to get the collar off," Jordan replied, leaping again. Four more leaps and he reached the valley floor, skidding a long furrow in the dry dirt. It was odd that it was dry during a storm of this magnitude, but hardly surprising when you thought about what the storm was made of. "As it is, we don't have any choice. Even if we did, this dramatically improves my combat abilities. They even included missiles. All I need is a rifle of some kind."

He broke into a full sprint, glancing at the chronometer that overlaid his vision. Fifty-four fucking miles an hour. Holy. Shit. Jordan broke right, grabbing the side of an outcrop and flinging himself to the top of the next hill. Again and again he repeated the process, quickly eating up the ground as he moved away from the storm. Or tried to anyway.

The boiling clouds shifted suddenly, moving in his direction. High above, lightning split the sky, and the orange clouds were thick with fire. He could smell burnt ozone, even through the suit's air filters. A bolt traced the horizon in front of him, stabbing into the earth with incredible brilliance. It sent up a massive geyser of earth and stone. Could lightning even do that? Another strike, then another. They rained down all around him, though the few surviving trees were thankfully acting as lightning rods.

The temperature gauge on his HUD read 118 degrees. Jesus, that explained why he was sweating so profusely. He blinked rapidly to clear his eyes, wishing he could touch his face. The armor prevented that, of course.

Could the vegetation here even survive the kind of heat and fury he was witnessing? It wasn't a god damned desert, or at least it hadn't been. After the storm, maybe that would be different.

A little red blip lit the upper corner of the mini-map in the corner of his display. It showed the surrounding topography, and the dot was ahead and to the right. He sprinted forward, leaping up a hillside and dodging another lightning strike as he crested the top. The storm was growing more furious, and the wind was strong enough to toss him off-balance each time he leapt. If not for the armor's internal stabilizers, he'd have been crushed against a rock. Or worse. Jordan kept moving, this time down to a wide plain.

In the sky above him, he saw the silver ship disappearing on a northern course.

Chapter 47- Breathing Room

Blair heaved a sigh of relief, shaking from the aftereffects of adrenaline.

"Blair, look at this." Liz's voice came from miles away. It took everything he had to raise his head and stare through the clear portion of the deck. He badly needed sleep.

Blair gasped as he took in the view. Orange and red clouds blanketed the entire southern horizon, their roiling mass flashing with occasional bursts of lightning. No one from this age had ever before witnessed such immense, beautiful power.

"It's amazing," Blair said, releasing the control pillar and moving to join her. "But honestly? I hope I never have to face one of those storms again."

"This one was mild," came a soft voice. Blair started, seeing Isis to his left, sitting atop a chest carved from dark red wood. She'd returned to human form, her silver hair loose as she stared at the storm. She was so tiny, so forlorn. "A strong sunstorm will boil away all life where it passes, scouring the earth of everything. Fortunately such storms are rare, and the first will not come for decades. Centuries if we are lucky."

"Well, let's just hope we don't have to fly through one any time soon," Liz said, her tone light and optimistic. She beamed a perfect smile his way, eyes twinkling in the strange glow of the storm.

Blair wished they were alone, though he was grateful Isis had saved them. He blinked away those thoughts as Liz continued. "So now what? I know the whole plan was to find out what had happened to the Nexus. We know Osiris has something to do with it. Blair, do you want to fill her in?"

"Not really, but I guess I have to," Blair said, steeling himself. It wasn't every day you told a goddess her estranged husband had become an evil overlord, apparently bent on world domination. "Hades said he was willing to give us the slipsail, because we had to be able to carry news to you."

"News of Osiris," Isis said, brow furrowing. "Tell me."

"Hades claims that as soon as the hibernation began, Osiris launched a war," Blair explained, trying to make sure he got it all right. "He created an army of what Hades called demons. I'm guessing you know more about those than I do."

"I'm familiar with their ilk," Isis said, anger darkening her features. "The term was coined by Set to describe his minions. One of the chief uses Ark Lords put their Arks to is the creation of new life. They craft minions the way a potter makes vessels. Demons are black things, incapable of any emotion save hate. They are violence incarnate, the perfect servants with which to flood a battle field."

"Well, Osiris used these troops to conquer the underworld," Blair continued. He turned to face the rail, gazing off at the storm. "They pushed Hades back, and eventually severed the conduit connecting Olympus to the Well. Hades also believed Osiris was severing all connections to the Nexus."

Blair trailed off as he looked to Isis. She was silent for a long moment, then finally turned to face them. Her green eyes sparkled in the storm's fading light, and a single tear slid down one cheek.

"If Hades is not deceiving us, then it seems my husband has done dark and terrible things during my long hibernation," she began, slowly, as if the words were forced from her. "I do not want to believe it. Osiris was the best of us, a leader for uncounted centuries. The idea that he would sever the connection to the Nexus is unthinkable. That would mean the destruction of the Ark network. What motivation could he possibly have?"

Blair looked at Liz, but she offered him no help. He turned back to Isis. "I don't know. I don't even know if Hades was telling the truth, but he certainly seemed scared. It also seemed like Olympus was stuck between dimensions somehow, for whatever that's worth."

"That's troubling," Isis admitted. She shook her head slowly. "It should have returned when the sun changed. The fact that it has not means the Olympian pantheon may be dead. Even if they aren't, their faction is lost to us. If Osiris has gone insane, then we'd have to face him alone. That is not a fight we can win."

"They're dead," Blair said, leaving it at that. He didn't want to dwell on the strange, empty city. Or on Hades's obvious grief.

"So we'd have to find allies then," Liz said. She looked determined, as always. "Lots of allies. If the Director was right, Osiris controls Mohn corp. That gives him a lot of firepower, especially if he has an army of demons to back it up. How do you plan to fight him?"

"There is only one way," Isis said. The tears were gone now, blown away by the hot wind that somehow seeped through the slipsail's skin. "We'd have to ally with Sekhmet, my near-sister. Only together would we have a chance, though even then our odds are slim. Osiris has had thirteen millennia to learn this world and to grow stronger. All that time he could have used the Well to create minions, and build weaponry."

Something about that tickled the back of Blair's mind. There was something obvious here he was missing, but he wasn't sure what. At least not yet. "Liz and I discussed places like ancient Egypt. We had a theory about the Great Pyramids. Is it possible structures like that were built to drain energy from sleeping Arks?"

Isis blinked several times, then cocked her head. "It is definitely possible. I've never directly inspected these pyramids, but their placement and composition are consistent with energy retrieval."

"And since Osiris was awake while the rest of you slept, he's the most likely person to have built these right?" Blair asked. An idea was forming.

"Most likely," Isis conceded. "Where are you going with this?"

"If Osiris had access to the near infinite power in the Well, why spend decades building pyramids to siphon a trickle of energy from the pyramids? What was the point?" Blair asked, connections forming. "I mean, I get the reasoning behind influencing cultures. If you wanted the world to be a certain way when the Arks returned, it would make sense to shape it. But why all the effort to make structures like the pyramids?"

Isis and Liz were both silent for long moments.

Isis finally spoke. "An interesting question. The energy gained from such work would be minimal, useful only to the desperate or miserly. Perhaps Osiris sought to rob his enemies of strength."

"Maybe," Blair said, shrugging. "The point is, we don't know his motivations. We have nothing but supposition. We need more data before we commit to a course of action. I've had enough of rash plans and mistakes. Let's do this—whatever this turns out to be—right."

"Agreed," Liz said, giving a tight nod. "We paid a heavy price back in San Francisco. I don't want to pay a similar price here, especially not with so much on the line."

"You speak with much wisdom, Ka-Dun," Isis said. She reached out and squeezed Blair's forearm, which nearly made him wet himself. She wasn't cruel, but she'd made it clear she didn't regard his opinion very highly. This was a definite reversal. "For now, I believe our course is clear. If Osiris is the enemy, then we need allies. The only ally strong enough to help is the very one we just fled. We will have to not only convince her of our intentions, but also make reparations for the hideous damage I wrought to her army."

"Yes, that giant worm thing was pretty messed up," Blair said, giving a half smile. "I'd be pretty pissed if someone unleashed it on my army."

"What if Ra isn't willing to work with us? If we wait for her, she could just attack and kill us," Liz pointed out. She was biting her lip, a habit he'd first noticed back in Peru.

"Trevor is with her," Blair pointed out. "He's not going to let her harm us."

"Your friend is powerful, but young. He would be nothing but a gnat to Ra," Isis said, snorting as she gave a dismissive gesture. "If Ra seeks combat, it will come down to her and I. You two will have to do the best you can against Ra's underlings. Pray that she does not bring Horus,

Wepwawet, or Anubis."

"I don't think he'll have to fight her," Blair said, giving a grin now. "Trevor hasn't been enslaved and he hasn't been killed. Wepwawet told us he'd been adopted into her court. Put yourself in Ra's shoes. You've been asleep for thirteen thousand years and a guy who studies the sun is dropped into your lap. Trevor is a warrior, a scientist, and an all-around badass. I bet you this ship she's taken him on as an advisor. Trevor will advise that she talk to us, at the very least. It isn't much but, hey, I'll take what we can get."

"You raise an interesting point," Isis conceded, glancing to the glowing clouds in the west. "There is a place of great significance in the land you'd know as France. How far are we from there?"

"I don't know exactly; we don't really have GPS," Blair said. His tone drew a sharp glance from Liz, so he moderated it. "I know what direction it is at least. I'd guess our speed at about two hundred miles per hour. We'll probably be there by morning."

"Excellent. I will use the time to meditate. When we arrive in the land of France, fetch me and we will discuss our next move," Isis commanded, her imperious demeanor back in full force. She turned on her heel and headed for the far side of the cabin, leaving them in silence.

"I hope you're right," Liz said, reaching out to squeeze his shoulder.

Blair sucked in a breath, and summoned the courage to act on an urge he'd been suppressing for weeks. He put his arm around Liz and pulled her close as they stared at the sunset.

Chapter 48- Now What?

Trevor eyed Wepwawet with concern as their party exited the crumbling building, emerging back onto the surface. Thankfully the storm had abated, though a hot wind still whipped sand and grit into Trevor's eyes. Still, it was preferable to being below.

The underworld, what little he'd seen of it, wasn't a place he'd like to visit again. It stank of coal and fire, and reminded him a little too much of depictions of hell. He'd been interested in the armor and weaponry Vulcan had been constructing, but not enough to spend much time there.

"What course now, mighty Ra? I itch to do violence," Wepwawet said in a strangely digitized voice, pausing next to Ra. If anything, he was even more intimidating in the strange black armor. It covered him from head to toe, with bulky contraptions around the right wrist and left shoulder. Those looked familiar. Too familiar. They brought Trevor back to San Diego, where Mohn Corp had invaded his house. If this armor was similar, both the wrist and shoulder likely packed missiles.

"Fetch Anubis. Tell him to begin marching northeast. We make for The First Ark. You will have your chance to kill soon enough," Ra commanded. She strode up a hill, pausing at the top. The keening wind twisted her scarlet hair wildly around her.

Trevor watched Irakesh follow her up the hillside, Steve not far behind. Steve always lurked in Irakesh's shadow, and it wasn't hard to guess his game. He was ingratiating himself, fading into the background until he saw an opportunity.

Jordan's departure worried Trevor, at least a little. It meant he was alone against Steve and Irakesh, and he doubted he could take them both. Steve definitely, but Irakesh was canny and powerful, and had more knowledge of his abilities than Trevor did.

That left him alone in an enemy camp, of course. He'd been embraced here, in a way, but he had no illusions about how far he was trusted. Ra seemed to like him, but he'd seen her moods shift quickly. She could just as easily decide to kill him as elevate him in rank. That meant in many ways he was playing a political game, something he'd never been very good at.

You've done well so far, my host. Yet you must exhibit more caution, or risk the ire of your more powerful brethren. Anubis is the greatest threat, though you are wise to fear Irakesh. We will overcome that one in time, but we are not ready for such a confrontation yet.

Trevor started walking toward the base of the hill. The wind prevented him from hearing the conversation between Ra and Irakesh, but Irakesh looked angry, his mouth an animated snarl. Ra raised one hand, silencing him. The dark-skinned deathless turned on his heel, stalking away from Ra with the grace of a jungle cat. He glared hatefully at Trevor as he passed, Steve trailing in his wake like some housebroken puppy.

"Trevor," Ra called, beckoning him to approach.

He did so, walking quickly up the hillside to join her at the crest. He didn't say anything when he got there, instead waiting for her to explain what she wanted. Silence was a powerful weapon, one that came naturally to introverts like himself. Let the other person tell you what they wanted. Sometimes they revealed more than they intended; even if they didn't, at least you didn't have to make awkward small talk.

"I am deeply troubled by the events of the past day," she finally said, turning those emerald eyes on him. Her gaze was searching, and also softer than it had been before. He wasn't sure what to make of that. "Irakesh has asked that I punish you. Did you know that? He believes you should have kept a closer watch on the Ka-Dun Jordan, and he blames you for the escape."

"He's not wrong," Trevor admitted with a shrug. "I left Jordan to watch over Wepwawet. If I'd kept him with me, then he and Hades wouldn't have met. He wouldn't have escaped."

"Does his escape displease you?" Ra asked, raising a delicate eyebrow.

"No," Trevor admitted. "I didn't like the fact that you put a collar on him. He's a real bastard, but he's a good soldier and he's fighting on the right side."

"The right side being Isis and her pack," Ra said, her tone curiously neutral. Perhaps dangerously so.

"Yeah, exactly," Trevor said, meeting her gaze. Thus far, honesty had worked pretty damned well, so he saw no reason to change that now. "I know I'm one of you. A deathless, I guess. But that doesn't take away my ability to know right from wrong. *Wrong* is murdering the entire world. *Wrong* is turning everyone into a walking corpse."

Ra cocked her head to the side, eyeing him curiously. "I like you, Trevor. Your honesty is refreshing, as is your raw ignorance. It affords a different perspective than I am used to."

"Ignorance?" Trevor shot back, bristling in spite of himself.

"Indeed," Ra said, folding her arms and giving him a smile that dared him to press the issue. When he didn't, she continued. "Try to look at this from my perspective. You are, among other things, a scientist, are you not?"

"Where are you going with this?"

"Patience, Trevor. It's a quality scientists should possess, yes? I want you to imagine that you will live forever. This should be easier for you, since you *will* live forever. You understand biologically how your body has changed, and that you will progress through the millennia without aging," Ra said, pausing as she watched him. She licked her lips, exposing a mouthful of inhuman fangs. "What if you saw countless generations rise, then die? Generation after generation, century after century, millennia after millennia. Always, people make the same mistakes. They are forever trapped in their narrow perspective of the world. They understand only what is important to them in this instant."

"I get what you're saying," Trevor said, shaking his head. "It doesn't mean you should devalue life, though. Isis still values it, and she has the same perspective you do."

"Isis is weak," Ra said, eyes glittering dangerously. "She makes foolish decisions of the heart. I use reason. The kind of logic you should understand, being a scientist."

"Okay, then explain to me why you murdered the world? I had a conversation with Irakesh a few months back, but his reasons for so much death were shit," Trevor said, recalling his former master's argument that the Deathless were stewards not just of humanity, but also of nature. Keeping mankind in check also kept a natural balance, because otherwise man would do…exactly what man had done. Pollute the world and wipe out thousands of species.

"No doubt they were. My son is many things, but a wise orator is not one of them," she gave back, smiling cruelly now. "Listen to my reasons, and judge for yourself. What if you knew that enemies far worse than the deathless were coming? What if the only way you could fight them was to breed an army of incredible size? There are seven Arks, Trevor. You've met the lords of two, and, if I understand it, your companion has become the lord of a third. The remaining four are not kind, nor are they inclined to share. I assure you their plans for humanity are far more abhorrent than mine. You heard what Hades had to say about Osiris, and he is not the worst of us."

"So the ends justify the means then?" Trevor asked, clenching his fists.

"Of course they do," Ra said, raising an eyebrow as if he were a foolish child. "Win. At any cost. Because if you lose nothing else matters. I have done as I have done to ensure that humanity has a future. If I took the timid path of Isis, there is every chance humanity would be obliterated, our entire race nothing but a memory of those who'd twist us to their own uses. You've never seen such enemies. Right now, I am the worst thing you have ever encountered, a monster in your eyes. Is this not so?"

Trevor had a difficult time answering that question. Ra was beautiful. Oh, there was savagery to that beauty, like a lioness, but she was breathtaking too. Something he could stare at all day, simply appreciating. "Yes, I do think you're a monster, at least by my standards. Maybe these enemies exist, and maybe they're worse than you. The thing is, when you fight a monster, you risk becoming one. In your case you've made too many compromises, too many concessions to win. I'm willing to bet that's why you and Isis don't see eye to eye."

Ra began to laugh, a thick musical laughter. She smiled warmly at him. "Yes, I definitely like you, Trevor. Not a single one of my followers would have the courage to say something like that, but perhaps that is the kind of counsel I will need in the coming days. If that treacherous snake of a god Hades is telling the truth, Osiris is the gravest immediate threat. We must wrest the First Ark from him, but that is something I do not believe I can do without help. Especially since Sobek has stolen the Primary Access Key. Without it, my powers are limited."

"So what do you plan to do?" he asked, more than a little grateful the topic had changed. He'd been treading on dangerous ground, and the last thing he wanted was to piss her off to the point where she killed him. He might not like what he'd become, but he was definitely attached to being alive. Well, un-alive, to be accurate.

"I'm unsure, a rare state for me. I need allies, but the only one who might possibly be of use would be Isis herself," Ra said, brushing a lock of scarlet from her face. "Unfortunately, she is blind to the truth and does not see Osiris as a threat. He must be dealt with, so I will marshall my forces, and make for the First Ark. We will do our utmost to pry Osiris from its depths, and when we have dragged him into the light we will kill him."

She made it sound so easy, but Trevor heard something he'd never expected from the seemingly implacable goddess: fear.

Chapter 49- France

"Set down there," Isis commanded. Blair did as she asked, guiding the slipsail slowly into the valley. They were surrounded by high cliffs of bare white stone, broken by a smattering of green trees. More trees lined the valley floor, which had a wide, slow moving river flowing through it. The place was familiar, though Blair wasn't sure why, since he'd never been to southern France.

The ship settled to a halt on a narrow ridge, about midway up one of the cliffs. He held his breath as it stopped, praying it wouldn't tumble into the valley below. Several moments later, he finally released his link to the control obelisk. Isis and Liz had already passed through the ship's skin to the rock below. Blair joined them, shifting as he did so. It was damn cold, more so than he'd have expected. Sometimes having fur was nice.

"Where are we going?" he asked, looking around for any features of note. There was nothing about this place to suggest why they'd come here. No landmarks, and no structures of any kind. They were in the wilderness, the largely untouched south of France.

"To a sacred place," Isis said, trotting up the trail. She moved quickly, and they struggled to keep up. Long minutes passed as they wound up a narrow trail. Isis eventually stopped, though Blair couldn't see any particular reason why she should have. She turned to face them, a wide, childlike smile lighting up her features. "We have arrived. It is still here, by some miracle."

"What is it?" Blair asked, stopping next to her. He followed her gaze to a hole in the ground, just barely large enough for an adult to crawl through.

"Is that a cave entrance?" Liz asked, teeth chattering as she rubbed her arms. She hadn't chosen to shift, for some reason.

"Yes," Isis said, kneeling next to it. "Let's get inside and out of the wind. It will be warmer in there, particularly after we start a fire."

She moved to a nearby bush and started breaking off small branches, then quickly gathered larger ones that had fallen from a neighboring tree. Her movements were quick and economical, as if she'd practiced them hundreds of times. When she'd finished she ducked into the cave entrance, shimmying through with surprising familiarity.

Liz gave a shrug, following her inside. Blair waited a moment longer, blinking a few times as he began considering where they were. He thought he knew why this place was familiar now. He'd seen a documentary about it. The Cave of Forgotten Dreams. If this was the same place, much of what the world knew about Cro-Magnon culture had originated here. Blair shifted back to human form, squeezing into the narrow opening.

"Isis," he called, rising from a crouch just inside. His eyes began adjusting to the dim, but he could still barely make out anything. "Where are we, exactly?"

"This was my home, once," Isis called back, her voice echoing from deeper in the cave. Liz was already disappearing into the gloom, so Blair followed. His vision was much sharper than it had been as a mortal, and the slight light from the cave entrance lit the place like day.

He slid down part of the cave floor, catching himself against a stalactite. This place couldn't have been more different than the underworld. It was slick and damp, the sound of water dripping everywhere. Blair rose into a stooped crouch, inching past the low ceiling until he reached a place where he could stand. Liz and Isis stood before a wide wall. Both stared up at something painted there, and Blair's jaw dropped when he saw what it was.

"My god. We're in Chauvet. See those brown lines on the rock above? That's a wooly rhinoceros. This place is even older than you, isn't it?" he asked, moving closer to join them.

"It is," Isis said, her tone reverent. "My tribe lived in the valley below. We hunted game when it was warm, and retreated here when the snows grew too fierce. I don't know who painted those. They were created countless generations before my people. My grandmother taught me that they'd always been there."

Blair was beyond shocked. It was one thing to understand how old Isis was, another to see proof. The cave paintings of Chauvet came primarily from two periods, one called the Gravettian, about twenty-six thousand years before the present. The other was thought to be older, perhaps as old as thirty-two thousand years.

"Most of the creatures drawn here are extinct now," Blair said, leaning in close to study the art. A beast had been captured there, the towering predator taller than a man even on four legs. "This one is a cave bear. I bet those must have been fierce."

"Fierce enough, when we were mortals," Isis said, giving a shrug. She turned to face him. "We never returned here after we changed. I wasn't even sure it would still be here. But it is, and that gladdens me."

"Do you think Ra will come here?" Liz said. She ran a hand along the stone, tracing a horse drawn from some black material.

"Definitely," Isis said, giving a nod. Her smile vanished. "She and I were near-sisters, once upon a time. We made many fires here, shared many tales. She can feel the key Blair possesses, and as she gets closer she will track it to this location. It is my hope she will honor the sanctity of this place, and keep the peace."

"That's a lot of trust to put in an enemy," Blair said, more than a little skeptical.

"Ra was and is honorable. We may not agree on much, but she can be trusted to keep her word if she gives it," Isis said. She stood up and wiped her hands on her skirt. "I'll set up a fire. You two see if you can scrounge up some game. We'll likely be here for a day or two before Ra arrives."

"So we just wait for her, then what?" Liz asked, tone more harsh than Blair had heard her use with Isis. "We're trapped, and if she attacks us we're done."

"I don't know," Isis said, eyeing Liz soberly. "It may be that we meet our end in this place. Fitting, as it is where it all began."

Chapter 50- Heavy Price

Jordan slid down the cliffside, using the armor's internal gyroscope to help keep his balance. He landed in a shower of rock sixty-three feet below the top of the cliff, on a narrow ledge with a few scrubby trees clinging to the white rock. Below, not more than a hundred feet distant, lay the ship he'd been pursuing ever since the storm. The hull had a silver sheen, despite the cloud cover. It appeared deserted, though it was possible the crew was below decks.

"Guess there's only one way to find out," he muttered, leaping to a ledge some forty feet below. Two more leaps and he was standing on the wide area where the ship had set down. Jordan expected his beast to make some comment, either about caution or rejoining his pack. Yet there was nothing. The trip here had been extremely lonely, highlighting just how dependent he'd grown on having that inner voice at his disposal. With the beast, he knew he was never truly alone, and that kept despair at bay when he was going through the worst of the things he'd had to endure. Where had it gone? The last time he'd spoken to it had been the day he'd donned the armor.

"Blair? Liz?" he bellowed, using the armor's internal microphone to amplify his voice. It echoed off the surrounding cliffs, disturbing a smattering of crows who winged their way skyward. There was no other response. Jordan walked to the ship, unsure how to proceed. "Blair? It's Jordan."

Nothing. He walked a full circuit around the ship, which was featureless. Not a single rivet, bolt, or discernible means of entry. Jordan knelt next to it, peering under the ship to see if there was a hatch. Nothing. He activated the powerful light above his right shoulder, panning the beam slowly across the bottom of the ship.

Jordan was completely unprepared for his sudden flight. One moment he was kneeling there, the next he was soaring into the sky like a very ungainly bird. He twisted, facing the ship. A massive silver werewolf crouched there, amber eyes narrowed as she watched his flight. For a split second, Jordan thought he was seeing Bridget, then noticed this werewolf was larger. A terrifying memory of having his arms torn off leapt to mind, and he realized with a shudder that he'd just run afoul of the Mother. Again.

He gathered the suit's armored legs underneath him, landing in a crouch. The heavy armor pulverized the rock, sending a spray of gravel shooting out. He kept his balance, though. "It's me, Mother. Jordan. I've escaped from Ra."

The Mother blinked twice, then slowly straightened. She stopped baring her fangs, and began walking toward him. Three paces later she was in human form, the shift happening all in a blur. She paused a few feet away, staring up at him. "You made enough noise to wake the slumbering dead. When I saw you, I feared the worst. What is that strange contraption you wear? I recognize it from your time among the house of Mohn, but this armor feels different. It smells…wrong."

"Hades gave it to me," Jordan said, walking back to the ship, though he kept his distance. No sense getting any closer to the Mother than he had to. "If it smells wrong, you can blame him and his friend Vulcan. You're right that it's very similar to Mohn's X-11. I don't know where Hades got the design, and honestly I don't care. I just wanted to get away from Ra. She collared me. I'm still wearing that collar, but the armor seems to have muted its influence."

"Collared?" Isis said, blinking. Then her mouth tightened. "That cruel bitch. She's used one of the shi-dun."

"Two," Jordan corrected. "She used a second collar on Steve. So far as I know he's still playing meek servant for Irakesh, and still spilling every secret he can to Ra. Anything he knew about you, or about us, she knows now too."

The Mother's scowl could have curdled milk.

"That cannot be helped. Steve will be dealt with in time," the Mother said, stalking up to Jordan. He wasn't quite as tall in the armor as he'd have been in wolf form, but she was still tiny beside him. She stretched out a hand and touched the armor, then closed her eyes. She was silent for a long moment before speaking. "It is as I feared. This armor is tainted. Dark iron was used in its forging. The suit you wear is demon-crafted."

"What the fuck does that mean?" Jordan asked, genuinely alarmed.

"On the one hand it means the armor is far more powerful than the simple steel used by Mohn to make its weaponry," Isis said, folding her arms as she stared up at him. "On the other, it means your armor has a primitive consciousness. It is neither alive, nor dead precisely. That consciousness is linked to something greater, a master you might say."

"Wait, the armor is alive?" Jordan said, struggling to keep up. "Alive how? It's just a piece of metal."

"Dark iron is imbued with the blood of a potent master," Isis explained, clearly disgusted. "A god will shed his own blood during the forging. This creates a link between him and anything created from the metal. Such creations are always powerful, but come with an awful price. They were first created by Set, used during his long war with Osiris. If Hades has spoken truly, which I still doubt, then my husband has now adopted the same methods as his treacherous brother. That gives him a tremendous advantage in the coming battle."

"How so?" Jordan asked.

"You are, in essence, wearing a part of the armor's creator," the Mother explained. "I do not know the extent of the influence that will grant, as you are a Ka-Dun. During our own age, those who wore armor or used weapons crafted from blood iron often fell under the influence of the item's creator. They could be made to kill their family. Turn on their liege. For this reason its use was banned by most Ark lords. Set was the exception, but when he was finally overthrown we thought all knowledge of dark iron had passed from the world. That is why I find the idea that Osiris might have adopted its use so troubling."

"Well, that's just fucking lovely," Jordan said, clenching an armored fist. "So my options are remove the armor and be controlled by the collar, or leave the armor on and worry that Osiris can seize control of my body at a critical moment. What the fuck do I even do with that?"

"Take heart. Taint takes time. Months, even for those of weak will. Someone with strong will can resist for years," the Mother said, giving a sympathetic sigh. "Why don't we start by removing the armor? Then I will see what can be done with the collar. Perhaps we can remove both. It will be difficult, but the shi-dun were crafted by Ptah. I know his work well and might be able to find a weakness."

"All right," Jordan said, through gritted teeth. He moved his thumb and forefinger in a very unnatural motion. It had been purposely chosen because it was something you'd never do on accident. That motion triggered the exit sequence. The armor would power down, and he'd be able to remove it.

Or that was what should have happened anyway. The HUD stayed lit. He tried the gesture again. Nothing. Jordan roared in anger, slamming a metal fist into the side of the cliff. Shards of rock flaked away from the impact. "I can't. The armor won't deactivate."

"Clever. Clever and incredibly devious," the Mother said, eyes narrowing. "I suspect once the armor has been donned it can only be removed by its creator. Such a measure makes you effectively a slave."

"A short lived one," Jordan countered, trying to calm his breathing. He wanted to kill something. Hell, he wanted to kill everything. "I can't eat with this thing on. Sooner or later I'll starve."

"That's unlikely," the Mother said, shaking her head slowly. The motion tossed her silver hair over her shoulder, exposing a pale neck. Jordan longed to wrap a gauntleted hand around that neck. "The armor will keep

236

you alive. It works much like sunsteel. It will absorb energy from the sun, and use that energy to sustain you. Unless we can get you to an Ark where I can experiment on the armor, you are trapped. Permanently."

Jordan closed his eyes, hanging his head. This was too much to bear, but with the armor he couldn't even end it. Even suicide was denied him.

So Jordan opened his eyes. He met Isis's gaze. "Then I'm going to make Osiris regret making me into a weapon. I'm going to kill that fucker, and I'm going to do it slowly."

Chapter 51- Dragons

"Sir," Benson said, bursting into the room. Her heart was thundering, the blood pulsing through her neck in a way that pulled Mark's attention from the ancient book. It took immense will to force his eyes up to her face, but he could still *feel* her heartbeat. She seemed to sense something, expression growing uncertain. "I apologize for the sudden interruption, it's just that—"

"What is it, Benson?" he asked, rising to his feet. He'd been at this for hours, to no avail. A lot of clues had been buried in human mythology, but the tome had yet to yield any great secrets.

"You're going to want to see this, sir." She spoke more rapidly than usual. "There's activity. At Stonehenge, sir."

"Show me," Mark said, stalking to the doorway and following her up the corridor.

The room he'd taken was tiny, with linoleum floors and cracked plaster walls. It had been a storeroom when he requisitioned it, and it stank of mildew despite the thorough cleaning that Facilities had given it. That didn't matter. His personal comfort was secondary to quick access.

Ops was only four doors up the hall, and he strode in briskly. People leapt to attention in a way they never had back in Syracuse. It wasn't that they hadn't respected him there, or even that they hadn't feared him. Both had been true. No, the difference was one of degrees. Before, they had feared he might fire them. Now they feared he might devour them, and with good reason. He could smell their fear, hear the symphony of heartbeats. He wanted to feed, and the primitive part of their brains knew it.

"What am I looking at?" Mark barked, striding to stand before the wall-mounted television. He missed the much larger screen in the Syracuse facility, but one worked with the tools at hand.

"It looks like we're just in time. We picked up seismic activity consistent with that in Peru," Benson said, tapping a sequence on her tablet. The screen's image changed, focusing on a moonlit field. The only recognizable landmark was Stonehenge itself, a tiny ring several hundred yards away from the field where the camera was centered.

The ground began to shake, trees swaying, though he doubted there was any wind. Then something burst from the earth, a black spear tip that shot skywards. Mark went cold, recognizing the enormous structure that bored from the earth. It was just like the others, a jet black pyramid visible only because of the moonlight. Up and up it climbed, emerging from the earth until the ground finally stopped shaking.

Mark studied the image, noting that the Ark hadn't destroyed Stonehenge the way the one in Cairo had the Great Pyramids. The ancient ring of stones sat at the foot of the Ark, just like the Sphinx sat at the foot of the Ark in Cairo. Was that significant?

He watched, trying to focus on the image and not on the thunderous heartbeats around him. He smelled sweat now—that and more thick, tangy fear. These people were right to fear him. Mark knew that if his composure slipped for even a moment one of them would die.

"Sir, movement," Benson said. She pointed at the screen. "Something is emerging from the Ark."

Figures emerged from the southern face of the Ark, a steady stream of them, bipedal but otherwise inhuman, completely black, bursting forth like bats fleeing from a cave. If not for the moonlight, they'd have been invisible. They scattered, disappearing into the night.

"Give me some data on these things. Telemetry. Size. What do you have, people?" Mark asked the room at large, but his gaze landed on Benson. Fear lurked in her gaze, but it was less than it had been the day before. Familiarity bred contempt after all. Even a monster became normal eventually.

She brushed dark bangs from her face, almond eyes going unfocused as she examined the data feed the other analysts were gathering. "Sir, at a glance the trajectory of the creatures covers a wide radius. If I had to guess I'd say they're scouting. If our read on their velocity is correct, they're going something like forty miles an hour. That means that the first wave will reach London in two hours, assuming they don't turn around."

"And you didn't see any of these creatures return to the Ark?" Mark asked, running his tongue along one of the sharp new incisors he'd gained from his transformation.

"No sir," she confirmed.

"Then these are almost certainly long range scouts," Mark theorized aloud. "Get six drones airborne. I want them combing the skies for these things. Go high altitude, and don't engage unless absolutely necessary."

"Of course, sir," she said, keying in commands on her pad.

Mark turned back to the screen, surveying the Ark. What was inside? Osiris had dropped hints, but beyond painting Set as some sort of tyrant he'd said little.

Chapter 52- Standoff

Trevor hadn't been this nervous since he'd defended his thesis. He was wracked by the same sense of being surrounded by people both more important and more powerful than himself, only this time there was also the foreboding that he was about to witness the most explosive battle ever recorded.

Five of them marched west into a thickly wooded valley. Wepwawet had been ordered to remain behind with the army, so Anubis led the way, fan-bladed axe slicing through any bush or branch that might impede Ra's path. Behind Ra trailed Irakesh, with Steve's servile form lurking like a shadow in Irakesh's wake.

Trevor brought up the rear, mainly by choice. Apparently it meant he was giving up some sort of prestige in the endless political maneuvering, or Irakesh seemed to think so anyway. He followed Ra with great delight, occasionally darting self-satisfied looks in Trevor's direction. Trevor was perfectly happy with the arrangement, though. He'd much rather be behind Irakesh and Steve than worry about a knife in the back.

"Mighty Ra, above us," Anubis rumbled, pointing up the cliff side. The strange silver ship that had escaped the sunstorm back in Olympus sat up there, apparently untended.

"It is as I suspected, then," Ra said, giving a sigh. A cool breeze came off the neighboring river, lifting a few strands of scarlet hair as she stared up at the ship. "It surprises me that she chose this place, though I believe I understand her reasons. It is here that we will complete a cycle that began twenty-four thousand years ago."

"Mother, is meeting her here wise? She has the high ground, and has had time to prepare any number of traps," Irakesh said, stepping up to join

241

her. "Could we not simply send in the Anakim to root her out, then attack in force?"

"I hope I do not overstep my bounds, master," Steve said, stepping up to Irakesh with a bow. "Such an attack would be costly, as Isis and her companions are likely to destroy much of mighty Ra's army."

"A small price to pay," Irakesh said, waving dismissively at Steve. Steve fell back, giving a low bow. Irakesh turned back to Ra, and he missed the hatred in Steve's gaze. "Mother, let us end Isis once and for all. She has nothing but a small pack to aid her. Allow me to destroy Blair. I'm sure Anubis will relish killing the Ka-Ken, Liz. That will allow you to face Isis alone, as it always should have been. She will have no place to run, no hole in which to hide."

Ra was silent for several moments, and Trevor couldn't help but smile as Irakesh started to fidget. The deathless was as self-important as anyone Trevor had ever met, even worse than some of the professors back in academia. The fact that Ra didn't immediately respond must cut Irakesh deeply.

"Tell me, Trevor," Ra finally said, without looking away from the ship. "What course of action would you recommend?"

"Send someone in to meet with her. Tell her you want to discuss...well, whatever you want to discuss," Trevor said, stroking his goatee as he considered. It made him feel like a villain in a Disney movie, which was somehow fitting. "Ask her to come to a neutral place, one where neither one of you has an advantage."

"Folly," Irakesh snapped, glaring at Trevor. "Why give up a powerful position for one of weakness? If we meet Isis, it should be on our terms, with overwhelming strength."

"She's in a cave, Irakesh," Trevor shot back, raising an eyebrow. "If we assault, she'll just flee. You know she can walk the shadows, probably better than anyone alive. We'll never catch her. What would that accomplish?"

"The pup has a point, most holy," Anubis rumbled, giving Trevor a rare nod of respect. "I do not like the idea of stepping into her trap, yet I also believe she will flee if forced to do so. She waited here for a reason. She seeks a true meeting, likely to discuss the treachery of Osiris. If you wish any chance at an alliance, then you will need to meet her in good faith."

"That is exactly what I plan to do," Ra said, turning to Anubis. "You will return to our encampment. Go back now and see that the deathless are properly fed."

"What of you, mighty Ra?" Anubis flinched, as if fearing to contradict a woman who barely topped his waist. "I would not leave you undefended,"

"I will wait here with my son and his slave," Ra said, then she turned to Trevor. "We will send this one as an emissary. In this way Isis will trust that the message we send is true. His companions trust him, and they will believe my intentions are honorable. Trevor, convince Isis to meet with me. Tell her I respect the sanctity of this place, and I will not enter it without permission. If she wishes to meet here, I will come. Yet I would prefer she come to my camp. If she does so, both she and her companions will have safe passage. Will you do this?"

"Mother, you can't—"

Ra's hand blurred so quickly it left a trail of light in its wake. Her fist slammed into Irakesh's jaw, shattering it and sending him sprawling to the ground.

"*Can't*? Some words are never spoken, not to me," Ra thundered, glaring down at Irakesh. "Boy, you go too far. Perhaps I have been too lenient. If you cannot hold your tongue, how can you ever hope to rule a district in my empire? Anubis, take him and his treacherous Ka-Dun back to camp. I will await Isis's answer alone."

She turned to Trevor, her expression expectant.

"I'll, uh, go tell her you want to meet," Trevor said, starting up the path toward the ship. He paused, turning to face Ra. "How do you know I won't just join her and flee?"

"Two reasons," Ra said, meeting his gaze evenly. "Firstly, if you flee then Isis will not have the alliance she clearly wishes. Secondly, because you are honor bound. If you join Isis, then you betray your word to me."

Chapter 53- Gone Native

"Are you sure about this?" Blair asked, probably for the fifth time in as many minutes. He couldn't help it. He'd tried to stay calm, but the bond with the ship revealed a great deal of data about the figures below. Ra had come with a powerful entourage, the most potent being a figure Blair recognized instantly.

He'd never seen Anubis, but then he didn't have to. He had both Jordan's rushed description, and his own knowledge of Egyptology. Anubis was an extremely common figure, and the god below was clearly the embodiment of that mythological lore.

"Do not ask again, Ka-Dun," Isis said, leaning over the cliff face as she stared at the figures below. "There, you see? They are not approaching. Most are departing, all save Sekhmet and the one she intends as emissary."

"How do you know she'll send an emissary?" Liz asked, giving an experimental swing of her sunsteel sword. She'd summoned it the instant Ra had entered the valley, though she was still in human form. One of the blade's properties was that it always seemed the perfect size for her, regardless of what form she wore.

"Because there are niceties to be observed. Ark Lords rarely approach each other without an intermediary. Too many have died as a result of treachery, and our memories are long. If she approached directly it could lead to combat, and if she wanted that she'd have attacked already," Isis replied, emerald eyes fixed firmly on Ra.

"I'll bet you anything I know who the emissary is," Jordan rumbled, his voice oddly digitized in the strange coal-black armor he'd shown up in. The commander hadn't told them where he'd gotten it, and Blair hadn't pressed this issue.

"Who do you believe they'll send?" Blair asked, genuinely curious.

"Trevor," Jordan shot back, as if it should be obvious. "It's a power play. For one thing, we're less likely to kill him, but more importantly it shows she's converted him to her side. If she can convert one of our own, what chance do the rest of us have? Real *Game of Thrones* shit."

Sure enough, Trevor began walking in their direction. Ra stayed where she was, scarlet hair playing in the wind as she folded her arms over ivory garments very much like those Isis wore.

"There's no way she's converted him," Liz said, bristling at Jordan. "I know you don't like him, and that's fine. Just remember he's on our side. If you try anything, I swear to god I'll tear you out of that armor and give you a proper ass kicking."

"You're welcome to try," Jordan said, folding metal arms over the suit's chest. "I'm not some meek little puppy, and I don't give two shits about the sentiment you feel for the thing that used to be your brother. He's deathless. Besides, you didn't see him in Ra's court. I did. He was perfectly at home there. They embraced him right from the first day. You want to turn a blind eye to that? Fine. But if he steps out of line, I'll turn him into pink fucking mist, period. I don't give a shit what you have to say about it, either."

"Be silent, both of you," Isis snapped, shifting to wolf form in the blink of an eye. She rounded on them. "Yes, the deathless are generally the enemy. I will remind you that Osiris was deathless, and he was an ally for many millennia."

"Yeah? Where is he now?" Jordan asked, taking a step toward Isis. "Oh, that's right. He betrayed us all, and now we have to figure out a way to stop him. I can see your point. Deathless are really fucking trustworthy."

Blair gawked at the Commander. Isis's eyes flashed, and a low rumble came from deep in her chest. She leaned closer to Jordan, her voice a bare whisper. "If you speak to me again—"

"You'll what?" Jordan interrupted. "Rail at me? Chastise me? Or kill me? Is that what you do, kill allies who disagree with you? Here I was under the impression you needed all the allies you can get. But if that's changed, just say the fucking word and I'll be on my way."

That cinched it. Jordan wasn't acting himself. He'd never been this aggressive, nor had he allowed emotion to rule him. Not ever. He was always in control, always making the best tactical choice. Goading Isis into attacking him was about as suicidal as he could get. Not the kind of move he'd make, unless something were very wrong.

"Hey," Blair snapped, stepping between the two of them. Both Jordan's armor and Isis's wolf form towered over him, but he didn't let that deter him. "Both of you need to stand down. In fact, all three of you. Jordan isn't going to do anything stupid, but you guys can't casually dismiss his paranoia either. Trevor's been an enemy. He's also clearly earned Ra's trust or she wouldn't be sending him to meet with us. We don't have all the facts yet, so let's reserve judgement. If he's an enemy, then we'll deal with it. Until we know he is, we treat him like an ally. Everyone cool with that?"

"Yeah," Jordan said, a bit sullenly. What the hell was wrong with him?

"You are correct in that I need you, Ka-Dun. For the moment. I will overlook your disrespectful tone, *this time*. Do not let it occur again," Isis snapped, spinning to face the cliff. She shifted back to human form as she did so.

Liz rested her sword on her shoulder, silent for a long moment before finally giving a tight nod. Fuck. Hadn't they learned from the whole Irakesh episode that they needed to band together? Blair had made mistakes back then. Mistakes like arguing with friends and not trusting the right people. He'd be damned if he was going to let Liz and Jordan make the same ones now.

"Why don't you guys let me do the talking?" Blair said. He didn't wait for an answer, instead leaping over the cliff to the rocky trail below. He waited there as Trevor approached.

His friend had changed, outwardly at least. His t-shirt and jeans had been replaced by flowing white garments very similar to what Isis wore. He also wore a sword belted to his side, a long, curved weapon much like an Arabian scimitar. The blade rode naturally there, as if he'd practiced often with it.

"Blair," Trevor called, perking up as he approached. He gave a wide smile, which was more than a little unnerving given the razored teeth. "How the hell are you, man?"

Blair rushed forward, embracing his friend. He clapped Trevor on the back, guiding him up the trail towards Liz and the others. "Eh, you know, on the run and outgunned as usual. You look, uh, different."

"Yeah," Trevor said, glancing down at himself a bit sheepishly. "I've gone a little native I guess. I wish you'd been there. There's so much I don't understand, but from the little I do I think you'd be fascinated by Ra and her pantheon. It's like witnessing all the history you're always talking about."

"Assuming she doesn't kill us all, maybe I'll get a chance," Blair said, laughing in spite of the dire circumstances.

Blair leapt up, seizing the lip of the cliff and pulling himself over it. Trevor landed a moment later, garments fluttering in the wind as he straightened. He stared curiously at each of them, gaze finally settling on Jordan.

"So, looks like Hades got to you too, eh, Jordan?" he said, his tone sympathetic.

"What do you mean?" Jordan asked, with more than a little hostility.

"Wepwawet donned a set of the armor too. They put it on him while he was unconscious," Trevor explained, resting a hand idly on the hilt of his sword. The gesture looked reflexive. "He hasn't been able to take it off. I'm guessing you can't either?"

That took Blair by surprise, especially when Jordan gave a tight nod of assent. So he was trapped in the armor. That explained why he hadn't taken it off. How did he go to the bathroom?

"Look man, I'm sorry about how things have gone down," Trevor said.

He stood a step closer, turning to Isis. "Ra put this collar on Jordan. I've got the bracelet that controls it. Is there a way to remove it?"

"Of course," Isis said, stepping up to Trevor. "Give me your wrist."

Trevor offered it willingly, and Isis put her tiny hands on either side of it. She closed her eyes, and a moment later there was a flash of bright, golden light. Then the bracelet opened with a click, and she gently removed it.

"Well that's one prison dealt with," Jordan said, more than a little bitterly. "Thank you, Trevor. You didn't have to do that."

"I still think you're a fucking pompous ass," Trevor said, but there was no heat to the insult. "But I also know you have more reason than ever to think I'm a traitor, especially after what I'm about to say."

"Oh?" Liz asked, finally entering the conversation. She eyed Trevor coolly, which surprised Blair. He'd expected her to be more enthusiastic at her brother's return. Maybe she'd just been burned too many times.

"As Jordan has no doubt told you, Ra has adopted me into her court," Trevor said, clearing his throat awkwardly. "I've chosen to embrace that role, for a good reason. Ra listens to my advice. I've been tempering some of her decisions. If I leave and rejoin you guys, I'll lose that influence."

"Oh my god," Liz said, eyes widening. Then they narrowed, clearly disapproving. "Jordan was right, you've gone native. You've got a thing for her, don't you?"

"No," Trevor shot back, just a little too quickly. "And by no, I mean yes. So what? It doesn't make me an enemy. Ra wants an alliance with Isis, but she's too proud to come herself. If we can seal that alliance then it means none of us have to be enemies, even if I stay with Ra's court."

"I don't like it," Jordan growled. "Ra is callous and cruel. Her son is a petulant little shit, and he listens to Steve. That gives Captain Douchey influence over Ra, even if indirectly."

"That's exactly why I have to stay," Trevor said, heaving a sigh. "Listen, guys, it's all very complicated, but here's the gist. If I stay, I can be a moderating influence. I can counter Steve and Irakesh."

"The decision is yours," Isis finally said. She'd been holding the bracelet pinched between two fingers, touching as little of the golden metal as possible. It was the same way Blair might have held a bag of dog shit. She looked at Trevor. "Like it or no, Sekhmet and her ilk are your people. I bear you no ill will, nor do I begrudge you seeking a place among your people. Your fate is secondary, however. What message did Ra send you with?"

"She wants to meet," Trevor said, squaring his shoulders. "She said she's willing to come here, but she offered her camp as a better meeting place. She's guaranteed your safety, and that of your pack."

"Are you fucking crazy?" Jordan said. He began laughing, a harsh, digitized sound. "Walk right into an enemy encampment with no support?"

"That is *exactly* what we shall do," Isis said, eyeing Jordan coldly. "Sekhmet—the one you call Ra—can be cruel. She can be callous. But she is a woman of honor. She'd sooner take her own life than allow harm to come to us while under an aegis of protection. We will be safe for the duration of the negotiations, and gods willing we will reach an accord in the process. Osiris must be stopped, and we will need her help to achieve that."

Chapter 54- Near Sisters

Isis strode boldly into the hastily constructed camp. She ignored the stench of death wafting from the army of deathless, their putridity an affront on the very land. She ignored the row of Anakim gathered near the mammoths Sekhmet was using for transport.

It would probably be more prudent to think of the woman as Ra, not as her near-sister. Yet she could not. She and Sekhmet had discovered much together, had fought uncountable threats together. They'd birthed the first empire together, with Osiris leading them into battle. She understood why her friend had adopted the name Ra, but she could not bring herself to think it, much less say it.

Isis stood tall, or as tall as she could. She was shorter than nearly everyone, especially the knot of figures waiting for her just inside the camp. Anubis was a good eight feet, taller even than Jordan in his tainted armor. Sekhmet was the same as always, a head taller than Isis and much more heavily muscled. Sekhmet's son had inherited that height, the dark-skinned whelp standing behind his mother with a petulant expression plastered across otherwise attractive features.

"Steve," Blair growled, low in his throat. His eyes narrowed, and the Ka-Dun tried to surge past her. She raised a hand, gently squeezing his shoulder. It was enough. Blair subsided, eyeing her apologetically. "Sorry. I owe the bastard, is all."

"A fact that will be addressed today," Isis said, eyeing Blair critically. He'd grown much, but was still far too impetuous. "Follow my lead. Do not speak, unless you are spoken to. That goes for the rest of you as well, especially you, Liz. It is possible Sekhmet may try to bait you into combat. Do not let her provoke you."

Liz gave a nod. She, at least, seemed calm. Jordan was a tangle of emotions, raging next to her like a bonfire. At least part of that came from the armor, though his own mind gave it fuel. The deathless Trevor was calm as well, walking next to his sister, just a few feet behind her and Blair.

It was a ragged little pack. Each possessed power in their own right, but they were all of them young. Too young to be fighting such battles. Unfortunately, they were all she had. Sekhmet had brought members of her pantheon with her, as evidenced by Anubis's presence. Would that Isis could have done the same. It almost made her wish she'd woken Jes'Ka, though after hearing about her father's apparent treachery, not doing so had proven prudent.

"Welcome, Isis," Sekhmet called, voice clear and strong. It sent a shock through Isis, the familiarity of it. It had been so long since she'd heard it.

"Hello, near-sister," Isis said. It was the best compromise she could come up with. She could not call her friend Ra, but neither would she dishonor her by using a name she'd discarded. Sekhmet was well and truly dead.

"I wasn't sure you'd come," Sekhmet said, her expression impassive. She wore her traditional garb, the flowing white garments very similar to Isis's own. She bore no weapon save a belt knife, though odds were good she had a sunsteel spear ready to summon. "Would you like refreshment before we begin?"

"I would not," Isis said, fighting to keep her tone even. She didn't want to know what food Sekhmet would have offered. "I am eager to conduct our business. Time is precious, if Hades is to be believed."

Sekhmet's face grew more grim, a darkness overshadowing her legendary beauty. "Indeed. I have prepared a tent for our use. I'd have my advisers close, unless you object."

She gestured at Irakesh, Anubis, and the Ka-Dun Steve. Isis considered a moment, then gave a nod. "I'd bring my pack as well. You've met the Ka-Dun Jordan. This is Ka-Dun Blair, Ark Lord of the Redwood. His Ka-Ken is

Liz."

"Well met," Sekhmet said, nodding graciously. She turned to the deathless Trevor. "Join us, my vassal. I'd have your counsel during these negotiations."

"Uh, sure," Trevor said, eyes flicking between Liz and Sekhmet uncomfortably. Isis could understand why. She recognized the depth of feeling in his gaze. He was loyal to his sister, but felt a growing affection for Sekhmet. That kind of pressure could break a man, if he were forced to choose between them.

Sekhmet turned for a large blue pavilion that had been erected in a meadow a little ways from the main camp. It had been set upwind, which mercifully cut the stench to a tolerable level. That had almost certainly been intentional, and Isis appreciated the subtle courtesy. It suggested that her friend still lurked in that undead body somewhere.

Isis filed in after Sekhmet and her retainers, blinking a couple times to adjust to the reduced light. A ring of fluffy pillows had been set at the edge of a massive rug that dominated the floor. It was simple, harkening back to their mutual roots. She made for one side of the ring, sitting gracefully as Sekhmet did the same. The retainers on both sides took positions around the ring, all save two. Jordan didn't sit, instead standing behind Blair with his metallic arms folded. A second figure moved on the far side of the ring, one who'd already been in the tent. He wore armor identical to Jordan's, and Isis didn't need to see his face to know she was looking at Wepwawet. She could smell the same taint that wafted from Jordan's armor, and felt a stab of pity for the wolf-headed god. She'd always liked Wepwawet, and not just for their shared love of the noble wolf.

Sekhmet waved her hand, and a vacant-eyed thrall moved about the tent with a pitcher of wine and a tray of bronze goblets. The thing was obviously dead, her stringy blonde hair matted to the side of her face as she mechanically served them. Isis waited for the process to finish before speaking.

"It is good to see you, near-sister. I hope that today, if we both find wisdom, we will somehow put aside the millennia of warfare and come together to face a common enemy," she said, her voice competing with the flapping of the pavilion's fabric from the wind outside.

"That's a title I wasn't sure I'd ever hear from you again," Sekhmet said. Her gaze was searching, the putrid green in her eyes still strange after all this time. "Before we can reach an accord that will satisfy both our people, perhaps we should discuss the nature of the threat. I'm willing to share what I've learned, if you grant the same courtesy."

The subtext wasn't lost on Isis. Sekhmet believed Osiris was the threat, and was gently rebuking her for not agreeing.

"A fair request," Isis said. She turned to Jordan, motioning him forward. "The Ka-Dun Jordan had the tale from Hades. As I was not there, I can not speak to the truth of it."

Isis noted Irakesh's reaction when Jordan stepped forward. The deathless's face tightened, and he shot a hatred-filled glance at Trevor. Wepwawet also took a step forward, though whether to protect Sekhmet or support Jordan she wasn't sure.

"Not much to tell," Jordan said in that strange synthesized voice. "Hades offered to help save Wepwawet, though he didn't mention he was going to encase him in cursed armor that can't be removed. He told me Osiris went to war on the underworld. Apparently he drove back everyone, and severed all conduits to the Nexus. Hades claims Olympus is trapped until he can reestablish the link, and he believes the only way that will happen is if the two of you work together."

"He gave me much the same tale," Sekhmet said, meeting Isis's gaze. "Osiris has been tinkering with demons for many millennia, while we slumbered. His strength has grown immensely during that time, and it's likely his power base vastly exceeds our own. Even with our combined strength, it is unlikely we can overcome any army he has gathered."

"It's worse than you know," Isis said, giving a heavy sigh. "When your son had his most unfortunate confrontation with Ka-Dun Blair, we learned something troubling in the aftermath. Osiris controls a powerful house known as Mohn. This group has mastered the best technologies this world has to offer, technology not unlike the armor both Jordan and Wepwawet now wear."

"So he has not only an army of demons, the kind we fought when we finally overcame Set, but he also possesses the best this new age has to offer," Sekhmet said, pursing her lips. "This is troubling in the extreme, if we can even believe what Hades has to say. Such a thing does not seem in keeping with Osiris. He was always sanctimonious, but he did what he thought was right. He considered himself a protector, not a destroyer or conquerer."

"Mighty Ra," Anubis rumbled from his place at her left. "Time changes all men. Perhaps the millennia have warped his mind, made him more like his twisted brother. Or perhaps the darkness was always there, and grew within him as he aged."

"Isis?" Blair asked, his voice soft, though not timid. She nodded at him and he continued. "Ra, I noticed something that I thought relevant. If Osiris controls the First Ark, and if he had a link to the Well, then he'd have effectively infinite energy right?"

Sekhmet's eyes locked on Blair, narrowing slightly. She'd ever been one for formality, and didn't like a Ka-Dun of Blair's lowly age using her title with such familiarity, that much was clear. Yet she gave a nod. "Indeed. He'd have near limitless energy, certainly enough to craft an army while the rest of us slumbered."

"Then that raises an interesting question. As I understand it, you and Isis seeded mankind with a sort of genetic memory, which is why we remember so many concepts from your age," Blair began. He sat up straighter, clearly excited by the topic. Isis watched Liz watching Blair, and smiled. Those two belonged together, and the seeds they'd planted were finally blossoming. It was a small consolation amidst all the horror. "Yet that doesn't explain why we know specifics like your name, or the history of your people. It would seem someone from your time guided our early cultures. You see proof of that in ancient Egypt, in the Mayan empire, and even in Cambodia. In each case the cultures built similar structures."

"Yes, the stone pyramids that aped the Great Arks," Sekhmet said, nodding. "What of it?"

"I've spoken to Isis, and we believe those structures were built at places of power to siphon energy," Blair continued, leaning toward Sekhmet as he drove his point home. "Why would Osiris go to such trouble if he had a nearly limitless supply of energy?"

"Because," came a strong, masculine voice that chilled Isis to the core. She rose slowly, clutching her hands to her breast as she turned to the tent flap. A tall, dark-haired man stood there. His chiseled jaw and glittering green eyes were forever etched into her memory. "I needed that energy to survive."

Chapter 55- Dramatic Entrane

Liz shifted in the blink of an eye, dropping back into the shadows as she drew her blade. All around her werewolves were shifting, deathless were drawing golden weapons. Both Wepwawet and Jordan activated a familiar metallic whirring she recognized as the cover pulling back over their missile launchers. The only person in the room not preparing to fight appeared to be the man who'd entered. She'd never seen him before, and wasn't entirely sure what to expect. Osiris, if that was who he was, was a handsome dark-haired man in his late thirties.

If she'd learned anything since this whole ugly werewolf mess had begun it was: get in the first shot. Liz glided forward, shifting into wolf form on the second step. She maneuvered behind her target. The sunsteel blade slid into the small of his back, drawing a wolfish smile as it met resistance. Part of her had feared he might be an illusion.

Then Osiris vanished. It wasn't a trick of the light. He didn't blur. One moment he was there, the next he was simply elsewhere. She glanced at the tip of her blade, still covered in blackish blood.

"I'd wondered where my sword had gotten to," came the same cultured voice from behind her. She started to pivot, but it was far too late.

A hand clamped around her sword hand like a vice, twisting until the weapon dropped from nerveless fingers. Even as it spun toward the ornate rug the man continued his attack. He launched a quick kick that shattered her right knee. It knocked her further off balance, and she tumbled to the carpet in a heap.

Osiris caught the blade inches from the ground, pivoting smoothly to plant the tip against Liz's neck. She read death in those hard green eyes, and knew nothing she could do would prevent it.

"Husband," Isis's voice cracked through the room like a whip. Osiris blinked once, taking a step back. Both Trevor and Blair had moved to support Liz, but each had drawn up short, stopped by that single word.

Osiris dropped the sword near Liz's outstretched hand, walked calmly into the ring of pillows. He gestured with one hand, and the pale-faced thrall brought him a goblet of wine. Osiris drank deeply of it, then looked up at all of them in mock surprise. "I'm a little hurt that I wasn't invited to this meeting, Sekhmet. There was a time when you called me chieftain. Don't you think courtesy ought to have included me?"

"An impostor?" the fiery-haired goddess asked, turning to Isis. Liz still wasn't sure what to call her. Trevor said Ra. Isis said Sekhmet.

"No," Isis rumbled, flexing her claws as she sniffed the air with her muzzle. "It is my husband. I would recognize his scent anywhere."

"Even were that not the case, I can prove it," Osiris said, extending his free hand in Liz's direction. An odd vibration began from her sword, then the weapon flew from the carpet like a falcon, sailing into Osiris's outstretched hand. Liz gaped in shock.

The sword recognizes its true master, Ka-Ken. It has served that one for an age of history far beyond knowing, and the weapon's primitive intelligence is happy to rejoin its master.

"I didn't realize the blade had even been found," Ra said, turning to Isis with narrowed eyes. "Why am I not surprised one of your bestial get had it?"

"Does it matter?" Isis shot back, turning to Osiris. "It's back with its owner now, whatever we might wish."

Ra took a step closer to Isis, standing shoulder to shoulder with her. Well, shoulder to waist, since Isis was much taller in wolf form. "You've always loved grandstanding, Osiris. If this is an attack, it's an ill-conceived one. What do you want?"

"Want?" Osiris said, blinking once. Then he smiled. "I want the world to survive, Sekhmet. I want humanity to live beyond the next few decades.

That, unfortunately, will not happen if events are allowed to unfold along their current path. Now, clearly you are surprised to see me. Just as clearly, both you and Isis bear me some sort of ill will. While I am thrilled to see the two of you speaking again, I'd rather not be the subject of your collective ire. So why not enlighten me on the cause of this animosity, and we'll see if we can come to some sort of accommodation?"

Osiris sank into a cross-legged position, lounging against a pillow. If he was alarmed by the sheer number of weapons aimed in his direction he certainly didn't show it. Whether that was confidence or overconfidence remained to be seen. Either way, Liz was more than a little annoyed he'd snatched her sword. She was tempted to try to take it back but, given that he'd handled her like a puppy, that would end badly. She barely used the thing anyway, though losing it like that was still humiliating.

"You play innocent, but you know quite well why Sekhmet and I have gathered here," Isis said, stalking over to Osiris. She shifted as she moved, somehow managing to look more threatening as a five-foot woman than she did as a nine-foot werewolf. "Do not play games with us, husband. You've been charged by Hades with the use of demonic weaponry, and also with a sustained assault that has resulted in the near destruction of the Nexus. Were it not for Ark Lord Blair's intervention, it would already have been destroyed."

"So the god Hades has charged me with these crimes, and you pronounce me guilty," Osiris said, raising a dark eyebrow. "Wife, you know me far better than any here save perhaps Sekhmet. Does that sound like something I would do? If I wished to conquer, why resort to the use of demons? I prefer my progeny to have their own will and, as you well know, I allow them to serve me or not as they choose. I have always commanded loyalty through respect, not the domination my brother preferred. Ask yourself, who is the most likely god to use such tactics?"

Isis snatched the goblet from Osiris's hand, and dumped the contents over his head. It ruined his perfectly coiffed hair, dripping down the shoulders of his Armani suit. She leaned closer, eyes narrowing. "I do not appreciate being spoken to like a child, *husband*. We are in dire peril, and I remain unconvinced you are not the threat. If these deeds were committed by another—if it is your treacherous snake of a brother—then speak plainly. You might be able to stand against me, or perhaps against Sekhmet. You cannot stand against us both."

"Peace," Osiris said, raising a hand defensively. He straightened his tie, apparently seeking to regain the smug superiority he'd exhibited when he entered the tent. "I'm sorry. I've gone about this badly. I like making a grand entrance. Maybe a bit too much. In my defense, I've been rehearsing this moment in my head for over a dozen millennia."

Osiris looked like a little boy who'd been caught stealing, and Liz had the sense his chagrin was genuine. Isis turned to Ra. "What do you wish to do, near-sister? This is your camp, after all."

"We have yet to reach an accord between us, Isis," Ra said, sweeping across the rug to stand next to the shorter woman. "Yet whether the threat is Osiris or Set matters little. We must save the Nexus, and that means stopping whoever is in control of the First Ark. That will take both of us, perhaps all three of us. I'd even accept Sobek's aid at this point."

"So what do you suggest?" Isis asked, glancing briefly at Osiris, then back at Ra. Liz held her breath, hoping against hope that the gods would see reason. They were a proud lot.

"Give me your terms. What will it take to seal an alliance? I will give you the night to think about it. In the morning we will discuss terms, and hopefully reach some sort of an accord. Assuming we can do that, we'll decide whether or not to include your wastrel of a husband," Ra said, shooting Osiris a glance every child who'd angered their mother knew and feared.

"Agreed," Isis said, extending a hand. Ra took it, pulling Isis into an embrace. It went on for several seconds before the two broke apart.

"I will give you this pavilion for the evening. If you have need of anything, send Trevor and I will have it seen to," Ra said. She turned to Trevor. "You will be my envoy this evening. Stay with your pack, and see to their needs. Gods willing, we'll all be allies come morning.

"Oh and one more thing," Ra said, turning to Osiris. "Do not think I trust you, Osiris. Do not think me weak, or stupid, because I allow you to remain with your wife. If you turn on me, or seek to turn her against me, then you will find me more than willing to fight such a battle. Anubis and Wepwawet watch your tent this night, and we are ready for war should you wish it. I can feel your weakness, my chieftain. That and that alone is why I allow you to remain unguarded."

Chapter 56- Demands

Blair waited as Ra and her companions filed from the tent. That left him, Liz, Jordan, Trevor, Isis, and the man they'd called Osiris. All eyes were on the latter two, who were eyeing each other with an unreadable jumble of emotions. Hardly surprising, given the vast gulf of time since their last meeting.

"You and I will speak later. Be prepared to meet at dawn. Until then, I ask that you find your own lodging," Isis said, her mouth a tight line. Osiris recoiled as if punched, and heaved a sigh before giving a quick nod. Isis reached up and squeezed his shoulder. "I am pleased that you yet live, and that Hades's slander appears false. If Set still lives, you will have our aid in stopping him."

"He does, I assure you. Do not deliberate too long. Set has been one step ahead of me for millennia. Even now I am sure he's set a dozen plans in motion," Osiris said, then he turned to Liz. She blinked up at him, blushing lightly. Blair bristled, and not just because Osiris was incredibly handsome. "I am sorry for stealing your weapon, Ka-Ken. You are a vassal of my wife, and I should not have assaulted you."

Osiris offered the blade back to her hilt first. Blair's jaw tightened, and his hands clenched. The man was scoring points with Isis, but both she and Liz seemed to be eating it up.

Liz looked at the golden blade for a long minute, then met the ancient god's eyes. "Can you use it to fight Set?"

"Without a doubt. The blade is powerful beyond measure," he said, eyeing her curiously.

"Then keep it, for now at least. If we survive all this, I'll want it back," she said, though there was no real heat in her words.

"I like her," Osiris said, giving Isis a grim smile. Then he strode from the tent, sweeping under the flap with a grace that made Blair grit his teeth. The man was the love child of James Bond and Antonio Banderas.

"Gather," Isis said, picking a spot near the center of the pillows. "We've much to discuss."

Blair settled in across from her, studying the others as they joined the circle. Jordan stood outside of it, and that felt like more than practicality. He must feel the outsider, for a lot of reasons. Trevor settled in next to Liz. Seemingly at home.

"Well that whole thing was pretty damn surprising," Liz said, breaking the tense silence. "How well do you trust Osiris?"

"Not at all, Ka-Ken," Isis said, giving a frustrated sigh. "I still love him, but his motives have always been his own. That will be more true than ever, now that he has spent countless millennia living on his own."

"That's the real question," Blair said, straightening as everyone turned to face him. "What is Osiris's goal? If he's on the level, it sounds like his brother Set is the real threat. That could even line up with what we learned from Hades. What if Hades works for Set, but was trying to turn us against Osiris?"

"It's a perfect strategy," Trevor said, stroking his goatee absently. "The last three powers we know of are the champions, Ra and her court, and Mohn Corp. If Hades can get us all to fight each other then no one is left standing to deal with Set. He just sweeps in and cleans up the mess we leave."

"Which we cannot allow to happen," Isis said. Blair saw something in her eyes he'd never thought to find. Terror. Not fear, which he'd seen occasionally. Not even despair. Stark terror. The certain knowledge that they faced something she wasn't sure they could beat. "Set is evil on a scale you cannot possibly imagine. Even as a mortal he was cruel. As an immortal he is infinitely worse. He has always sought to rework the world in his own image, which means transforming all living things into demons.

Each would be an extension of his will. In essence, we'd become one entity, an extension of Set."

"So our course seems pretty clear then," Jordan said, finally entering the conversation. "All three factions unite, and we take the fucker on. He goes down, no matter what that costs."

"That is precisely what we must do," Isis agreed, nodding at Jordan. "Tomorrow morning we work out the particulars of this alliance. We will need to establish a true leader, and we will have to hammer out the details of a truce."

"Isis," Blair said, rising to his feet. He clenched both fists, forcing down a knot of anger. "There's a stipulation we need to ask for. It's non-negotiable."

"What is it you wish?" Isis asked, raising a delicate eyebrow.

"Steve has to face justice for his crimes. He stole memories from you, stole a key from me, and he'll work with anyone if it advances his own cause. He's dangerous," Blair said. He knew his voice was rising, almost to a shout. He didn't care. "Too many times we've let him live and he's gotten away. He's betrayed us at every turn, and he won't hesitate to do it again. If he thinks Set is the side likely to win, he'll sell us out in a heartbeat. He's got to go."

Isis was silent for a moment, head cocked as she considered. Then her gaze swept the room. "Do the rest of you agree?"

"Fuck yes, I agree," Jordan said, stepping onto the carpet with a massive metallic foot. "Steve is the worst kind of douche, self-serving and conniving. We should have dealt with him back in San Francisco. Let's not make the same mistake again."

"They're right," Liz said, nodding.

"I think we can convince Ra to give him to us," Trevor said. "She doesn't have any love for the guy, and she's not going to jeopardize an alliance just to keep Irakesh happy. Let's ask her, but I doubt she'll refuse."

"Do we have any other demands?" Liz asked, scanning the room.

"I don't," Blair said. If he could finally deal with Steve, that was enough.

No one spoke for several moments, until Isis rose gracefully to her feet. "Then we have a course of action. Get some rest, those of you who can. I must meditate upon all that has happened. I will return before dawn."

Chapter 57- The Cave of Painted Dreams

Isis left the tent, walking through Sekhmet's camp with little attention for the myriad of deathless creations. She'd battled them all at one time or another, when her near-sister's armies had invaded the lands now known as the Americas. They no longer held the same terror for her, and not just because they'd soon be allies. She could crush them all now that she once again possessed a Primary Access Key. That was a fact Sekhmet and Osiris might both be ignorant of. One she'd have to choose carefully whether or not to reveal.

She made her way up the pathway that led back into the valley of the sacred cave, the place known as Chauvet in this age. It was no longer a place of power, but the images she'd crafted in the dark there all those millennia ago still gave her comfort. She remembered learning at her grandmother's feet about the mysteries of the world, and her ordination as a shaman.

They'd been wrong about so much, but in their own way her people had possessed more wisdom than any civilization that had come since. They'd lived in harmony with the world, living and dying as all animals did. It was only after the virus she herself had crafted that their species had changed, had begun dominating the environments they'd once merely lived in.

Perhaps that would have happened anyway. Surely the discovery of agriculture would have happened without their influence. By the time the Egyptians and Sumerians had come to power, all memory of her people had faded.

The cool wind stirred her hair as she mounted the pass, ducking under a narrow cliff as she entered the valley. The face of the land was a little different, but this place could have been the world of her childhood, if it was covered in snow. She pressed on, passing by oaks and a few pines as she climbed higher. Blair's slipsail glittered in the distance, the ship a rarity even in her time. The fact that Hades had parted with it was troubling, but she'd detected no trap. If it existed, it was cunningly hidden.

Isis climbed still further, eventually reaching the hidden entrance to the cave. In her own time, it had been a secret entrusted only to the shamans, those wise enough to guide chieftains. All of their prayers and meditations had taken place within its narrow confines, and it had been that way as far back as man had memory.

The fact that this place had survived pleased her, and she couldn't help but smile as she shimmied through the entrance into the darkness. She summoned her staff, extending her right arm as it flowed into her hand. Isis willed the barest hint of energy to the sapphire set in the thorax of the winged scarab at the staff's head. The room filled with sudden brilliance, more than she'd ever seen when she'd been first acolyte, then shaman, of her tribe.

The illumination showed her sights she'd never dreamed of. Thousands of tiny stalagmites dotted the ceiling and some of the walls, like tiny rain drops frozen by the breath of a god greater than she. Between them lay the magnificent cave paintings she'd known as a child. Some were drawn in black, those the work of the eldest tribes. Others were scarlet, traced using dye from berries she herself had mixed.

She smiled at one of her own works, a stallion rearing on the southern wall of the cave. She'd labored for days to create it, agonizing over every line. At the time, she'd been taught if she made the image perfect she'd capture the spirit of the creature itself, and in so doing would convince the beast to return. Then her tribe could slay it, taking the gift of its life to sustain them through the endless winter.

"Magnificent," came a warm voice behind her. She turned to see Osiris standing in the cave mouth, his hair coated lightly with dust from squeezing through the entrance. It did nothing to diminish his attractiveness; if anything, that was increased by the light of wonder in his eyes. "I always wondered what the inside of this place was like."

"It is not for your eyes," Isis said, more than a little crossly. She extinguished her staff, blinking at the sudden darkness. "This is a holy place, meant for shamans. You were a chieftain, and this place is forbidden you."

Sudden laughter echoed through the cave, warm and friendly. "Ah, my wife, I have missed you. You were always one for tradition, always mated so closely with nature, and with the old ways. I am chieftain no longer, as you are no longer a shaman. This is a new world, one neither of us is equipped to rule any longer."

That shocked her. Osiris had always been ambitious, had always believed in his divine right to rule. "Then you intend to step aside and simply allow a new generation to rule in our stead?"

"Hardly," he scoffed. A tiny ball of green energy appeared above the palm of his upraised hand. It cast hellish shadows over his features. "There are many threats the people of this world cannot face alone. They need us. But once those threats have been eliminated, then yes, I intend to step aside and allow others to rule. I'm tired, my love. I've spent countless millennia guiding the world, and it is a burden I wish to lay down."

She eyed him suspiciously. The Osiris she'd known would never abandon leadership, never give up his stewardship. That man had said the world would always need them, that he would always be there to protect it. "There will ever be more threats. You know that. Each time we vanquished one, another rose. It will be much the same in this age."

"You're right," he said, giving her a crooked smile she well remembered. "But in time there will be new champions to face them. I've made preparations in that way, just as you have. They just need time to find their footing, but once they do we'll be able to retire knowing the world's safety is in good hands."

Their conversation was interrupted by a scrabbling from the entrance.

Osiris tossed the swirling green ball into the air and adopted a combat stance. She noticed that he'd reached for his sword, an instinctive reaction he'd likely never outgrow.

"I'm not interrupting a tryst, am I?" came Sekhmet's voice, as the scarlet-haired woman ducked into view. She, too, was coated in a fine layer of dust. "I do hate it when you two gaze so lovingly into each other's eyes, though those episodes have been thankfully rare in recent millennia."

Neither she nor Osiris answered. Despite the cavalier tone, the tension was palpable. This was the first time they'd been together since they'd first founded their pantheon all those millennia ago. There had been so much war and strife since then, each championing their own view of the perfect world.

"So this is the vaunted cave of the shamans?" Sekhmet continued, staring up at the ceiling in obvious wonder. "I always wondered what happened in this cave. I thought real magic happened here. Imagine my surprise when I finally unlocked the mysteries of shaping and realized that everything that happened here was nothing more than superstition."

"Not so," Osiris snapped, with more ire than Isis would have expected. He'd never cared much for religion. Why had Sekhmet's comment bothered him so? "I've learned much about mankind while you and Isis slumbered, much about what makes us whole as a people. We were at our best when we were in harmony with the land, and part of that harmony came from our mythology. Myth grounds us; while what happened here may have been superstition, it was integral to our identity as a species."

"The years have not been kind, Osiris," Sekhmet said, giving him a cruel smile. "You were a warrior, once. It sounds like you've given that up to become a philosopher."

"And apparently you're still a mindless brute," Osiris said, voice heavy with weariness. "In the past I'd have let you bait me with insults, but I've seen things neither of you can really understand. Set is a grave threat, but we've even worse to deal with, assuming we can best him first."

"Worse?" Isis asked, fearing she already knew who he meant.

"We've always wondered who the Builders were, where they might have gone," Osiris replied, gazing at her with those serious eyes. "I've found answers while you slumbered. The Builders will return, and when they do the war that follows will make our war with Set look like feast day games. Thankfully, we have years before that event occurs. Which is why I suggest we deal with Set first." He turned back to Sekhmet. "I just want to make sure you understand the gravity of the situation. This cannot be like our past skirmishes, where we came together just long enough to complete a task. If we do not find a way to stand united, the world is doomed."

Sekhmet studied Osiris, expression unreadable. It was long moments before she spoke. "Perhaps you have gained a bit of wisdom. I have many questions about the Builders, but I agree that for now Set is the true threat. If we cannot overcome him, it won't much matter what happens afterwards."

"Then you believe me when I say I was not behind the invasion of the underworld?" Osiris asked, gaze roaming between the two of them.

"I believe you. I can feel your weakness. You are still gathering your strength, and had you been in control of the First Ark that would not be the case," Isis said, nodding. "Besides, Hades couldn't be trusted in the best of times. It makes sense that he'd agree to serve Set, though I am surprised Vulcan would agree to such a thing."

"I do not believe he has," Sekhmet said, pursing her lips. "When I met with him, he was clearly uncomfortable, likely because of what he'd done to Wepwawet. I do not think Hades has shared everything with him, and Vulcan may not even be aware of who it is he really serves."

"So what do we do now?" Isis asked. It warmed her to be working with her tribe again, just as they had when they'd been mortal.

"We gather our forces, and attack," Sekhmet snarled, face growing feral as her eyes flared green. "Set will pay for his treachery."

"It isn't that simple," Osiris said, folding his arms as he watched them.

"Set has grown powerful beyond measure. Developed abilities we cannot even comprehend. His spies are everywhere. My organization is littered with them, as are both of yours, I'm sure. If we wish to overcome him, it will take stealth and subterfuge."

"You have some plan then?" Isis asked.

"I do," Osiris said, grinning wickedly.

Chapter 58- Surprise

Jordan was more than a little irritable, partially because he now understood that the armor fueled his negative emotions. It made him angry, which made him angrier. It was a vicious cycle, one he'd have given just about anything to escape. In may ways, the armor was worse than the collar had been. He was more free, physically at least. Yet mentally he was trapped in a way he'd never experienced, and he hated it. Not breaking everything around him took every ounce of self control.

He watched as everyone filed into the tent. It was like a state dinner, each side bringing their respective dignitaries. Ra, Trevor, Irakesh, and Anubis took one side of the tent. Behind them stood Steve and Wepwawet. The former was a servile little fuck, while Wepwawet exuded thinly-veiled violence. Jordan could feel the god watching him through a faceplate twin to his own. Was the wolf-headed god experiencing the same things he was? Maybe, if they struck a real alliance here, the two could find a way to help each other escape their respective prisons.

Isis, Liz, and Blair dominated the other side of the tent. Jordan loomed behind them, trying to make up for Ra's larger force. He wasn't sure how much success he was having, but at least their faction was more impressive than the last one. Osiris sat by himself on another side of the circle, drinking from a cup of water and looking utterly unconcerned that he was the only one without backup.

"The last of us have arrived," Ra said, her melodious voice easily overpowering the wind outside. "We have come to discuss a treaty between the gods, a compact between Isis, Osiris, and myself. To this end, I'd suggest we discuss our respective terms. Assuming we can reach an accord, we will then nominate a leader for this alliance. Is this an acceptable format?"

Both Isis and Osiris nodded. The whole thing felt very rote, as if the three had already discussed this at length and were now merely going through the whole thing for show.

"Isis, why don't you begin by giving us your terms?" Ra asked, leaning forward and resting her chin on her hand.

"Our terms are simple," Isis said. She straightened. "We are willing to work alongside you and Osiris to stop Set. We will put our forces at the disposal of the elected leader. In exchange, we ask the following. First, we will be given safe passage back to our lands once the deed is done. Second, the group will help re-establish a conduit to the Nexus. Third, the Ka-Dun Steve will be turned over to us, to face justice for his crimes."

Whispering rippled through the room at the last, though it was doused like a candle caught in the wind. Jordan watched Steve's reaction carefully, and he couldn't help but smile at the fear he read there. Steve had been playing a dangerous game for a long time, and seemed to realize he might finally have lost.

"Osiris?" Ra said, shifting to half face him. "I would hear your demands as well before terms are set with Isis."

"My terms are simple," Osiris said, setting down his goblet. He gave Ra a hard look. "After Set is overthrown, I am again made Ark Lord of the First Ark. If we recover a Primary Access Key, that key is given to me. In exchange, I offer the following. I will use the key to forge a conduit to the Nexus. I will also offer the full might of Mohn Corp, and I assure you it will be needed to win this battle. When the fighting is done, I will grant all parties safe egress from the land now called England."

Ra was silent for a long moment. "Very well, I have heard both your terms. Now hear mine. Osiris will be made Ark Lord of the First Ark, this I can agree to. Yet I will not give up a Primary Access Key, if one is discovered. I know all gods will seek such a powerful tool, so I'd suggest that whoever personally vanquishes Set may claim the weapon."

Now that was an interesting choice. Jordan privately agreed with it. It gave all three of them incentive to kill whoever this Set was, and it prevented whatever pointless bickering would no doubt erupt over who got the weapon.

"As for your terms, Isis, I agree to them unilaterally. The Ka-Dun Steve will be turned over at the conclusion of our compact," Ra said, raising a hand.

Wepwawet seemed to know what she wanted, reaching out a metallic hand to seize Steve by the scruff of the neck. Good thing too, as Steve had already begun to blur. Fucking coward.

"In light of Osiris's request for the Primary Access Key, I'd suggest a compromise," Isis said, rising to her feet. She extended a hand, and a moment later gold flowed up her arm. It coalesced into the familiar staff with its scarab head. "I already possess one of the keys, and I have no need of another. In exchange for foregoing my claim to the weapon, I—"

Pain wracked Jordan. Fire shot through every nerve, and he began to twitch as if being electrocuted. The armor prevented him from falling, but he'd lost all muscle control. He felt woozy, as his bladder emptied of its own accord. The fire faded, but in its place left a heavy blanket smothering his entire body. He tried to shake his head, but found he couldn't move, not so much as his jaw. What the hell was going on?

A moment later his HUD flickered to life, entering combat mode. It began cataloguing people in the room. All were listed as enemies, and as he watched each was assigned a priority. All save one. Wepwawet was painted blue, the only friendly in the room. The implications chilled Jordan to the core. He strained, trying to force movement from his flaccid body. Nothing. It refused to obey him, instead moving of its own accord.

He could do nothing as the missile tubes on his shoulder opened, watching in horror as Wepwawet's armor mirrored the action. Isis had been wrong about the length of time it would take for the taint to seize control.

There was a small kick as both launchers delivered their entire payload.

Chapter 59- Flight

A wall of flame ballooned outward from the exploding missiles, blowing shrapnel through anything in its way. Trevor curled his body into a ball as the blast hurled him through the scattering ash of what had been the tent. His internal organs were perforated, his spine broken. He landed in a heap, his one good eye aimed in the direction of the carnage.

Jordan and Wepwawet stood in the midst of the destruction, with everyone else strewn around for a hundred yards, moaning, groping for missing limbs, clutching at bleeding heads.

Ra stood first, with more grace than one could expect, though her body remained whole and her golden spear emerged like an extension of her arm. Her eyes smoldered, and her lips were drawn back in a snarl.

Isis rose next, shifting into wolf form as she tore loose the tattered remains of her skirt. Osiris leapt to his feet immediately after, his suit nothing but a charred memory. Its absence exposed an athletic body criss-crossed with near-endless scars.

Ra's golden spear twirled in her hands even as she leapt into the air above Wepwawet. She thrust the weapon through the seam in his armor where the helmet met the chest plate. The sunsteel passed through the armor like it was paper, punching through the back of the throat. Even as Ra's feet touched the ground she reversed the stroke, using her momentum to fling the heavy power armor into the air. Trevor tracked its flight, eyes widening as he spied something behind and above it.

Something massive, with scaly black wings. Trevor had long been a fan of fantasy. He'd spent countless hours devouring novels, watching movies, and playing Dungeons & Dragons. The thing in the air, the thing descending slowly in their direction, was without a doubt a dragon. Of course the dragons he'd read about didn't have fifty caliber machine guns built into their backs.

It was like a fucking T. Rex with wings, and even as he watched, awful green mist burst from its mouth. Trevor used the blur to scramble out of the way, rolling to the right as the mist sizzled a wide path where he'd been standing. That path continued toward the smoldering remains of the pavilion, where most of his companions were still reacting to the sudden betrayal of Jordan and Wepwawet.

Fortunately, Osiris saw the danger. He sprinted forward, his passage so swift it kicked up a wind that tore at the remains of Trevor's pants. Then he leapt, not a human jump, but something superhuman. The kick sent him into the sky like a comet returning to the heavens, and as he rose Osiris summoned the sword he'd taken from Liz. He spun it in a circle until it became a single blur, like a plane's propellor. He used that to deflect the steady stream of bullets belching from the gun set into the dragon's back.

Then he was past the machine gun's firing arc, moving faster than it could track. The gleaming golden point of his sword was held above him, and it punched through the underside of the dragon's jaw with almost no resistance. There was an enormous crunch of bone, and the dragon's head exploded as Osiris's body impacted.

Then the god turned to mist, hovering in the air as the decapitated dragon plummeted to the ground. It struck with titanic force, the box of ammunition on its lower back exploding spectacularly. The crash was loud enough to be heard over the din of explosions and painful cries arising throughout the camp. Trevor looked around him, realizing several things at once. There were three more dragons in the sky, and dozens of smaller bat-like creatures as well. There was also a wall of muscular demons tearing through Ra's undead. It was a perfect ambush, and it was destroying their ability to fight before they even realized they were in battle.

"To me," Ra roared, launching herself into the air. Like Osiris, she hovered above the earth, a faint green glow suffusing her skin. Her hair whipped around her like a million tiny snakes, writhing about almost with a will of their own. "Gather to me!"

Isis didn't respond, instead seizing Jordan's armor by one wrist. She whirled around as if throwing a discus, then released Jordan. He shot through the air towards a knot of demons nearly a hundred yards away. His armored form slammed into two, crushing both as he rolled into the dust. Trevor doubted Jordan was dead, but the Commander didn't rise.

Liz had shifted as well, and held Blair's mangled body protectively as she stood behind Isis. Blair was already beginning to heal, but it looked like he was out of the fight in the short term. Neither Irakesh nor Steve had emerged from the wreckage of the pavilion, leaving Anubis as the only other member of their party. The jackal drifted into the air, moving to join Ra. His fan axe scythed with an almost casual ease through any demons who came close. That seemed like the safest place to be.

Trevor ignored the fiery pain of healing, instead willing himself to mist, drifting into the air to join them. He had no idea how they remained solid while hovering there, but now wasn't a great time to ask. He positioned his cloud between Anubis and Ra, drawing shadows closely about him until he was hidden. He had no illusions as to his place on this battlefield. He, Blair and Liz were puppies compared to the gods around them. The best thing they could probably do right now was just stay out of the way.

"Sekhmet," Isis roared. Trevor looked down to see Isis pointing at something in the distance. He looked that way and found a pair of truly frightening gods marching in their direction. Both were clad in black armor, more what he'd expect a knight to wear than the modern stuff Jordan was using.

"It's my brother," Osiris called, drifting close to Ra. Isis leapt up to join them, hovering just like the others. He'd never seen a werewolf do anything like that, though it made a certain kind of sense. Jordan had used telekinesis. If Isis had the same power, maybe she was lifting herself.

"There's no way we can win against him, not here and not now," Isis said, turning her attention back to the approaching gods. Set walked calmly in their direction, drawing an enormous black sword from a scabbard over his shoulder.

"My army has already been devastated," Ra said, nodding in agreement. "We have no choice but to flee, yet I cannot imagine how we'll manage that. There's no way he'll allow us to get away."

"Only one thing will keep him from pursuing, mighty Ra," Anubis rumbled, drawing the attention of the other gods. Trevor wasn't sure what he meant, but the rest of them looked gravely at the jackal. "Set has ever been prideful, and long has he desired my death. If I stay, he will take time to kill me personally. That will give the rest of you time to flee."

"Doing so will weaken us," Ra said, shooting a concerned glance at Set's approaching form. They had only moments before his arrival. "I am almost tempted to make a stand here."

"That would be beyond foolish," Osiris snapped, drifting closer to Ra. "We flee. Now. If we die here, then Set wins and the world pays. We must find safety and gather our strength. If that means losing one of our own to do it, then we must make that sacrifice."

"Very well," Ra said. She stretched out a hand and squeezed Anubis's shoulder. "Fight well, nephew. You will be remembered long after this age."

"Trevor," the jackal said, turning those ancient eyes in his direction. "I will not have time to finish my teaching. Tell Anput why I must dishonor myself so, and see that she learns the nature of my death."

That surprised him. The idea that Anubis would trust him with anything seemed odd. The jackal had made it clear at every point that he detested Trevor, yet here he was asking a favor that would have been better left to Ra. These people were damned strange.

"I'll tell her," Trevor said, dropping the shadows. "Good luck, Anubis."

Anubis nodded once, then glided to the ground. He casually dispatched a pair of the tall muscular demons, then turned to wait for Set.

"Are we sure this is going to be enough for us to get away? What about

Set's troops?" Trevor asked. The dragons had finished with Ra's army, and were heading their way.

"Do not concern yourself," Osiris said, giving him a crooked smile. "I have just the thing for the fodder."

Osiris looked skyward, and Trevor followed his gaze. Something twinkled above them. Whatever it was, it was getting larger quickly. At first he thought it was a meteor, but then he recognized it.

"Holy shit," Trevor said, looking at Osiris. "You're using the Skyhammer aren't you?"

Chapter 60- Last Stand

Anubis twirled his fan-bladed axe in lazy arcs as he waited for Set to approach. The ebony-armored figure walked slowly toward him, despite the fact that he could have blurred across the distance in the space between heartbeats. It was hardly surprising; Set loved theatrics.

Dragons? Anubis thought with a chuckle. Seriously? Each took centuries to grow and consumed an enormous amount of flesh daily. They were notoriously difficult to keep and, while they were impressive in combat, a god of any decent age could best one easily. They were hardly worth the effort. Yet Set had a fondness for them.

Anubis glanced up as a sudden downdraft tickled his fur. For a moment he thought one of the dragons was attacking, but all three had passed him in pursuit of Ra and her companions. The wind came from a strange glittering object that plunged from the heavens like a star.

A molten hunk of metal the size of a small mountain screamed to the earth, catching all three dragons. The first creature took the full brunt of the blast and was crushed easily. The other two were caught in the wake, knocked spinning from the air like lions kicked by an elephant.

Anubis laughed, a warm hearty laugh. Little had impressed him in this new world, but it seemed these moderns had invented at least a few interesting weapons. He turned toward Set, who'd paused in his approach to study the carnage where his dragons had been. Anubis couldn't see his face, but he imagined it locked into a rictus of rage, and that pleased him.

"How many more dragons do you have, Set?" Anubis taunted, walking slowly toward the demonic god. Ra was safe now. Set and his terrible wife Nephthys wouldn't pursue so long as Anubis lived, and by the time Set killed him Ra would long since have fled.

"Don't goad me, jackal," Set snapped, his armored visor turning to focus on Anubis. His eyes were twin pools of flat black, utterly alien. What had he done to himself? "Your death will be painful as it is, but if you push me I will keep you alive for centuries. I will make you eat your own entrails. You will beg for death, whimpering like the cowardly animal you resemble."

"We've battled before, Set. Have you forgotten? Perhaps if you removed the helmet occasionally you could see the scar I gave you all those millennia ago," Anubis taunted, enjoying it perhaps more than he should.

"Ah, I forget," Set said, barking out a sudden laugh. He reached up with both hands, removing the demonic helm and tucking it under one arm.

All mirth crumbled to ash. Set had been handsome once, perhaps the most handsome of all the gods, excepting only Osiris. The only thing marring that had been the single scar on his right cheek, a wound Anubis had the dubious honor of having given him. The scar was gone. Everything that had made Set human was gone.

A bulbous head of ashen grey housed eyes of flat black, and Anubis found his death reflected there. Set smiled, a sea of shark fangs glittering as he spoke. "You've slumbered for thirteen millennia, jackal. I have not. See the changes the Builders have wrought. See what I have become, the power I now wield."

"What are you?" Anubis took a cautious step backwards.

"You ask the wrong question," Set said, stepping forward with a terrible smile. "What am I becoming? The progeny of the Builders have shared much with me. I am being shaped into their image, so that I might join the Builders when they return. All that I do, I do to further the return."

"As a slave?" Anubis growled, spitting in the dust at Set's feet.

"Oh no," Set corrected, taking a step closer. He waved a hand dismissively, and Nephthys retreated to a safe distance. "As an overseer. I will enslave mankind to my will. All will become demons, an extension of my mind. Those who do not will be slain. I will present a vast army to the Builders upon their return, to execute their will in reshaping this world."

Prudence said Anubis should have let Set come to him, that he should have waited as long as possible to prolong the battle. Yet he could not. Everything in him cried out to end the abomination before him. He charged, executing a hundred-blade attack.

Countless images burst from him, each a perfect mirror, down to the fan-bladed axe. The images attacked from a hundred directions. Only one was real, but to deal with that attack the victim had to be able to pick out the real Anubis. It had been precisely this attack that had given Set the scar all those centuries ago.

Set simply vanished. A hundred copies of Anubis struck nothing but empty air. He took a moment to regain his balance, then began to spin. Set was behind him, and he was already attacking. His gauntleted fist punched through Anubis's chest, ripping out his heart.

Anubis stumbled back, propping himself up with his axe. As a deathless he no longer had a heart that beat, but the blow still staggered him. He expected Set to press the attack, but instead the abomination began eating his heart. Slowly, as if relishing a great treat.

Anubis roared, blurring toward Set in a fury. This time his attack was unsubtle, but as fast as he could make it. As expected, Set disappeared again. This time Anubis studied the movement. He wasn't blurring. He was in one place, then he was in another. Just like a vampire.

Again Anubis attacked, a powerful strike, as fast as he could make it. Again Set teleported, laughing this time. That laughter ended when Anubis drove his axe backwards, ramming the second axe head through Set's chest. Armor crunched, twisting as the sunsteel found flesh.

He capitalized on the attack, swinging a clawed hand at Set's still exposed face. He felt a moment's elation, but then Set's jaw distended. His mouth opened impossibly wide, and he struck like a snake, snapping his jaws around Anubis's outstretched hand. There was a moment's pain, then Anubis fell back with a roar as he stared at the stump where his hand had been.

Set gave him no quarter, driving brutally forward. He slammed a gauntleted hand into Anubis's jaw, shattering it and knocking him backward. Set snatched Anubis's fan axe out of the air, whirling it over his own head once, then down in a low sweep. The move severed both Anubis's legs at the knees, spilling his mangled body to the dusty earth.

Anubis used his one good arm to pull himself backward, but it was a feeble gesture. He was about to die, and he knew it.

"Not so, jackal," Set said, leaning close with that bizarre, alien grin. By Ra, was Set in his head somehow? That was a trick for Ka-Duns, yet he'd clearly heard Anubis's thoughts. He displayed powers from Isis, Osiris, and Ra. What did that mean? "Oh, yes, jackal. I can hear your thoughts. But what you will find more terrifying? I can control them as well."

Set plunged all five fingers of one hand into Anubis's chest. White fire flooded Anubis's body, and his back arched. He screamed and screamed, praying for death.

Chapter 61- A Fitting Fate for Baldy

Irakesh came to with a groan, pulling himself from under a singed section of the pavilion. Everything ached, especially his head. He stared around dumbly, unable to comprehend what he was seeing. Smoke rose in little plumes, a whole sea of them. Each came from a cooked corpse, a mixture of humans, anakim, and…worse things. One looked like a creature he'd heard of but never seen, one he'd longed to test himself against. A dragon. The corpse had no head, and its sickly green blood had congealed into a great stinking pool around its body.

"Hello, nephew," came a feminine voice from behind him. Irakesh froze, unable to even turn and face the voice. He recognized it from his early childhood, and it still terrified him. "Are you not happy to see me?"

You must face her, and quickly, my host. Convince her you are her servant, or she will burn us to ash.

Irakesh turned, painting a smile on his face. "Ahh, Aunt Nephthys. You are looking radiant. It would seem you and Mother had a bit of a disagreement."

"Not so," Nephthys said, cocking her head to the side. She wore form-fitting black armor, a million tiny scales much like that of the dead dragon. The armor highlighted her generous curves, but one look at the inhuman face erased any beauty an observer may have found there. Ebony eyes, lacking an iris or cornea, latched onto him. Her skin was the pallid white of a new corpse, her head disproportionate to her body. Somehow the worst part was her hair, which had fallen out save for a few stringy patches of grey. "We were in perfect agreement. She ran like a frightened child, so I didn't kill her."

"Ahh," Irakesh said, feeling queasy in a decidedly un-deathless-like way.

"Husband," Nephthys called, her melodious voice at odds with that strange face. She turned to face another figure, one that would have made Irakesh wet himself were he still human.

Set approached, face grim. What a face it was, too. It looked almost exactly like Ka, the servant the Builders had left behind. Save where Ka appeared harmless, Set was terrifying. It meant Set was shaping his helixes to match that of the Builders.

Set carried a limp body in his hand, dragging it through the dirt as he approached. Irakesh blinked, recognizing Steve's bloody form. Steve still breathed, but he hung there limply. Set had a hand around the back of Steve's neck, his fingers curled around the golden collar, which he was using to carry the Ka-Dun.

"Ahh, nephew," Set said, tossing Steve at Irakesh's feet. "I can see by the bracelet on your wrist that I've found something that belongs to you."

"Erk," Irakesh said, staring down at Steve. He could tell the Ka-Dun was awake, but Steve lay there as if unconscious. Irakesh envied him that. He looked back up at Set. "Y-yes. The Ka-Dun belongs to me."

"I see," Set said, wrapping an arm around Nephthys's waist. His voice was warm and friendly. "Tell me, nephew. Would you like to continue your wretched existence?"

"Of course," Irakesh said, wiping soot from his forehead with the back of his hand. How was he going to get out of this situation? He looked around, but all of his allies were gone. He was well and truly on his own.

"Excellent, I'm pleased to hear that," Set said, giving him a truly alarming smile. "Swear fealty to me, accept the gift of the demon, and I will elevate you to a commander within my forces. You will answer only to me and your aunt. How does that sound?"

Irakesh considered his options. Set was asking him to betray his own mother. More, he was asking Irakesh to allow Set to sink his hooks in. Those hooks would begin to erode Irakesh's will, and someday would take over his mind. With each year Irakesh's will would belong less to him and more to Set, until one day he was a mindless thrall.

"I'm afraid I can't do that, Uncle," Irakesh found himself saying. The words were strange. He didn't know where they'd come from. Irakesh sank to his knees, and met Set's awful gaze. "I suppose you'll have to kill me. I won't betray my mother, and I won't give up my identity to be one of your servants."

Steve leapt eagerly to his feet, dropping the pretense of being unconscious.

"I will." He was bloody and battered, but his gaze was steady as he looked at Set. "Take me, my lord. I have no love for Ra, and even less for Isis. Give me power, and I am happy to assist you in killing your enemies."

"Interesting," Set said, laughing. He stalked over to Irakesh, drawing an enormous black bastard sword from the scabbard over his shoulder. He gave a quick flick, severing Irakesh's wrist. There was a moment of hot pain, but Irakesh ignored it as the hand with the bracelet clinked to the ground at Steve's feet. He said nothing as Set turned to Steve. "I accept your offer, Ka-Dun. I will free you from the collar, and give you the gift of the demon."

Set gave Irakesh a truly wicked smile, one full of tiny razored teeth that made Irakesh's own look harmless. "As for my quivering nephew here, he will be your first thrall. You may enslave him, just as he so thoughtlessly enslaved you."

Irakesh watched in horror as Steve approached. The Ka-Dun wore a gleeful smile, staring cruelly at Irakesh as he snapped the collar around his neck.

Chapter 62- Our Best Plan Sucks

Blair stared back over his shoulder, but none of the demons approached. They'd blurred several miles, finally stopping at an empty freeway.

"You were ready for this," Isis said, gesturing at a massive jumbo jet parked on the road. The cargo hold in the back was open, a wide ramp beckoning for them to enter. A single figure stood there, waving frantically at them to board.

Blair sprinted up the ramp. He was one of the last to board, joining the cluster of figures in the center of the little hangar.

The man who'd been waiting had salt and pepper hair. He wore a deep blue Armani suit, one that matched the quality and cut of Osiris's own—pre-dragon goop, anyway. Whoever it was had the faint green glow Blair had come to expect from the deathless, and his familiar nod to Osiris reinforced that judgement.

"Where's Commander Jordan?" the man asked, scanning their ranks as the wide ramp behind Blair began folding up into the plane.

"I'm sorry, Mark. He didn't make it," Osiris replied, grimly. "He's trapped in a suit of armor derived from our X-11s."

"Trapped?" the man asked, raising an eyebrow.

"Yes, trapped. Using tech stolen by Set's spies," Osiris explained, giving a sigh as he sat on one of the benches set into the wall of the cargo hold. Isis joined him, though Ra and Trevor remained standing.

Blair looked to Liz, who seemed just as shell shocked as he was. He moved to her, wrapping an arm around her waist. She seemed a little surprised, but gave him a tentative smile. At least there was still something good, something to hold onto amidst all the chaos.

"Okay, so they've stolen our tech. That's alarming, but I don't understand what you mean by Jordan being trapped," the man Osiris had called Mark seemed agitated, and the flippant way he spoke to Osiris suggested he was used to being in charge.

"The armor is tainted," Osiris explained, accepting a silk handkerchief from Mark, which he used to clean grime and dragon ichor from his face. "It's demonic. In essence, it makes Jordan a slave to the will of the person who created the demonic taint. In this case, that's my brother Set. Normally that taint takes months to seep in, sometimes years. Set managed to do it in just a few days."

"So, Jordan's been compromised. Can they force him to work against us?" Mark asked, grabbing a bulkhead as the plane began to move.

"I'd say so, Director," Liz said, disengaging from Blair and approaching the man. "He fired a bunch of missiles into the middle of our gathering, and might have tried to do more if Isis hadn't used him like a frisbee."

"Ms. Gregg," the Director said, giving her a smile that revealed a pair of elongated incisors. Just like the ones Osiris had. "I'm pleased to see you're still alive."

"Likewise," Liz said, accepting his handshake. "Well, living-ish. It looks like you've become deathless."

"Something like that," the man said. Blair finally knew who he was now. "Though I'm not a deathless, as I understand it."

"No, you're not," Osiris interrupted. He smiled at them, face finally clean. "Mark is a vampire, Ms. Gregg. One of my progeny."

Trevor and Ra had been whispering in a far corner, but she turned to look at Osiris as he spoke.

"What's the difference?" Liz asked.

"Osiris couldn't stomach what we'd become," Ra said, walking a few feet toward them. The plane began to shake as the engines roared outside. They gained momentum quickly, and Blair was forced to grab the bulkhead. "He altered the virus so he would appear more human, and his children have the same lineage. They hide what they are. Deathless revel in it."

"We can argue the aesthetics of our respective bloodlines later," Osiris said, turning back to the Director. "How did you know where we were?"

"You asked me to follow Ra's progress," the Director said, shrugging. "It wasn't hard to figure out this was where you'd go, so I kept an eye on things. When creatures began emerging from the Ark in England I thought it prudent to move material here in case this was where Set planned to hit. Looks like I was right."

"Your decision may have saved us all," Osiris replied, nodding in apparent thanks. "Set will be after us soon. He'll likely gloat over his victory for at least a small time, but we'll need to prepare for the next attack."

"Next attack?" Blair asked, finally joining the conversation. "How will he know where we're going?"

"Because he has spies everywhere," the Director said, picking a piece of lint from the arm of his suit. "If he knows where Mohn is headquartered in London, then that's where he'll strike."

"Then why don't we just go somewhere else? Somewhere he doesn't know?" Blair asked. It seemed foolish to walk into a trap you knew about.

"Because Set knows we have no choice," Isis said, heaving a great sigh. "We know his scheme now, which is nothing less than the destruction of the Nexus."

Blair was silent for a long moment, considering. "So you think Set will use the First Ark to get back into the Nexus, since his previous plan to cut off its power source didn't work. I've restored a conduit to it, and for him to destroy the Nexus he has to sever the conduit. That about right?"

The plane engines screamed, then the front wheels left the runway. There was a moment of weightlessness, then they were airborne.

"Precisely," Osiris said, giving a tight nod. "Had it not been for your actions, the Nexus would already be destroyed. I don't know why its destruction is so important to Set, but the reason doesn't matter, really. The Nexus is critical to our eventual defense against the Builders. Without it, we lose the Ark network, and they'll be able to pick us off easily."

"I keep hearing the Builders brought up," Liz said, folding her arms as her gaze roamed the elder gods. "I get that they made the Arks. I get that they're a threat for some reason. How do they relate to Set, though? We have too many damned enemies, and I'm not even sure which is which anymore."

"Doesn't matter," Trevor said, crossing to join Liz. Ra shot him a look as he moved, expression unreadable. Interesting. Blair wondered if there was something more going on there. "What does matter is our immediate actions. Maybe these Builders are a threat, but they're a distant one as I understand it. The immediate problem is Set. We know what he wants. He knows we know. It sounds like he'll bring everything he has to stop us."

"That he will," Osiris said. He looked deeply troubled. "We don't have the resources to resist him, either. You saw what he brought to bear back there. He'll bring a stronger force to London, one we can't stop. If he catches us we'll be wiped out, and there will be no one left to oppose him."

"So we bring the battle to him then," Ra growled, stalking over to stand next to Trevor. That made Blair smile.

"Sekhmet is right," Isis said, straightening. "We have to stop Set. We cannot run, or he wins by proxy. He destroys the Nexus unopposed."

There was a long moment of silence as everyone seemed to weigh their options.

"Let's blow up the First Ark," Blair found himself saying, even as the idea crystalized in his mind. Everyone eyed him in shock, so he continued. "If we assault The First Ark, Set will have no choice but to stop us. Once he's in the Ark we find a way to overload the reactor. Someone, or several someones, keep Set busy until it goes critical. The Ark detonates, killing Set along with it."

"There is a serious flaw with that plan," Isis said, eyes boring into Blair. "The Arks are linked to the Earth's magnetosphere. They use it to evenly distribute sunstorms during the height of the sun's fury. It's all that keeps the surface of our world from being burnt to a crisp. If you destroy one of the Arks, you risk destabilizing that network."

'What would that mean, exactly?" Blair asked.

"A pole shift," Trevor said, stroking his goatee. "That would be some nasty business. It could cause the continents to shift, meaning we'd see some of the worst earthquakes and volcanoes since the Late Cambrian."

"Does anyone have a better plan?" Liz broke in. She reached down and took Blair's hand, giving it a supportive squeeze.

Silence, until Osiris finally spoke. "Blair's plan is workable. Set has to die, that much is clear. None of us have the power to kill him, and even if we did he still has an army of demons to deal with. That army will be centered in or under The First Ark. Blow up the Ark, and you wipe out that army."

Chapter 63- Well and Truly Fucked

"I bet you have a really small penis," Jordan said. He kept his tone light, matter of fact. It had the desired effect.

Set, the pompous ass wipe he was standing next to, turned toward Jordan. His expression was unreadable behind the dark, demonic helm. But Jordan liked to think he'd scored a point.

A choking sound came from the freakish hag standing next to Set, and her all-black eyes blinked furiously as she stared at Set. She looked as if she wanted to run. Jordan guessed Set probably had some serious spousal abuse issues to effect that kind of reaction in his wife.

Irakesh and Steve cowered in the corner. Jordan, Wepwawet, Set, and his haggish wife Nephthys stood near the control rod of the slipsail Blair had used to escape Ra. The room was spacious, but it suddenly felt cramped.

"Can you give me a single reason why I shouldn't incinerate you where you stand, whelp?" Set rumbled, taking a threatening step toward Jordan.

"Because you're a megalomaniac with a serious Napoleon complex. If you kill me, you'll have to find another dog to whip—you know, since that's the only way you can actually get hard."

"He's right, you know," Wepwawet said, surprising Jordan. It was the first time the wolf-headed god had spoken since he'd donned the armor. "You do have a small penis. Osiris spoke of it often, usually with a great deal of pity."

Set roared, grabbing Wepwawet and slamming his armored body to the deck. He rounded on Jordan, armor clinking as he trembled visibly. "I am not so foolish as you think. Death is a release, your only escape. I will make you suffer for a thousand lifetimes, each worse than the last. Your insolence will earn you nothing but pain. I'll make you kill your family. I'll make you—"

"Blah, blah, fucking blah," Jordan interrupted, grinning.

A buzzing began in the back of Jordan's mind, like a thousand cicada on a hot summer night. The buzzing intensified, growing louder until he could hear nothing else.

Every fiber of his being screamed that he should run, and his bowels emptied themselves. Jordan finally collapsed into a fetal position, drawing his armored legs against his chest as he prayed for the terror to abate.

"I can make the terror permanent," Set said, eminently smug. Just like that, the fear vanished. "I can make you lust for corpses, or fill you with hatred until you will beg me to kill your closest companions. Tell me, whelp, do you have any further insults you wish to offer me?"

"No, sir."

"Excellent. You can learn, then," Set said, leaning down next to Jordan. "See that you remember your place. If you speak again, for any reason, I will offer you a kind of torment far worse than anything you can possibly imagine. Do you understand?"

Jordan almost said yes, but realized the trap that had just been laid. He nodded, rising slowly to his feet.

"What of you, Wepwawet? Any further insults you wish to offer?" Set asked, shifting his attention to the wolf-headed god. Wepwawet rose slowly to his feet, shaking his head. "Wonderful. Ready yourselves for battle. In the morning, we invade the sanctum of your vaunted Osiris. Together we will kill him, his wife, and that awful bitch Ra."

Chapter 64- The Builders

Set waved a hand, erecting a shadow sanctuary around himself and the control obelisk. Neither light nor sound could penetrate it from without, though he could still see the rest of the ship. It afforded him the privacy he needed for the task he was about to undertake. It was unpleasant at the best of times, but circumstances would make it far worse than usual.

He took a deep breath. He was wrestling with an unfamiliar emotion, one he was far more used to causing than experiencing. Fear. In his hundreds of centuries he'd almost never run across a being that could give him pause, especially the last hundred. With Osiris withering outside the Arks, and the rest of Set's contemporaries asleep, he'd had little to fear.

He'd subjugated the underworld, killed any god who resisted, and pressed the remainder into service. He had spies and vassals all over the world; his demonic taint spread far and wide. He'd touched dozens of powerful beings, and each now bore a shard of his existence, in much the same way he still bore a shard of Ka's.

Yet all his power, all his control, had left him ill-equipped to deal with the progeny of the Builders. In them, he glimpsed the Builders themselves. Their power was vast and incomprehensible. It had created the Arks, shaped entire species, and ultimately carried them from this world to one somewhere at the fringes of space.

All the vast power they'd discovered in the First Ark was merely the leavings of the Builders. Who knew what abilities they'd discovered in the millions of years since they'd departed? Their progeny were terrifyingly advanced, which was why Set was experiencing such a base emotion.

He withdrew a small golden triangle as thick as a finger. It had seven gems arranged across the surface, and as he concentrated they began to glow. A moment later, a tiny translucent figure appeared. It looked much like Ka, its head too large, and eyes too black. Yet where Ka's skin was green, this being had a pallid grey. He still found it alien, despite having adopted the same disturbing visage himself.

"Greetings, exalted one," he said, bowing his head. The need to do so galled him, yet there was little choice in it. If he served the Builders, there was a place for him. If he did not, then he'd be annihilated alongside all other sentient life.

The creature's mouth didn't move, yet it emitted an odd chittering. Set hadn't been able to learn their language, but images appeared in his mind. They showed the Nexus, crushed by the ocean. They showed vast numbers of humans morphing into grey men through the use of the chrysalis the progeny had provided.

Set glanced at the corner of the slipsail where the device sat, a coffin-shaped block of stone just larger than a man. The idea that it could change a being into a grey man was in itself terrifying. It was by experimenting with it, and with the heart of the First Ark, that he'd effected such changes on himself.

"Soon, master," Set said, bowing his head again. "The Nexus is being supported by a single Ark. Tomorrow I will kill its lord, and kill all the elder gods who would oppose us. Once they are dead I can remove the conduit, and the Nexus will collapse."

More chittering. More images. Mostly emotion, or what passed for it in the mind of the grey men. They were deeply dispassionate, yet they could feel anger. As this one did now.

"Colonization can begin soon," Set said, aware that he was almost pleading. It wasn't dignified, but it *was* smart. "Once the Nexus is destroyed, I will begin linking the vessels Vulcan has created to the First Ark. My slaves will convert night and day. Then we can begin conquering other Arks to speed the process."

The chittering sounded almost mollified, then the image broke into fragments and disappeared. Set shuddered. He'd met the grey men in person only once, but that had been enough to cow him. Their ships were incredible—smaller versions of the great Arks. Smaller versions that could fly through the vast emptiness of space. Their power was considerable.

Yet that wasn't truly what terrified him. It was the knowledge that the few hundred grey men were merely forerunners. Countless others would come, and when they arrived the war would begin in earnest.

Chapter 65- Holding Action

Trevor shifted his weight from foot to foot. The anticipation was killing him. They'd arrived in London two hours ago, and had hastily erected defenses throughout the facility. Trevor, Liz, and Blair had been assigned to guard something called Object 3—a teleporter, from the brief explanation The Director had provided.

Their instructions were simple. Keep the enemy away until everyone could fall back, then use the teleporter to invade the First Ark. Only, Trevor doubted it would be simple. Heavy footfalls sounded in the distance. Far too heavy to be human, and the stampede was growing closer.

"Incoming," Trevor roared, sprinting down the tunnel back into the narrow hallway. He dove behind a stack of crates, rolling to his feet next to the machine gun emplacement. The woman manning the weapon wasn't anyone he knew, which might be just as well. It was unlikely she'd survive the next few hours.

"How many?" Blair asked, crouched in werewolf form across the hall, behind another stack of crates. There was no sign of Liz, but Trevor knew she was there somewhere, in the shadows.

"At least a dozen, the big bruiser types," Trevor answered, slipping into the shadows himself. "You want to fall back to Object 3?"

"Not yet," Blair said, shaking his furry head. "We need to make this believable, or they'll know something's up. That means making them pay for every inch they take."

The first lumbering figure emerged from the room beyond, pausing to bellow a challenge as it entered the narrow hallway. It was a little over eight feet tall, and had to stoop to enter. Both broad horns carved furrows in the ceiling, dusting its shoulders with white plaster.

The woman next to Trevor opened up with the machine gun, ringing Trevor's ears like gongs. The vibrations shook the floor as a sea of spent cartridges clattered to the ground around them. The stream of rounds punched into the demon's chest and face, driving it backward. Most of the rounds ricocheted off, which showed just how tough these things were. A few punched through, sending out gouts of black blood. The demon answered with an angry roar, and tried to force its way up the corridor.

The machine gun kept firing, until the creature finally collapsed in a pool of its own black blood. There was a moment of blessed silence, then a second demon tried to crawl past the body of the first. The machine gun howled death again, and Trevor covered his ears. The floor was thick with spent shell casings now, and the room reeked of gunpowder.

The second demon stopped moving. A third tried clawing its way past, but was having a hard time managing the bodies of its companions. Then the demon disappeared back the way it had come. Trevor waited for long moments, praying for the ringing in his ears to fade. Nothing. No further attempts by the demons to gain the corridor.

"Where do you think they went?" Liz called from behind him, her deep voice confirming that she was in wolf form, despite the fact that Trevor couldn't see her.

"Regrouping, maybe?" Blair asked, peering over the crates on the other side of the all.

"I doubt it," Trevor said. "We only killed two of them, and they have a whole hell of a lot more fodder."

"Then why did they—" Blair began, but a wall of flame and shrapnel erupted up the hallway. Trevor blurred, ducking behind the machine gun emplacement. The soldier wasn't quite fast enough to get her head down, and took a face full of flame and pain.

The rapid staccato of automatic weapons fire came from the far end of the corridor, and the crates that had survived the missile blast crumbled under a withering hail of high caliber bullets. Blair crouched across from

Trevor, his fur singed, but seemingly unharmed otherwise.

"Fall back," Trevor roared, unsure if anyone could hear him beneath the deafening weight of the gun fire.

Either Blair heard him, or had the same idea. He blurred up the corridor, disappearing into the room beyond. Trevor did the same, rolling through the doorway and scrambling to one side of it. A moment later, Liz emerged from the shadows. She swung the heavy iron door shut, dropping the kind of crossbar he'd expect in a medieval dungeon.

"That's not going to hold them for long," she roared, spinning to face Trevor. "Did you get a look at whatever was firing?"

"No," Trevor said, shaking his head. The muffled roar of bullets finally ceased, but they still had to shout to be heard over the ringing in their ears.

I did. Blair's voice echoed in Trevor's head. *Or I felt the person, anyway. It was Jordan. He wasn't alone either. Steve is out there too.*

"That will mean Irakesh. Maybe Wepwawet too," Trevor yelled back. "All working for Set, you think?"

Definitely. It doesn't surprise me about Steve or Irakesh, and we already knew Jordan was compromised. Blair's voice rang through Trevor's mind again. *That means we're outnumbered, and likely outgunned. That might change the plan.*

Trevor looked at the platform dominating the room. Object 3, Osiris had called it. A triangle of black stone sloped up to a golden disk about six feet across. "Should we use that thing, then?"

"We can't," Liz called back, shaking her auburn-furred head. "Not yet, anyway. We have to wait for Isis. There's no point in going to the Ark without her, Osiris, and Ra."

"How long will it take you to warm that thing up, Blair?"

"I don't know," Blair said, turning to face Object 3. "Osiris says it works just like a light bridge, but it feels a little different."

"He said this thing was built by the progeny of the Builders, right?" Trevor said, eyeing the thing uneasily.

"Yeah, that explains the difference. It's a more modern version of the light bridges. Let's just hope it works like we expect," Blair said, trotting toward the disk at the top. "I'll see if I can get a feel for how it works. Just keep them from getting through that doorway."

"Will do," Trevor said. He put his back to the wall on one side of the door, while Liz did the same on the other. They had to hold, whatever it took.

Chapter 66- Distraction

Isis seized one of the bulkier demon shock troops by its leg, then blurred as she swung it toward a neighbor. Bodies crunched together, slamming into a pile of large, wooden crates in an explosion of wood. She flinched as she was drenched with black ichor.

Something flashed by on her right, and she rolled into the shadows before realizing it was Sekhmet. The fiery-haired goddess bounced between a half dozen more brutes, her golden spear piercing an eye on each target. She vaulted off the last one, hooking a leg on the metal shelving that held an array of smaller crates. Sekhmet flipped up toward the warehouse's high ceiling, then she too disappeared into the shadows, each of her victims collapsing bonelessly to the ground.

"Show off," Osiris yelled, striding through the warehouse with his blade held casually in one hand. The ancient sunsteel contrasted with the thoroughly modern high-tech communications device he wore hooked over one ear. "You could have left one for me."

"It's not my fault you're slow," Sekhmet shot back, stepping from the shadows to join Osiris. She wore a familiar smile, one that warmed Isis. It was almost like a journey back in time, back to when they'd been a real tribe. A family that fought together, no matter what.

"I'm just saving myself for the real fight," Osiris said, clapping her on the shoulder. He turned to the shadows. "Isis?"

"I'm here," she said, stepping into the light. She shifted back to human form as she did so, wiping ichor from her face. "Those things stink abominably."

"Just another way for Set to make himself feel superior," Osiris said, rolling his eyes. He turned to the far side of the warehouse. The wall had several demon-sized holes in it, and most of the dirty windows had been shattered during the assault. "They'll come again soon, I'm sure. Set is nothing if not cautious. He'll probe our defenses at every point, then mass and hit where he thinks we're weakest."

"Not here, certainly. He must sense us," Sekhmet said, frowning.

"Likely," Osiris replied. He tapped the mouthpiece he wore, whispering into it. "Mark, give us a status update." He was silent for several moments, listening. Then Osiris turned to them. "Set's forces have hit us from below, as we expected."

"How do the whelps fare?" Isis asked, concern bubbling up. She hadn't liked the plan. Leaving Trevor, Liz, and Blair on their own was dangerous.

"They're fine, for now," Osiris said. Roars sounded in the distance, then perhaps two dozen demons rushed through the hole in the warehouse wall. "More fodder. Husband your strength. This is Set's attempt to bleed us, so we're weaker when he faces us himself."

Chapter 67- Sacrifice

Mark wished, for the millionth time, that he was back in Syracuse. The London Ops center was cramped, understaffed, and under geared. Not the best place to orchestrate a battle, particularly one as violent as that about to take place.

"Sir, falcon one and three are down," one of the techs called. Mark watched the readout impassively, hands clasped behind his back.

"We've lost warehouse six, sir. They've breached the perimeter on level two," another tech called. Mark didn't answer this one either. This was expected. Most of it had been his plan, in fact. They didn't know that, of course. Didn't know he'd agreed to sacrifice them all.

"Benson," he barked, glancing in her direction. She looked up, brushing her dark bangs from her face. "What's the situation on level four?"

"They've breached the loading dock," Benson said, showing uncharacteristic concern. "Your, uh, team has fallen back to Object 3. If they breach the door, we lose the Object."

"Noted," Mark said, fishing his smartphone out of his pocket. He tapped the button on the top of his ear piece, speaking in a low voice. "The situation has changed, sir. Object 3 is in trouble. If you don't get down there in the next two minutes we've lost."

"Understood," Osiris shot back. The words were clipped, as if he were distracted. In the background came the sounds of combat. Demons were dying noisily.

Mark turned back to the monitor. A large group of demons had entered the facility, directly above this room. That, too, had been expected. All command signals were being broadcast from this room, and Mark had theorized that Set would have a way to listen to them.

The infernal god would have no choice but to crush Ops. It was too tempting a target. Doing so would cost Set time, time the other gods would use to reach Object 3. Then they'd spring the trap Mark had left, the reason they'd lured Set here.

"Sir," Benson called, clearly alarmed. "They've breached the elevator shaft. They're on their way here. We should get out. Now."

"Take the techs and go," Mark said, gesturing toward a metal cabinet that had been pulled away from the wall. Behind that cabinet lay a tunnel Mohn corp had dug for just such an occasion. He didn't bother telling her there was no escape, that she couldn't hope to outrun death.

Benson didn't wait for further instructions. She didn't even try to convince him to go with her. Professional to the very end. "Move, people. In the tunnel, NOW."

Then she leapt through. The others followed her.

Mark was left alone in the room. He pushed the cabinet back in front of the hole, then sat in his chair. He propped his feet up on the desk, interlocking his fingers behind his head as he waited.

A few moments later, the heavy metal door exploded into the room, crashing into the wall with a deafening clatter. A figure in midnight armor strode through, six feet tall with a horned helm. His black eyes scanned the room, narrowing as they landed on Mark.

"Where is he?" Set snarled. Mark didn't answer as several demons ducked into the room. There was no sign of Nephthys. Unfortunate, but also expected. It was unlikely Set would have left the Ark entirely undefended.

"Who?" Mark asked, giving Set an innocent smile. He knew it would show off his fangs, reminding Set that Mark was a child of Osiris.

"My brother," Set spat, taking a threatening step toward the desk. "He's too proud to give command to another. So where is he?"

"See for yourself," Mark said, nodding at the monitor. It flickered to life, showing a dim view of warehouse five. Osiris stepped into the light, smiling broadly at the camera.

"Hello, brother," Osiris said, grinning wickedly. "As stupid as always, I see. Rushing forward without any understanding of the cliff before you, just like the mammoths we used to kill."

"I will tear out your heart, brother. I will turn your life to ashes. I will—" Set roared.

By that time Mark had gotten his hand into his pocket and wrapped it around the detonator.

Chapter 68- Cutting it Close

Blair closed his eyes, feeling the platform beneath him. Object 3 was unlike anything he'd ever encountered, more advanced than even the Nexus had been. Unlike the light bridge in the Ark, this thing seemed to possess its own primitive intelligence.

It enjoyed being used, and was happiest when it served the needs of others. That manifested in sending them wherever they wanted to go. Doing so drew partially on the strength of whatever power source Object 3 was connected to, and partially on the person powering it.

"Better make this fast, Blair," Liz roared, an edge of panic to her tone. Blair opened his eyes.

Deep booms sounded as demons pounded on the thick steel door. Dent after dent appeared, and the frame anchoring it to the concrete was beginning to give. Liz had her back to the door in an attempt to reinforce it, but wasn't having much luck. Trevor struggled to assist her, looking comically small next to a nine foot werewolf.

"I can make it work," Blair finally called, certain he could do so even as he said the words. "I think things are going to go south pretty damn quickly if we do this without Isis, though."

Your survival depends on your escape, Ka-Dun. The Mother will have to fend for herself.

Blair refused to heed the beast, even if it was right. They had to give Isis as long as possible to reach them, right down to the very last second.

The door exploded inward, fragments of metal bouncing from the walls. Liz rolled out of the way, vanishing into shadows. Trevor took a large section of door to the face. It knocked him to the concrete, and he was still struggling to rise when enemies began pouring through.

The first was a brute, larger than the others they'd seen. It paused next to Trevor, driving a massive meaty fist into the small of his back. Bone cracked, and Trevor gave an agonized cry.

Then Liz was there, snapping and biting. She savaged the demon's throat, rolling back into the shadows as its corpse tumbled to the ground. Trevor exploded into green mist, which flowed into the shadows and was gone. Blair felt a moment of elation that Trevor had escaped, but then realized he was the only visible target in the room.

The staff, Ka-Dun. Use the Primary Access Key.

Blair had completely forgotten about the staff Isis had entrusted to him. He extended his right hand, willing the weapon to manifest. The sapphire in the thorax of the scarab throbbed with power. Several more demons flooded the room, and Blair aimed the staff in their direction.

"Uh, kill them," he said, willing the staff to incinerate his enemies. He knew shaping was all about visualization, so even though he didn't know precisely how the staff worked he was hoping it would manifest some wonderful ass-saving ability.

A wave of blue light flowed from the gem, a wide beam that swept the room. It washed over the mass of demons, and Blair understood on some deeper level exactly what it was doing. It was breaking the molecular bonds holding each creature together. Effectively, a ray of disintegration. All eight demons collapsed, and within moments were nothing more than a pool of black sludge.

"Jesus," Liz rumbled, appearing next to him. "That thing is crazy."

"Let's hope it can keep doing that," Trevor's disembodied voice said.

More demons rushed the room, but this time they weren't alone. Two sets of familiar black power armor followed, spraying the room with bullets as they entered. Jordan and Wepwawet. Behind them, just past the doorway, Blair could sense Steve lurking. That probably meant Irakesh as well.

"I'll take the armor on the right," Liz growled, disappearing into the shadows.

"I've got the left," Trevor replied.

That left Blair as the target. Rounds tore through his legs, severing the right below the knee. More rounds punched through his back and shoulder, and he spilled to the surface of the platform with a cry of agony.

Then Liz appeared, grabbing one of the suits by the right arm, and slamming it into the wall. It started to rise, but she stomped on the helmet, knocking it back to the concrete.

Trevor appeared behind the second suit of armor. He seized the arm holding the gigantic rifle, and twisted it to fire at the mass of demons rushing Blair. The weapon cut them down with ruthless efficiency, until the suit was able to stop firing. By that time only one demon remained, and Blair downed it with a quick blast from the staff.

He struggled into a sitting position, gritting his teeth in pain as his knee began to heal. Then a wave of familiar green energy burst from his right, washing over him like acid. He collapsed, dropping the staff. He had enough time to register Irakesh's bald black head and mouthful of razored teeth before the deathless snatched up the staff.

Curiously, Irakesh's face was a mask of grim determination. There was no gloating, no twisted smile. None of the behavior Blair had seen when Irakesh had fought back in Panama, or later in San Francisco. Then Blair saw the golden collar around Irakesh's neck, and suddenly he understood.

"Give it to me," came a familiar, cultured voice. Steve appeared next to Irakesh, blurring next to him from across the room. He extended his right hand, which bore a golden bracelet to match the collar. Irakesh passed the staff over to Steve, though the gesture was reluctant. Steve smiled, then looked down at Blair. "Beaten by your own pride once again. You should have fled when you had the chance, but once again you've made the wrong decision. Once again you—"

Blair blurred, launching three separate attacks. First, he buried the claws of his right hand in Steve's groin. That made Steve reach down to defend himself, which exposed his throat. So Blair tore it out with his fangs. Lastly, he seized the staff in his left hand, then planted his newly regrown leg against Steve's gut. He kicked as hard as he could, hurling Steve from the platform.

"I can't believe I caught you monologuing. Didn't you see the Incredibles?" Blair asked, aiming the staff at Steve's broken body. He fired a wave of blue energy, but Steve blurred away and the energy washed harmlessly over the wall.

Irakesh started to laugh. "I owe you a boon for that, Ka-Dun. It's a pity that—"

His words were choked off as he went pale. Blair turned to see Ra approaching the platform at a fast walk. She casually eviscerated a demon with her spear, then backhanded Irakesh so hard his jaw shattered. He was launched from the platform, landing in a heap on the far side of the room.

Blair glanced back to see Osiris and Isis each battling one of the suits of armor. It was like watching cats play with mice. He actually felt bad for Jordan and Wepwawet.

"Enough," Ra called, her voice ringing through the din. "We must be away. Leave them."

Trevor limped onto the platform, and Ra moved to assist him. Liz appeared a moment later, her fur slick with black blood. Isis approached next, dropping a mangled suit of black armor and leaping onto the platform. She glanced down at Irakesh, then back at Ra. "You're not going to bring him?"

"No," she said, shaking her head. "He's made his choices, and now he has to deal with the consequences. I cannot know if Set has tainted him, and we dare not risk it."

"Just as well," Osiris said, finally stepping up on the platform. He paused as his jacket began to chime, then withdrew a smartphone. He set the phone to video, smiling at the screen. "Hello, Brother. As stupid as always, I see. Rushing forward without any understanding of the cliff before you, just like the mammoths we used to kill."

He paused for a moment, as if listening. When he spoke again, Osiris wore a huge, predatory grin. "Enjoy the explosion, brother. As you survey the shattered wreckage of your army, know that I've outwitted you once again. The First Ark is mine."

Then Osiris hung up, turning to Blair. "Let's get out of here."

"Is there any chance he'll die in the blast?" Blair asked, though he was fairly certain he knew the answer.

"None," Ra said, shaking her head. "Though the blast will destroy his troops. That's some benefit, at least. If we wish to kill him, your plan is the only way."

Blair nodded, then focused on the platform. He willed Object 3 to teleport them, and they disappeared in a veil of brilliant white light.

Chapter 69- Boom

Jordan was not having the best of days. A thick crack ran down the center of his HUD, and the left ankle of the suit screeched as servos groaned. Nor were those the only problems. The little paper-doll style status icon in the bottom left of his vision showed a half dozen blinking lights, each indicating a problem of one kind or another.

That was to be expected, of course. It wasn't every day a werewolf goddess slammed you repeatedly into the concrete, and all things considered he'd made out far better than the last time he'd gotten on her bad side. At least she hadn't torn his arms off.

"Status report," Steve said, sweeping back into the room with far more dignity than he should have been able to muster after having fled out of it just moments before. Jordan ignored him. So did Wepwawet, who was just climbing to his feet. Steve turned in a slow circle, his eyes narrowing. "I said, status report."

Neither of them answered. Steve's response was to aim the wrist with the golden bracelet at Irakesh. He adopted a look of concentration, and a moment later Irakesh shrieked. Then he came to his feet, eyes narrowing hatefully on Steve. Jordan decided right then that he actually liked Irakesh more than he liked Steve. That was saying a lot, because Irakesh was very near the top of his shit list.

"What happened, slave?" Steve barked, stalking closer to the still-groggy deathless.

"I don't know, master," Irakesh hissed, infusing the last word with a healthy dose of scorn. That made Jordan smile beneath his mask.

Metallic footsteps rang on stone from the hallway outside. Someone was approaching, and it wasn't hard to figure out who it might be. Jordan was momentarily grateful he wasn't in command. Hopefully if Set blamed someone it would be Steve. He'd love to see Captain Douchey taken down a peg.

"You allowed them to escape?" Set roared as he stalked into the room. His flat black gaze fixed on Steve.

"Yes, master," Steve groveled, falling to his knees. Jordan expected Irakesh to do the same, and was genuinely shocked when Irakesh chose to remain standing. "I do not know where they have gone, but they used that object to light walk away."

"No matter," Set said, gesturing behind him. A pair of brutes entered, carrying a familiar figure between them. Jordan blinked in shock, realizing he was looking at the Director. Or a version of him anyway. He was no longer human, as evidenced by the glowing green eyes and elongated canines. "You, where did they go?"

"Oh, I'd be happy to sell out my companions," the Director said, sarcasm thick. "Let's see, where did they go? I'm pretty sure they went to the land of go fuck yourself."

"Release him," Set ordered the demonic guards. They dropped Mark, who landed in a heap. His suit was shredded, and several bones were still broken. The fact that he hadn't yet healed was telling. He was close to the brink of collapse. Set stalked over to him. "I will give you one more chance. Tell me where they've gone and I will grant you a swift death. Defy me, and I will turn you into a tool of destruction, one I will use to hunt your own companions to extinction."

"Hmm, let me think," Mark said, seeming to genuinely consider the offer. "That does sound like a pretty good deal. I have a counteroffer though. How about I blow the fuck out of you?"

Mark withdrew a hand from his pocket, and Jordan realized Mark held a tiny black cylinder with a single red button on the top. Even as Jordan recognized the detonator, Mark pressed the button. There was a series of distant clicks that grew closer. They were coming from the walls. Then everything went white as the walls around them exploded.

Chapter 70- Prep

Liz-wolf stumbled on the uneven ground, catching herself against a giant standing stone. A moment ago she'd been standing atop Object 3, the strange teleporter Mohn had apparently liberated from the progeny of the Builders. Looking around, she realized she'd arrived at Stonehenge. It wasn't unexpected, but it still caught her off guard.

She'd traveled a lot of the world, but the sight of Stonehenge in the moonlight was unlike anything she'd ever witnessed. Of course, it would have been more impressive if not dwarfed by the massive, black Ark just a hundred yards away.

"To me," Ra called, her voice heavy with long-accustomed authority. Liz did as asked, moving to stand next to Blair. He looked up at her with a toothy smile, his silver fur catching the moonlight. She smiled back, resting a hand on his shoulder.

Trevor emerged from the shadows next to them. A bit creepy with those hellish eyes and razored teeth, but there was still something of him in the boyish smile. Especially in his tone. "Get a room, you two."

"If we survive this, we will," Liz said, shooting Blair a wink.

"Silence," Ra hissed. Liz turned to face her, resisting the urge to stick out her tongue. She knew Trevor liked the woman, but Liz was too loyal to Isis to feel the same. Ra moved to join them, beckoning at Osiris and Isis to do the same. The latter pair were off by themselves, sharing what looked to be a quiet moment between lovers. "Good, we're all here. Osiris, are your forces ready?"

"They are," he nodded, looking up guiltily from Isis. "I've held back over sixty percent of Mohn's local forces, including all our heavy armor and air units. We've also got the Skyhammer standing by. We're a little light on the ground though."

"Leave that to me," Ra said, folding her arms and leaning her back against one of the standing stones. "I've called every nascent deathless within five miles, and they're shambling their way here now."

"Too late, I think," Isis said. She'd gone back to human form, but still leapt nimbly to the top of one of the stones. "There, demons are approaching. I can see Nephthys at their head. She's moving to engage us."

"Let's not keep her waiting," Osiris said, grinning. "I'll order an initial artillery strike, then we can rush them. Sekhmet, your forces can pin them down after the initial attack."

Ra looked less than pleased that Osiris had assumed command, but she merely nodded.

"What do you want us to do?" Liz asked, shivering even with her thick fur. She wished she'd brought a werewolf-sized jacket. It was funny the things your mind dwelled on right before you did something insane.

"Your task is clear," Isis said, leaping from her perch to land before Liz. "You must safeguard Blair to the heart of the Ark. We will keep Nephthys busy, and deal with Set when he arrives."

"All right," Liz said. She had a feeling it wasn't going to be nearly as easy as Isis made it sound.

"I'll watch your backs," Trevor said, though his gaze went to Ra. Something passed between them, and Liz found herself softening a bit toward the harsh goddess. Ra wasn't kind, but she clearly cared for Trevor and that scored her some points.

Then the scarlet-haired goddess pressed her hand to Trevor's forehead. She adopted a look of concentration, face tightening as her entire body began to shake. There was a flash of silver, then a series of sparks as something passed from her into Trevor.

"What the hell was that?" Trevor said, blinking. He staggered, but Ra caught him.

"A burden I must pass to you, Trevor Gregg," Ra said, in a tone more tender than Liz had ever heard her use. "If I survive, you can return it. If not, then I can think of no one else I'd ask to sit my throne. Use the power well, should it come to that."

"I'm not really sure what to say," Trevor said, pulling Ra a little closer. He gave a start, backing a step away when he realized what he'd done.

"Would that we had more time," Ra said, smiling at him. "You'd have made a worthy consort, I think."

"Incoming," Osiris said, leaping to the top of one of the stones. His golden sword appeared in his hand, and Liz felt a stab of jealousy.

"Liz," Blair said, effecting a strange parody of a narrator. "It's dangerous to go alone. Take this."

He offered her the na-kopesh he'd taken from Irakesh, and she accepted the curved blade. She got the feeling she was missing some sort of inside joke from the way Trevor giggled at the comment. She gave the weapon a few experimental swings. It was different than the heavier broadsword, but she thought she could make use of it.

It looked like she was about to find out.

Chapter 71- Bait

Isis watched the approaching mass of demons warily. She counted at least two hundred, and that didn't include the winged ones circling above. It wasn't anywhere near the size of the force that had devastated Sekhmet's army back in the land now called France, but it was a substantial number.

Still, Isis trusted Osiris. The thought of him drew her eye to where he stood, a little ways off from the stone monuments comprising the place these moderns called Stonehenge. He looked resplendent in his dark blue suit, tie fluttering in the wind. She didn't know when he'd found time to change into a new one, but it didn't surprise her. Osiris raised his golden blade skyward, then brought it down in a chopping motion.

Chaos erupted. Several trails of fire streaked into the demon's ranks, exploding as they impacted. Then something glittered above, falling like a comet. It landed in the central mass of demons, hurling black bodies into the night, each one melting like wax.

The surviving demons scattered, not that she could blame them. Grouping together was an invitation to fiery death, and they knew it. The sudden chaos infusing their ranks seemed to enrage Nephthys, who was leading from the rear. Isis could hear her shrill voice barking commands, which it seemed the demons were ignoring.

Then a wave of corpses emerged from the tree line, shambling their way toward the demons. They weren't strong, and by themselves no single corpse was a threat. Yet they seemed endless, and at the very least the demons had to deal with them. That distraction was exactly what she'd been waiting for.

"Are you ready?" she asked, knowing Sekhmet lurked in the patch of darkness at the foot of the stone pillar she stood next to.

"I am. Let us end this," Sekhmet said. Isis melted into the shadows, blurring across the field toward Nephthys. She couldn't see Sekhmet, but knew her oldest friend was right beside her.

Isis shifted as the gap between herself and Nephthys lessened. She almost tried to summon her staff, before realizing she'd given it to Blair. Her claws would have to do. Isis whipped past a few confused demons, then leapt into the air. She came down on Nephthys with the avenging fury of all the poor souls the woman had corrupted.

Her claws bit deep, but Nephthys's black armor was strong. Isis knocked the smaller woman on her back, but wasn't able to deliver any serious blows. Nephthys planted a booted foot in Isis's midsection and kicked with all her strength. Isis flew backwards, crushing a hapless demon with the impact. Several dull-eyed deathless stood around her, but wandered off to find easier prey.

"It's not like you to be so brave, Isis," Nephthys said, flipping to her feet. She drew a long thin blade, forged from the same black metal as her armor. "You were always the weakest of us, until you adopted that furry form. Even now you're but a shadow of the true warriors."

"It's a good thing she brought one then," Sekhmet taunted, her golden spear emerging from Nephthys's throat, silencing the woman. "You talk too much, Nephthys. You always did."

Then Sekhmet spun back into the shadows. Isis gave a wolfish smile and did the same. "You're outnumbered, and your husband isn't here to protect you."

That last was designed to do more than anger her. She wanted Nephthys to panic. Her husband would feel that, and it would bring Set running.

"You think I need his protection?" Nephthys rasped, her ruined throat already healing. The armor had begun to repair itself as well. That could be a problem. "Come and find out."

Nephthys spun in a slow arc, shifting on the balls of her feet. It was a warrior's stance, and it drove home how right the woman was. She'd always been a better warrior than Isis, though Sekhmet was Nephthys's equal. Or had been anyway. Who knew how strong Nephthys had become during the time the other gods had slept?

A wave of green energy shot from the darkness, competing with the explosions from the artillery falling around them. Nephthys sagged to her knees, but immediately began struggling to her feet. Sekhmet didn't give her any quarter, gliding forward and ramming her spear through the knee joint on Nephthys's right leg.

Isis bounded forward and seized the injured leg. She pulled with all her might, and gave a wicked grin when Sekhmet seized Nephthys and began pulling the opposite direction. The leg tore free with a pop and a spray of gore, drawing a shriek of pain from the black goddess.

"You'll pay for—" she began, but another form emerged from the darkness. Osiris-rammed his sword through her breastplate. The weapon pierced the armor with a sickening crunch; before Nephthys could react, pulses of sickly black light began flowing out of her corrupt heart and up the weapon.

"A bit anticlimactic, I know," Osiris said, gritting his teeth as the flow of pulses came more quickly. "But we're pressed for time. Just die, so we can do the same to your husband."

Chapter 72- On Four Legs

Blair ran fast and low through the mist-coated grass. He moved with a light blur, but was careful not to expend too much energy. He savored the thin trickle of moonlight, though it wouldn't provide much power before he reached the Ark.

There was no sign of either Trevor or Liz, but he was confident they were lurking in the darkness near him. He wondered for the millionth time why Isis hadn't given males the ability to use that power, as it left them at a great disadvantage compared to the other supernatural predators he'd battled.

We have other advantages, Ka-Dun. If you wish more stealth, trust in me and I will guide you.

He trusted the beast in the same way he trusted his arms or legs. It was part of him, and he ceded control willingly. There was a rush of heat through his entire body, then something like the change from human to werewolf. This change was different though. Instead of growing larger, he grew smaller.

Within a few steps he found he had four legs; instead of hands he had paws. His fur was thicker, his muzzle longer. He'd become a wolf, the same way he'd seen Ahiga do all those months ago back on the beach in Peru.

Despite the dire circumstances and impending battle Blair felt better than he had in months. There was something harmonious about the wolf. It bonded him to the land, and he longed to surround himself with his pack.

He loped through the darkness, bounding over a grassy knoll. It carried him to the base of the Ark, near the far corner, away from the fighting. Explosions and gunfire split the night, broken by cries from the dead or dying. He ran low and fast next to the Ark, and not a single demon turned in his direction. They were too busy getting shelled by Mohn's artillery, or crushed under the orbital bombardment from the Skyhammer.

Blair finally reached the mouth of the tunnel at the wall's center. He slowed as he approached, carefully peering around the corner. Nothing. At first he thought it curious the place was undefended, but it quickly occurred to him why Set hadn't bothered leaving more of an internal defense. He was the lord of this Ark, and even another Ark Lord couldn't do much to harm the place. Unless they had a Primary Access Key. As he understood it only two existed, and Osiris had theorized that Set possessed one.

That meant Set only had to fear the remaining key, and what were the odds of a small pack sneaking into the Ark with it? Pretty damn high, as it turned out. Blair gave a wolfish grin, trotting up the corridor into the darkness. His enhanced vision allowed him to see, especially with the soft glow from the diamonds set into the wall.

He wasn't sure he wanted to, though. This place had a stench to it, layered decay that made him want to vomit. Refuse and worse had been smeared on the walls. It was as if this Ark had been inhabited by squatters for a very long time. His lupine senses allowed him to detect every nuance of the stench, and he found himself sneezing repeatedly. It was terrible.

Blair tried not to notice the smell as he made his way deeper into the Ark. He was so focused on his progress that he leapt into the air with a yelp when Liz appeared beside him.

"Sorry," she whispered. She'd returned to human form, and was peering around at the walls. "What the hell happened to this place?"

Blair shifted back to human form, sighing in relief as his sense of smell returned to normal. Now he just wanted to gag, instead of vomit. "I don't know. Guess Set isn't much for housekeeping. Maybe his demons haven't been housebroken."

"Whatever the reason, this place makes me long for a shower," Trevor said, shimmering into existence next to Liz. "Let's do what we came to, and get the hell out of here."

Chapter 73- Set Arrives

Jordan smiled grimly inside his armor as he stood at rigid attention behind Set. His armor was damaged in so many places now that the entire paper doll in his HUD was lit with red. He was still a prisoner, but if the armor were destroyed he'd be free. All he had to do was watch for an opportunity, and he could probably hasten that destruction.

"Stop your groveling and gather to me," Set growled at Steve, stepping atop the smoking remains of Object 3. "I will show you the kind of power the other gods only dream of."

The rest of them moved to the platform, though Steve was the first to reach it. Typical. To Jordan's immense surprise, a faint white light came from the platform. Apparently it was at least partially functional. The light flared, then washed over the five of them.

There was something like a clap of thunder, then he was elsewhere. His ears were ringing, and his head felt like he'd spent the last six hours drinking shots of Jaeger. Or something even fouler.

Irakesh and Steve looked just as bad, maybe worse. It was hard to tell with Wepwawet, as he was enshrouded in armor just like Jordan. Only Set seemed unaffected. His lip curled up in a snarl, as he stared at the battle unfolding before them.

They'd arrived at Stonehenge, near the center of the giant stones. In the distance lay a sea of black, twisted bodies—Jordan guessed they were probably the remains of the defense force Set had no doubt left to prevent his enemies from gaining entrance to the Ark. In the distance, four figures battled. Jordan recognized Isis, who towered over a figure in ebony armor.

"Steve, take this motley lot to the central chamber. Ensure that no one reaches the heart of this Ark. Do this, and I will reward you greatly. Fail, and

I will give you to my wife as a plaything," Set growled, not even turning to see if his order was heard.

Set began to grow, gaining height as he knocked stones out of his path that had stood for millennia. His footsteps thundered on the turf as he began a loping run towards Isis, Osiris, and Ra, who were ganging up on Nephthys. It looked like she was getting the worst of it, too. Good on them

"You heard him," Steve snapped. He waved toward the Ark. "Move, if you wish to live."

Jordan's armor started forward of its own accord. He considered resisting it, but this wasn't the place to make a stand. That should happen when and where he could make a difference.

Chapter 74- Intercepted

Isis's wolfish ear twitched, angling toward a new sound—a savage yell of unparalleled ferocity. She half-turned to face the sound, careful not to release her hold on Nephthys. The goddess wasn't thrashing much now, but Isis wasn't taking any chances. She'd hold her until Osiris finished siphoning her essence.

A figure was sprinting toward them with impossible speed, the type of blur that could only be sustained by the eldest of gods. It would make it here before Osiris could finish his work, and she could see enough of the figure to realize the ebony armor belonged to Set. Their distraction back in London hadn't bought them nearly as much time as they'd hoped.

"Sekhmet," Isis growled, meeting her friend's gaze. "Hold Nephthys. I will deal with Set until she is no more."

Sekhmet nodded, and Isis released the black goddess. She slipped into the shadows, interposing herself between Set and Osiris. She began her blur, considering as she did so. Was Set using illusion? He could be approaching from an entirely different direction. She studied the grass in his wake, noting both mist and dew evaporated in his passing. It was possible that was illusion. Set possessed enough strength to create one of that size and detail, certainly.

Yet she didn't think so. Set had been a cautious god in his youth, but age had fueled his overconfidence. He was all too willing to engage his foes if he thought he had the advantage, which he very likely had here. Then there was his very real concern for his wife. Set was an evil, tainted, bastard. Yet his affection for Nephthys had always been consistent. If he had anything approaching a weakness, that was it.

Isis braced herself, praying she was right. She blurred as fast as she ever had, pouncing upon Set as he passed her. She wrapped a thick arm around his neck, using her momentum to arrest his. Then she flung him hard to the muddy earth, creating a deep crater with him at the bottom.

She stilled her elation at having been right. It *was* Set and not an illusion, but now she had to deal with him. Alone, at least until her allies finished Nephthys. Set wouldn't respond to taunts or threats, not while he was concerned with his wife. The only way to stop him was overwhelming force.

Isis leapt into the crater, seizing Set's arm and attempting to rip it from its socket. Set merely tensed, and she couldn't move that arm even an inch, no matter how she strained. Set's black eyes glared at her from beneath his twisted helm, and he struck back in a fury.

His fist punched through her gut, exploding her innards and spine into the grass behind her. His other hand seized her neck, dragging her face close to his. "It ends tonight, Isis. There is no escape this time, no bringing Osiris back from the dead. I will kill you all, and consume your memories. Before you die, know this, little sister. If you'd not meddled, not created the virus, we'd all of us be dead. This world would be free. Because of your actions, I exist, and every crime I perpetrate can be laid at your feet."

Isis knew despair then, because Set was right. Had she left well enough alone, had she never entered the Valley of Forgotten Voices, they'd have died as humans. That moment of weakness had created a chain of events that led here, and she had only herself to blame. Yet she wasn't dead yet.

"So overconfident," Isis choked out. She blurred, willing her body to shift as she did so. Faster than thought, she became a tiny fox, dropping from Set's grip and rolling back into the shadows. A heartbeat later she'd gone back to wolf form, bounding out of the crater. A third shift brought her back to werewolf form, even as she spun to face Set.

The black god had leapt to his feet, spinning in place as he sought some sign of her. He gave a roar, raising both arms to the sky. A pulse of black and green energy rolled out from him, a mixture she'd never seen before. It burst in all directions, and she was caught in the blast.

The energy was pure pain, but that she could deal with. What filled her with terror was the energy's residual aura. It clung to her like paint, exposing her in a way no ability ever had. Set had found a way to reveal her in the shadows, a way even more potent than that Blair had discovered.

Set leapt from the pit, stalking in her direction. Isis turned and ran for the Ark, knowing she'd never reach it.

Chapter 75-The Repository

Blair took his first step into the repository. Words were insufficient to describe what he was witnessing, the majesty and complexity exhibited by the Builders. This stadium-sized room was the pinnacle of an entire civilization—the outgrowth of, he presumed, millions of years of technological advancement.

"Wow, look at the size of the crystal in the center," Trevor said, walking past Blair to lean on a railing that lined a walkway ringing the entire chamber. "What do you think it's made out of? It's too light to be a sapphire."

Liz walked past Blair as well, stopping at the railing next to Trevor. "I'd guess it's a diamond from the clarity, but I don't really know a lot about gemstones."

Blair finally moved to join them, still struggling to find words. The smooth walls below the railing sloped down to a platform holding the single largest gemstone Blair had ever seen. It had to be at least a hundred feet tall, and could have been two or three times that, depending on how large the room really was. It was difficult to say without anything to give it perspective.

"It's an aquamarine," Blair said, absently. The walls leading to the the stone were bare, but those leading to the ceiling were covered in gemstones that matched the one below.

"Hey Blair, I'm guessing that thing is important," Trevor said, drawing Blair's attention. He was pointing at a spot along the wall a couple hundred yards away. The railing was broken by a wide platform, with a roughly person-sized blue aquamarine in the center.

"That's the control locus Isis told me about," Blair said, trotting along the railing. He needed to focus. This place was amazing, but he didn't have time to study it. That killed him, as he knew he was witnessing the very thing he'd sought his entire life.

He'd always wanted to know the origins of mankind, and many of those answers lay in this room. Yet if he were successful in the next few minutes he'd be blowing it up, denying the world of all the precious secrets it contained.

"Better speed this up," Liz called, darting a nervous glance back the way they'd come. Her wolfish ears twitched. "I hear something behind us. I'm guessing whatever it is, it isn't friendly."

Blair blurred down the walkway, crossing the the gap to the control locus in a couple seconds. He skidded to a halt next to the platform, stepping onto it as he examined the crystal. There was a sort of socket at the base, one that looked about the right size and shape for the base of the Primary Access Key.

Behold, Ka-Dun. This is the very place where the Mother brought our species into being, the place where she first crafted the virus that gave birth to the deathless. It is here that she became more than a simple woman, adopting the first Ka to become the first Ka-Ken.

Blair extended his hand, summoning the key. He reverently placed the base in the socket with a satisfying click. There was a thrum of energy in the staff, which flowed down into the man-sized aquamarine. The gem began to pulse with light, and the giant counterpart in the center pulsed in time.

He sensed a vast array of data, some of it incomprehensible, but much of it readily identifiable. In that instant Blair understood why this place was called an Ark, and why this room was called the repository. It was a genetic repository, and he was seeing every species this place had ever catalogued. Their DNA was stored here, to be drawn upon by a shaper like him. He could create entirely new life forms, or return ones that had been long extinct to the world.

Yet that was only the surface of what this room could be used for. It tapped into every system in the Ark, and the enormous power reservoir driving the place lay directly under the giant aquamarine.

"Blair!" He heard Liz's frantic voice as if across a vast gulf. "We've got company. Whatever you're going to do, you need to do it now."

Blair looked up from the staff, glancing at the entrance to the room. Several figures had burst in, and were charging along the railing in their direction. Several familiar figures. Jordan and Wepwawet were in the lead, then Irakesh, with Steve predictably bringing up the rear.

"There's no way I can finish before they get here," Blair said, shifting as he spoke. "We're going to have to deal with them first, then I can set this place to self-destruct."

"Guess it's a fight then," Trevor said, slipping into the shadows. "I'll deal with Irakesh. Liz, see if you can keep the armor out of the fight while Blair deals with Steve."

Blair gave a grim smile, removing the key and aiming it at the walkway. He summoned the same energy he'd used back on Object 3, firing a trio of blue pulses at the lead armored figure. As expected, the armor dodged out of the way—but, also as expected, that left an opening for Liz.

A nine-foot auburn werewolf burst from the shadows, seizing the first suit of ebony armor by one leg and flinging it over the side into the valley below. The second set drew a bead on her, but by the time a pair of missiles corkscrewed from the shoulder launcher she'd already disappeared. They detonated harmlessly against the wall, cracking several of the aquamarines and extinguishing their light.

Blair blurred, sprinting along the narrow railing as he glided toward their enemies. Irakesh vanished into the shadows, but Trevor would deal with him. That left a clear path to Steve. Blair saw red.

Chapter 76- Free

Jordan tumbled off the railing, falling for what seemed like forever before crashing to the hard ground below. The blow caused warning klaxons inside the armor as still more red appeared on the paper doll. Several systems were now listed as nonfunctional, and many, many more were listed as critical.

Above he could see the two sides squaring off against each other, Blair, Liz and Trevor engaging Wepwawet, Irakesh, and Steve. If this had been a movie the armor would have forced him to fight his friends, but he'd somehow have escaped at the last minute. The good guys would win, and the critics would lambaste the movie as being predictable. Particularly because Trevor had done the same thing back in San Francisco.

Fortunately, Jordan had been planning for this for some time. The armor made him a prisoner. It could exert control over his nervous system, and would resist any attempt to remove or damage it. Even with all the punishment it had endured he still couldn't override that basic control.

So he did something the designers had probably never expected. Jordan concentrated, forming a skin-tight bubble of telekinetic energy around himself. It was a much smaller, more tightly controlled version of the bubble he'd used to save everyone from the nuclear blast back in San Francisco. Once Jordan had created the bubble, he began expanding it outward with all the strength he could muster.

He gritted his teeth, pushing harder, and harder. At first the armor refused to give. A bead of sweat trickled down his forehead, and he could feel the vein in his temple throbbing. He pushed harder. Harder still. There was a groan as a seam popped, then another. The groan became a shriek as multiple seams began to give. Metallic fragments sprayed out in all directions, littering the ground for dozens of yards. Jordan grinned like a fool, giving a whoop of joy.

Well done, Ka-Dun. You have freed us from the armor's demonic taint. You are a true warrior, worthy of your bloodline.

"You know what? I actually missed having a psychotic beast in my head," Jordan said, laughing out loud and giving another whoop.

He reached up to feel the golden collar along his neck, probing with his fingers until he found the catch. The collar came loose, and he dropped it to the ground triumphantly. He was fucking free, and it was time to dish out some god damned payback.

Chapter 77- Turning the Tide

Trevor crouched in the shadows, waiting. He knew how this would go, because he could see the bracelet on Steve's wrist. Steve was about to be attacked by Blair. He'd force Irakesh to intervene, and the second that happened Trevor would attack Irakesh. Irakesh had to know that too, and the real question was how would the deathless react? He was older and stronger than anyone else here, save Wepwawet. Trevor had no idea how old the wolf-headed god was, but that wasn't his problem. Hopefully Liz could hold him until they could help her.

Blair blurred past Trevor, kicking up a wind as he moved along the railing. He'd nearly reached Steve when a familiar green glow came from a spot behind Blair. Trevor blurred as well, launching himself at Irakesh. He caught his former master around the midsection, and they went down in a tangle of limbs.

Irakesh gave off a pulse of green light, one Trevor had seen him use before. Trevor faded to mist, allowing the light to pass harmlessly over him. He phased back to solid form, swiping at Irakesh's face with his claws… and his hand passed harmlessly through the illusionary version of his former master.

Trevor wasn't surprised when Irakesh's fist emerged from his chest, or when a booted foot kicked him to the smooth metal walkway He was surprised when no followup attack came.

"Get up," Irakesh snarled. Trevor heard the rasp of a sword leaving its sheath. "You're wearing a blade. If I'm going to kill you, I'll do it with steel. Come, learn what a true master can do."

Trevor rolled to his feet, drawing his own sword. The long slender blade felt at home in his hand, more than a gun ever had.

"No blurring, no illusions. You know I can best you in both those arenas anyway. I have every advantage. Die like a true deathless, Trevor," Irakesh said, gliding forward on the balls of his feet. Trevor moved to meet him, blocking Irakesh's probing strike. He parried a second and third strike as well, each coming more quickly than the last.

"You don't have to do this," Trevor said, attempting a low slash at Irakesh's knee. The deathless batted it casually aside. "I know you hate Steve. Serving your mother is one thing, but Set? Join us, Irakesh. We should be fighting on the same side."

For just a moment Irakesh faltered. Trevor saw doubt in that putrid gaze. He backed up a step, weapon at the ready. But then Irakesh flowed forward, striking like a viper. He rained blow after blow at Trevor, and it was everything Trevor could do to parry. Each one was more wild than the last, and finally Irakesh batted the sword from Trevor's hand.

Irakesh followed up immediately, burying his weapon in Trevor's chest. Trevor felt a moment of terror, but then remembered the sword wasn't sunsteel. Irakesh couldn't drain his life. Trevor planted both legs in his former master's midsection, launching the deathless into the wall as the sword pulled loose with a popping sound.

"Die. Just die, you worm," Irakesh screeched, launching another attack. As Irakesh rushed toward him, Trevor saw something blonde flash in the corner of his vision. A male werewolf landed on the railing. Jordan raised a hand, palm facing Irakesh.

A wave of invisible force blasted Irakesh into the wall with a sickening crunch. Irakesh was pinned, the force remaining as Jordan hopped down and walked over to Trevor.

"Get up, you lazy fuck. We have work to do," the Commander offered Trevor a hand. Trevor took it, allowing Jordan to help him to his feet.

"Took you long enough," Trevor said, smiling in spite of himself.

Chapter 78- Desperate Gamble

Wepwawet was both stronger and faster than Liz. His armor made him damn hard to hurt, and her only advantage seemed to be that the armor was hideously damaged. If it had been anywhere near full strength, she'd have already been dead.

A metallic fist crumpled the railing next to her, and she rolled away from the followup blow as the other fist smashed a dent into the walkway where she'd been standing.

If you wish to win, then you must use the blade, Ka-Ken. Your only prayer is draining his life essence.

"And how the hell am I supposed to do that?" Liz growled, flipping into the air over Wepwawet. She gathered the shadows around her, bounding off the wall to change the angle of her flight. Good thing, too.

A trio of wickedly sharp claws erupted from an armored fist, smashing several crystals in the wall where she'd have been if she hadn't altered course. They flickered and died, creating more of the shadows that were her only advantage. Liz responded by summoning the curved blade Blair had given her, landing in a crouch as the weapon coalesced in her right hand. It was smaller than her previous sword but, because it weighed less, it was also faster.

She lunged forward, ramming the weapon between the plates around Wepwawet's elbow. He roared in pain, blurring. She never even saw the backhand that smashed her away from her quarry. Her jawbone shattered and her head rang from the blow. Liz shook her head to clear it, willing her face to mend and fighting desperately to retain her grip on her weapon.

Through the heart, Ka-Ken. It is the only way.

Through the heart. How the hell was she going to land a blow like that?

Doing so would open her up to a vicious counterattack, and once those armored hands wrapped around her she knew she'd never escape. But maybe she didn't have to.

Liz gave a tight smile, launching a frontal assault. She batted one arm out of the way, then buried her sword right through the armored chest. Wepwawet might have been able to stop the blow, but as she'd expected he was more focused on catching her. Impossibly strong arms wrapped around her chest, crushing the air from her lungs as he drew her up against his metallic body.

Black spots danced across Liz's vision.

Chapter 79- Final Deception

Isis fled, but she could feel Set gaining ground on her. Every step he took thundered in her ears, and no matter how quickly she blurred he was still narrowing the gap. It seemed he'd abandoned his quest to save his wife, and was now focused to the exclusion of all else on killing Isis.

She leapt over a small knoll, barreling toward the entrance of the Ark. If she was going to die, she had to do it as close to the Ark as possible. Gods willing, she could lure Set inside.

"Isis," Set roared, so close she could feel his hot breath. "I will eat your heart. I will make Osiris watch as I visit the same fate upon you that he visited upon Nephthys."

It occurred to her that Set must be linked to his wife. Perhaps that was the reason he still gave chase. He already knew Nephthys was dead, so there was no point in going after Osiris.

"Will you now?" came Osiris's strong voice. He appeared ahead of her.

Her husband swept forward in a combat stance, golden blade held high. Isis ducked under it, skidding to a halt behind him. She scanned the shadows, but saw no sign of Sekhmet yet.

"At last," Set roared, extending his left hand. A massive ebony claymore flowed into his hand, painful to look upon. It behaved like sunsteel, but was corrupted somehow, just like the armor. "It's time to die, brother. But before I kill you I *will* make good on my threat. I will force you to watch me consume Isis's essence. I will do the same with—"

"Sekhmet?" came a feminine voice from behind Set. A golden spear erupted from his chest. "Was that what you were going to say, Set? This isn't the first time my spear has found your flesh, but I promise it will be the last. Your wife is dead. You will not survive the day."

The words were brave, but Isis knew the truth. Set was beyond any of them, and there was no way they could overcome the titanic strength he'd displayed. Still, Sekhmet's words had the desired effect. Set roared in rage. He brought his sword down in a one-handed sweep.

His blade sheered through Sekhmet's sunsteel spear, lopping the end off. The gold fell to the ground, melting into a shapeless mass. Set was already moving, spinning faster than thought to ram his weapon through Sekhmet's face. She gave a choked cry, dropping the remains of her weapon and tumbling back in a spray of blood.

Set pressed the attack, and Isis knew Sekhmet was doomed if she didn't do something. So she charged, barreling into Set from behind. The blow knocked him to the dirt, and she continued forward, scooping Sekhmet up in both arms. She gathered the shadows close about them both, cradling her friend's limp body.

"It will be okay, Sekhmet. Rest. Heal," she whispered, terrified at the hideous blow Set had inflicted.

"Take the staff into the Ark, Isis," Osiris roared, striding forward to meet Set. "I will deal with my brother. Take control of the Ark, and lock him out, just as he did to me all those centuries ago."

She could have kissed him. Set roared in rage, clearly buying into the deception.

Chapter 80- The Fate of Captain Douchey

Blair leapt from the railing, time slowing to a crawl as he gained altitude. Steve was blurring as well, tracking Blair's movements with those heavy brown eyes. They shifted at precisely the same instant, Steve into a midnight-furred werewolf, and Blair into silver.

Steve no doubt expected Blair to grapple—to claw, and snap, and rend like the beasts they resembled. But while they might possess a beast, a second consciousness, they were men. Blair decided to fight like one. Smart, and lethal.

He came down with a leg extended, kicking Steve in the chest. The blow caught Steve off guard, flinging him back into the glittering wall. It didn't do any real damage, and from the comically confused expression on Steve's face, he thought it made absolutely no sense. All the better.

The move put distance between Blair and Steve, just enough that Steve couldn't close the gap. Blair raised the access key and leveled it at Steve like a rifle. He willed it to fire, and a trio of azure pulses lanced into Steve's furry face.

Steve collapsed into a heap, screeching through his hands as he raised them to cover the terrible wound. Blair fired again, but apparently Steve was less injured than he'd pretended. He leapt straight up, narrowly dodging the pulses fired by the staff. Steve landed on the railing, glaring at Blair through that ruined face.

"Are you a fucking coward, Blair?" Steve growled, barring his fangs. "Too weak to face me in combat? I watched Bridget die, and I laughed. I robbed Isis of her memories while she slept, and betrayed her to Ra. Now I've given everything to Set. Doesn't that infuriate you?"

Blair smiled. A younger version of himself would have fallen for Steve's very transparent ploy. Hell, even an older version of him had made mistakes. Had trusted Steve and gone running back to Bridget within days of being separated from Liz. He'd made mistake after mistake in combat, all because he was fighting with his heart, and not his head.

"Yeah, it kind of pisses me off," he replied, keeping the staff leveled on Steve's chest. He was ready, hovering at the edge of a blur.

"Then put down the staff, and let's end this," Steve said, a light of triumph entering his gaze.

"Or I could gun you down with this handy Builder weapon," Blair said, blurring as fast as he could. Time slowed, but Steve matched his movements perfectly.

As expected, Steve leapt from the railing, aiming straight for Blair. Blair fired two blasts, each with a very specific target. The first was aimed at the clawed hand coming for his face. Not because he feared the blow, but because of the golden bracelet wrapped around the wrist. The blast incinerated bone and flesh, melting everything between his elbow and hand.

The hand spun away in slow motion, no longer blurring. The second blast caught Steve in the crotch, incinerating everything that made him a man. Childish, maybe. But the fucker deserved it.

Steve crashed to the walkway, dropping his blur. He stared up in pain, and horror, mouth already opening to form some sort of plea. Blair didn't give him that chance. He rammed the scarab end of the staff into Steve's neck, choking off whatever the bastard had been about to say.

Are you going to kill me? Steve asked, the thought echoing hatefully in Blair's mind.

"Nah," Blair said, grinning wickedly. "I've never been very good at cruelty, and I want your death to be as painful as possible."

Steve looked confused, which only made Blair smile wider. "Hey Irakesh, guess what? You're free."

Steve suddenly understood. He struggled into a sitting position and stared in horror. Blair turned to face Irakesh, who was pinned against a wall.

Jordan turned, sized up the situation, and gave a wolfish grin. He released Irakesh, nodding in Steve's direction. Irakesh's face twisted in fury, and he blurred to Steve. Irakesh flew into a flurry of blows, punching, kicking, and clawing as Steve desperately sought to ward off the blows.

Then Irakesh finally picked Steve up, drawing his face close. "You are an honorless cur. A stain upon both your kind and mine. I have long considered Isis and her bestial get enemies, but the Ka-Dun Blair has my respect. He is a worthy foe. You? You are nothing. Contemplate that as you die."

Irakesh tossed Steve high into the air, the arc carrying him over the railing. Before he could plummet to his death, Irakesh fired a thick pulse of green energy, melting Steve's legs. Blair added a trio of blasts from the staff, unraveling Steve's torso. Just like that Steve dissolved, his scream abruptly cut off. Blair began to laugh.

"Man, I hated that fucker," Jordan said, glancing over the railing as all that remained of Steve splattered to the ground below. Blair felt something stir there, a familiar energy that resonated with the key within his chest.

A streak of silver shot from Steve's remains, crashing into Jordan's chest. Every last strand of blonde fur stood on end for a few moments, leaving Jordan looking like he'd just been through the dryer. Then the Commander heaved a deep sigh, blinking in wonder. Blair knew what he was experiencing, the sudden link to an Ark.

Blair turned to Irakesh. "You have a choice, now. Help us end this, end Set. Or meet your own end here. You know you can't take us all. Jordan, Trevor and I are all Ark Lords. Choose, and choose quickly."

"So be it," Irakesh snarled. "There is peace between us, until Set is dealt with."

Chapter 81- Broken

"You can set me down," Sekhmet said, though her gaze was a little unfocused. Isis did as Sekhmet asked, placing her friend next to the central obelisk. It was the first time Isis had returned to the First Ark in over twenty millennia, and she couldn't help but shudder as she saw what had been done to the place.

Set's demons had defaced the walls, destroying both the glyphs she and Osiris had carved, as well as those left by the much older Builders. The place reeked of feces and worse things, a foul miasma that seemed strongest in the central chamber. That, more than anything else, showed her they'd made the right decision. Sacrificing everything to stop Set was the only possible course.

"Listen," Sekhmet said, nodding at the doorway.

Heavy booted steps approached. Isis had expected the battle between Set and Osiris to last longer. It seemed they'd underestimated their foe. Just how powerful had Set grown? Would even an explosion such as the First Ark might make be enough to kill him?

"Iiiiiiississs," Set taunted. A moment later, his armored form strode imperiously down the ramp into the central chamber. All damage to his armor had been healed, and the black metal looked as if it had been forged that morning. "Ahh, there you are. I've brought you a gift."

Set reached back into the shadows, dragging forth a limp body. He tossed Osiris on the ramp ahead of him, grinning manically as her husband rolled to a stop near the base of the ramp. Then Set tossed something golden and metallic. It flashed through the air, landing next to Osiris.

Osiris's mighty blade had been shattered. The piece Set discarded was nothing more than the hilt and the first foot of the blade. The rest was gone, cut off cleanly just as Sekhmet's spear had been.

"Oh, don't worry, little sister," Set said, all mock sympathy. "I haven't killed him, not like last time. There's no need for you to craft a virus to bring him back. I want him alive, just as I want you alive. Your torment will last millennia. I will make you kill everyone and everything you have ever loved. You will not only watch this world burn, you will participate. And when at last nothing of our species remains, I will sacrifice you to our new masters."

Isis licked her chops, rising to her feet. She was a terrifying beast, yet it was she who quailed. She glanced at Sekhmet, who'd risen as well. Sekhmet looked exhausted, but she drew a small golden dagger from her belt. Isis gave her a quick nod, and the two turned to face Set.

"Is that your plan?" Set asked, clearly amused. "Make me kill you? It won't work. I'll thrash you as I have your husband, but you won't die. Not yet. Come, let us dance one last time."

Isis winked at Sekhmet, and her sister shot her a quick smile. They were all about to die.

Chapter 82- Detonation

Blair looked up from Steve's remains on the valley floor with a grim smile of satisfaction. In so many ways, killing Steve represented atonement for Blair's monumental fuck-ups in Panama and San Francisco. The job wasn't done yet, though.

He took a moment to survey the rest of the combat. The last active fight was between Liz and Wepwawet. Blair's hackles rose and he began sprinting along the railing when he saw Wepwawet crush Liz to his chest. He blurred, crossing the space between them in a couple heartbeats. Blair was fully prepared to tear Wepwawet's armored form apart, but slowed to a halt when he got close enough to see what had happened.

Liz had been crushed to the black-armored chest, and it looked like several ribs and both her arms had broken in the process. However, she'd rammed the sword Blair had given her through Wepwawet's heart. As he watched, bright pulses of sickly green energy flowed up the blade, just the way they'd done when Liz had mercifully ended Cyntia back in San Francisco.

Wepwawet twitched weakly, then lay still. Liz pushed his body off her, the armor tumbling to the walkway with a clatter as she rose to her feet. Blood matted her auburn fur, but her bones were already popping back into place. If anything she looked stronger than she had at the start of the fight, strengthened by consuming the essence of an elder god.

"Oww," she said, rolling her shoulder as it popped back into place. She turned to look back up the walkway. "So we won?"

"Looks that way," Blair said, shifting back to human form. Liz did the same, her black t-shirt and camo pants replacing thick auburn fur.

Jordan shoved Irakesh up the walkway toward Blair. Irakesh looked like he might say something, but apparently seeing both Jordan and Trevor ready for a fight gave him pause. His shoulders slumped, and he marched up the walkway until he stood just a few feet away.

"Thank you," he muttered sullenly. Blair assumed the words were meant for him, though Irakesh didn't meet his gaze. "You freed me from that pompous fool. More than that, you allowed me to exact revenge on the treacherous Ka-Dun. You could have claimed that vengeance yourself, but you gave me a chance to redeem my honor. I owe you a debt for that."

"Good," Blair said, giving Irakesh a grin. "Don't think I'll forget it."

"So what's the plan?" Jordan boomed. He'd shifted back to human form. "I'm guessing you guys have a way of dealing with Set."

"We're going to blow up the First Ark," Trevor said, leaning on the railing next to Liz.

"Come again?" Jordan asked, blinking.

"Are you mad?" Irakesh asked, jaw falling open. He looked comical, despite the razored teeth and glowing green eyes.

"You guys explain it to them. I have work to do," Blair turned back to the stone on the platform, inserting the Primary Access Key into its slot once more.

He closed his eyes, thinking to his beast. *Any advice?*

What you seek to do is beyond me, Ka-Dun. Beyond even the Mother, I think. You must draw upon your knowledge of this age, of technology. Perhaps there you will find an answer.

"Thanks," Blair muttered, trying not to be too sarcastic. He wasn't much for technology. Sure, he could use a computer, but his geek-fu was weak.

He focused on the system itself, a vast array of mental options sort of like a folder full of computer programs. After a little bit of study he thought he understood how the system worked, more or less. A conduit extended deep into the earth, like some sort of power line piping energy into the Ark's enormous battery.

It didn't look like it would be possible to overload the battery, because it seemed to have a nearly infinite capacity. So how could he blow this place up? Why couldn't there be some button labeled 'self-destruct'?

Another glance at the system revealed something interesting. The massive aquamarine in the valley below was designed to create life. It channeled huge amounts of energy to do so, and could make everything from a dinosaur to a twelve-legged dragon. But the gem had limits. There were safeguards put in place so a shaper didn't channel too much energy.

What if he removed the safeguards? Blair focused on the Primary Access Key, willing those safeguards to lower. They obligingly disappeared. Blair smiled, then he focused on pouring all the energy from the conduit into the crystal. The flow was immense, a torrent of power that rivaled the nuclear detonation back in San Francisco—only this flow was continuous, not the quick burst he'd seen there. Once the flow to the gem was stable, he disengaged from it.

"What did you do?" Liz asked.

Blair wasn't sure what she meant, until he felt something begin to vibrate behind him. He turned to see the enormous gem in the center of the valley begin to glow. It gave off a brilliant blue light, emitting a high pitched whine.

"Uh," Blair said, turning to face the others. "I have a feeling we're not going to want to be here when that thing blows."

"I still cannot believe it. You're detonating the Ark," Irakesh said, grabbing the rail with both clawed hands. "This place is priceless, and you are destroying it."

"Yeah," Trevor shot back, already starting up the walkway back to the passage that led out of the room. "Better we blow this place up and kill Set along with it, than leave it here for him to use to enslave the world."

Irakesh still looked pissed, but he gave a nod and started after Trevor. Jordan came next, with Liz and Blair bringing up the rear. They ran for all they were worth, sprinting up the walkway.

"Where to now?" Trevor asked, once they'd all reached the hallway.

"The light bridge," Blair said, taking the lead and darting up the corridor.

"It's not far from here. We can use it to get back to the Nexus before this place blows."

The high pitched whine had grown louder, which was all the motivation Blair needed. He turned to Liz. "Ride my shadow. The rest of you get ready to blur. I'm guessing we've got under thirty seconds to get the hell out of here."

Liz flowed into his shadow, and Blair didn't wait for the rest to respond. He blurred, zooming through corridor after corridor until he emerged into the chamber with the light bridge. It looked like a low-tech version of Object 3, just like the one back in his own Ark.

Blair waited on the light bridge as the others appeared one by one. Trevor arrived last, and the instant he appeared Blair triggered the light bridge. Brilliant white light flared around them, but something was different. Blair could feel the power surging through the Ark, overloading every system at once. Including the light bridge.

He struggled to control it, praying he could somehow master the flow. If he couldn't, they were doomed.

Chapter 83- Gloating

Isis shifted back to human form, praying it would somehow lessen the pain. She was only half-conscious as Set hoisted her body into the air. He stared at her with those flat black eyes, no trace of compassion or humanity lurking in their depths.

"I've waited a long time for this, Isis," Set purred, reaching up with his free hand to remove his helm. She flinched as he exposed his horrible face. The too-large head was like an evil, pasty version of Ka. It, more than anything else, showed that his humanity had been sacrificed on the altar of power. "You know, I've never really forgiven you for choosing Osiris. I wonder how things would have been different if you'd chosen me. Perhaps you'd never have gone to the Valley of Hidden Voices. Perhaps we'd never have discovered this place."

A high-pitched whine began in the distance, and Set cocked his enormous head. He seemed curious, but not alarmed. "It seems your companions are up to some mischief. Perhaps the Ka-Dun I recruited is less competent than I hoped. I may have to deal with this myself."

"I'd never have chosen you," Isis said, drawing his gaze back to her. She had to stall, for just a few more seconds. If they succeeded in detonating the Ark the center of the blast would be here, in the central chamber. It would flow up the obelisks around her, obliterating them all. "Even if I'd never met Osiris. He wasn't just the better man; he was the only choice. You were weak even then. Flawed. That hasn't changed."

Isis spit in his face, smiling at the sudden rage. It didn't matter what he did to her, not after what he'd already done to Osiris and Sekhmet. The pair lay a few paces away, neither moving. Both were still alive, though Isis knew if it were in their power they'd choose death over what Set had planned for them.

Set hurled her into the central obelisk with bone crushing force. Isis mercifully blacked out for a moment, but came to with his face mere inches from hers. He wore a too-wide smile with a million tiny teeth, ready to rend her psyche as well as her flesh.

"That was unwise, Isis. You will have centuries to consider the wisdom of provoking me, I assure you."

"I doubt that," Isis forced a smile. Every part of her hurt, but that didn't matter. "You're a fool, Set. Easily deceived. Now, it is you who will pay."

Set looked confused. The high-pitched whining was much louder now, and confusion became concern.

Something rumbled deep beneath the Ark, then the loudest sound she'd ever heard split the air, split her ear drums. The entire room vibrated, until she was engulfed in painful white light. Her last thought was of Yukon.

Chapter 84- TSDS

Blair stumbled from the light bridge, catching the wall as he sought to right his center of balance. He was dizzy, though not sure why. That hadn't happened during previous light walks.

"Wh-what happened?" Liz asked, blinking as she lurched from the platform. Blair caught her, helping her into a sitting position. A moment later she emptied the contents of her stomach all over the floor next to the platform.

The others were in the same state. Even Irakesh tripped, sprawling to the ground between Jordan and Trevor.

"I don't know," Blair said, licking his lips. He felt more than a little queasy himself.

"I can explain," came a hollow, disembodied voice. Blair glanced toward the door to the chamber and found a holographic projection of Ka hovering there. "What you are experiencing is a type of distortion that was once theorized by scholars among the Builders. They called it temporal spacial displacement sickness, or TSDS."

"What's the cause?" Trevor asked. Blair wasn't surprised. Trevor would always be a scientist first, even if he did look like some crazy redneck vampire.

"Theoretically, TSDS would be caused by the destruction of an anchoring Ark during transit," Ka said, cocking its strangely oblong head to the side. The eyes were more than a little terrifying, especially after having seen Set. "The fact that you survived at all is a testament to the redundancies of the system."

"Wait a minute," Blair said, weaving drunkenly across the chamber to stand before the hologram. "You said temporal. I get the spacial displacement, that makes sense. Temporal displacement is time. When are we?"

Ka cocked its head the other direction, eyes flickering as if calculating. "It has been four years and eleven months since you last passed through the Nexus."

Blair sank to his knees. He felt Liz wrap him in a hug, but he was too numb to respond. Five years, just gone. What had happened in that time?

"What happened to The First Ark?" Jordan asked, seemingly unfazed by the sudden news. "Was Set killed?"

"Unknown," Ka said, giving something like a shrug. "Observe."

A second hologram appeared, this one showing a view of earth from orbit, centered over the British Isles. A moment later something red and white bloomed in the south of England, working its way outward. It covered much of the island, and it wasn't a stretch to imagine what it was.

"My god," Trevor whispered. "Look at the size of that explosion. There's no way Set could have survived that. Most of England didn't survive that. It might have taken Wales and Northern France with it too."

Blair rose to his feet, forcing himself to concentrate on the present. He couldn't change what had happened, only move forward. "Has there been any sign of Set, Isis, Osiris, or Ra since the explosion?"

"Negative," Ka said, voice far too cheery.

"Who controls the Ark of the Cradle?" Irakesh asked, pulling himself to his feet.

"Unknown," Ka said, turning to Irakesh. "If a new Ark Lord has arisen, they have not established a conduit to the Nexus."

"Ra could still be alive," Blair said, cautiously turning to face Trevor. He knew Trevor had been close to her before the end.

"It's possible," Trevor said, shrugging. His face shifted into a scowl. "There's only one way to know, though. I need to go to the Cradle and speak with Anput. If anyone knows, she will. Besides, I have the key. I guess that gives me a responsibility."

"I'll go with you," Irakesh said, giving a magnanimous smile.

"Like hell you will," Trevor shot back. "You'd backstab me at the first opportunity, and we both know it. I'm wondering why you're even still alive, now that I think about it."

"That's a great question," Jordan said, taking a threatening step toward Irakesh. "Why is he walking around free? Hell, why is he even still breathing? Or not breathing, I guess."

"It's so nice to see you two getting along," Liz said, beaming a smile their way. "Maybe you can bond by ending this pathetic twerp's life."

"Wait," Irakesh said, raising a hand to forestall them. He reached into a satchel hanging from his belt, and removed two golden items. The collar, and the bracelet. He offered the bracelet to Trevor. "If you need assurance that I won't betray you, then use the collar to control me. It's preferable to death, and my situation is still better than it was under Steve. You'll treat me better than he did, and maybe someday I'll earn your trust."

Blair was taken aback. "You'd go into slavery? Willingly?"

"Of course," Irakesh said, snapping the collar around his own neck. "Isn't it preferable to the alternative? Death is very final. With life, who knows what will happen?"

Trevor stared hard at the bracelet, then looked up. "Jordan, you wore one of these things. What do you think we should do?"

Jordan looked surprised, then gave a shrug. "He won't be able to escape. God knows I tried. It's still possible for him to cause mischief, but if you keep an eye on him you're probably safe. He might even be an asset, since you don't know what you'd be walking into. If nothing else, he proved he had more honor than Steve. He refused to serve Set, even though it cost him his freedom."

"Liz? Blair?" Trevor asked, turning to them.

"I say let him live," Liz said, she turned to Blair as well.

"I'd agree," Blair finally said. "If it were Steve I'd say kill the fucker, right here and now. Irakesh is different. He's evil, but at least he has some honor."

"All right then," Trevor said, snapping the bracelet around his wrist. "Looks like I'll be heading to the cradle. What about the rest of you?"

"I need to find out where we stand with Mohn," Jordan said, folding his heavily muscled arms over an even more heavily muscled chest. "The Director probably died in the explosion back in London. With him and Osiris out of the picture, that means the person most likely to be running the show is the Old Man himself. I need to find out if that's the case, and what Mohn's operational directive is now. Can I hop a ride with you two to San Francisco?"

"What about the key to the Ark in Peru?" Liz asked, rising shakily to her feet. She took a big step back from the mess she'd made. Blair did the same.

"Good point," Jordan said, heaving a sigh. "I guess I have a responsibility too. The thing is, we don't know what's gone down while we were away. At the very least it makes sense that we stick together, in the short term anyway. I'll head to San Francisco with you guys."

Blair gave Jordan a nod, then turned to Liz. "Of course. Liz, I assume that's where you want to go?"

"Yeah, we need to see what happened with Angel Island, plus you have an Ark to run. If possible, we need to rebuild there. They need leadership, and we can provide that. Not to mention, Jes'Ka is still asleep. We have to decide what to do about her," Liz said, eyes taking on that determined cast.

"When we get there, do you want to grab dinner?" Blair knew it wasn't the right time, but was it ever?

"Are you finally asking me on a date?" Liz brushed her hair from her face, looking away for a moment. Was she blushing?

"Hell yes, I am," Blair said. He wrapped an arm around her waist.

"Yeah, I'll have dinner with you. Just take me somewhere nice," Liz leaned into Blair. It felt good. Damn good.

"Ka-Dun, if I may interrupt," Ka said, a hint of impatience leaking into its tone. Blair turned toward the hologram, giving it a nod. It bobbed its head once, then continued. "The signal broadcast from the Arks just prior to our first encounter has had time to arrive at its intended destination. The Builders are now aware of the state of affairs on this planet. They will be coming."

Dead silence fell as everyone took that in. Trevor took a step closer to Liz and Blair, Jordan joining them a moment later. Even Irakesh looked frightened.

"In addition, this planet's magnetosphere has been unstable since the First Ark's detonation," Ka continued, frown deepening. "I believe you will find much has changed in your absence."

Epilogue

Mark came awake by degrees. He felt different, though it was difficult to say how, precisely. It was dark and moist, wherever he was. He reached out, fingers probing some sort of membrane. It gave a little at his touch, but refused to tear. A shiver of anger lanced through him, and claws burst from his finger tips. They were long and dark, much longer than they'd been when he transformed into a vampire. How was that possible?

He used the claws to shred the membrane, gasping at the cool air that rushed into the strange cocoon. He tried to lean forward, but something on his back prevented the movement. He felt an odd tingling back there, and realized he could feel something he shouldn't have been able to. An extra pair of limbs. He flexed them experimentally. Were those…wings?

Mark scrambled from the chrysalis, clawing desperately at the membrane until he tumbled free. A slick substance coated him and made it difficult to grab onto anything. Mark fell heavily to a stone floor, dimly aware of a reddish glow in the distance. Where was he? Panic and revulsion warred within him as he struggled to understand.

"Ahh, you're awake," came a gravelly voice. He squinted up at the speaker, an elderly man with a thick beard and long white hair.

"Who—who are you?" Mark rasped. His throat felt strangely unsuited for speech.

"I am called Hades," the old man explained, kneeling next to Mark. "Do you know who you are, or where you are?"

"I'm…Mark Phillips," he said, the full name coming to him from the dim recesses of his mind. "I don't know where I am. Or what's been done to me. What the hell was that thing?"

"Ahh, the chrysalis. Set sent you here to be reborn, one of his final acts.

The chrysalis has changed you, made you far stronger than you were," Hades explained with the tone of a concerned grandfather.

It has also gifted you with me, Set-Dun. A deep voice thrummed through his mind. The voice was familiar, yet different. It didn't sound like the risen he'd been given when Osiris transformed him. This, whatever it was, felt darker. *You have been elevated. You are the first to survive the transformation, the herald of our return.*

Mark didn't respond to the voice, but he knew for damn sure he didn't like it. He focused on the old man instead. "What happened to Set?"

"I was hoping you could tell me," Hades said, resting a hand on Mark's goo-covered shoulder. He looked at that shoulder, eyes widening as he took in the smooth, black skin. It had the tough, marbled texture of a lizard's hide. Mark shuddered, appalled by what he'd become.

"I'm not sure," Mark's thoughts were racing. Where was he? What had happened?

"What of Isis and Ra? Osiris?" Hades asked, betraying a bit of concern. His grip tightened on Mark's shoulder.

"I don't know," Mark replied. If the plan had worked, then England was nothing more than a crater, and they were all dead.

"No matter," Hades said, releasing Mark. He rose to his feet. "Come, you have much work to be about. Our enemies are many."

Mark took his first awkward steps with his horrifically deformed body. They emerged into a wide tunnel that passed between pools of lava. Mark found himself enjoying the unbearable heat. "Our enemies?"

"Yes," Hades said, turning to meet his gaze. "All sentient life on this planet. It must be eradicated."

Made in the USA
Middletown, DE
23 March 2021